I0632829

Rise of the Champions

By

Nicholas Joslin

This story is a work of fiction. Any names, characters, places, or events are products of the author's imagination. Any resemblance to actual persons living or dead, or actual events, is entirely coincidental.

ISBN: 978-1-7321627-1-6 (Paperback)

The Five Clans of Forthoton and Notable Clanspeople

The Narsho Clan

Jonis Barod – Chieftain
Anna Myhre – Scout
Titus Fardson – Champion
Ragnor Jarult – Guard Captain
Olaf Tobar – Shaman
Roy Matkon – Elder

The Narsho is a proud clan that has always balanced their skill in battle while seeking better ways for their people. They begrudgingly fight a war against the Highrock Clan, which stems from an old disagreement few can remember. They seek only to end the war, preferably through peaceful means.

The Highrock Clan

Vlad Mace – Chieftain
Garon Mace – Prince of Highrock Clan
Lorag and Glora – Champions

The Highrock Clan is extremely aggressive and puts battle before everything else, seeking vengeance against the Narsho Clan over an ancient grievance. Their war with the Narsho consumes them, and defeating their foes is their upmost priority. The title of Chieftain is usually passed down from father to son, maintaining a royal bloodline.

The Forud Clan
Herold Wooll – Chieftain
Goreth Destro – Champion

The Forud Clan is an ally to the Narsho Clan, though they do not fight alongside them against the Highrock Clan. They live peacefully among the western woods.

The Linta Clan

Richard Yarmot – Chieftain
Becca Yarmot – Niece of Chieftain and trader for
Linta Clan
The Linta Clan has developed the strongest economy
of any of the clans and remains neutral in the conflict.
While they trade to both sides, they recognize the
borderline brutality of the Highrock Clan. They are quite
skilled with sailing and building.

The Ancient Clan

Lorenz Mordou – Seer
Valon – Seer's Apprentice
The Ancient Clan lives in seclusion within the Great
Swamp, as it is distrusted by the other clans. They are the
only clan whose members use magic regularly and study
the old ways of magic use. They are led by a Seer, a
powerful mage that can see through time and space itself
when assisted by his clanspeople.

Prologue

As the crude wooden gates opened, all eyes were on the strange man entering the large village. His face was hidden by a hooded cloak, which slowly trembled behind him in the harvest season's wind. His robes seemed rather simple at first glance, being brown and rather plain. The only thing about him that remotely stuck out was the silver colored trim on his robes, a strange symbol on the chest of his robe, and a blueish light coming from beneath the hood. Still, the hesitation of those around him had nothing to do with his attire.

"You, Seer, lower that hood if you know what's good for you," one of the village guards grunted, his hand resting on the pommel of his sword.

The Seer turned to look at the guard, hesitating. He knew if he wanted to get his message through, he'd have to abide by the customs of this clan. After all, his message was far too important.

The Seer lowered his hood, revealing the face of an older man. His hair was still black, but beginning to grey, and was cut very short. At first glance his face seemed as plain as his robe, no scars or other signs of battle. However, his left eye was covered by an eye patch, and a strange blue light was trying to creep its way out between the patch and his clean-shaven face.

"By the gods! You're not foolish enough to use your magic here are you? Take that patch off!" the guard ordered, lifting his poorly fitted bronze helmet to get a better view.

"As you wish. However, as Seer, I cannot stop the flow of magic," the Seer replied.

He removed the patch, revealing his strange eye. While his right eye was simply hazel, his entire left eye was a glowing teal color, covering all other parts of the eye, or at least blending them together. The strange light unveiled the guard's face in the poor evening light, revealing his worried visage and clenched teeth.

"Why have you come, Seer? You know your people are not welcome here. You know that magic isn't welcome here either," the guard asked, tightening his grip.

"I must speak to your chieftain, guardsman. I have a message of great importance. In fact, all your clan should hear my words," the Seer replied, remaining calm.

"Hah. You think I'd let you near the chieftain looking like that? You look as though you are working some sort of nefarious spell. Perhaps if you can stop that strange glow, I can bring your message," the guard replied firmly.

"I cannot stop this magic. It isn't mine to control. As a Seer, magic flows through me no matter where I am. I now see the future, of a time of ruin that could befall us. Please, I beg of you, at least pass on my message to your chieftain," the Seer pleaded.

By now a small audience of guards and clanspeople had begun to gather, all quietly talking about the strange Seer that stood before them. Some spoke more quietly than others, and some spoke briefly of tales of the past, of a time when magic had almost destroyed the Narsho people. This was the first time a member of the Ancient Clan had visited the Narsho clan in decades, putting all on edge.

"Well, I, er," the guard stuttered, now noticing the crowd.

The Seer smiled softly, looking at the weary clanspeople that had joined the crowd. He knew many of the Narsho potentially hated him. Just being part of the Ancient Clan was enough for all the clans to distrust him. It was more tradition at this point, as no living Narsho Clan member had been alive during the great betrayal. Still, it didn't stop new generations from being raised to mistrust the Ancient Clan and their ways. Some here probably even hated him, or at the very least, his magic. Despite it all, the Seer didn't hate them back, he never could. A young redheaded woman suddenly caught his eye, but his interest was interrupted.

"What's the meaning of all this?!" a booming voice said from behind the crowd.

In an instant, the mass of people made way for their Chieftain. He was heads taller than some of his clanspeople, bursting with muscle and vigor. His apparent stamina was surprising, considering his age, which only gave itself away through weathered grey hair and a long beard.

"Chieftain! A Seer of the Ancient Clan has arrived," the guard answered quickly, pounding his chest against his bronze chest piece as a salute.

"Chieftain Barod, it is an honor," the Seer greeted, kneeling to the dirt and staring down.

"Rise, Seer, but do not try any of your tricks. I am in the mood to rip a man apart," Chieftain Barod replied, crossing his arms and staring at the interloper. "Stand and speak."

"Thank you. I promise I am not here for any other reason than to give you, and all your fellow clanspeople, a message," the Seer answered.

"Oh? And what message is that?" Chieftain Barod asked suspiciously, stroking his grey beard.

"It's a warning, perhaps from the gods themselves, Chieftain. I have been gifted the ability of farsight. Through magic, I am able to see throughout our realm, and sometimes through the veil of time itself. Both what I have seen and what my people have sensed portends something truly dark for our realm," the Seer began, pointing to his eye and beginning to speak louder.

"The gods, eh? Was it Ty'roel? Svune? Yrollshama perhaps? Or does the mad god Faraldo himself whisper into your ear?" Chieftain Barod mocked, gathering chuckles from the nearby clanspeople. "The gods remain silent, just as they always have."

The Seer wasn't deterred, looking around at everyone, then back at the Chieftain. He had to listen, or at least someone else would. He couldn't waver now, not when their entire land was at stake.

"A great enemy rises to the far east. I know not the origin or identity of this enemy, but I see it is a terrible one. It is already here, infesting our land, preparing itself for us. All five clans must unite if we are to have any hope of stopping it. Time is running out, and before long it will consume us one clan at a time!" the Seer yelled, looking to all that would listen to him.

"The far east? The Cursed Lands? Nobody of any clan has traveled there in my lifetime. That is as preposterous an idea as the clans themselves uniting," the Chieftain replied, his voice losing all essence of mockery.

"If we strike soon, it won't be too late to save our land!" the Seer urged.

"Enough! That is enough. Seer, your words are volatile and sound as though you wish to bring fear to my people. Begone! Leave our clan and do not return!" the Chieftain yelled, his pose becoming more aggressive.

The Seer simply nodded, knowing there was no more he could do. As he placed his eyepatch back over his glowing eye, he looked at the clanspeople that were watching him. They did look afraid, some looking angrier. He wasn't sure if it was from his message or merely his presence. Regardless, he had done all he could. He quickly lifted his hood and bowed once before the Chieftain, wanting to show his respect.

He walked through the opened gate once more, not looking back. Despite how it appeared, he knew the Narsho clan had taken the news to heart. He could sense something had changed. Someone had heard his message and would likely see the threat for themselves. Someone in the Narsho Clan had listened.

Chapter 1

As the two scouts reached the top of the mountain, they yelled to the heavens in elation. They then looked at each other and embraced, both grinning ear to ear. They shared a quick yet passionate kiss, then looked back to the land ahead.

Beyond the small, rocky mountain in front of them was a long, unnaturally beautiful valley carved into the surrounding land. It was lush with vegetation and other untapped resources. It was surprisingly plain. To Anna, it seemed far from cursed.

"Anna, we've made it! We're further than any Narsho has ever been! We've made it into the Cursed Lands!" the man cheered, looking to the young woman next to him.

"I am proud, Fredrik, and to think so much land still lies unclaimed. Why is it even called cursed anyway?" Anna replied.

"A good question indeed," Fredrik replied, gazing into the unknown land ahead. "It seems to be anything but cursed."

As Anna stared at the verdant valley, her green eyes were drawn to something at the very farthest point from them. She squinted, seeing something white and as tall as a tree, if not taller. She finally gave up, knowing she wouldn't be able to see from here.

"Do you see it too? That white object?" Fredrik asked.

"I do. Shall we go take a closer look?" Anna asked.

"I think so," Fredrik replied with a smile. "If you're up for it, my love."

Anna couldn't help but blush, still not used to this romantic side of Fredrik. She knew this was only temporary, as they couldn't reveal their true love when they went back to the clan. Scouts and warriors of the Narsho Clan were forbidden from taking each other as a companion while they served. The fact they both were in love would be frowned upon, calling their service into question. However, they had hidden it well, something both Anna and Fredrik hated to do.

"Of course. At least the climb down will be easier than up," Anna replied, quickly kissing Fredrik.

"Do you think that is what that Seer tried warning us about?" Fredrik asked, staring back down into the distance.

"I do not know. However, I still would take his words with a grain of salt. I only hope we don't run into the Highrock Clan," Anna replied.

"He sounded so sure of himself. I don't know, I just worry about him being true. That's how I've managed to talk Chieftain Barod into letting just us explore out this far alone. He normally wouldn't let only two venture this far, let alone without any soldiers. And I doubt we'll see Highrock Clan scouts out this far," Fredrik replied.

Anna sighed, staring at Fredrik as he moved his hand through his long, golden blond hair. He had been increasingly worried about the Seer's words since he had visited two months ago, almost to the point of worrying her. She had known Fredrik her entire life, and he had never been one to get caught up in superstition or care about any sort of magic. But since that day, he had been focused on getting to the Cursed Lands to see for himself. While Anna did find some of the Seer's words provoking, it was Fredrik that truly believed them.

"I know. We have enough supplies for another day or two of walking. Then, we'll have to turn around unless we start replenishing them, which isn't guaranteed," Anna added, grabbing a piece of cured meat from her bag and taking a large bite of it.

"Well, we can reach whatever that is before the sun falls from the sky. I think we should at least try to see what it is, don't you?" Fredrik asked, withdrawing his own chunk of meat and taking a few bites.

"Of course; I already suggested that, you rockhead," Anna chuckled, putting away her food and kissing him on the cheek. "Now let's get a move on, swiftly and silently."

The two shared one quick kiss and set off down the hillside, determined to reach what they had seen in the distance. Fredrik was more excited than Anna and she realized this. However, she had enjoyed the journey and his company so much she almost dreaded going back to their clan where their love had to remain secret.

As they worked their way down the rugged hill, Anna felt herself smiling brightly. Even though it was called the Cursed Lands, they hadn't seen any signs of a curse yet. In fact, it seemed the opposite. The land around was fertile, filled with life, as though no clans had been here in some time.

They didn't speak much for the next hour, saving their breath as they moved quickly through the lush forest. They kept a jogging pace the whole time, both in superb physical shape. Then again, it was the Narsho way to move swiftly and silently, their scouts being their eyes and ears everywhere.

"As peaceful as it seems, I'm still keeping my eye out," Fredrik finally spoke, his ocean blue eyes darting from enormous tree to tree.

"Rightfully so. There has to be some reason this place bears the name it does," Anna replied.

"One would think," Fredrik quietly replied.

They pressed on for another hour, knowing their destination had to be close. Based on how far it appeared, they had to be moments away from stumbling upon whatever it was. That fact filled Anna with some trepidation, as it had been some time since she had seen any sort of combat. While she didn't doubt her training as a scout, she knew it only took one moment of indecision or one mistake to be dealt a lethal blow.

It wasn't long after that they found exactly what they had seen from the small mountaintop. Now, standing before the two, was an incredible yet damaged white stone arch. Most of it was intact, but the center of the top had fallen onto the overgrown cobblestone path below. Thick vines twisted around it, and other flora grew around the base. Beyond that archway lay more buildings of the same impressive, white stone and impeccable architecture.

"By the gods, look at this," Fredrik said in disbelief.

"It looks like the home of the gods themselves, does it not?" Anna asked, walking ahead and resting her hand on the pillar of the stone archway.

"That it does, albeit a seemingly abandoned, overgrown one," Fredrik added.

Anna looked closely at the stone pillar of the archway. It was finely carved, and the stone was nothing like the crude rock they used back in their village. The Narsho buildings were made of wood and comparatively ugly grey, basic stone, and she knew whoever had built this was skilled in craftsmanship.

"Shall we continue in?" Fredrik said, looking at the mossy cobblestone path before them.

"Of course. If there is a threat to our people somewhere in the Cursed Lands, I'd be surprised if these ruins had nothing to do with it," Anna said, walking onto the cobblestone path.

The two forged ahead down the cobbled path of the ruined town, both in awe of their surroundings. All the buildings were finely made, boasting white stone, pillars, and superior designs. It was like nothing they had ever seen before, and neither could find the words to describe what they were feeling.

They continued to walk in silence down the ancient path, heads turning as they passed building to building. There were no signs of present life, just of those lives that had once thrived here. Some items like pots, carts, and other objects found in daily life were scattered around, most smashed or aged beyond usability.

Reaching what appeared to be a well in the town center, they stopped, staring at each other in awe. Over a dozen buildings stood in the town, most of them larger than any building in the Narsho village. It was hard to think a town like this could exist, and even more strange to find it abandoned. By the looks of it, it had been abandoned for some time.

"Hello!" Fredrik boomed, looking around after he yelled.

"Is it really wise to yell here?" Anna asked, caught off guard by her lover.

"I find it difficult to believe there is nobody here. Should we perhaps look in some buildings?" Fredrik asked.

"Perhaps. There isn't much else to do out here than stare at their craftsmanship," Anna replied.

As she began to look, she noticed what appeared to be a blacksmith's residence close by. She quickly walked over, leaving Fredrik to follow her. She figured if anyone would be home, it would be the blacksmith. In their village, Thorvad was always busy at work.

Reaching the outdoor covered forge area, she slowly touched the forge. It was cold with no signs of warmth or life. She then grazed her hand over the large anvil, her eyes wandering around the long-abandoned workshop.

Heavily rusted metal was strewn across the place, including what appeared to be ancient swords. It all looked so old, and nothing of any value. Suddenly, she noticed a wooden container resting on a shelf next to the forge.

"Did you find something?" Fredrik asked.

Anna, focused on her finding, slowly found a latch and opened the wooden container. There was a small poof as she did, the container taking some force to open. Inside was what appeared to be a blacksmith's hammer, still in pristine condition and looking of high quality.

"It's the smith's hammer. It somehow hasn't fallen to the elements like everything else. The container must've saved it," Anna replied.

"How strange. It looks to be made with incredible skill as well. Before we press on, I want to investigate the large building at the head of the square. I'd wager that is the home of their chieftain, and we may find something there," Fredrik explained.

"I agree," Anna replied, returning the hammer back to its container before placing the container in her leather backpack. "Let's go."

She followed Fredrik to the largest of the buildings, standing tall with two enormous pillars on either side of the entrance doors. As they neared, they noticed the doors were wide open. It seemed suspicious to her that anyone would leave doors open like that.

Fredrik stopped at the doorway, waiting for Anna to stand next to him. It was dark in the building, with only a few streams of light finding their way through the open windows. She knew there could be wildlife sleeping inside. The worst thing they could encounter was a raptor, but they would've probably already smelled or seen the decomposing kills of the ferocious creature as well as seen the territorial clawing.

"Swift and silent," Fredrik said with a smile, kissing Anna.

"Let's go," Anna replied with a reciprocating smile.

Entering the dimly lit abandoned building, Anna instantly noticed the elements had breached their way inside. Leaves, dirt, and other debris of nature lay scattered in the entryway and close to nearby windows. Not only that, but some grass had begun to grow through the floor. Nature itself was retaking the building, and she knew this place had been abandoned long ago. But now the burning question on her mind was why it had been abandoned.

They split up, and Anna found herself drawn towards a huge, well carved round table in the center of many cobwebbed chairs. On the table lay various parchment and other tomes. She had only ever seen two books before—one was passed down from chieftain to chieftain; it was rarely shown to people, and she knew nothing about it other than it was ancient. The other was a book the Clan Elders used to teach the young to read. Everything else were either carved stone or crude paper.

Various decomposing tomes lay on the table, some in much better condition than others. She looked through them, all filled with symbols she didn't understand. Too focused on the tomes, her free hand slowly curled around the one longest lock of her straight red hair, a habit she greatly disliked. Finally, there was one book that called out to her.

Amongst the scattered, abandoned tomes lay one that seemed to have held together much better than the others. Gold symbols were inscribed on the parchment of the tome, and something about them enticed her. She neared it, staring at the old book.

Anna slowly picked up the tome, careful not to damage the strange work. Dust and other debris of the strain of time slowly fell from it as she lifted it from the table. She stared at its pages for a moment, not able to understand any of the writing. She carefully closed the book after shaking off more dust and looked at the cover.

The book was bound with gold material and looked to be of great importance. More symbols were on the leather cover, as well as a drawing. As she brought the tome slightly closer to her face, she saw the crude drawing was of some strange creature.

The two-legged creature almost looked to be human, but was drawn to have a sinister looking face, claws, and black lines drawn on either side of its head. She had never seen anything like it and took a moment before placing the old tome in her backpack.

Suddenly, as she went to take a couple more of what appeared to be maps from the table, she heard a harsh, loud cry from somewhere outside. She spun around, quickly folding the parchment and stuffing them into her bag. She looked across the room to see that Fredrik had heard it as well and was already heading towards the front door.

Anna quickly ran over to meet him, and together they poked their head outside the building. They looked at each other, then back outside, but didn't see anything waiting for them. Then suddenly, again, the cry came. It was a harsh, primal shriek that pierced the peaceful wind like an arrow through hay. Anna shuddered as she heard it.

"What in the Dark Depths is that?" Fredrik whispered as he looked to Anna.

"No familiar creature's call, that's for certain," Anna replied.

They paused, waiting in silence for another sound. Sure enough, the mysterious, almost desperate cry came from somewhere even closer. A chill went down Anna's spine as she heard it, her eyes widening. Whatever it was, it sounded nefarious.

"It's getting closer. Could it be tracking us?" Fredrik slowly asked.

"I say we track it," Anna replied, finding courage within herself.

"Agreed. Let's go," Fredrik said, patting her on the shoulder.

She nodded, unsheathing her short sword. Fredrik nodded to her, taking his battleaxe from his back. Together, now armed, they made their way back into the warm afternoon light of the early autumn sun.

They walked side by side into the cobbled town square, looking in every direction for their potential foe. This time, they heard which direction the piercing howl came from, and they looked toward the blacksmith's home. They both stood still, frozen as the creature finally walked around the home and into the end of the town square.

Anna had never seen any animal or other creature like it. It was a horrible, tormented, menacing looking being made of flesh and hatred. Rough, almost purple leathery skin wrapped the burly, odd looking being. It walked on all fours, its front two arms enormous in size. Even walking down like an animal, it was almost as tall as Anna. However, something about it seemed unnatural, and as Anna stared, she made eye contact with the creature's almost glowing solid red eyes.

"By the gods ... what is that thing?" Fredrik said, readying his axe.

"It looks like some creature from the Dark Depths itself," Anna replied, holding her sword in a defensive stance.

As the creature noticed them, it stood on its back legs. It was easily eight feet tall now, and as Anna stared, she noticed what appeared to be small tentacles were growing on random spots on the creature's warped purple skin. Suddenly, it roared, its mouth filled with terrible teeth and a violent looking large tongue.

"You there! I don't suppose you speak the tongue of the clan?" Fredrik asked aloud to the creature before them.

The creature simply roared again, slamming its burly fists on the cobblestone, shattering it and sending shrapnel flying. Anna flinched, having to move her head to miss a small piece of shattered rock flying her way. She could tell whatever the creature was, it wasn't capable of communication.

"Ready yourself," Anna quietly said, shooting a glance at Fredrik.

"Oh, I'm ready," Fredrik replied with his confident smile.

The two watched as the creature howled once more, hitting the ground a couple more times. Then, it ran at them with full speed, its pulsating muscles working on overdrive. Surprised by the large creature's unnatural speed, the two jumped aside, the creature clumsily running through them and hitting one of the pillars of the large building they had just exited.

Anna turned, seeing the creature easily recover from smashing headfirst into the rock. It hadn't been phased by the hit and immediately turned to face them again. It snarled and charged towards Fredrik. Fortunately, Fredrik was ready.

The creature ran a bit slower and let loose an aggressive slash from its clawed hand at Fredrik, who nimbly dodged the attack. Using the moment, he swung his axe hard and true at the beast, striking the blade into its gnarled flesh. Thick, black blood flew from the wound, but before Fredrik could dislodge his axe, the terrible creature swung at him, knocking him back a few feet.

"Fredrik!" Anna yelled, charging at the beast and swinging her sword at it.

She swung her sword overhead with as much force as she could muster, intent on killing the nasty creature. It raised its barely wounded arm to defend itself, Fredrik's axe still lodged in its flesh. With vigor, Anna brought her sword down on the creature's arm, striking it hard enough to dislodge the axe and have it drop to the shattered cobblestone below.

More black blood spewed from the creature, some of it hitting her shoulder as she slashed open a decent wound on the creature. It howled with rage, taking a step back from her before lashing forward with both of its claws. She dodged to the side, barely fast enough to escape its grasp.

She continued stepping back as the creature let loose a flurry of attacks, dodging a few and parrying others with her sword. The way it fought was ruthless, desperate, and like no beast she had fought before. As she caught a glimpse of its face up close, it seemed tormented, in pain somehow, but not from the wounds they had just inflicted.

Then, an arrow struck the back of the creature. It quickly spun around to face Fredrik, who had hit it square in the back with his hunting bow. However, the arrow was expelled from the body of the creature, as though it had some sort of control over its flesh.

Before Anna could attack again, she noticed something out of the corner of her eye. She quickly turned to see what looked to be a dozen more creatures coming from behind the buildings to her right. To her surprise, they didn't all look alike. They were an assortment of hideous amalgamations of gnarled flesh, teeth, claws, and tentacles. Anna felt her heart drop as she witnessed the horrible sight, and looked to Fredrik, who had now retrieved his battleaxe from the ground.

"Fredrik! We need to get out of here, there's more coming!" Anna yelled, pointing to the others.

"No! Dammit! Get out of here, Anna! Make a run for it!" Fredrik yelled, running forward and unleashing a flurry of attacks on their original foe.

"I'm not going to leave you!" Anna yelled, holding her sword tight and running at the beast.

Fredrik's axe struck hard on the creature, but it couldn't cut deep enough into its thick flesh to truly do damage. Still, it bled, and hot, tar-like blood dripped onto the ground beneath them. Anna took the opportunity to stab the beast clean through with her sword, thrusting with all her might through the back of the standing creature.

It howled in pain as it looked down to see her blade clean through its body. Yet, this seemingly grievous wound did not stop it, and it swung itself around with rage and speed, taking its large arm and striking Anna so hard she was tossed back ten feet.

She struggled to breathe, having the wind knocked out of her. However, the adrenaline of the situation helped her get back on her feet. She noticed her bow had been snapped in half from landing on it. Cursing, she saw the other creatures were closing in, only about twenty meters away now. They couldn't possibly fight them all, but she would not leave Fredrik, she would not leave her love.

"Anna! Go! You must tell the chieftain what we've found!" Fredrik boomed, taking his axe and throwing it at their enemy.

His axe struck the creature hard in the neck, and it gurgled a horrible sound as nasty blood wept from its head. Fredrik didn't stop, taking his bow and unleashing two quick arrows. His attacks seemed to work, and creature fell back on all fours, slowly crumbling to the ground.

"Fredrik! Quick! Let's make a run for it!" Anna pleaded.

Before Fredrik could respond, some sort of projectile flew from the incoming creatures, striking him hard in the leg. Anna gasped, seeing the gnarled looking spike that had impaled him. Not only that, but the enemy they had been fighting began to crawl away, her sword still stuck in its torso.

"Gah! No! If you love me, leave now and save yourself! Save our clan! Destroy these… horrors!" Fredrik yelled, pain lacing his voice.

Anna took a step back, tears beginning to run down her face. She had no weapons, and no choice. She watched as Fredrik shot more arrows into the horde of creatures, his quiver running low. She knew how important this had been to him, and that if she truly wanted to help, she needed to leave. She had to listen to him.

However, as she stared at him, her chest felt heavy. Even her legs were controlled by her heart, ignoring pleas from her brain to escape now. If she left, the man she loved would most certainly die. If she stayed, she would likely die too. But as she stared at him, he knew the look in his eyes meant he truly wanted her to save herself.

"I-I love you!" Anna called out, gritting her teeth as she began to sob.

Fredrik, in obvious pain, looked to her, smiling as he nocked another arrow.

"I love you too."

Anna quickly turned and began to run, covered in tears and a mixture of her blood and the creature's. It pained her, but she didn't look back, even when Fredrik began to scream as he entered battle with the other beasts. Every moment felt like being trapped in some sort of waking nightmare as she ran, her tearing heart beating rapidly.

She knew she could be followed, and in an adrenaline-fueled frenzy, Anna ran strange patterns, over rocks, around trees, and did whatever odd pathing she could to throw them off. Determined to live and fulfill Fredrik's last request, Anna didn't stop running—and later, slowly jogging—at all until she reached her village almost an entire day later, falling unconscious as she approached the gate.

Chapter 2

The father and son sat in cold silence, rowdy cries of distant clanspeople the only sounds barely making it into the room. The darkness of the evening was only chased away by two candles between them, their flames flickering as a gust of wind made it inside every few moments. As the son cut through his steak, he watched as the slightest bit of blood was squeezed from the rare cut, which briefly and uncomfortably reminded him of a past battle. He shook his head and looked to his father, who ravenously assaulted his food. Suddenly, his father stopped, looking up briefly.

As the son went to speak, the door to their hall quickly opened, letting some of the cooler evening air in. He watched as a young warrior quickly approached them, his red dyed armor looking worn. He saluted and stood at attention. The son then looked to his father, who either didn't realize or didn't care one of their warriors stood before them.

"Father," the young man whispered, then took a sip of his ale.

"Please, speak," the father said, adjusting the crudely made gold crown on his head.

"Chief King Mace, Prince Mace, we have sighted another Narsho scout, this time heading west. It appears to be one of the two we spotted heading east days earlier," the young warrior reported.

"Two enter the Cursed Lands and one returns … How curious," Chief King Mace grinned. "Is there anything else to report?"

"No, Chief King," the warrior answered.

"Then leave us."

The warrior quickly turned and left their hall. Prince Mace was worried about the report, the Seer still on his mind. He wasn't as convinced as his father that the war with the Narsho clan was their top priority. In fact, he had never been convinced the war had been necessary to prolong.

"Could it have something to do with that Seer from the Ancient Clan? He did say the threat came from the east," Prince Mace asked, looking at his father.

"Bah, the Ancient clan is full of madmen. We cannot let them distract us from disposing the Narsho. We have them on the ropes now, we must follow through," Chief King Mace answered gruffly, running his bony hands through his overgrown black hair.

"Father, why are you so intent on their destruction? I've never actually been told the entire story," Prince Mace asked, hoping his father wouldn't overreact.

"Why am I intent on their destruction?" Chief King Mace grumbled, slamming a fist on the table. "Those Narsho are traitors and cowards."

"How so?" Prince Mace asked with a non-confrontational tone.

"Their tale of treachery comes during the end of the Great Clan, which as you know was when our clans stood together, unified. These end times were called the Week of Midnight, or at least that's what our ancestors refer to it as. The Great Clan fought and lost to an unknown enemy. This enemy was strong, vicious, and moved like a shadow. It was apparent to the Great Clan that they could not win, but instead of rolling over like prey, they decided to fight, to lead a strike against their enemies. The Narsho, of course, were against it. They wanted to give up, leave the city, and run into the hills like the cowards they are. The other clans sided with the Narsho and tried to flee the city. But our clansmen, particularly our bloodline, still decided to fight. They courageously pressed into enemy territory and fought the enemy back, probably buying enough time for the rest of the clan to run away like they wanted. However, they all perished. Every single warrior with Highrock blood who fought ended up sacrificing themselves for the rest of those cowards. Only the Highrock too young or unfit to battle lived on. But it was the Narsho that persuaded everyone else to abandon the fight. Who knows, if they had stood together, they could have succeeded in pushing the enemy back and your great, great grandfather may have lived to have more children," Chief King Mace explained with anger, clenching his fists the entire time he spoke.

"Oh, I see," Prince Mace replied, surprised at the story.

He had never sought out his people's history before. He had only known about the Great Clan's existence, but that was about it. Still, these events must have happened well over a hundred years ago. Nobody alive then could possibly be alive now. It seems the grudge of the ancestors had outlived them. The prince wasn't sure how he felt about the continuation of the war, as he personally had no grudges against the Narsho, despite having fought them. But unfortunately, it was not his call to make, it was his father's. If he wanted it to change, he would have to convince his father, not an easy task.

"Which is why we must make them pay. If it wasn't for their cowardice, who knows what we the clan could've become. We must avenge our ancestors," Chief King Mace insisted.

Prince Mace only nodded, understanding his father's rage. He knew he should feel the same anger, but he simply didn't. He found it almost hypocritical that his father wanted to know what the Great Clan could've become yet was too far gone in his hatred to focus on restoring the Highrock clan to its former greatness. It seemed his father, the chief king, could only focus on war.

They returned to silence, the prince looking back at his steak. He didn't know what else to say to his father. He knew by now it was pointless to try to change his mind. When the chief king put his mind to something, he saw it done. If he wanted the Narsho gone, he would likely accomplish it. However, the war had been long and rather unsuccessful so far. But he knew it only took one battle to change everything.

The prince watched as his father slowly stood from the table, leaning heavily on his large, old mace. He felt bad for his father, who had never fully recovered from a great wound in battle against the Narsho almost a decade ago. Since then, the chief king had become frail, his strength sapped away by not only the wound, but also age. Yet despite his frailty, his father had surprising agility, making him still fierce in battle.

"Garon, please convey my orders to the warrior general. We strike the Narsho in one week's time. This time, we assault their home directly. We'll evade their scouts, outposts, and whatever else stands between us and them if possible. We will finish this war," Chief King Mace snarled, looking over to his son.

"Of course, Father, I will go now," Prince Mace nodded.

Just before he left, he saw his father quickly look around, as if hearing something. His father cocked his head, as if trying his hardest to listen. Then, he looked back at his son. He seemed paranoid, and Prince Mace certainly didn't know what his father was trying to hear.

"Did you hear that? Is someone outside whispering?"

"What? No, I didn't hear anything father," Prince Mace replied, trying but failing to hear anything.

"Fine then. Keep an eye out when you leave," Chief King Mace ordered before sitting back down.

The prince nodded and headed toward the door of the hall, feeling his father's piercing gaze hitting his back. It almost felt as though his father didn't trust him or had a lack of faith. However, it was a justified feeling, as Prince Mace didn't want to fight the Narsho if he could help it. There was nothing he could do about it, however, and would carry out his father's will.

Stepping from the hall, the prince was greeted by a cool night breeze gently caressing his fair-skinned face. He took a deep breath, savoring the moment. Their ancestral home, Highrock, was aptly named after the tall rocky hill their village sat upon, leaving them with an almost constant breeze. He had always found this wind calming, at least when the village wasn't preparing for battle. Unfortunately, that was about to change.

He looked around, not seeing anyone nearby. In fact, there was nobody up here with them. Being at the top of the peak, the chief king's hall stood alone at the highest possible point. It was this way to be both symbolic and defensive. He shook his head, continuing on to deliver the message.

He began to walk down from the peak, his boots scuffing along the worn stone. He could see fires roaring and his fellow clanspeople enjoying the night while it was young. He sometimes wished he could partake as well, but there had always been a divide between him and the rest of the clan.

Unlike the other clans, the Highrock clan's chieftains were the result of a long bloodline. Their leaders were bred, not chosen, and while not everyone in the Highrock clan liked it, that's how it had always been. Prince Garon Mace knew that's why some of his people disliked him, that and the fact he didn't have the same barbaric rage they had to fight. His father didn't have that issue.

He continued down to the large barracks building at the lowest point of their village. Just beyond that were the sharp wooden palisade walls that protected them. With the wall and the village being on a hill, their village was a superb defensive position. Their ancestors had chosen their settlement well.

Approaching the barracks, Prince Mace could hear the rowdy warriors from inside. They usually enjoyed drinking copious amounts of ale and gambling away their silver to each other. To no surprise, that's exactly what they were doing when Prince Mace entered.

He saw some eyes dart to him as they entered, but most went back to whatever they had been doing. While it was technically customary to greet any member of the bloodline when they entered your presence, Prince Mace had never liked it and told them not to bother. Fortunately, they managed to listen to him over the years.

"Ah, Prince Mace, good evening," a short, stocky man wearing an eyepatch greeted as he approached him.

"Good evening, General Klon. I am here to bring you our chief king's orders," Prince Mace began, looking to see that others were listening.

"Oh? Will we be heading to battle again soon?" General Klon asked excitedly, twisting his moustache in delight.

"In a week's time we strike the Narsho village," Prince Mace replied simply.

"The village? What about the outposts and scout patrols?" General Klon asked, concerned.

"We are meant to find a way through or around them if possible, so we may have the element of surprise on our side," Prince Mace explained.

"I suppose we have some work to do then. You will be joining us on the battlefield, I hope?" the old general asked, as if to force the prince to say yes.

"Of course," Prince Mace answered with a fake sense of excitement.

"Very well then, we do as the bloodline commands. I shall brief the men," General Klon nodded, turning and motioning for the warrior leaders to gather.

Prince Mace did not linger and went back outside. He stared up at the clear night sky, not a single cloud to dim the sight. The thousands of glowing stars in the sky entranced him, and he couldn't help but smile at the majesty of the sight. He truly didn't know what he was looking at, but part of him thought they were the many eyes of the gods looking down upon them. Whatever it was, it seemed peaceful.

He slowly walked back toward the hall, wondering if the other clans were looking up at the same sky at the same moment he was. The Linta Clan was the closest of the clans to them, being not too far southwest. That clan had always taken pride in their craftsmanship and trading, and Prince Mace frequently bought goods from them.

Then, far west and close to the Narsho clan was the Forud clan. The Forud people had strong, unbreakable ties to the Narsho, and Prince Mace wondered why they didn't simply become one. If anything, it was the war that stopped it, as the Forud people refused to fight alongside the Narsho. However, Prince Mace figured if it looked like the Narsho would be defeated for good, the Forud may finally join the Narsho in combat. This was why he was particularly worried about their attack on the Narsho Clan. That attack may be enough to drag the Forud people into the fray. If that were to happen, Prince Mace figured they would be defeated by the allied clans.

He sighed, sitting on a nearby stump and staring to the sky once more. Ever since the Seer had visited their village, the prince had become more interested in the Ancient Clan and their magic. From what he had learned speaking to many different clanspeople over the years, magic was all around them and could be used by anyone, provided they had the knowledge and training. However, due to its supposed malevolent and unstable nature, it was forbidden to be used by all the other clans. Only a clan shaman was allowed to use it, and strictly for healing purposes. If anyone else was to try to use it within a clan, they would be exiled. This fear of magic was the one thing shared by every clan except the Ancient Clan. Still, it didn't stop Prince Mace from being curious.

As he stared at the stars, he felt a sense of dread overcome him. Between the upcoming battle and the Seer's warning, the prince felt as though he should be doing something. However, his place was to follow his father's orders, and with that he had no choice. For now, he could only keep his wits about him.

NICHOLAS JOSLIN

Chapter 3

As Anna slowly awoke, she immediately felt uneasy. She sat up in a fit of fear, her panicked breathing loud in the silent hut. She reached for a weapon but couldn't find anything. She looked around frantically, noticing that she was wearing someone else's clothing. She didn't even know where she was. At least, not at first.

"My, my! Scout Myhre! Please, try to calm down!" a familiar voice pleaded from nearby.

Anna looked to see their shaman, a wise old man named Olaf Tobar, rushing toward her. Being tall, he knelt beside her, stroking his white beard as he slowly rested the back of his hand across her forehead. Then he stood back up and walked to a nearby table.

"What? What's going on?" Anna asked.

"That's what we would like to know. You've been sleeping for almost a full day. You made it to the entrance of our village and then collapsed of severe exhaustion. Your condition was so critical I even had to perform a brief stamina restoration spell because I feared for your life, and you know how much our people distrust magic," Olaf replied, fiddling around with some herbs and other things on the table.

Anna took a deep breath, realizing she felt horrible. She remembered running from the ruins, and then it was all a blur. Fredrik, the creatures, she had to tell the chieftain as soon as she could. For all she knew, they would have followed her back.

However, she must've been in a dire condition for the shaman to use magic. Magic was forbidden by all the clans, except for the borderline hated Ancient Clan. Anna knew only a shaman was allowed to use magic in life-threatening situations, and for that reason, she knew she should take it somewhat easy.

"Olaf … Fredrik, he's dead," Anna slowly said, trying not to tear up.

"Scout Johanson is dead? By the gods, he was a true fighter. What happened?" Olaf asked, leaving his herbs and placing his hand gently on her back, his eyes filled with empathy.

"First, we found ruins in the Cursed Lands, far east from here. These ruins were, I don't know, complex? Their buildings were far better than ours, at least they looked nicer. But then they came. These ... horrors, abominations, they attacked us and killed Fredrik. He saved my life. Without his bravery, I would be dead," Anna explained, tears running silently down her face.

"Gods ... The chieftain will want to hear about this," Olaf said, walking back over to his table. "And Anna, there is something else."

"What is it?" Anna asked, unable to stop the tears from flowing down her face.

Olaf finished preparing a drink and brought it over to Anna. However, now noticing her tears, he stopped talking. Instead he shared a moment of eye contact with her, unable to find his words.

"Er, it can wait. However, I urge you to drink this formula. It should help restore your health and vigor. Also, do avoid the impure vices we enjoy—smoking anything, drinking alcohol—as it will delay your healing for now, alright?" Olaf asked, handing her the cup.

"I will try," Anna replied, taking the blue colored formula and cringing at the bitter taste.

"Good. Feel free to keep those clothes, as yours were, er, rather soiled. When you gather your strength, the chieftain wants to speak to you. He also currently has your backpack, in case you were wondering," Olaf explained. "Is there anything else you need?"

"No. Thank you, Olaf," Anna answered, finally finding the strength to stop her tears.

"Then I shall leave you alone for now," Olaf replied, stroking his beard as he left the hut.

Anna lay back down in silence, already feeling the effects of the shaman's brew. She liked and trusted

Chieftain Barod, but it would be hard for her to go into the details of her ordeal. It was too soon, and too painful. However, she had no choice. They needed to know there was a threat, one that seemed greater than their current war with the Highrock Clan. After all, Fredrik would want her to. She had to finish his task.

She then rested for a while before finding enough energy to leave the shaman's hut. It was a cloudy day, and she could tell the nice part of harvest season was soon ending; before long, a harsh winter would likely befall them.

Eyes of her fellow clanspeople were on her as she walked through the village, and she could tell she was the current gossip, yet nobody dared approach her. At least, the civilians wouldn't, not before the chieftain spoke about it. A cheeky warrior might risk it, but they were all likely either in training or patrolling for Highrock warriors.

She looked down at the muddy ground, smelling the recent rain she must've just missed while asleep. Trudging forward, she felt immense grief lingering within her. Yet she knew that she must press on and tell the chieftain of the threat.

She walked through the muddy paths of the Narsho village, keeping her eyes to herself. It didn't take long to make it to the large hall of the chieftain, and with a deep breath, she entered.

Inside she found Chieftain Barod, Guard Captain Jarult, and Titus, Champion of the Narsho. It was no surprise their leader of the chieftain's guards and the Narsho's most gifted warrior would be joining. If anyone needed to know the threat, it was those three men. Unfortunately, Titus Fardson, Champion of the Narsho and only a few years older than Anna, was often described as not only the strongest, but also the rudest of the Narsho.

"Ah! She joins at last," Titus bellowed, staring at Anna with an almost condescending look as his enormous muscles twitched.

"Greetings, Scout Myhre, please join us," Chieftain Barod boomed, slamming his fist down on the wooden table and causing a great sound.

Anna saluted her chieftain, placing her left fist over her right shoulder, then proceeded towards them. By slamming his fist, she knew her chieftain had officially started the meeting. As she approached, she realized the items she had found in the ruins were now spread out on a large table in front of the men with her blood-covered backpack on the floor next to them.

"We're glad to see you up and well, Anna. Unfortunately, our shaman has just let us know that Fredrik did not make it. His loss will affect all of us, for he was a great man and a great scout," Chieftain Barod mourned.

The others nodded, even Titus showing brief sympathy. Anna gulped, mentally readying herself to retell everything that had happened. Something about those creatures had haunted her, and just thinking about them gave her chills.

"It was horrible, Chieftain. The monsters we fought were like nothing we had ever seen before. Hideous, brutal, warped, and hard to kill. Fredrik saved me and took on at least a dozen of them so I could come back and tell you what we saw. It was his final request," Anna slowly explained, managing to hold back tears.

"Monsters? I didn't think monsters were more than tales to keep children in line," Titus sneered.

"Do you doubt I know what I fought?" Anna replied with angrily squinted eyes.

"Okay, easy," Guard Captain Jarult urged, holding his hands up and mainly looking at Titus.

"Yes, we must remain calm. Monster or not, Anna faced a brutal beast that killed one of our most adept scouts. The fact you saw at least a dozen more is worrying too. Where did you encounter these beasts?" Chieftain Barod asked.

"We found the ruins of an old yet seemingly advanced town far east of here in the Cursed Lands. The buildings' designs are impeccable, made of fine white stone and carved with master craftsmanship. It is like nothing we or any of the other clans have made," Anna explained as she stared at the tome on the table. "That is where we found those monsters."

"Is that where you found these as well?" Chieftain Barod asked, noticing her stare.

"It is. We briefly looked through the building and I recovered that tome and those other pieces of parchment. A couple look like maps; however, I cannot read any of it," Anna replied.

"It's like nothing I've ever seen," Titus added.

Anna thought she saw the guard captain roll his eyes as Titus spoke. It was likely nobody had ever seen anything like it. Almost nobody wrote or read the tongue of the clan, though she knew the chieftain and Shaman did. If anyone could read what she found, it would be them.

"Unfortunately, the same applies to me," Chieftain Barod admitted. "I cannot decipher any of these symbols, although the drawing on the cover of the tome is most interesting. Still, these odd letters are nothing any of us can read. The hammer is especially well crafted, but nothing like we would make. I thought it may be remnants of the Great Clan, but nothing leads me to believe that."

"Great Clan?" Anna asked, having not heard of it before.

"Ah, I forgot our Elders do not teach the young about the Great Clan. You must be, what, in your early twenties? They stopped teaching when I was a little younger than you, almost forty years ago," Chieftain Barod began.

"A Great Clan? How interesting. I wonder if they had a Champion that could stand against me," Titus boasted.

Guard Captain Jarult chuckled to himself, looking to Chieftain Barod. The chieftain also let loose a small laugh, shaking his head. This caused Titus to purse his lips together in slight embarrassment. It seemed the Champion's thought was funny to the clan Elders.

"The Great Clan was the most powerful clan in all our realm of Forthoton. They numbered in the tens of thousands and were quite powerful. We know little of them now, only from what's been passed down by those before us by way of tongue. Their grand achievement was driving those wretched green devils, the goblins I think they were called, from this land. But unfortunately, they fell to an enemy far greater than we can imagine, which are only referred to as the shadows. Part of me wonders if what you encountered were those shadows, but that's something I couldn't know," Chief Barod explained, almost sounding disappointed at his lack of historical knowledge.

This was the first Anna had heard of such history. Between the Great Clan, goblins, and the shadows, she was perplexed. It seemed their people had more history than she had thought. She had no idea if the creatures she had encountered were the supposed shadows of which the chieftain spoke, but her gut said they weren't the same.

"I don't see those beasts being called shadows. They were loud, aggressive, and hardly a shadow," Anna slowly replied, unsure of what else to say.

"Perhaps they were not shadows then," Titus pondered.

"Regardless, I believe we should send a group of warriors to where you encountered these demons," Chieftain Barod began, ignoring his Champion. "Who knows what else may be afoot there."

"While I agree with sending warriors, I am worried about the Highrock clan attacking us," Guard Captain Jarult added.

"I worry about that as well. However, if what Anna says is true, we may not have an option," Chieftain Barod replied.

The room went silent for a moment, each person realizing their chieftain was right. Anna knew from their silence she had convinced them but was in no rush to face those enemies again. However, part of her also knew she would likely have to lead the warriors back to where she found the beasts of torment. She didn't want to face her lover's killers, but figured she may be able to at least avenge him with the opportunity.

While she hadn't seen Fredrik die, she had begun to accept that outcome; despite being a fierce fighter, she knew no one person could fight those horrors alone. They were too strong and fierce with hatred to take on by oneself. She knew in her heart he had to be gone.

"You are right, Chieftain. If an enemy like that exists, we must slay them before they reach us or our allies," Titus said with courage.

"Now that I agree with. Even if we must spare some of our better fighters, I will ensure we remain as well defended as possible with who we do have," Guard Captain Jarult affirmed.

"Well, then go find twenty or so warriors you'd trust for this," Chieftain Barod said, looking over to Titus.

"I would be honored, Chieftain," Titus replied with a salute.

"As for getting there, could you possibly help create a detailed map for our warriors?" Chieftain Barod asked, looking at Anna.

"I, er," Anna began.

"A map? Could she not lead us there? It would be easier than following some map," Titus interrupted.

The chieftain grimaced at Titus's lack of respect and subtle understanding. He turned to Anna, his eyes saying he didn't want to ask but now had to. He sighed.

"Anna, I know this is much to ask of you, but would you be able to bring the warriors to the ruins? You could leave in a couple days, allowing you to rest. I do understand if you are not able," Chieftain Barod asked, feeling put on the spot.

"I will lead them," Anna replied confidently, feeling a thirst for vengeance grow within her.

"Aha! That's the spirit! Together we can slay the servants of the mad god Faraldo!" Titus grinned, reaching over and patting Anna on the back.

"Very good, Anna. Your competence as a scout will certainly make the trip quicker. As for beast slaying, the primary purpose of this mission is to see how many there are. Kill those you can, but more importantly, figure out just what we're facing. Understood?" Chieftain Barod asked, looking at Anna and Titus.

"Of course, Chieftain," Titus said loudly.

Anna simply nodded, now pondering the beasts they faced. She could hardly think of those beasts as servants of a god, at least none she knew of. Even the mad god Faraldo was supposedly not malevolent, and those creatures knew nothing but evil.

"Then leave me. I have much to consider. Anna, please stay behind a moment," Chieftain Barod ordered.

Titus and Guard Captain Jarult saluted and left the Chieftain's Hall. As Anna watched them go, she wondered why she had been asked to stay. As she looked at the chieftain, she noticed he had a somber look on his face.

"Anna, I must ask. You and Fredrik, were you...?"

"Yes, we were. I ... I loved him..." Anna replied, fighting back the waves of sorrow that crashed over her.

"I appreciate your honesty, and I'm sorry for your loss. I know technically all scouts or warriors aren't allowed to be together, but that's not a rule I implemented. In fact, I really don't care. What I mean to say is, I'm sorry you could not be together more because of it," Chieftain Barod explained with absolute sincerity.

"Thank you. But you shouldn't have to apologize, it wasn't your doing," Anna replied, comforted by her chieftain's words.

Chieftain Barod nodded and there was a moment of silence. Anna realized she probably looked ragged, and tried to fix her once straight, red hair. She felt a bit better now, knowing the chieftain was supportive. It was reasons like this that made her decision of going back to the ruins easier.

"Again, thank you for offering to lead our warriors back there. It seems that Seer may have actually known something. You shall leave at dawn in two days' time. Does that sound reasonable?" Chieftain Barod asked.

"Yes," Anna simply answered. "I'm merely worried about what we may find."

"I am too, from what you described. We may be dealing with something … unnatural. For that, I am sending a runner to the Forud Clan. I am going to invite Chieftain Wooll and his best warriors here a couple days before you arrive back. That way, they can hear from our best face to face. This will make them more likely to aid us if we require it," Chieftain Barod explained.

"That makes sense, Chieftain," Anna replied.

"I'm glad you agree. Now, go get some well-deserved rest, brave scout," Chieftain Barod said, handing Anna her backpack.

Anna nodded and left the hall. As she stepped back outside, she felt the tiniest raindrops beginning to fall. She felt drowsy and slightly chilled, as this was a far cooler day than she was used to. She spared no time and made her way back through the village to her home.

Her small wooden and stone dwelling paled in comparison to the homes she had seen at the ruins. But she didn't care about that. Anna loved her small home, and quickly opened the door and walked inside.

Everything was just how she had left it. She passed through her small dining and kitchen area and into her bedroom. She fell like a rock onto her bed, the sheep's wool catching her softly. She was overwhelmed with various emotions to the point where she was beginning to shut down. Fortunately, she recognized this, and knew sleep would be her best choice. After all, there wasn't anything else to be done for two days.

Anna would follow the chieftain's orders and rest for two days straight. During this time, she mourned Fredrik, trying hard to remember all the good memories they had made together. Unfortunately, her dreams were often turned to nightmare by the memory of the creatures they had fought. Every time the horrors appeared in her dream, she swore she could hear a strange, muffled whispering, which would cause her to wake up in a panic. But each time she awoke, the whispering would fade back into the shadows.

Chapter 4

A dozen people in simple brown robes sat silently in a large circle, all staring blankly at their Seer in the middle. A faint blue glow emanated from their hands, with small wisps of blue light streaming toward the Seer. Only their magic illuminated the dark cavern they sat in. One other person stood in the back of the cave, leaning on one of the cool stone walls that surrounded them. This lone apprentice, a thin and well-groomed man in his early thirties named Valon, had no role in aiding his masters farsight.

Both of the Seer's eyes were engulfed in blue light, and he sat in a trance, disconnected from the world around him. He was now one with the magic that surrounded everything. As the apprentice watched his master utilize his ability of farsight, he wondered why it was taking longer than it usually did.

A few more silent minutes passed before the magic surrounding them all turned from the kind blue into a light red. Almost in a trance of boredom himself, the apprentice didn't notice the change at first. However, when he did, he almost fell as he pushed himself off the wall to look closer.

He stepped closer to the mages surrounding his master, all in a state of meditation. They were unable to recognize that something about the magic had changed, but the apprentice did notice how the pure, relaxed nature of the magic had changed into something harsh, festering, and almost so pungent he could smell it. While he watched in worry, he was too well trained to panic.

While the mages couldn't break the spell, his master the Seer could. At least, in theory he should be able to. Not only that, but Valon could end the spell as well. While the apprentice had never undergone farsight, from what he understood the user remained conscious the entire time, it just gave the user an altered form of consciousness. However, the apprentice also knew magic was a wild, powerful thing that served no one person. It was because of this he was trained in another method of interrupting the spell, albeit a cruder and slightly dangerous method. He wouldn't attempt to use this method unless the situation seemed dire.

Small specks of dark green began to mix with the red color magic, something Valon had never seen, making him nervous. As the magic warped from a light red into an almost blood red, the apprentice swore he could feel a presence around them. No, this wasn't just the presence of magic, but that of something sinister. He had never felt the feeling before and had no idea what it could be. However, as a bit more time went on, whispers began to echo in the cave.

Upon hearing the contorted whispers fill the room, the apprentice made his way over to his master. He stared at the Seer, watching his master's blue-filled eyes begin to flicker. While he wasn't sure if this qualified as a dire situation, he knew something wasn't right. He reached to touch his masters head, but his arm was suddenly grabbed by the Seer.

"Not yet!" the Seer hissed in a voice that almost wasn't his.

"Master Mordou?" Valon asked quietly, almost in shock.

The magic surrounding them almost seemed to crackle, as if it was amongst a fight with itself. Valon felt conflicted, knowing that it was possible this wasn't his master's voice. As the unintelligible whispers continued, he forced his hand down to place it on Seer Mordou's head.

"Do ... it..." Seer Mordou slowly whispered.

Immediately after hearing his master's words, he began the spell. He focused and closed his eyes, never having used it before. However, he was a proficient magic wielder, and knew how to bend the exotic energy to his will.

Valon tried to visualize the magic around them in his head as he always did. Magic was an oddity in that to use it one must only know how to traverse it. It was as if it was just another limb of the body, an extension of the mind with its own sense. Being here always meant being surrounded by magical energy. One only had to open their mind and focus to utilize it and hone their skills to be able to make use of it.

The spell was quick and brutal. In the blink of an eye, Seer Mordou was ripped out of his farsight and cut from the influence of magic. Valon watched his spell work as intended, the blood red magical essence being thrust from his master's body. The other mages feeding him slowly waned in power, however the magic did not dissipate as it should. No, it continued to congeal together into what looked to be a mass of floating blood. Valon helped his master up, whose eyes had returned to their normal state, the right being of birth and the left blue again with a permanent magic connection.

"No, no," Seer Mordou sputtered, trying to catch his breath.

"Master, are you alright?" Valon asked, not taking his eyes off the coalesced energy floating before him.

Suddenly, the magic burst into the nearest mage, violently forcing its way into the man's body. Valon watched in horror as the man grabbed his throat as though he couldn't breathe, looking to his still fatigued comrades for help. But before anyone could even comprehend what was happening, it was too late for the man.

Whatever had taken hold of the old mage succeeded in its bid for control. The man transformed before everyone's eyes; his entire body began to contort from the inside out. His skin tore apart and reformed into a leathery, sickly whitish purple color. The structure of his body warped as well, turning him from a frail, thin man into a muscular being. Bone claws ripped out from his knuckles and his teeth became sharper. His entire body was being remade from a human into a beastly predator of sorts.

"H-help!" the man cried out in a vain effort to save himself.

But it was too late, and only seconds later his eyes were consumed by a pungent red glow. Valon looked to his master for wisdom, having no idea what was happening. To his surprise, Seer Mordou looked just as lost as he was.

"Brother! Are you well?" a nearby mage asked, her voice quivering in fear.

"Don't get too close," Seer Mordou cautioned.

But his warning came too late, and the beast lurched forward and struck her with its sharp claws. She was thrown by the blow, her blood spilling to the stone floor of the cave. With the magic gone, darkness filled the cave, only the beast's red eyes and the Seer's blue eye piercing the shadows around them.

Valon was quick to conjure light, bright blue strands of magic dancing from his hands into the air above them. He illuminated the dark cave just in time for him to see another mage being attacked by the creature that was once their friend.

As the aberration struck another mage, Valon could feel blood spatter strike his face. He shuttered, running his hands through his thin beard, trying to get the blood out. It seemed they were out of options.

Seer Mordou quickly unleashed a barrage of pure magic energy at the monster. The sizzling bolts of blue knocked the creature back hard into the wall of the cave, causing it to drop to a knee. Normally, this assault would be enough to either kill or knock out any human. However, as Valon watched the creature slowly stand again, it didn't appear to be as effective.

"Concentrate your magic on this abomination!" Seer Mordou ordered.

The other mages looked at each other in a moment of hesitation. However, seeing three of their own lying wounded on the ground made their decision easy. The mages all unleashed a similar attack on the creature.

A torrent of magic projectiles flew at their once-friendly foe, striking it hard.

Valon maintained the light above them as he watched the creature's demise. The combined magic of the mages tore through the creature with relative ease. Its body was brutalized, ripped apart and scorched from the raw energy of the magic. Still, Valon had never seen anything require so much energy to kill.

Finally, it was over, and the creature lay dead in a pool of tarry black blood. Valon simply stared in horror, having never seen anything like that happen. However, he knew magic was still a mystery, despite thinking anyone had control over it. He just wondered what other terrible things existed within their realm.

"Mages! Tend to your brothers' and sister's wounds. Then bring that creature to my study. I need to speak to my apprentice alone," Seer Mordou ordered.

The mages nodded and spoke affirmations and quickly got to work. Valon watched as his master began to walk from the cave, motioning for him to follow. It seemed that in his farsight, his master had stumbled upon something sinister.

They left the ritual cave and emerged back into the foggy swampland of their home. Valon was surprised by how quickly his master was walking after what they had just gone through. He followed his master through the board fused paths of their village to the Seer's Tower.

The tower stood tall in the center of the village, made of stone and good craftsmanship. It dwarfed the other huts and trees surrounding it, its height allowing the occupants to be closer to the sky and see the surrounding area. Although, there wasn't much to see in the swamplands. Seer Mordou had always been fascinated with the sky, something Valon didn't quite understand.

Before he knew it, Valon found himself sitting in a chair in his master's study room on the bottom of the tower. He remained silent as his master tore through tomes and scrolls on the shelf in his study. He had so many questions but knew they would be answered in time. Valon was completely obedient to his master, who to him was a man that had never been wrong in his life.

Seer Mordou led the Ancient Clan and was the only one able to use farsight to gaze not only at distant things, but sometimes ahead in time. This passed-down ability is how he was declared the next Seer just before the previous had passed away. While seeing ahead in time was difficult and more dangerous, Seer Mordou could do it when necessary.

Valon knew someday he would replace his master, but not before being gifted the ability of farsight. In truth, he was immensely nervous, as the ability was nothing like any other in the realm of magic they were aware of. He could only train and practice other magic until that day came.

Part of his anxiety came from the fact that nobody, including his master, knew how magic exactly worked. They could use it, for it was abundant in the world and it flowed around them like water surrounding a stone in a river. But beyond that, its origins and many secrets remained a mystery. It also didn't help that only the Ancient Clan studied magic.

"Cursed, useless tomes! Not even one of the texts say anything of what I just saw," Seer Mordou yelled before giving up his fruitless effort.

"Master, if I may be so bold, what did you see?" Valon asked, unable to sit idly by any longer.

Almost surprised at Valon speaking up, Seer Mordou's brow ruffled. He sat across the table from his apprentice, nervously scratching at his chin, still perturbed by what he had seen.

"Valon, my apprentice, I've seen what may be the demise of our realm. You of course remember how I sensed a great disturbance in magic energy from the east, yes?" Seer Mordou asked, staring at Valon.

"Of course, Master. We all sensed that day, that brief explosive tear in the fabric of magic. Since then, the magic essence from there still flows as though it is ongoing. Did you see what caused it?" Valon asked, leaning forward with curiosity.

"Perhaps, perhaps not. But I saw what exists there now. There is something strange. It is a gateway, a portal, some sort of connection to another realm. But that oddity is not what I fear, no, it is only the method of transportation for the foul creature. I cannot describe it because I do not know the proper words," Seer Mordou explained, his narrowed eyes showing confusion and possibly fear.

"Creature? A creature of magic?" Valon questioned, eyes wide.

"Of magic, using magic—regardless, it is powerful. You saw what it did to our dear brother Francis. It corrupts, controls, and only grows in strength. I saw the portal; it shimmers in clearing with dozens of strange aberrations making their way through. Not only that, but festering tendrils have forced them through and defile the land around the portal. This is far worse than what I originally thought. They appear like a cruel … living infection, of sorts. We need to act, or we may lose everything," Seer Mordou declared.

As his master explained his vision, Valon leaned back in his chair, chills running down his back. The emotion and descriptive language painted a grim picture in his mind. He had never heard or read anything about this kind of creature before, but it sounded dire. This was the first time in his life he had seen his master this worried.

"That is terrible. What can we do?" Valon replied.

"That is a good question for which I wish I had an answer," Seer Mordou replied, shaking his head.

"Master, I'm sure you will think of something, you always do," Valon urged.

Valon watched as his master smiled briefly before placing his head in his hands, staring down at the knotted wooden table beneath him. It was no wonder his master didn't want the other mages here to see him so distraught. He was always confident and knew exactly what to do.

Something had changed, and Valon figured it was from his farsight connection.

"I know it's a stretch, but could you perhaps try to see our future? I know that many paths may exist, but perhaps we could find something, some hint as to how we defeat it?" Valon asked, knowing his question was based on theory more than knowledge.

"For me to see the future is difficult enough. But there's no telling if I will be able to see what we need. I don't know," Seer Mordou muttered.

Valon sighed, knowing he alone could not solve their problem. No one person could, by the sound of it. Something seemed off with his master, however. He had never been so hesitant to use his farsight, not like this. It seemed whatever he had seen truly scared him.

"Master, please forgive my insolence. But you seem afraid to use your farsight. Did something else happen?" Valon asked slowly.

He watched as Seer Mordou struggled with something in his own mind. Something seemed to have left a mental wound within him, and his eyes looked almost lost. Valon felt badly for pushing, but knew this was not the time for indecision.

"Valon, my keen apprentice … you are right…" Seer Mordou began, shaking his head and focusing himself. "Whatever this being is … it tried to overtake me. If you had not snapped me out of it, what happened to Francis could have happened to me. I feel partially responsible for his death, however we all know the consequences that may result from delving into magic. I cannot stop thinking about the whispering I heard."

"I heard the whispering too. It was … concerning, to say the least," Valon said with a chuckle, trying to lighten the mood.

Seer Mordou let loose a brief chuckle and shook his head. He appeared slightly more confident than he had moments ago. Valon only wished to see his master snap out of whatever mood he was in. Right now, the Ancient Clan needed a leader.

"I believe you are right then, Valon. Our best course of action would be to gather the rest of the clan for me to use my farsight. Perhaps we can see what the future holds and work backwards from there. I only hope I know what to look for," Seer Mordou conceded.

"Or who to look for," Valon added as he lifted an eyebrow.

Before anyone could speak, someone knocked at the front of the tower door. Seer Mordou yelled for them to enter, and Valon stood to see who it was. As expected, it was the rest of the mages from the ritual carrying the remains of the beast that had once been their fellow clansperson, Francis.

"Seer Mordou, we gathered what we could, but it's rather messy," the mage leading the group explained, dry heaving as he spoke.

"That's fine, please bring it to the cellar," Seer Mordou ordered, standing from his chair.

"What now, Master?" Valon asked.

"Now, apprentice, we examine the remains of this abomination closely," Seer Mordou replied, following the other mages to the cellar.

Valon nodded, already feeling sick from the strange odor. As he followed them towards the cellar, the scent of death began to fill the tower. While Valon wasn't looking forward to having to dig through the oozing remains of the corpse, he knew it may yield answers. He took a deep breath and entered through the cellar door, ready for whatever came next.

Chapter 5

Anna could feel herself gritting her teeth as she walked through the once silent forest. Behind her was the cause of her annoyance. Twenty Narsho warriors and their Champion chanted an old marching song as they followed her, singing loud and proud. She had already explained that it would be wise to stay quiet in case the creatures or Highrock Clan were near, but her suggestion had fallen on deaf ears. Instead, the men chose to continue singing with everything they had.

Worst of all was Titus's attitude, who constantly had been delivering small jabs at her anytime she tried to speak. He tried to come off as playful, but Anna knew better. She had briefly wondered if it was because she was a woman, but seeing their Champion act that way to plenty of men too had helped her find the true answer. Titus Fardson, Champion of the Narsho Clan was just extremely arrogant.

As she continued walking, Anna adjusted the metal armor she now wore. Typically, she wouldn't wear such armor as a scout, but they could very well end up in combat. Now, she wore chainmail armor on her entire torso and even had a metal plate covering each of her thighs. That wasn't the only change in her loadout either. Since her sword had been lost, she had been given a replacement one by their blacksmith, Thorvad. It was a little heavier and slightly longer, but she was still confident in her ability to use it. Not only that, but she also chose to take a reinforced wooden buckler shield as well. While it wouldn't help as much as a large shield in combat with a human, she figured the maneuverability of the shield would do well against the weaponless creatures. She had also gotten a replacement bow and quiver full of razor-sharp arrows.

In return for his quick work, Chieftain Barod had given Thorvad the well-crafted hammer Anna had found in the ruins. He had been shocked to see such quality, and was immediately impressed by its power and elegance. He swore that in return, he would make the finest weapons and armor the clan had ever seen. Anna hoped he was right, as they would likely soon need it.

Most of her fellow clansmen behind her had similar armor and weaponry, except for Titus. He had a specially forged set of full plate metal armor, a beautifully made two-handed greatsword, a much smaller sheathed shortsword, and even a Narsho green colored cloak trailing behind him. Anna did recognize that Titus was an incredible warrior and had cut down many Highrock warriors over his twenty years of fighting. She only hoped his combat skill translated from humans to walking horrors.

As they continued, she noticed Titus had suddenly begun walking next to her, no longer singing. She didn't know what to say and waited for him to speak. As she thought, it didn't take long for him to start talking.

"So, what do we call them anyway?" Titus asked, his voice coated in confidence.

"Call what?" Anna asked in return.

"Those things you fought. I've heard you refer to them as probably a dozen other names. What should we call these foul spawns? By your description, they sound as though they've crawled out of the Dark Depths of Folm itself," Titus explained.

"Oh, hm. I don't know," Anna briefly answer, not wanting to think about the enemy they'd soon face.

"Based on how you've explained them, I think horror fits quite well," Titus reasoned, almost talking to himself more than Anna.

"Then Horror it is," Anna affirmed with disinterest.

She watched as Titus turned to the men behind him, walking backwards. He raised his arms around his mouth and took a breath.

"Men! Are you ready to slay these Horrors that dare invade our realm?" Titus yelled loudly.

Anna listened as the men cheered, their morale high. She only hoped they wouldn't waver when they encountered the Horrors. None of them had ever fought such a foe, and unlike the Highrock warriors, this foe did not seem to slow until you inflicted a near-killing blow. In fact, Anna still had to explain what she had learned to everyone. However, she had already planned on going over everything tonight as they camped, for she knew that by this time tomorrow, they would be at the ruins where Fredrik fell.

She stared around at the large trees around them. She recognized some of the sights, and knew they were in the Cursed Lands. She still wondered how the land got its name. From what she could tell, not even the chieftain knew why it was named such. Her only guess was the name may have originated from whatever had left the abandoned town in the ruins it now was. While she had at first thought it was the Horrors that overtook the town, something told her they weren't the cause.

Suddenly, she saw some sort of animal moving ahead. She held up her hand to signal spotting something, but lurched forward as Titus ran into her, not paying attention from walking backwards. She barely steadied herself from falling, shooting the Champion an annoyed look.

"Why are you stopping?" Titus asked loudly.

"Sh!" Anna briefly replied, turning to see what was ahead.

Unfortunately, the animal heard them. It stood straight on its two legs and put its long, feathered nose to the air to smell. Anna could instantly tell they had stumbled upon a forest raptor, a nasty birdlike predator capable of tearing apart even the most trained warriors. She only hoped it was an older male, as they were the only ones who often walked without their pack.

"What is that?" Titus said slightly quieter, trying to block the sun from his eyes.

Anna could hear the men whispering behind her, some louder than others. She quickly turned to quiet them, briefly explaining that a forest raptor was ahead. Unfortunately, by the time she turned back around, it was gone.

"Titus, where did it go?" Anna asked, laying down her sword and taking her bow from around her.

"I don't know, it put its head back down and disappeared into the vegetation," Titus answered, not seeming too worried.

Anna's heart sank as she heard his reply. That could only mean the raptor had caught their scent and was preparing to attack. Even a single raptor would go after a group of humans, trying to grab whatever it could. It was that scavenger ferocity that made them so tough, that and their sharp teeth and claws.

"Keep an eye out; it's stalking us!" Anna shouted to the rest of the warriors.

"Stalking? That doesn't sound good," Titus said to himself.

Anna watched closely for any sign of the raptor from within the many ferns, bushes, and other flora on the forest ground. She had an arrow at the ready, knowing the raptor would have to be dealt with quickly. She continued scanning her surroundings, finally seeing the rustle of a group of ferns from behind them. At least this confirmed the raptor was alone.

"There!" Anna shouted, pointing to the ferns.

Unluckily, her warning was just a moment too late. The raptor leapt from the ferns at the closest warrior, who only gawked as the beast charged him. The raptor lunged forward with a primal slash, its talons ripping through the arm of the warrior as he tried to defend himself. While Anna's warning came too late, her arrow did not.

Just as the raptor went to grab at the warrior with its beaked mouth, it was struck by one of Anna's arrows in the shoulder. It flinched, taking a few steps back. Anna nocked another arrow, ready to deliver a killing shot. However, Titus had already run towards the creature.

"Foul beast!" Titus yelled, running forward and holding his sword high above his head.

The raptor ran at Titus, falling for his taunt. Anna watched in anticipation as the two closed in. The raptor lunged forward, trying to slash Titus with its claws as it had with the other warrior. However, Titus had apparently anticipated this move.

Titus dodged left, and as he did, he shifted his sword from over his head and used the weight of it to swing back around, delivering a fast yet powerful strike at the raptor. The blow struck clean through the neck of the beast, causing its head to topple down on the forest floor.

"Aha! Looks like we're eating well tonight!" Titus cheered as he held the decapitated head of the raptor high into the air.

Seeing that their threat had been neutralized, Anna ran to the wounded warrior, taking some wraps and other medicinal things their shaman had given her out of her bag. She had to push her way through the other warriors who had crowded around their comrade. When she finally got to the wounded man, she was glad to see the laceration wasn't terrible.

The slash hadn't done much damage, but an open wound was the last thing they wanted in a situation like this. Anna had to think for a moment to remember the older man's name, having never talked to him directly.

"Bernol, is it only your arm?" Anna asked, now noticing Titus was bending down to take a look.

"It is, and it hurts," Bernol replied, cringing at the sight of his bleeding arm.

"Ah, a simple flesh wound. Be glad it did not tear muscle or bone, or else you'd really be in bad sorts," Titus said loudly, patting the man on the shoulder.

Anna watched as the man squirmed from Titus's heavy pat as she began to bandage him. All things considered, it could've been much worse. Had she not struck the raptor with her arrow the beast could have dragged him away. If that had happened, the man may be dead right now.

It didn't take long for her to bandage up the warrior, and Anna helped the man stand. He was covered in his own blood, which didn't seem comfortable. However, he was lucky to be alive. She just wished she had been able to shoot the raptor before it had the chance to strike.

"We shall press on now, yes?" Titus asked, looking at everyone around him. "A couple of you find a way to drag that raptor along so we may cook it later."

They all agreed, still in fine morale. However, Anna did notice they were slightly less enthusiastic than they had been only minutes earlier. It did make sense though, as raptors were very uncommon to find. She figured most hadn't even seen such a beast in person before. She was only happy it hadn't been a whole pack.

"I suppose so. There is a certain spot where I'd like us to make camp for the night," Anna replied to Titus.

Titus nodded and looked to Anna to follow. She led on through the forest, Titus walking beside her. Again, she could tell the man wanted to say something. She waited for him to speak.

"That was a fine shot with your bow. You're quite quick," Titus slowly complimented with a small smile.

Anna was shocked at his words, not expecting anything kind to come from the Champion's mouth. She continued walking, not wanting to make a big deal out of it.

"Thank you. I had good mentors," Anna responded, realizing she should at least return the compliment. "You are quite skilled with that sword; the raptor didn't even touch you."

"Ah, thank you. I pride myself in swordsmanship. Though fighting a beast is different from fighting a human; the movement, the awareness, it's an entirely different battle. Fortunately, that is not the first raptor I've slain. In fact, someday I hope to slay one of every beast in this land with my sword," Titus rambled, oozing with pride. "It will be a glorious accomplishment."

"Is that so?" Anna responded, not particularly interested in Titus's story.

"It is! However, I wonder if we do not even know of all the beasts in our realm. Forthoton is a large place. At least I'll be able to cross these Horrors off my list," Titus replied.

"Since you recognize that fighting beasts and humans are different, you should know the Horrors fight more like beasts. They have some sort of primal rage about them. However, as a group they seemed to communicate," Anna described.

"Good to know. But what do you mean they communicated? Did they speak?" Titus asked with great curiosity.

"No. Well, nothing besides beastly roars and angry bellowing. But that didn't seem to communicate anything. Anyway, I plan on telling everyone this over the fire tonight as we camp, for come tomorrow, we will be in combat," Anna explained.

"I see," Titus simply responded.

Anna was surprised at Titus's brief response. It seemed he was actually listening to her for once. Then again, Titus was a very combat-focused man. She could say anything about fighting and he would listen. While it didn't make for great conversation in times of peace, she knew his one-track mind and fierce courage would benefit them in the fight to come.

As they continued, part of her mind began to wander. She hadn't actually seen Fredrik die. While she had already mourned his loss, she now wondered if he was truly gone. Nothing was impossible, and perhaps he had found a way out of the situation. It was only because she would be there tomorrow that she thought such things. Had she not been returning, she would've considered him gone. While she was smart enough to not get her hopes up, the smallest flicker of hope did still exist within her heart.

As they reached a plateau adjacent to the mountain she and Fredrik had stood on when they first looked down upon the ruins, the group quickly set up camp. Their small tents and good-sized campfire were now nestled between the large trees of the plateau. As darkness came, the bright stars of the night sky watched over them.

The raptor made a delicious meal, however the wounded man Bernol opted to eat his previously packed cured meat ration instead. As Anna bit into the rare raptor meat, she looked at the others sitting around the fire. They seemed quiet, as if the reality—and accompanying dangers—of their situation was now dawning; they were going to be fighting a fierce enemy the following day. She had made sure they knew what they were getting themselves into, but Anna knew there was a world of difference between describing a situation and being in the middle of it.

After they finished eating, Anna told the rest of the warriors what she had told Titus earlier. As she explained the Horrors, she could see the smallest glimpses of fear within the eyes of those listening. However, she didn't want to leave out any details, as the last thing she wanted was for them to freeze up when they entered combat. Describing the Horrors in thorough detail now would benefit them all later.

After she finished her small speech on what was to come, she asked if any of them had questions for her. Unsurprisingly, they did not, and began conversing with themselves out of nervousness and to distract their minds.

Anna left their campsite and walked to the edge of the plateau not too far away. She stared over the Cursed Lands, wondering what other secrets it held. There wasn't one fire or any other light in her entire view, which was quite something given the distance. Now, the only light she saw was their own fire and the stars above.

She almost didn't hear Titus as he approached, turning quickly as he heard him step closely behind her. He looked embarrassed for startling her, but then continued walking forward to stand next to her.

"I believe everyone will be ready to fight tomorrow. However, I won't be able to get your description of the Horrors out of my head tonight," Titus chuckled.

"Oh, just wait until you see them. I haven't been able to sleep well since it happened," Anna replied with a half-hearted, almost desperate laugh.

There was a moment of awkward silence, neither knowing what else to say. Anna didn't feel like trying to keep a conversation going if there wasn't one but didn't want to be rude. After all, they would fight side by side tomorrow. She knew the bonds that could form in combat.

"This plateau is a fine spot for camp. Did you stay here on your trip out?" Titus asked.

"No, we passed it as we climbed up the mountain," Anna replied, pointing to the barely visible silhouette of the small mountain nearby. "It was on that mountain top we saw the ruins in the distance."

"Ah, so we are close then?" Titus asked with subtle nervousness.

"Somewhat. Since climbing the mountain is unnecessary, we will need to go around it. Then, at our speed, probably two or three hours walk. At least, that's how far the ruins are. Whether or not we run into those Horrors beforehand is impossible to know," Anna answered.

"I see. Well, then I guess I shall prepare and get a good night's rest. Goodnight, Anna," Titus said with a small nod.

"Goodnight," Anna replied.

Anna watched as the Champion walked back towards camp, his walk looking less confident than it typically did. She wondered if maybe Titus was worried about the fight tomorrow. She hoped he was, as the Horrors were like no enemy she had faced. She was lucky to have escaped, and had it not been for Fredrik's brave sacrifice, she would be dead.

She looked back over the Cursed Lands, shrouded in darkness from a cloudy, almost moonless night sky. Her mind raced with thoughts of Fredrik, the Horrors, and what tomorrow would bring. She sighed, knowing it wouldn't help to overthink things.

Anna turned and walked back toward the camp, trying to stop thinking of Fredrik. If she let emotion overcome her tomorrow, she could pay the price in combat. She needed to remain focused and thought back of her training as a child.

Wanting to be a scout from a young age, the chieftain had let her tag along with other scouts when she was only nine. From then on, she had trained hard. Her entire clan was her family, and she had been raised by random people at various times. Since her father and uncle had died in battle before she was born and her mother had died in childbirth, the Narsho Clan as a whole was her family.

With a deep breath, Anna focused her mind. The best way she could repay her clan was to successfully complete her mission. As a scout, it was up to her to lead the way for her warriors. This wasn't the time to think of the past, no matter how recent it had been.

With this newfound focus, Anna found it easy to sleep well that night. Unbeknownst to her, this would be the final night she would sleep well.

Chapter 6

A foul spray of saliva hit Prince Mace directly on the face as the warrior in front of him barbarically screamed at him. Moments like these were when the prince realized he had no choice but to fight. He held his two swords in front of him, waiting for the Narsho warrior to make the first move.

Watching the hate in his enemy's eyes, Prince Mace easily parried the first blows of his opponent. He continued staring into his foe's eyes, which he saw constantly glance to the raging battle around them. While the prince knew awareness was important, this Narsho warrior seemed to be borderline distracted. For Prince Mace, this was a good thing.

The next time his foe glanced away, Prince Mace lunged forward with his offhand sword, an attack meant to misdirect his Narsho foe. It worked, and the entirety of the man's defense went into deflecting the sword. However, by doing so, the unskilled warrior couldn't react to Mace's other sword, which was thrust directly through his chainmail and into his chest.

Prince Mace felt the small rush of victory as the warrior fell before him, the fatal wound pumping blood from beneath the chainmail. While the prince didn't enjoy killing, he did enjoy the art of swordsmanship. It was that appreciation that allowed him to become the fighter he now was, as he didn't have the fury the other warriors seemed to possess. He would have been just as satisfied to win without killing his opponent.

Prince Mace looked to see his father smashing their ancestral mace down on a wounded Narsho, hatred bursting from his eyes. The finely made weapon was more an artifact than a weapon and had been created by their ancestor and aptly named after him. He knew it was a sign of vanity and pride that his father carried the weapon. Plus, he didn't often fight directly in battle due to his weakness but was always ready to finish off any enemies that still drew breath. While his father didn't have great physical strength, his anger made him stronger in the worst of ways.

Looking around, it appeared their ambush on the outpost had been a success. This outpost had been the closest to the Narsho village, and they had figured it made sense to attack it. Now any Narsho runner from their main village would waste their time coming here. With the other outposts being farther away, they would have enough time to strike the village before any backup could arrive.

As Prince Mace approached his father, he heard the soft rustling of something behind him. Not only that, but his father began pointing behind him, his face still seething with rage. As he turned, Prince Mace saw a Narsho woman trying her best to sneak away from the receding chaos.

Knowing she could warn her people, Prince Mace sprinted after her. She turned to see she had been spotted and began to run. However, she tripped over a large tree root and was sent hurtling down to the forest floor. He quickly approached, swords at the ready.

She turned over to face him, backing away on the ground for a moment before realizing she had been caught. She firmly gripped a dagger in one hand and a small piece of parchment in the other. There was no fierce determination in her eyes, only fear.

"Finish her!" Chief King Mace yelled as he walked toward his son.

The woman lay shaking on the ground, the dagger held in front of her. Prince Mace watched as she held it in a death grip, knowing her fate. The prince held his sword to her throat, feeling nausea grow in his stomach.

This wasn't who he was. Armed or not, man or woman, Prince Mace did not enjoy killing. No, he enjoyed the swordplay and that was it. The killing was done out of basic survival and a necessity to his people. Unfortunately, he'd have to do it once more.

"I'm sorry," Prince Mace whispered to the woman, his voice filled with sorrow.

The prince wasted no time in killing the woman, delivering a clean slice through the Narsho's neck. He flinched as he did, feeling acid rise in his throat. When he was young, he used to throw up in this sort of situation. Fortunately, or perhaps unfortunately, he had become desensitized to it.

"Good work, Son. If she had made it back our attack would've been lost," Chief King Mace lauded, removing his winged metal helmet and holding it at his waist.

"Thank you," Prince Mace replied, not wanting to gloat over such an easy kill.

"Warriors! Grab this corpse and put it with the others!" Chief King Mace yelled, turning to the men back in the camp.

Prince Mace passed his father and headed back towards the camp. Soon, the body of the woman he killed would be placed on the fire their warriors were now constructing. It was another part of his father's obsession. In their tradition, all clansmen were to be buried upon death, that way their body would be reclaimed by the land and their soul would be put at rest. To burn their bodies was to disrespect them, to send their soul to the Dark Depths. While Prince Mace was skeptical of the existence of the terrible realm of Folm, it seemed his father believed with passion.

As he entered the now torn apart camp, he realized they had lost two warriors in the fight. Fortunately, they had brought most of their warriors with them. Over seven hundred men and women lingered around the camp now, readying themselves for the large battle to come. Still, Prince Mace estimated that the Narsho clan had a similar number of troops around their large village.

In fact, given they had been fighting since the fall of the Great Clan, the two actually had similar populations and warrior counts. Prince Mace remembered hearing their own clan's last estimate was almost two thousand five hundred clanspeople, and the Narsho was close in size. Because of their constant fighting, they had lower populations than the Forud and Linta clans. If war ever broke out against them, they'd be far too outnumbered.

There was so much to consider that nobody else seemed to worry about. In times like this Prince Mace wished he could shut it out easier, but he couldn't. Someday he would be able to do something about it, but until then he would have to wait. As he thought in silence, he didn't hear his father approach him.

"Son, you should look happier in front of the warriors. Any victory is a good one," Chief King Mace urged, patting his son on the shoulder.

"My apologies, Father; I'm just deep in thought," Prince Mace replied.

"Thought? About what?" Chief King Mace asked, his tone suggesting the question was more of a formality.

"Nothing important; forgive me," Prince Mace replied, turning to look at his father.

"That is alright, just make sure to have a clear head for the battle ahead. We shall camp here all day tomorrow to rest, then the following day we shall attack. With any luck, our people will finally get our revenge," Chief King Mace replied, almost salivating at the thought.

"Of course, Father."

"Good. Now, I will go deliver a speech to our brave men and women. I urge you to stand amongst the crowd and make your presence known. While you may fight well with that, well, with that fancy dual-wielding technique the old weapons master taught you before he died, not everyone sees your skill in battle," Chief King Mace suggested, then walked away from his son.

Prince Mace didn't respond, only following his father toward the center of the camp. The fire pit had already been dug and began to roar. Bodies of the deceased were thrown in with reckless abandon, except the Highrock warriors of course, who were getting a proper burial just outside of the outpost.

After the warriors formed a huge circle around the fire and their chief king, Prince Mace put on a confident face and stood next to his father. As his father began to speak, he zoned out once more. He knew his father would only speak of their strength, their history, and to fight hard against the Narsho. While his words were somewhat hollow, his passion and determination were not. It was those qualities that filled his warriors with a similar righteous zeal.

Fierce roars of the warriors echoed out as his father spoke. Prince Mace even felt it difficult to not get worked up. Between the violent flame lashing out as more bodies were tossed into it, and his father's passion, even the prince felt a sense of pride run through him. It was moments like this that he wondered if his father was right, and that their war was just and should be finished. However, the prince knew it was merely the heat of the moment, and once he returned to logic he would think differently.

Of course, a large feast took place after the speech. More campfires were made, parts of the ground were cleared, and it began. Ale flowed and the warriors of the Highrock cheered with vigor and anticipation. While the prince didn't particularly feel like he fit in, he still took part in the celebrations, more for his father's sake. If nothing else, he had to keep up an appearance; part of him knew if he was to succeed his father he would want to do so with good relations with his people. After all, not everyone appreciated the ancient bloodline of the Highrock clan. Prince Mace often worried what would happen when that day came. His father had three advisors, none of whom the prince had a close relationship with. Whether they truly liked his father or feared his wrath was uncertain, but if anyone would try to steal control it would be them.

Prince Mace was dragged out of his own mind by someone calling his name. He looked around for a moment, seeing who could've called him. Eyes were on him, and finally he realized it was General Klon standing across the fire.

"Prince Mace! Have you had too much to drink?" General Klon asked with a cheeky grin.

"Of course not; I was thinking about the fight to come," Prince Mace replied.

"I only wanted to applaud you on your swordsmanship," General Klon continued, his tone borderline snide. "Your elaborate dual wielding is something to behold."

"Why, thank you," the prince replied slowly. "Trov, the old weapons master, taught me everything he knew before he died." Prince Mace took a drink of his ale to further calm his increasingly agitated nerves.

"Ah, it must be nice. And to think some people consider it a crutch for a man that cannot fight with a single sword or axe alone. How foolish they are," General Klon rambled.

Prince Mace felt a mix of embarrassment and anger. It seemed the general was the one who had imbibed too much golden ale. Prince Mace closed his eyes briefly, trying to calm his frayed mind. He was sick of feeling like an outsider in his own clan, like he hadn't earned their approval or trust. Having spent most of his time with Trov made him spend less training with his clan. Of course, that wasn't the only reason. Trov had been a severely outspoken clansman who wanted the war with the Narsho to end. Prince Mace had been largely influenced by him, and as he thought of his old mentor, he opened his eyes, feeling a fire ignite within him.

"I'd hardly call it a crutch. If anything, it can only be achieved by a proper swordsman who can handle such an artform," Prince Mace responded, finishing his ale and standing.

The nearby warriors watched in anticipation as the two glared at each other, only the crackling of the fire disrupting the silence. Prince Mace saw the general was surprised by his reaction but wasn't ready to quit.

"Ah, an artform, that is a good way of calling it. After all, art is something made by those who lack the will and skill to fight, and those who have too much free time on their hands. I suppose if one's expectation of skill was low enough, they could be talked into wasting their time on such an art," General Klon replied with a mocking chuckle.

Some of the warriors around him laughed, others looked on with confusion and bewilderment. It seemed the day of someone challenging the prince had already come, just in a different form and objective. However, Prince Mace was not in the mood to surrender.

"Enough of this!" King Mace yelled from nearby, looking away from his advisors.

"No, Father! If General Klon wants to speak, who are we to stop him? Even if what he says is unintelligible and a waste of our time, the good general should be allowed to speak," Prince Mace yelled, looking from his father to the general.

"Now his true colors show. You are painted in arrogance, boy! Covered in it! You think you're better than all of us because you have the blood of the Mace line!" General Klon yelled, pointing at Prince Mace.

"Again, you are wrong, General. I don't care for the bloodline; while it's a part of me, I rarely consider it. No, I care for the future of our people. I am focused on making the Highrock clan great. If you have a problem with me, let us settle it here and now!" Prince Mace challenged, stomping hard onto the dirt beneath them.

"Fight you? I could not. What fool would fight their own prince? Certainly, that would lead to exile," General Klon retorted, pretending it wasn't his skill he was worried about.

"Oh, that issue can be solved. Father, promise me you will not interfere if the general and I duel? This is a personal matter and must be settled," Prince Mace implored, looking at his stunned father.

"I…" After a moment's hesitation, the chief king replied, "I will certainly not. You both know dueling is a sacred right to our clan. If you wish to duel, I will not stop you. If you wish to duel to the death, I will not block the axe as it cleaves your skull." An almost excited look gleamed on his weathered face.

More warriors from around their camp came over to watch what was unfolding. Whispers had turned into antagonizing yells, and the sound of it all continued to fuel the fire. Most cheered for General Klon, others cheered for the prince. However, Prince Mace was only focused on the older man standing across the crackling orange fire.

"Well then. That solves that problem. So, General, my question is this: will you see this through and request a duel? Or will I have to do it for you?" Prince Mace asked, feeling more fired up than he ever had in his life.

Everyone stared at the general, whose face had slowly lost its confidence. The smallest cracks of disbelief and worry began to undermine his facade of bravery. However, he soon realized this from the looks he received from nearby warriors and stood up a little straighter before speaking.

"Of course, I will see it through. Prince Garon Mace, I challenge you to a duel!" General Klon yelled, picking up his battleaxe from beside him.

"And I accept," Prince Mace replied, drawing both of his swords.

They waited, knowing they required one more person to begin the duel. It was customary to have a watcher for the duel, a warrior or even a clansperson who acted as a sort of referee. That way, if any banned methods such as magic, poison, or throwing weapons were used, the user could be brought before the chief king.

"I shall act as your watcher," a deep female voice said from nearby.

Prince Mace looked to see one of their two clan Champions, Glora, crossing her muscular arms and watching the two of them. Prince Mace held her in regard, knowing she was immensely tough yet simple enough to not choose a side and let anything slide.

"I agree," General Klon affirmed.

"I agree," Prince Mace repeated.

"Then, as your watcher, I will ensure the sanctity of this duel. I need not explain the rules to you two. I shall count down from ten," Glora began.

Prince Mace felt a rush of adrenaline as he realized this was happening. General or not, he would defeat Klon. He was sick of being looked upon like an outsider. He was tired of his bloodline being the reason some disliked him. He hated that even thinking differently invited Highrock clanspeople to object to him. Now he would show them he could be as fierce as any of them, as they all hoped he could be.

As Glora counted down, time slowed to a crawl. Prince Mace watched General Klon, who nervously spun his battleaxe around within his hands. While the prince recognized the man had obvious talent in combat and a fine technique, it seemed his emotions could be used against him. He could tell the general was filled with hatred, perhaps even fear. He would undoubtedly strike hard and fast, as to end the fight before it became too prolonged. This was not only his way, but the way of the Highrock people.

Prince Mace unhooked his dark red cloak from his back, not wanting it to slow him down. He stared intently at his opponent, time barely creeping along. He waited with bated breath for Glora to finish her countdown.

"One!" Glora yelled, motioning for all her clanspeople to step back.

At that moment, General Klon almost leapt from where he was standing. Dust from the ground kicked up as Klon sprinted around the fire towards Prince Mace. The frenzied look in his eyes told the prince he had assumed correctly; the general was going to try his hardest and use all his strength to kill him.

The harsh sound of metal rung out through the silent air, cutting the rising tension like a knife. General Klon was growling as his battleaxe struck against Prince Mace's two blades, trying to force his weight upon the prince. However, despite being thin, the prince had more muscle than he appeared.

Prince Mace forced the battleaxe from off his blades, taking a leap back before the general would attack again. As predicted, he did, leaping forward and swinging his axe from a low position. Prince Mace easily deflected it, letting loose his own attack. But his parry was deflected almost as easily, General Klon quickly recovering and smacking away the prince's swords with his axe.

Prince Mace quickly deduced the general had speed and power but lacked the technique to combine them together. The general pushed himself harder, unleashing a flurry of blows at the prince. Prince Mace parried or dodged them all until the final strike came. The blade of the battleaxe barely nicked the prince's arm, drawing blood. While it stung, the prince didn't flinch or even acknowledge the wound. Instead, his focus was tempered, and he finally went on the attack. Now, he wouldn't stop until the general was dead.

Their blades clashed as both stayed on the offensive, neither giving an inch to the other. Neither held back, the general's brutal axe swings dancing off the dual blades of the prince. Dirt was kicked up as they fought, always rushing back to engage the other directly. The onlookers yelled, some in favor of the general while others in favor of the prince.

Prince Mace could feel an animalistic sort of energy rising within him, and he tried to suppress it the best he could. His technique relied on a focus and a clear head, which was hard to keep in battle. Not to mention a part of him feared the kind of person he would become if he gave in to primal rage. He had seen such depravity on the battlefield earlier. Despite his challenge to the general, Prince Mace did not want to be a killer. Besting the general in front of their clan would suffice.

As sweat and his own saliva began to drip into his well-trimmed goatee, the prince felt it hard to concentrate. Luckily, he realized the general was already waning. Through the chaos he spotted his father, whose face was contorted with a strange prideful pleasure. It appeared he would finally do something worthy of his father's attention, and as he thought of their strained relationship, he strangely found himself focusing better.

He unleashed a flurry of blows onto the general, his fine blades dancing around him in a performance of beautiful death. General Klon was unable to keep up, the blades lightly cutting across his arms. Prince Mace watched as the general leapt back, shocked at his inability to block the blades. He stared at the body language of his opponent, seeing the anger and distress in him. Based on how the general fought, the prince knew what was next. He changed his stance, ready for the assault.

General Klon let loose a battle cry, riling up the warriors around him. Prince Mace watched intently as the general charged at him with his battleaxe held high. As expected, the prince smiled, having an idea of how to finish this fight.

General Klon grabbed the axe by both hands and brought it down hard on Prince Mace, who artfully sidestepped. In a moment, the prince managed to disarm the general by forcefully lifting it out of his now weakened grip using one of his swords. Before General Klon even had a chance to react, Prince Mace struck with years of withheld contempt.

With the fast slash of his sword, Prince Mace slashed through flesh and bone, sending the general's dominant right hand falling to the torn-up ground beneath them. Not giving any quarter, Prince Mace swung both his blades at the general's neck, barely stopping in time to slightly draw blood.

The entire forest was now silent, watching in shock as their general knelt helplessly on the ground, looking as though he were a captive about to be executed. Only the muffled sounds of pain from the general and whispers from onlooking warriors filled the air; not even the king said a word.

Prince Mace looked over to his father, whose eyes were wide with absolute pleasure. This was the first time the prince had ever seen his father look at him with any sort of pride. And in that moment, he knew exactly what his father wanted him to do. He wanted him to slay the general here, in front of their warriors.

Prince Mace looked back down at the nearly sobbing general, who was trying to stop his wrist from bleeding out. The prince knew killing the general would send a message that the bloodline was not to be trifled with, let alone himself. As he pressed his blades against his opponent's throat, knowing what he must do, a sudden wave of emotion overcame him, battling his earlier animalistic rage—as it had in the midst of battle—and he immediately felt disgusted. Prince Mace ripped his swords away in a sudden act of restraint, holding the dripping blades at his side.

Whispering filled the air and he turned to his father, whose smile had begun to fade. The prince's display of mercy was not customary in Highrock dueling, and the chief king appeared to be having just as difficult a time reconciling his son's action as the rest of the warriors.

"Thank ... you," General Klon whispered, also in a state of shock.

Prince Mace didn't respond and walked toward his father. The look of disappointment he was used to had returned to his father's face, but the prince did not care. He had won in his own way, without any help. But, the battle had unleashed something within him.

As he stared at his father, the prince noticed his father's attention divert as he cocked his head and appeared to listen intently to something no one else could hear, staring off into the distance. He didn't spare a look for his own son.

The prince walked past his father, refusing to acknowledge him as he fixed his gaze on the dark forest ahead, pain and conflict tearing at his soul. Now that he had left the battle, and though it had been a victory, his mind raced, and he hated it. As he strode off into the darkness, Prince Mace only focused on the battle ahead, knowing it may very well lead to the end of their fighting.

Chapter 7

As Chieftain Barod looked over his ever-expanding harbor, he felt the slightest sense of pride emerge. In his old age he began to frequently reflect over his almost thirty years of leading the Narsho people. It wasn't perfect; he hadn't gotten them out of war, but it hadn't been the worst of times ever. Nonetheless, he sought more for his people, and for that reason, he had begun constructing a small fleet of ships over the past year.

The morning's mist was beginning to leave, slowly revealing seven large ships and a few smaller ones. He had heard tales of islands and other mysterious places somewhere across the sea from Linta sailors over the years, and he wanted to see these places for himself. He yearned to explore more of Forthoton and hoped he could find something that would aid his people.

He waved to some passing workers, who were clad in their warmer clothes as they headed towards the harbor to begin the day's work. He loved his clan, and from what he could tell they loved him. He only wanted peace and prosperity for them but didn't know how to attain it. He thought perhaps exploration could help them.

"Good morning, Chieftain!" an old man greeted with a wide smile as he walked past.

"Good morning, Nort!" Chieftain Barod replied to the man he had known his entire life.

As the sun slowly emerged through the clouds, the chieftain smiled, knowing it would be a good day. He turned from the harbor and began walking back up the dirt path towards the heart of their village. Chieftain Herold Wooll of the Forud Clan would likely be arriving any moment now, and he wanted to be ready to greet his old friend.

Given their non-aggression alliance with the Forud, it was common for Narsho and Forud to stay in each other's villages for prolonged times. While the

Forud wouldn't help the Narsho fight the Highrock, they didn't trade or interact with the Highrock at all.

While Chieftain Barod wished his old friend would assist them in their long fight against the Highrock Clan, he knew why he wouldn't; war was terrible, wasteful, and expensive. Chieftain Barod thought of an old saying the previous chieftain used to tell him: "If the blacksmith was properly compensated for his work, he'd be the richest man in all of Forthoton." He chuckled, continuing back towards his hall.

Suddenly, a voice from nearby called out, "Chieftain!"

Chieftain Barod looked to see their shaman waving to him as he slowly walked over. He had always liked Olaf, but sometimes the man was known to unnecessarily exaggerate the state of things. Still, he was a skilled man of medicine and magic, although Chieftain Barod didn't like magic and often shut the nasty concept out of his head.

"Good morning, Olaf!" Chieftain Barod waved, walking in the shaman's direction.

As the two approached, he thought he heard Olaf muttering something out loud, too quietly to hear. He couldn't help but chuckle to himself, knowing they were both old men now. Once it had seemed such a distant concept, and now they lived it every day. He waited until they were only feet from each other before speaking.

"Olaf, I couldn't hear you; what was that?" Chieftain Barod said softly as they approached.

"Chieftain, where is Anna Myhre?" Olaf asked with slight worry in his eyes.

"She left to lead our men to the ruins, did I not tell you?" Chieftain Barod asked, almost certain he remembered telling the shaman.

"Oh no. If you did, I didn't realize it. Oh, my," Olaf worried.

"What? Why? Was she not well to travel?" Chieftain Barod asked.

"Oh, she was well I suppose. Perhaps too well," Olaf replied, brow furrowed in concern.

"What do you mean?" Chieftain Barod asked in confusion.

He watched as Olaf thought for a moment, as if running various scenarios in his head. He wasn't sure if he should say something or let the shaman think. Fortunately, he spoke again quickly.

"I believe Anna is … with child," Olaf whispered, looking around as he did.

"Anna is pregnant?" Chieftain Barod replied, eyes wide.

"Yes! I'm almost certain. I did not have a chance to tell her, as I wanted her to relax without concern. Oh, I made a mistake," Olaf groaned regretfully.

"Olaf, Olaf, great shaman. You made no mistake," Chieftain Barod replied, wanting to calm the man. "If there is fault, it is mine."

"Chieftain, had I told her then she might not have gone, for fear of the child's life," Olaf argued.

"Or she may have still gone. She isn't far along, is she?" Chieftain Barod asked.

"No, no," Olaf mumbled.

Chieftain Barod didn't reply immediately, feeling guilty for asking her to go. He wasn't sure if she would've gone on her own had she known, but because he had asked, she was now on the mission with her unborn child. In his wisdom, he knew he shouldn't feel guilty or regret it, but he still would. The human mind was never as controllable as logic itself.

"Well, we must not worry, Olaf. She is a capable scout. And once she returns, we can tell her immediately—together, if you'd like," Chieftain Barod replied.

"Thank you, Jonis; I can always count on you," Olaf said, then realizing his lapse in proper address, amended, "er, chieftain. I only wonder who the father is."

Chieftain Barod was surprised to hear his given name spoken, having not heard it in so long. As for the father, he was sure it was Fredrik. However, he would not reveal Anna's secrets, not even to his old friend.

"I shall wonder too," Chieftain Barod replied.

Before either of the old men spoke again, the chieftain noticed one of his gate guards running down the village path toward him. He already knew what the man would say and tried his best to temporarily forget about Anna. There was nothing he could do about her now, but he could convince the Forud Chieftain what she had seen was a real threat. That was how he could best help her now.

"Chieftain! Chieftain Wooll and the Forud have arrived!" the guard yelled as he approached, saluting his chieftain.

"Very good," Chieftain Barod replied, sending the guard off.

"I shall leave you now. When Anna returns, we shall tell her together in private," Olaf affirmed mainly to himself.

"Yes, we will. Goodbye, Olaf."

The two parted ways, both partially bound by the smallest of secrets. Olaf was a good man, and the worry in the old man's eyes made the chieftain respect him that much more. His clan was everything to him, and he would do anything for them.

As he turned to walk to the gate, he knew his people could be helped. With the threat of the horrors out in the world, they would need as much help as they could get. If he wanted to create a peaceful world, he had to convince the Forud Clan to aid them in battle against their common enemy. As he strode up the dirt path, Chieftain Barod felt a swell of purpose, knowing how he may be able to best help his people.

Chapter 8

Looking upon the terrible sight with absolute horror, Anna found herself speechless. In fact, none of the other Narsho clansman made a sound. Not even Titus spoke a word, standing silently next to Anna.

Anna removed her sword from its sheath, staring at the blade, then at the slowly pulsating ground before them. She slowly touched her sword to the sickly purplish, black-colored flesh covering what had once been the forest floor. As she pressed the blade into the fleshy surface, black ooze seeped from the wound for a moment before it slowly began to seal itself.

As she peered into the distance, it seemed the entire forest ahead of them had become defiled by something. She knew it was probably connected to the Horrors and that the ruins were close by; however, she wasn't sure she wanted to walk on the strange, seemingly living surface covering the ground.

"Er, Anna, was this here last time you were here?" Titus asked, slowly touching the ground with his foot.

"It wasn't. The land was like the rest of the forest. The ruins are close ahead as well. It seems that something is destroying, or perhaps controlling the land here," Anna replied.

She nearly held her breath in anticipation as she stepped on the almost spongy surface. It quivered under her step, and she almost fell ill as she stared down at the nasty, black ground. She knew they had to press forward, but something didn't feel right.

"It's like the land is living…" commented one of the warriors from behind her.

Others agreed as they all hesitantly stepped onto the strange living flesh. To Anna, it felt as though she was walking in a semi-dried puddle of mud, but the sound, appearance, and slight odorous smell of it prevented her from pretending it was anything but a strange growth.

"The ruins are just ahead," Anna said quietly over her shoulder. "Let's slowly make our way there. Keep your eyes open."

"Oh, I won't have a problem looking away from this disgusting abomination," Titus replied, frowning at the ground.

As they continued, Anna was stunned to see all the flora of the forest had fallen victim to the strange material as well. Plants on the ground had begun to wither, and the bark of nearby trees had turned dark black as the living ground crept up their surfaces. It was a terrible sight, and she shuddered to think what was causing it.

They continued through the tainted forest, finally coming to the abandoned town. As they walked through the town, there were no signs of the Horrors. In fact, the quiet was tormenting Anna more than the sight of the Horrors themselves. There was no way they had simply vanished, and she knew their group was probably walking into a trap, but they had to press on and see what was going on.

"This is incredibly strange. These buildings are so … decently constructed," Titus said, clenching his greatsword.

"Yes. Whoever lived here had superior craftsmanship. I wonder if whatever is happening now happened to them," Anna replied.

"I only hope they were not as strong as we are," Titus quickly added.

Anna had the same fear. If these lost people had fallen to this strange enemy, then what chance did the Narsho people have? Everything pointed to these ruins being from a more advanced, or at least more intelligent group of people. If the Horrors had caused their demise, Anna feared for her people.

Continuing down the flesh-covered cobblestone path, Anna noticed her warriors entranced with the surroundings. Interestingly, the buildings didn't seem to be covered by the strange living ground. She looked closer at a small home they were passing and saw that it appeared as though the strange fleshy substance was having a hard time taking hold of the buildings. In fact, it appeared to overtake anything living with great ease.

As they continued toward the town square, Anna's anxiety mounted with each fleshy step. She could see the well in the distance, which was only feet away from where she had seen Fredrik fall. She knew what she may see, his lifeless body still lying there. In fact, she had tortured herself over every scenario in her head. Still, she was ready for whatever came, or at least she hoped she was.

However, as they reached the center of the town, there was nothing in sight beyond the strange ground and untouched buildings. Fredrik's body was nowhere to be found. Briefly forgetting about the world around her, she looked around the cobbled square, scanning around all the buildings. She even ran into the large building they had searched together.

Unfortunately, there was nothing inside the large building either. The growth had already seeped in through the open doors, yet Fredrik was nowhere to be found. Not only that, there were also no Horrors around. She closed her eyes for a moment, part of her feeling cheated at being denied closure. A tear dropped from her eye as she felt a mix of anger and sorrow.

It took a few moments to regain her composure, knowing her job here was not yet done. No, it seemed the foul growth was spreading from a certain direction, and if they found the source, they may be able to find out how to destroy the deadly new foe. She straightened herself out, took a deep breath, and walked back outside.

She found the warriors had spread out, examining the nearby buildings and heading down the other paths to other parts of the ruined town. Titus had been standing by the well looking at the building she had been in, obviously waiting for her. She approached him, not in the mood for his usual sarcasm or rudeness.

"Is this where you fought them?" Titus asked, the slightest hint of suspicion in his voice.

"It was. Right here. I'm sorry I ran off like that. I just expected to... well, find Fredrik's body here," Anna admitted.

"That's understandable. I'd want to try to find one of my men if I had to leave him. Although, I'd do anything in my power to not leave them in the first place..." Titus replied, seemingly unaware at how offensive his statement was.

Anna ignored it and simply walked off, shutting Titus out of her head. Based on the direction she had come, she could somewhat tell where the start of the corruption might have been. However, she didn't want to venture too far, and felt slightly defeated. Between Fredrik and not finding anything here besides the living ground, she began to lose hope.

She sighed, staring at the wretched land around her. Now the Cursed Lands truly began to look like their namesake, though part of her believed it had gotten its name under different circumstances. After all, it hadn't been here only a week earlier. If this odd sickness had been what wiped out the prior people here, why would it have disappeared? Wouldn't it have spread? She didn't know, but something in her gut told her this was a new threat to their realm.

"Champion Fardson! Scout Myhre!" a young warrior yelled as he sprinted up the farthest pathway out of town.

Anna quickly walked toward the man, Titus following her. As she neared the warrior, he looked as though he had something truly disturbing. She recognized him as Wil Tukor, potentially the youngest of the group. If she remembered, he was still but a teenager.

"What is it?" Anna asked as they approached each other.

"I found something strange, I don't even know what to call it. Please, you should see it for yourselves," Wil replied as he caught his breath.

"Alright, lead the way," Anna replied, glancing at Titus. "We should bring everyone."

"Warriors! We're leaving!" Titus barked at the top of his lungs, looking around the town square.

The group formed as Anna followed Wil, wondering what the young warrior had found. Based on his lack of description and the fact he was still breathing, she knew it wasn't a Horror, or Fredrik for that matter. He must have found something quite out of the ordinary.

They followed him down the relatively short path leading out of the city, and as they turned a corner around the final home, Anna's eyes were instantly drawn to something. Not far from them was a strange, large object on the ground.

"There, that's it," the warrior said, slowing his pace as though he were afraid to get near it.

Anna didn't hesitate and passed Wil, walking closer. It was a strange looking thing, like a sort of tendril, root-like object that had grown straight along the ground for so far that she couldn't see where it began. It was quite large and easily was six or seven feet in circumference. If it wasn't for the sickly, purple color and flesh-like appearance, she could have been convinced it was the emerging root of an enormous tree. Interestingly, the living ground didn't try to take control of the tendril and was just as far in the distance as the tendril was.

"Anna, be careful!" Titus yelled from behind her.

Anna ignored him, now standing inches from the tendril. The closer she examined the foreign object, the more disgusted she was. Its flesh seemed hardened, with only small holes here and there coating it. It looked like it was made of the same substance as the Horrors. She could only assume following the tendril would lead them to the heart of the issue.

"We need to follow it back," Anna quickly said, turning and facing her stunned warriors.

"Er, are you certain it is necessary?" Titus asked, trying to hide his fear.

"Yes; the chieftain must know the size of this threat," Anna quickly answered, turning back around and walking.

She could hear Titus swear under his breath before ordering the warriors to follow her. At least the Champion's pride wouldn't let him turn back, something Anna could use. She needed to know what lay in the distance, and if possible, find Fredrik's fate in the process.

She pressed on, following the tendril through the thick, corrupted forest. A strange odor was in the air, one that reeked of death. The tendril had carefully wrapped its way through any opening between the trees, rocks, and other obstacles in the forest. While the path was not a straight one, the tendril itself could easily be followed, and as they did so, its size increased slightly.

"This is disturbing," Titus said, quickly walking his way next to Anna.

"Yes. Yes, it is," Anna replied, noticing she too began to feel some fear.

The world around them now looked like an entirely different realm. Between the pungent, black flesh covering the life of the forest and the large tendril, she could only wonder if they had crossed into Folm, or if this is how the legend had been created.

As they continued forward, she noticed even the leaves of the trees had been corrupted and now sprouted nasty black tendrils of their own that reached out to other leaves. It almost looked as if they sought to darken the sky above them, merging the trees together that were close enough.

Anna shuddered at the thought of the artificial darkness, hoping they wouldn't have to find a torch somewhere. Given that it was midday, she didn't think she would need anything of the sort. However, as they followed the growing tendril, the leaves had progressed further along in their dark goal.

Finally, after walking for what was probably twenty minutes, they found themselves shrouded in darkness. Only small beams of light managed to penetrate the few openings here and there. The trees of the Cursed Lands were thick and copious, allowing the strange affliction to overtake it with ease. Anna felt dread rising within her and longed to see more light. Out of nervousness, she found herself curling her one long lock of red hair around her finger. She thought she felt eyes watching her, and she constantly looked around for the source, but saw none. Fortunately, they were only minutes from her desire.

Light from the distance protruded through the forest, and Anna picked up the pace. She and the warriors quickly ran towards the light, following the tendril, which had almost doubled in size. Anna felt slight hope as she began to emerge in the light, but it only took a moment for it to be crushed.

In the middle of the forest was an enormous, treeless clearing. The only thing in the clearing was the center of everything they sought to follow. Dozens of tendrils were split out from one central location, which somehow seemed empty. As Anna stared in shock, it looked as though the space where the tendrils met was somehow contorted, or blurry. She had no idea what she was looking at.

"What … What is that?" Titus asked.

"I don't know. But whatever it is, it looks to be draining or controlling the life around it. I'm sure the Horrors must've come from here," Anna replied.

Tendrils from the strange shimmer in the air shot out along the ground in all directions. Not only that, but the strange plague covering the ground also seemed thicker there, making her believe it all must be centered in this location. She could only stare in horror, unable to speak. However, it wasn't long before something else did.

"...Anna..." a pungent, dark voice whispered from somewhere close.

Anna spun around, feeling a violent chill run up her spine. She looked everywhere, not seeing anything. She began to breathe heavily, trying hard to remain calm.

"Did you hear that?" Bernol asked aloud.

"I did! It knew my name!" Wil replied.

"What? It said my name!" Titus insisted.

"I think we should go," Anna said, looking at everyone else.

"Anna ... Join us. You can be with Fredrik again..." the thick, nasty voice whispered.

"Anna!" Fredrik's voice called out.

Anna's heart stopped as she heard the voice of her former lover. She felt frozen in time, and slowly turned back toward the shimmering air. As she saw him standing there, she forgot everything else—her mission, the warriors with her, they all were tossed away as she saw him again: walking to her from the strange anomaly was Fredrik.

"Fredrik?" Anna asked quietly, feeling her eyes water.

She stumbled toward him, enamored by his beautiful bright red eyes. He was as handsome as she remembered, and she almost tripped as she continued to walk toward him. He was only twenty or so meters away now, and she longed to be in his arms.

"Anna! My love!" Fredrik called, holding out his arms and stopping.

Anna continued forward, picking up her pace. She felt so desperate and knew the hole in her soul was from his absence. Now she could be with him forever; she could find somewhere safe and live happily. Thoughts ran through her mind as she approached him, unable to focus, but someone else was loudly calling her name from behind her, though she could barely hear it. She turned to see Titus running toward her, waving his arms in the air.

"Anna! Get away from that thing!" Titus yelled, his greatsword at the ready.

As she turned back to Fredrik, she shrieked, stumbling back and falling in terror. The man she remembered wasn't standing before her any longer. The Horror standing only feet away may have been Fredrik at one point, but now it looked to be consumed by the corruption around them. It lurched toward Anna, gnarled claws for hands.

Anna flinched, unable to do anything but stare at the familiar yet distorted face of her love. She braced for the worst, feeling her heart sink.

"Fredrik…" Anna whispered in sorrow.

"No! Foul beast!" Titus yelled, charging forward and ramming his heavy metal pauldron shoulder first into the Horror.

Anna watched as the Horror flew back and fell onto the fleshy ground. Titus quickly helped her up, but she couldn't take her eyes from what once had been Fredrik. She almost reached back, wanting to somehow save him.

"Anna, we need to leave now!" Titus urged, holding his hand down to help her up.

She shook her head, trying to snap herself out of it. She grabbed hold of Titus's metal gauntlet and was quickly lifted by his great strength. He put his arm around her and began to run, Anna barely able to keep up.

Hearing yelling, she looked back to where the warriors had been standing. To her shock, they were now fighting Horrors that were emerging from the forest around them. She winced at the sight of the terrible looking creatures; while they all had the same purplish, gnarled skin and other abnormalities, she noticed they did not all have the same bodies, not like a same group of humans or other animals.

Tempered by her desire to fight, she lightly pushed herself away from Titus and grabbed her sword and buckler. There was no question this was the center of it all, but now they had to escape from here. She found it hard to concentrate, but knew their best bet was to follow the same tendril back out to where they had come from. But first they had to deal with the Horrors.

Anna prepared to strike as she neared the Horrors, taking aim at a thin, tall looking one that was trying to flank the now encircled warriors. The Horror turned around just before she reached it and flailed its long-clawed arm at her.

She ducked under it and let loose a mighty slash at the Horror's leg. She managed to slash almost clean through it, sending spurts of putrid black blood spraying. It bellowed a nasty yell, its mouth full of teeth, and hobbled back for a moment as other Horrors took its place.

Anna turned to see Titus hacking his way through more of the creatures, his greatsword looking like a metallic flurry in the air. However, it seemed he had forgotten her advice and wasn't aiming at the heads of any of the creatures. She knew if anything, that's how they could be stopped.

"Aim for the heads!" Anna yelled to the nearby warriors.

She wasn't sure if they heard her, but she knew this wasn't the place to fight. She was suddenly blocked by a larger, six-legged Horror that began to roar at her, nasty bile erupting from its mouth. She took a step back, now shoulder to shoulder with Titus.

"We need to break through, get to our warriors, and get out of here!" Titus said.

"I couldn't agree more," Anna replied, sharing a glance with the Champion.

They fought side by side, barely holding their own against the Horrors. Given they were outnumbered, Anna found herself frequently having to dodge and deflect the attacks of other Horrors around her. They seemed to fight in a strange unison, somehow knowing the move each other made. This made anticipating their movements difficult, and Anna soon felt outmatched by the creatures. Fortunately, the power and skill of both her and Titus allowed them to clear a path, joining the group of warriors that was still valiantly fighting. As they merged, Anna realized three had already been killed, including young Wil. She knew if they stayed, they'd share the same fate.

"Warriors! We need to move into the forest and follow the tendril back!" Titus yelled as he took the head clean off a Horror, sending the body crumpling to the ground.

Anna found herself barely deflecting a blow with her buckler, being knocked back. She felt a moment of panic as she took in the dire situation—more Horrors were emerging from the woods and shimmering area in the field. Their numbers seemed endless.

"Fight toward the forest! Defend your brethren!" Titus ordered, taking a nasty blow that luckily didn't penetrate his armor.

Primal roars, clashing of metal against flesh and bone, and heavy breathing of the warriors filled the air as they began to move toward the forest, their defensive circle managing to hold the Horrors back for the time being. Anna could tell fatigue was already setting in, as fighting the Horrors was nothing like fighting another human.

As they reached the edge of the forest, two more warriors were stuck down by Horrors. Sharp claws tore through their chainmail, the warriors letting loose cries of agony. Anna wanted to help them, but knew it was too late. As it happened, their line began to collapse, a couple of the warriors fleeing into the woods too early.

"No! Stick together!" Titus yelled as he continued to fight, his blade coated in black blood.

Barely avoiding the attack of another mangled Horror, Anna looked to see a disturbing sight. The fallen Narsho warriors were slowly standing back up, their skin and eyes the same colors as the Horrors. They looked as corrupted as Fredrik had been. At that moment, Anna knew he was unquestionably dead.

"Titus, we need to make a break for it," Anna said through gritted teeth.

"Unfortunately, you are right. Our formation has collapsed, and we'll die here if we're not careful," Titus agreed.

"… You will join me, willingly or in death…" the terrible voice whispered directly into Anna's head.

Ignoring it, Anna fought harder as they pressed into the darkened forest of corruption. They had thinned the numbers slightly, but they were still surrounded. She wasn't sure how they would get out of this and began to panic. As her own will slowly crumbled, so too did that of the other warriors. The living half dozen began to run off into the forest, only a few following the tendril. Realizing they were about to be left behind, Anna grabbed Titus's arm and pulled him along with her.

"They've left us! Cowards!" Titus yelled with a fearful voice.

"We need to run! Don't lose sight of that tendril or we may be lost in here!" Anna yelled as she dragged him.

She released him as he reached her speed, and they sprinted through the infested woods. The Horrors were close behind them, and as they ran, she could see two warriors who had ventured astray being taken down by their pursuers.

Suddenly, unable to see in the growing darkness, she felt her foot being grabbed. She toppled into the fleshy ground, her face hitting the damp, living forest floor. Fueled by adrenaline, she quickly turned to see a disgusting purplish tentacle had burst from the living ground and had grabbed her leg. She could feel the suction of it hold tight against her leg, only the cloth of her pants preventing it from touching her body. She looked for her sword, but it was just out of reach. She tried to pull herself free, but it was no good. She looked to see Titus hadn't noticed, still running forward.

"Help!" Anna screamed, desperately reaching for her sword and buckler lying only inches out of her reach.

Titus spun around as he heard her cry, his eyes wide with terror. Despite his fear, he began to run back, greatsword at the ready. Anna felt hopeful as he returned, but quickly realized the Horrors chasing them would get to her first.

"Anna! Watch out!" Titus yelled.

She watched as he held his heavy greatsword in one hand and grabbed the other small sword from its sheath with his other hand. He took a moment before throwing it at Anna, a dangerous but necessary move. Luckily, his aim had been good enough, and it plunged blade-first into the ground next to her, which briefly shot out a small spray of black ooze.

She quickly grabbed the sword and hacked at what had grabbed her. She slashed and stabbed, extraordinarily fatigued. The tentacle bled and writhed in pain, but still held her. She slowly tried to stand but found herself unable to walk anywhere, but as the Horrors neared, she knew she had more to worry about.

As a large, sprawling Horror jumped at her, she barely dove out of the way in time, the tentacle still attached and slamming her back onto the ground. She was winded and struggled to flip over on her back. She saw Titus arrive just in time, entering combat with three other Horrors that had followed.

"I can't break free!" Anna coughed.

Titus glanced at the tentacle mid-combat, being slashed in the armor as he did. Anna knew he would be dead without the heavy armor he wore, which was now stained with black blood and covered in scratches and dents. As he cut down one of the Horrors, Anna knew Titus was rightfully their Champion.

She managed to stand just before the large Horror circled back around to attack her. This time it stopped short, swinging three clawed hands at her. She used Titus's sword to parry two of the arms and slice the third one off. As it flinched back from the shocking loss, she plunged the sword into the Horror's head, the blade ripping out blackened blood and organs from the other side. She withdrew the sword as it crumbled to the ground in front of her, and again tried to tug herself free. Seeing her failure, Titus quickly dodged the two remaining Horrors and brought his greatsword's blade down hard on the tentacle. It was chopped cleanly in two and immediately let go of Anna's leg, wriggling and writhing uncontrollably as black blood spraying everywhere.

Now free, Anna leapt at the Horrors fighting Titus, using nearly all her strength to unleash a flurry of stabs. As she did, Titus brought his greatsword around to nearly cleave the other in half, both the Horrors letting out loud primal shrieks. As she breathed heavily, Anna grabbed her sword from the ground, but before she could give Titus back his sword and retrieve her buckler, two more yellow sets of Horror eyes had already engaged him.

"Make a run for it!" Titus yelled with weary breath. "I'll hold them off!"

This time, Anna wasn't going to leave anyone. She was tired of watching others die around her. She would ensure Titus would make it out of here alive—she wouldn't let the Narsho Champion die.

Anna leapt forward, wielding a sword in each hand. The second Horror looked at her and charged, bringing a fleshy paw down on her. She blocked it with the two swords, barely having the strength to push it off. She could barely stand, her energy fading quickly. She felt a wave of dread crash over her as she saw more Horrors in the far distance shambling towards them.

"I'm not leaving you behind," Anna declared.

Titus cut the two arms off the beast he fought, but it didn't stop the Horror; it lurched forward, biting his metal pauldron with incredibly sharp teeth. Titus punched the Horror in what appeared to be its head with his gauntlet, black blood spraying his face. Slowly, the Horror released its grip and fell back, seemingly stunned.

Titus then leapt over and brought his greatsword down onto the second Horror, delivering an incredible blow. Nearly sliced in half, it collapsed.

"Let's go," Titus quietly said, barely able to catch his breath.

The two caught sight of the tendril on the ground and ran as fast as their bodies would allow. Anna's entire body began to burn, her lungs feeling like they were tearing. Even the great adrenaline rush of the fight could barely suppress her need for rest.

As they continued for minutes, they noticed the forest was even darker than it had been when they first walked through it; the infected leaves had interwoven into a pitch-black web above them, almost looking like an artificial night. Anna's mind was too exhausted to process just how disturbing and deadly this mission had turned; she only searched for light that would signal the end of this forest.

Finally, Anna and Titus saw light glimmering from ahead. She quickly looked behind her, seeing no sign of the Horrors. Doubting their fatigued running had outpaced the beasts, she could only guess they had stopped their retreat for some other reason. Regardless, she was glad there weren't any. As the two plummeted out from the dark corrupted forest, she stopped, completely out of breath. Even Titus found himself hunched over, desperate for fresh air.

As Anna breathed in the fresh air, she noticed it was much cleaner than the tepid, odorous air inside the afflicted forest.

"Thank the gods! You're alive!" a nearby voice said.

The voice startled her, making Anna jump. She looked over to see Bernol and another warrior hiding behind a small white stone wall. Bernol looked terrible, his wound open and saturated in both Horror blood and his own. The other warrior had some scrapes too but looked far less worn down.

"Where ... is everyone else?" Titus asked, barely starting to catch his breath.

"We are the only ones here, Titus," Bernol replied, wincing as he spoke.

Anna finally felt as though she could move again and started down the cobbled path. She glanced at the others, then at the forest behind them. As she stared, it seemed as though the Horror's corruption had further spread since they had entered.

"Come; we must return home now," Anna slowly said, turning and continuing down the path.

"You heard her, we need to tell Chieftain Barod what we've witnessed," Titus nodded, looking to the other two.

Anna had never felt this exhausted before; she had no thoughts, only the animalistic drive to survive remained. With each step she felt part of her body wear down but knew she couldn't stop here. The Horrors were too close and her home too far. For all their sakes, she had to press on.

As she passed through the town square, thoughts of Fredrik came into her mind. She had finally seen Fredrik's fate with her own eyes. While his body and form somehow still partially existed, he was certainly dead. Whatever he had become, or what had taken his body, it wasn't him any longer. Between that and managing to find where the center of this all had started, she had succeeded. It hadn't been without loss, but it hadn't been a failure either. So, as she slowly walked back to her home, at least her will and soul remained strong while her body began to fade. She had survived, for now.

Chapter 9

As Valon took a sip of the hot, vegetal tea, he found himself unable to let go of his concerns. He stared across the small table at his aging parents, who simply smiled at him. He knew they could tell he had something on his mind, but they were too polite to inquire. Given what he was worried about, he found it hard to begin speaking.

Valon gazed at the nearby fireplace, thinking about his master. Lately, it seemed the Seer required more assistance with farsight than he had in the past. On his own, Seer Mordou could sense imminent things— whether it was something that created a large ripple in magic or was happening to him, his master was permanently connected to magic in a way that other mages were not. That connection was the reason Seers required so much training and didn't become a Seer until the middle of their life. If someone had that connection without training, they could easily lose their mind. Between his masters waning power and their age, Valon knew he would soon be given the gift of farsight and become the next Seer. While his master's connection would remain, he would no longer be the one leading the farsight ceremony. However, it was the connection that slightly worried Valon.

"Is the tea alright, dear?" Valon's mother asked.

"It's great, as always. I'm just … I don't know, deep in thought," Valon replied, looking at his parents.

"We can tell," Valon's father chuckled, the scar under his left eye looking more pale than normal.

"I know you can. I'd hope after thirty-four years you'd be able to anyway," Valon replied with a laugh, then stared back off into the distance.

"If you'd like to talk about it, you know you can always talk to us," Valon's mother added.

Valon nodded, desperately wanting to vent to them. However, he didn't want them to think he was doubting his master or even himself. As the next Seer, he knew he would succeed his master in leading their clan, and the last thing he wanted was to project uncertainty.

"It's just the farsight ritual the other day. You've probably heard all about it by now. It was disturbing, and I am worried about what's happening," Valon explained, withholding his other concerns.

"Indeed, it was troubling," Valon's father said, looking over at his spouse.

"But it's nothing our people can't handle I'm sure. We were almost this worried when the unbound elementals appeared before you were born. But we managed to dispel each of the... anomalies," Valon's mother added.

Valon remembered frequently hearing tales of the elementals when he was a child. Just years before he was born, a mysterious disturbance in magic had created a multitude of elementals—somewhat sentient beings made of pure magical energy. Normally such creatures could only be summoned by a mage, and by doing so were loyal to their creator, but these unbound elementals served no one and wreaked havoc through the realm.

However, their new foe seemed far more intelligent and dangerous.

"I suppose that is a good point; they could be similar in severity," Valon replied, not truly believing his own words. "We will have to see what tonight's farsight holds."

"Indeed, my son. It is odd for a Seer to need so many mages for a ritual. But I suppose that's due to the depth of what he needs to see, and the fact he is growing old," Valon's father pondered.

"Mm. Soon, you will likely be given the gift of the Seer. You must be close to complete with your training. It has been almost two decades now, has it not?" Valon's mother asked.

"I cannot say for sure, as I would not ask Master Mordou. However, he has alluded to it a few times lately

… I shall do nothing but follow his instructions and await my time," Valon replied.

There was a moment of silence, and Valon didn't know what else to say. He looked back at the warm, crackling fire, finding something soothing about its almost rhythmic burning. He wanted to tell his parents more, but he didn't want to worry them. What his father asked next surprised him.

"Son, are you worried about becoming a Seer?"

Valon froze, shocked his father was being so direct. Normally the man would tiptoe around topics and stay far away from anything too personal. For him to ask was out of the ordinary. Or, more likely, a sign of his old age and growing wisdom. Valon looked back to his parents, seeing his mother was giving his father the same surprised look.

"Honestly, I am. But not for the reasons you may think," Valon replied, already feeling better.

"Then what are the reasons, dear?" Valon's mother asked with slight concern.

Valon took a moment, figuring out why he felt the way he did. While he knew why he did, it was hard to put into words. Still, it was too late to avoid the topic now. If he could confide in anyone, it was his parents.

"I'm not worried about leading the clan. It's the connection itself, the gift of farsight. I cannot reveal everything I have learned, but to be a Seer is to have a gift and a burden. Master Mordou is permanently connected to the flow of magic; at all times, even if he wants silence and peace, that connection is there. He sees moments ahead of time often without seeking it out. It is taxing for a man to be constantly bombarded with that sort of … information. And while he's taught me incredibly and told me almost all there is to tell, there is no way to emulate or even imagine what that presence is like without actually having it. Not only that, but it's a taxing gift. Magic doesn't just affect your body, it affects your mind and soul too. With each moment that passes, Master Mordou becomes that much more drained from the presence of magic within him. That will soon be me. I suppose more than anything, it's the unknown that I fear, and that cannot be solved until I am a Seer," Valon explained, each word lifting a weight from his chest.

He was out of breath as he finished, yet felt so much better. He felt himself smiling, so happy he could tell someone how he felt. As he looked toward his parents, their emotions seemed mixed, though he wasn't worried; he knew he had just told them more than most clanspeople knew about Seers. In fact, he was sure they didn't know people were Seers for life. Most assumed it was something that had to be given up, taken from someone else.

"Son, that is ... I can see why you may have concerns," Valon's father stumbled.

"I'm glad you were honest with us. That sort of ... connection, as you described, it does seem intimidating," Valon's mother added, her wrinkles scrunched up in worry.

"It is," Valon agreed, taking another long sip of his tea.

"However, you can handle it. Between your natural strength, intelligence, and your training, you will do spectacularly," Valon's mother spoke, her voice filled with motherly warmth.

"Indeed! We have faith in you, Son. You can handle anything—this we know," Valon's father added, filled with pride and assurance.

Valon couldn't help but smile, knowing he had the most supporting parents in the realm. He loved them and watching them age had become difficult. This was another worry he would never tell them, not wanting to make them think it was their fault. He wouldn't be able to take care of them as easily when he became the Seer, but he knew worrying now wouldn't do anything. The Ancient Clan was supportive and cared for its own. He'd do what he could, but the clan would do whatever he couldn't.

"Thank you both," Valon began, interrupted by knocking at the door.

"My, my! Are we expecting anyone, dear?" Valon's mother asked, looking between her son and husband.

"No, I don't believe so," Valon's father answered, slowly standing from the old wooden chair.

Valon stood, already sensing the presence outside. He knew who it was, and chances are his master had already managed to hear his worries in one form or another. While Seer Mordou was not a purposefully invasive man, he sometimes couldn't stop the smaller visions that came to him. Valon knew he couldn't hide from his master, not that he'd want to.

As Valon's father opened the creaky door, Seer Mordou stood just outside, his eye glowing bright in the waning sunlight. He smiled, nodding toward Valon's father, then saw the others inside.

"Good evening! I thought I'd find my fine apprentice here," Seer Mordou smiled.

"Seer, please come in," Valon's father offered.

"Unfortunately, I have come to ask Valon to come help me prepare for the coming ritual," Seer Mordou replied, shaking his head.

"I thought I wasn't to be a part of this ritual?" Valon asked curiously.

"That is true, as we cannot risk you stopping the farsight like you did before. However, I will need your assistance with other matters first, if you have a moment," Seer Mordou explained.

"Very well, let us go," Valon nodded.

"Thank you for visiting, dear," Valon's mother smiled, trying to stand from her chair.

Valon quickly walked over and hugged her, sparing her from having to get up. He then shook his father's weathered hand, receiving a nod of approval from the man. Valon looked to his master, seeing the man had the smallest glint of worry in his eye.

"Thank you for agreeing to come," Seer Mordou said as they closed the door to Valon's parents' house.

Valon simply nodded, following his master down the boardwalk path. They did not speak as they trudged through their swamp village, but Valon had some idea what it could be about. Regardless, the ritual was supposed to begin within the hour just after sundown, so whatever this was it had to be quick.

They both remained silent until they had shut the door to the Seer's Tower. As they took a seat in their usual places, Valon looked at his master, awaiting his orders. Certainly, they hadn't come here just to talk. Every moment he had spent with Seer Mordou had been for a reason, almost always to learn.

"Valon. Tell me what's on your mind," Seer Mordou insisted, taking an old wooden pipe from his pocket and stuffing it with a dark brown herb.

Valon knew the herb well. Magleaf was a special, hard to grow herb that when smoked increased the user's magical perception. However, it certainly wasn't good to use often, and could cause fits of coughing. It was no surprise his master was using it before the ritual.

"Correct me if I am wrong, but I believe you will soon be gifting me with the power of the Seer," Valon replied, knowing his master likely knew this already and was simply asking out of formality.

"Oh? What makes you think that?" Seer Mordou asked with a cheeky grin.

Valon didn't know how to reply. His master often teased him in situations like this, holding back and making Valon try to wriggle out of his self-made situation. However, Valon wasn't in the mood for his master's usual games. The fact he was acting this way before a ritual worried him most of all. Normally, Seer Mordou would be serious.

"I think that because of the situation. I'd rather not go into the details because I know you know what I mean, Master. In fact, I'm willing to bet you know what

I'm worried about as well," Valon replied, remaining stern but respectful.

Seer Mordou chuckled to himself, taking a large inhale of his pipe. He held it for a moment before exhaling a puff of dark grey smoke and a tiny cough. He looked back at Valon with a perplexing expression.

"Of course, I do know. You're understandably worried about the connection a Seer has. And you're right. I imagine I'll be giving you the gift of the Seer shortly. In fact, I believe tonight's ritual may help me figure out exactly when it will happen," Seer Mordou answered.

"I understand. But Master, why am I here right now? How can I help you with the ritual if I cannot be there?" Valon asked.

"My apprentice, I've invited you here to commend you, to thank you," Seer Mordou said with a small smile, taking another smoke of the pipe.

"Thank me? For what?" Valon asked, not knowing what was going on.

"For your studious behavior. Valon, you've been my apprentice almost your entire life. From the moment you were found to have that special talent in magic when you were young, you have been here learning from me with absolute attention and loyalty. I was not half the student you were when I was an apprentice all those years ago. I don't know if we've ever even had an argument. There's no telling how this strange, terrible situation will play out. Your time to lead is likely coming soon, and I wanted to thank you while I still could and tell you that you will make an even better Seer than myself," Seer Mordou explained, his words laced with pride and sincerity.

Valon was caught off guard by his master's kind words. Never had they had this kind of emotional conversation. He stared at Seer Mordou, finding it hard not to smile. Sure, his master was supportive and told him when he did a good job in his training, but this was something more, like his master was worried about the road ahead. Hearing that he had Seer Mordou's confidence bolstered his own. He wasn't sure what to say but knew he couldn't continue to sit in silence.

"Thank you. That means a great deal to me," Valon replied.

"I'm glad to hear it. Now, I must prepare for the ritual alone. No matter what you hear, do not enter the cave. You cannot pull us out like that again, not considering the power being used. You must remain outside, and I will find you when we are done," Seer Mordou explained, standing from his chair.

"Of course, Master. I will await your instructions," Valon replied, standing and heading to leave the tower.

"I shall see you in a few hours' time," Seer Mordou affirmed.

Valon left the old tower, stepping back into the humid swamp air. He could hear the swamp frogs call loudly through the quiet village as fog gently rolling in. It seemed peaceful, and he began to walk down the boardwalk back to his own small home, though part of him wondered if this was merely the calm before the storm.

Chapter 10

Trudging through the thick forest, Anna saw something through the clearing of the leaves overhead. She quickly walked left into a more cleared area, worry taking root in her heart. Smoke billowed in the distance, soaring tall over the trees.

"Anna, we must slow down," Titus spoke as he managed to catch up with her.

"Titus, do you see that smoke? That's in the direction of our village," Anna replied.

Before Titus could respond, they heard a loud thud and a quick scream. The two spun around, seeing that Bernol had fallen to the ground, the other surviving warrior, a much younger man named Falu, standing over him in surprise.

"Bernol!" Titus yelled, jogging over slowly in his heavy armor.

"He began to moan and made some weird gurgling sound and just fell over!" Falu explained in a panic.

Anna made her way over, her mind more focused on the mysterious smoke. She watched as Falu and Titus flipped Bernol over, revealing something horrible. The man's eyes had rolled back in his head, and his skin had begun to change. She instantly knew what was happening—he was turning into a Horror.

"How did this happen? Did he bleed out?" Anna asked, slowly unsheathing her sword.

"No! He was fine—well, wounded, but managing. I don't know what's going on," Falu answered.

"He's turning into one of them," Anna replied, walking closer as she gripped her sword tightly.

"What? That's impossible. He was alive! They can only take the bodies of the dead, right?" Titus asked nervously.

"Kill … me…" Bernol gurgled, his mouth thick with black ooze.

"By the gods!" Titus said loudly, jumping back from the fallen warrior.

"No, Bernol, we can help you! I'm sure the shaman can do something," Falu insisted, trying to pick his wounded comrade up.

"No, Falu, get back!" Anna yelled.

Bernol started changing even more as Falu slowly stood him up. His body began to morph, horrible sounds piercing their ears. Anna knew it was too late for the old warrior; she would grant him his final request.

Before the transformation could finish, she lurched forward, thrusting her sword clean through his eye socket. A very dark red, almost black blood oozed out as it happened, her strike causing the other two warriors to flinch. As she removed the blade, Bernol's corpse slowly fell to the ground, completely lifeless.

"No!" Falu yelled, beginning to cry.

"By the gods … Anna, are you sure that was the right decision?" Titus asked, his words plagued by fatigue.

"Yes. He was turning into a Horror. That's why he asked to be killed, Titus," Anna insisted, looking back at the smoke.

"Let's give him a proper burial at least," Falu managed to speak between tears.

"There's no time! Do you see that smoke? Our home may be under attack!" Anna replied harshly, pointing to the darkened sky in the distance.

Titus and Falu looked at each other, knowing Anna was right. Bernol deserved a fine burial like any other Narsho warrior, but there was no time. Not only that, but the three of them were exhausted as it was. Digging such a large hole without any proper tools would be far too taxing on their bodies. They had to leave him, for now.

"You are right. If our people are being attacked then we must assist them," Titus agreed, pressing forward.

Falu didn't reply and simply followed the two. Anna felt mentally exhausted more than anything. After all she had seen, all she had fought, she was running out of willpower. However, they weren't far from home now, and from what she could tell there was one fight remaining.

As they crested over the last hill before their village, Anna's suspicions were confirmed. She audibly gasped as the terrible sight in front of them became clear: well over a thousand warriors were engaged in a large battle just feet from their village walls. Anna knew immediately the attackers were from the Highrock Clan.

"Those dishonorable mongrels, they dare attack our home?" Titus snarled, gripping his greatsword in anger.

"Is that the Highrock Clan?" Falu asked, not having fought them directly before.

"It is. And it looks as though they've brought all the warriors they could muster," Anna answered, unsheathing her sword.

Titus turned, taking the short sword from his side and presenting it to Anna.

"Would you care to use this again? You seemed quite skilled with both blades before. Plus, your buckler is gone," Titus offered.

Anna simply nodded, taking the second sword. She had only played around with the idea of using two swords before, as it was highly irregular. However, she would rather have two than one, and her buckler was gone, as Titus had stated. She figured she may throw off some of the opponents with her style.

"H-How are we going to do this? Approaching from behind is suicide," Falu asked nervously.

"We shall head to the very edge of the fighting and outflank their line. Then, if we fight well, we may collapse it," Titus answered, looking at Anna to see if she agreed.

Being a scout, Anna never found herself in these large-scale types of battles. She had to admit this was

Titus's specialty, and his knowledge and experience was greater than hers. She would follow his lead.

"I'm behind you, Titus," Anna nodded.

"Good, then let's move," Titus ordered, taking one last drink from his now empty waterskin.

They stayed within the trees as they made their way toward the farthest part of the fighting. Anna watched as the hundreds upon hundreds of warriors fought, screams of both pain and bloodlust erupting before them. She took a moment to see how each side was faring, but couldn't easily see who had more warriors from this distance. She did know that fighting this close to the village was bad; part of the wall already smoldering in flames.

Finally, they were close to the edge of the line, where warriors of both sides were engaged in fierce combat. Blood and bodies were strewn across the ground, the signature red-dyed armor of the Highrock warriors seeming more numerous than the green of the Narsho. She took a deep breath, readying herself for the moments to come.

"Are you both ready?" Titus asked, making last minute adjustments to his battered yet intact armor.

"Yes," Anna answered, looking over at Falu.

"I guess," Falu replied with obvious fear.

Titus didn't reply, turning away from them and sprinting toward the fray. Anna followed behind, knowing her entire clan's life was at stake. They quickly closed the distance from the tree line to the battle, the Highrock Clan not even realizing they were being flanked.

Anna followed close as Titus brought his greatsword down on the nearest Highrock warrior, inflicting a mortal wound in the single blow. Realizing what had happened, the other warriors nearby began to yell, trying to shift to fight their new foes.

Powered by a mix of exhaustion, adrenaline, and determination, Anna clashed her swords into a nearby warrior. He barely deflected it, staggering back and knocking his comrade right into a spear of a nearby Narsho warrior. Anna cleanly parried the axe of her opponent, quickly bringing twin slashes at both the man's arms. Unable to dodge them both, he took a terrible gash to his weapon-wielding arm. He dropped it, taking a swing at Anna.

His weak, unbalanced swing hit her in the jaw. Fortunately, it had little power behind it, and she quickly dispatched her foe with a clean stab through the chest. She kicked him off the sword, feeling absolutely numb to the carnage.

She looked to see Falu struggling to fight. He was remaining defensive, unable to counterattack. Anna ran over to ambush Falu's opponent from behind, stabbing the Highrock warrior-woman directly in the back. A spurt of blood hit Falu as his opponent fell, and he staggered back in surprise at the sight of Anna.

As Anna stared at the young warrior, she could tell he was not cut out for warfare. She knew he would die out here, likely without even taking anyone with them. She put her hand on his shoulder and looked into his young eyes.

"Falu, get back to the village. Tell Chief Barod we're here and fighting," Anna ordered.

"Y-yes! Of course," Falu answered, taking a moment before trying to figure out how to get back to the village.

Hearing a loud metal clanging, she looked to see two warriors fighting Titus. His armor was taking a beating, and certain spots had begun to crumple and split from force, but before she could assist the Champion, he spun around, using his greatsword as a counterbalance, bringing it through the unprepared warrior's stomachs.

The two fell over in a pool of gore, desperately clinging to their fatal wounds. No normal warrior had the protective armor like Titus and would be helpless to a direct blow from his greatsword. As they fell, the Narsho line began to push through, enveloping the entire corner of the fighting. Seeing their Champion in front of them filled the Narsho warriors with hope.

"Titus! You're back!" a Narsho warrior yelled in excitement.

"I am!" Titus boomed, cutting down another nearby Highrock warrior. "We must drive these cowards from our land!"

The nearby Narsho let out cheers and ran headfirst into the Highrock line. Anna watched the chaos unfold, their warriors now filled with vigor at the sight of their Champion. She took a moment to catch her breath, watching her people collapse the line of the Highrock Clan. It seemed even the smallest of chaos could interrupt the once-stagnant battle. However, they were still close to their village, and pushing their foes back would be their top priority.

As the Highrock Clan's line began to fold in on itself, Anna could discern they were barely winning; constantly having to readjust to prevent being outflanked, the Highrock warriors had to move backward, but, then they moved aside, revealing an incredibly tall, buff, and fearsome looking warrior woman. Anna had never seen her, but figured it was one of the two Highrock Champions: Glora.

"Titus of the Narsho! Face me!" Glora yelled loudly over the chaos.

Anna watched Titus turn, seeing the foe that had called out his name. The fighting slowed as eyes shifted toward the strange display. Titus spit out a mouthful of blood and approached Glora. The two stood ten meters apart, surrounded by their warriors.

"Glora, one of the two Highrock Clan Champions. It will be the ultimate glory to take your head in front of your people today," Titus growled, his face a beastly visage.

Glora simply chuckled and sprinted towards Titus. She held her large greataxe with both hands and swung it hard at Titus. Parrying it with his greatsword,

Titus stepped back a few steps, seemingly surprised by the woman's strength.

Anna's concern spiked as the two engaged in battle, their powerful strikes sending small sparks as metal clashed with metal. She knew Titus, despite his great strength, must be exhausted too. Not expecting a battle, they had taken very little time to rest on their way home. Because of that, Anna assumed Glora had the upper hand.

Suddenly, her attention was drawn by someone fighting not far from her. She saw twin blades dancing through the mayhem of battle, cutting down her own people. She stared, now seeing a man in fine armor and a red cape cutting down Narsho warriors, his face contorted in a strange anger. His wavy black hair spun around his neck as he struck down the Narsho in front of him, his bare face covered in blood. Something about him called out to her, but her attention was ripped away by the sound of Titus yelling.

Anna looked over to see one of Titus's large pauldrons had been crushed in by the axe, dark blood seeping out from his shoulder underneath. The cries and cheers of nearby warriors rang through the air, and Anna instinctively stepped forward. However, she knew not to interfere with such a duel.

"Ha! Is that all you have?" Glora laughed, pounding the wooden bottom of her axe against the ground and causing a nearby eruption of cheers from her comrades.

Titus looked sluggish as Anna watched him stand. Even his posture had begun to wither, not holding himself as tall as he once did; despite this, he looked as determined as ever, and ignored his shoulder wound.

The two Champions rushed forward to meet each other again, their powerful weapons clashing with great force. Each swing made Anna's heart jump, half expecting Titus to be cleaved in half by the woman's large axe. As much as she desperately wanted to help Titus, she knew it would be dishonorable. As Titus parried another blow from Glora, she quickly brought her axe around, hitting him across the face with the large wooden handle. He stumbled back, digging his greatsword into the ground to prevent himself from falling. Not moving, he simply stayed there, hunched over his greatsword and staring at Glora.

"Surrendering so soon?" Glora mocked.

Titus didn't respond and remained still. Glora slowly approached, her ego dominating those around her. Anna could tell the Champion thought highly of herself and believed the battle already won in the Highrock favor.

"I will give you a quick end, poor Titus," Glora chuckled darkly.

Still, Titus remained, barely shifting his weight as he leaned on his sword. He continued to stare at Glora, as if waiting for something. Anna feared the worst as Glora approached Titus, her greataxe ready to strike.

Suddenly, Titus roared, his eyes nearly flaming with determination. The Narsho Champion brought his greataxe from the earth below with great speed, delivering an uppercut of sorts at Glora's greataxe. Splinters flew as he cut it in half, sending both parts flying from the Highrock Champion's hands. Moving with a desperate fury, Titus brought his sword around and cut hard into Glora's lightly armored leg, sending her stumbling down on her other knee. She grabbed for a dagger at her waist, lurching forward and slamming it through the armor of Titus's leg. He roared in pain but did not stop, instead he brought the greatsword over his head, all in one swift motion after his initial strike. Using the last of his strength, he brought the sword down on Glora, taking her head with one clean, brutal blow. A torrent of blood sprayed as her body crumbled to the ground, shocked yelling emerging from the nearby Highrock onlookers. Anna saw a large, heavily armored Highrock run towards Glora's body; she figured it was Lorag, the other Highrock Champion.

Titus wavered, his energy gone. He walked back towards his comrades, his steps unequal. As his massive body began to fall, Anna and another Narsho warrior ran forward to catch him.

The two could barely hold him, but managed to drag him safely behind the line of battle that had quickly resumed after the duel had finished. Anna herself was wavering in strength, and as they sat Titus down, she collapsed next to him, feeling spent.

"Anna … Thank you," Titus managed, looking as though he may pass out.

"Don't thank me, Titus. You would have done the same," Anna replied, looking at the warrior that had helped her. "Go get the shaman! Now!"

Despite not knowing who she was or why he should take orders from her, the warrior nodded as Anna spoke with confidence. He ran behind their lines and to the gates, which weren't too far anymore. Anna watched as the Highrock and Narsho warriors continued to fight but noticed some of the Highrock had begun to retreat, though she figured their retreating was based on personal fear, not an actual order.

"Help me back up … I can continue to fight," Titus slowly spoke, blood trickling from his pauldron and leg.

"I don't doubt you could, but you shouldn't. You're bleeding too much as it is," Anna replied, staring into the distance for the shaman.

Titus didn't reply and didn't struggle to stand. Anna became increasingly worried as he looked as though he may collapse. She grabbed his hand, not wanting him to give up. As he closed his eyes, her heart sank.

"Titus, don't fall asleep, now's not the time," Anna urged, patting him on the face.

"I, er, sorry," Titus mumbled, shaking his head.

Anna looked over again, but fortunately this time she saw others heading her away. Behind the line of chaos walked their shaman, Olaf, Chieftain Barod, and a few others with blue trim on their armor; Anna didn't recognize them but knew they were with the Forud Clan. She didn't stop holding Titus's hand until they arrived. She stood to greet her chieftain, her legs barely having any energy left in them.

"Anna! By the gods!" Chieftain Barod yelled, quickly running forward and helping her stand.

"Titus is wounded, he needs the shaman. I believe he's bleeding out," Anna said, pointing to the wounds.

Olaf shuffled past them and slowly knelt next to Titus. He had a small bag with him, containing bandages and other medicinal supplies. He examined the wound for a moment before turning for help.

"You two, help me get his armor off," Olaf ordered to nearby Narsho.

"By the gods, is that Titus Fardson?" the old, unknown man standing next to Chieftain Barod asked.

"It is," Chieftain Barod affirmed, then realized Anna likely had never seen the other man. "Scout Myhre, this is Chieftain Wooll of the Forud Clan."

"Hello, Scout," Chieftain Wooll greeted, his white beard stained with blood.

"It's an honor to meet you," Anna replied, out of breath.

"Anna, the Highrock have ambushed our village. The battle was looking grim until now. I'm assuming you both have something to do with it," Chieftain Barod yelled over the noise of battle.

"Yes, we flanked behind the corner of their line. Chieftain, I have much to relay after this battle is over," Anna replied, beginning to tear up.

Seeing Anna in distress, the Chieftain frowned. He motioned for her to sit, helping her to the ground. He gave her his waterskin and patted her on the shoulder.

"You've completed your mission. We will speak after the battle is won. Rest now, and we will finish this," Chieftain Barod urged.

"Yes, Chieftain," Anna replied, feeling as though her body was sinking into the ground.

"After seeing this carnage, I am sorry we have chosen not to fight alongside you," Chieftain Wooll apologized, glancing out at the fray.

"Do not apologize, Herold. Nobody should have to go through this sort of brutality. If you want to help fight now, then help me push back this dishonorable clan and save my village," Chieftain Barod offered, extending his weathered hand to his old friend.

"My guards and I will join you," Chieftain Wooll agreed, shaking his fellow chieftain's hand.

Anna sat back, finally regaining the slightest amount of energy as she watched the two chieftains and the Forud guards walk toward the fighting, their weapons at the ready. As she rested, she watched the battle in front of her unfold.

Chieftain Barod and Chieftain Wooll rushed forward, both carrying heavy battleaxes. Seeing the leaders fighting alongside them, the Narsho warriors let out a cry, their morale bolstering. Now, it was readily apparent the tide of war had shifted.

The two Chieftains and Forud Guards fought hard, taking down opponent after opponent. Of course, Chieftain Barod had far more experience, and truly led the charge. While he was an old man, the chieftain had been fighting his entire life. He probably had more experience than any other warrior on the battlefield.

As they continued to push back the invaders, Anna turned her head to look at Titus. Olaf and the men assisting him had made quick work of the wounds and had patched up their Champion. She had even seen Olaf use magic, a sign of a desperate measure. Titus was still understandably exhausted and did not move.

"He will be alright. Just don't let him try to fight," Olaf began, feeling guilty as he looked at Anna. "And Anna, Chieftain Barod and I must speak to you after the battle is over."

"Oh, er, alright," Anna replied, finding the shaman's cryptic demeanor odd.

"Good. Now, I have many others to tend to," Olaf quickly said, wandering back towards the scores of wounded warriors scattered amongst the blood-soaked battlefield.

Anna looked back, seeing the Highrock warriors had collapsed into a mess, but something seemed off; like with Titus's duel, the warriors stopped fighting, as if watching something. She struggled to stand and make her way toward the front line.

She staggered through the muddy, blood-drenched field whose grass had been torn away. She walked around bodies, limbs, and other atrocities as she reached the line about thirty meters away. She quickly pushed through the Narsho warriors, none trying to stop her. When she finally reached the front, she saw what everyone else was watching. Chieftain Barod and a thin, sickly looking man wearing a crown were standing about ten feet apart, both staring at each other with absolute hatred. Standing just behind the older man in the crown was the fine-looking warrior with dual blades. As she made eye contact with the warrior, something about him called out to her again.

Chapter 11

As Prince Mace eyed the redheaded woman about his age standing across from him, he felt a strange sensation. It wasn't her rough yet elegant beauty, and it wasn't the impressive fact she was wielding two swords. No, he couldn't place his finger on why he felt a connection of sorts. But for now, it was a waste of his time to fixate on it. He looked back toward his father, who took another step toward the Narsho Chieftain.

"Chieftain Barod! I demand you face me alone!" Chief King Mace yelled, slamming his ancestral mace on the muddy ground.

Prince Mace watched as the Narsho Chieftain took a step forward, his battleaxe dripping with blood. The chieftain's chainmail didn't have a scratch on it, and he looked to be full of energy. The man was intimidating, and the prince wondered if his father could actually defeat his opponent.

"Mace! You coward! You attack my home directly? Why should I duel someone so dishonorable?" Chieftain Barod yelled back.

"You dare call me dishonorable! You come from the most dishonorable group of people that has ever existed in this realm! Fight me, coward!" Chief King Mace bellowed, his words seething with hatred.

"If it is a fight you want, then so be it! Come, strike the first blow!" Chieftain Barod responded.

Prince Mace watched as his father stewed in his own hatred, so close to the nemesis he had been wanting to defeat his entire life. He knew his father had been fueled by that hatred, that skewed sense of justice since he was young. Whether it was enough to let him defeat Chieftain Barod he wasn't sure. Regardless, something told him this wouldn't turn out well for anyone involved.

Chief King Mace ran at Chieftain Barod, swinging his heavy, sharp-spiked mace at the man. The Narsho chieftain dodged the first couple swings and parried another, then he swung his battleaxe at Chief King Mace, who sidestepped to avoid it with ease. If Chief King Mace had anything, it was his agility.

The two continued to clash, equally matched in their own ways. Chieftain Barod had superior strength, while Chief King Mace had quickness. Roars from the crowd reached each of the leader's ears, causing them to fight that much harder. With each swing of the Narsho leader's battleaxe, the prince found himself wincing, knowing at any moment he could lose his father.

Chieftain Barod swung a hard hit down on Chief King Mace, who barely had the strength to parry it. The Narsho leader held his battleaxe against his opponent's mace, trying hard to shove the blade forward into his enemy's face. It was a tense moment, and the prince watched as his father withdrew one hand, now barely holding out against the strength of his enemy. Then, the chief king conjured a dagger from somewhere beneath his clothing with his suddenly free hand, and quickly stabbed Chieftain Barod in the gut.

The Narsho leader stepped back, the sharp dagger penetrating his chainmail. He instinctively touched the wound and looked at his fingers, which were now soaked with blood. He brought his hand to his face, seeing something strange mixed with his blood. A moment later, his fears had been confirmed.

"Poison? You would use poison in an honorable duel?" Chieftain Barod yelled for all to hear, whisking the blood from his hand.

"I'll do what is necessary to avenge my ancestors!" Chief King Mace yelled, his voice crackling with delight.

Prince Mace shook his head, disappointed at his father. Poison was not the Highrock way and would have led to the exile of any other clanspeople had it been them using it. However, since it was his father, the people roared with excitement. The prince found very little honor to be had in such a move.

From the corner of his eye, Prince Mace saw General Klon at the front of their warriors, arms crossed, watching. As their eyes met, he felt a seething hatred emanating from the general's visage. His own anger flared, and Prince Mace longed for the distraction of combat yet again.

"Your ancestors left the rest of the clan behind!" Chieftain Barod yelled, swinging his battleaxe wildly at his foe.

Chief King Mace struggled to deflect them all, taking a couple of minor strikes on his arm and side. He lurched back, surprised his opponent hadn't fallen yet. He placed the dagger back beneath his robe, knowing the poison had already been delivered.

"It was the other way around! My ancestors fought the shadows when nobody else would! Without their sacrifice, the entire Great Clan could've been lost!" Chief King Mace yelled, swinging and missing as Chieftain Barod sidestepped.

Being struck hard across the back by the blunt part of the battleaxe, Chief King Mace coughed violently, the wind knocked out of him. He fell to a knee and scrambled through the mud to escape his opponent. He slowly stood, seeing he was being approached faster than anticipated.

Chieftain Barod leapt forward, smashing his battleaxe down on the Highrock leader. With a brutal sound, his ancestral mace cracked from the strike. The spiked head of the weapon slowly slid apart, the metal finally giving way. Shocked by the destruction of his family heirloom, the chief king cried out in anger.

"No! The council decided together to flee their home. It was the arrogant Chief King of the Great Clan who ignored his council and led his warriors into a slaughter!" Chieftain Barod yelled, coughing up the slightest bit of blood.

Chief King Mace's clothes were now stained with blood from his wounds. He looked to General Klon, who quickly ran out and gave him a sword in lieu of his destroyed mace. He adjusted the crown on his head, and slowly approached his foe.

"Chief King Mace the First was an honorable warrior and great leader! I will continue his legacy as chief king and will unite the clans after the Narsho are defeated!" Chief King Mace yelled.

"You are no chief king! You are a dishonorable, cowardly warmonger!" Chieftain Barod roared, charging his opponent with all his strength.

Prince Mace watched as the two collided, his father unable to match the Narsho leader's strength. The self-proclaimed chief king was sent hurdling into the ground, his crown flying into a nearby bloodied mud puddle. However, this wasn't before the Highrock leader got a partial stab through Chieftain Barod's left arm, causing him to drop to a knee.

Prince Mace instinctively took a step forward as his father fell, part of him wanting to help his old father. He stopped himself quickly, knowing his father wouldn't intervene if it was him. Besides, anyone else like General Klon could've stepped in, and they still hung back. It wasn't normal to interfere with a duel.

"Damn you, Barod! Damn you and the Narsho Clan!" Chief King Mace howled from the ground, still not standing.

Chieftain Barod said nothing, only coughing up blood. He couldn't quite stand on his own and was still stuck on his knee. It looked as though the poison was finally taking effect. Prince Mace noticed the young red-haired woman was walking toward her chieftain despite protests from nearby warriors. They seemed to address her as Anna.

"What are you doing?" Prince Mace asked loudly, walking toward her.

"I'm not letting him die of poison!" Anna yelled back, her two mismatched swords at the ready.

"I cannot let you interfere with this duel," Prince Mace warned, drawing his own twin swords.

"But we have bigger things to worry about! The Horrors to the east get stronger with each moment!" Anna yelled back, desperation plaguing her voice.

Prince Mace stopped, noticing her words seemed genuine. Could she have been talking about the same thing the Seer had warned them about? Had he gone to every village? If so, it sounded like she had seen what the Seer had foretold.

"What? Do you speak of the Seer's warning?" Prince Mace asked, slightly lowering his swords.

"Son! What are you doing?" Chief King Mace yelled as he slowly stood from the ground.

"Yes! We've seen them!" Anna yelled for all to hear. "There are powerful, terrible beasts we call Horrors running amok in the Cursed Lands! They are infecting the entire forest and will eventually reach us if we do not act now!".

Prince Mace listened intently, judging her words to be genuine. Based on the look in her widened blue eyes, he could tell she had seen something that tormented her. He lowered his swords so their tips touched the ground, not interested in fighting. He wanted to speak to her more, to figure out just how much of a threat lay east of them.

"Garon Mace! Stop consorting with that wretched Narsho," Chief King Mace demanded, having just pulled his crown from the mud.

"Quiet! Has your hate blinded you so much, Father? She speaks of what the Seer warned us about!" Prince Mace protested.

"My hate does nothing but focus me! Your enemy lies before you and you speak to them like an acquaintance," Chief King Mace berated as he approached his son. "Now step aside and I shall finish that weakling Barod once and for all.

"No!" Prince Mace yelled, holding out his arm to stop his father.

"Father or not, you dare stop your chief king?" Chief King Mace yelled, pushing his son.

"I only want what's best for our people," Prince Mace yelled. Then, fueled by his anger and conflicted feelings toward the man, the prince shoved his father back with both hands, careful to keep his blades pointed away, but it only took him a moment to realize his mistake.

He quickly looked behind him at those he was trying to protect and noticed Chieftain Barod had already been removed from the battlefield. Now, only Anna stood behind him. Prince Mace watched as General Klon grabbed his battleaxe with his one hand and charged towards him.

"You insolent little worm!" General Klon yelled, swinging his battleaxe wildly at Prince Mace.

The agile prince parried and dodged the general's sloppy attacks. Having lost his dominant hand the night before, the general's attacks were anything but deadly. Prince Mace found it easy to keep the general's attacks at bay. This time, however, the prince would not let the general walk away alive. Fueled by frustration, Prince Garon Mace made his decision. He didn't waste his breath on the man that hated him and began his own flurry of attacks. His twin swords were too fast for the one-handed general, whose face was contorted in loathing. As they fought, Prince Mace's eyes kept being drawn to the Highrock warriors standing behind his father. They were staring at him with a hatred close to that of the general. While the duel last night had been about status within the clan, their fight now proved the prince wasn't truly a part of their clan, at least not to them. While their looks and jeers toward him weighed heavily on his heart, it did not stop him from fighting with all he had. No, Prince Mace was full of his own righteous fury.

As the general waned in strength, Prince Mace found his opening. Parrying the general's battleaxe with one sword, he quickly brought the other around and sliced clean through his foe's wrist. With a tiny thud, the general's hand fell to the ground, fingers still angrily gripping the weapon.

"You—" General Klon began to cry out.

Prince Mace plunged his sword through the heart of the general, sending him into an instant state of shock. The prince neared the man, bringing his face close. As he stared into the general's eyes, all he could see was anger and fear.

"Traitor…" General Klon coughed bloodily.

Prince Mace simply smiled, knowing he had finally killed the man who had mistreated him his entire life for no other reason than jealousy. In fact, the prince had never done one wrong thing to instigate such aggression. Thoughts of their past quickly raced in the prince's mind, but he knew there was no point in reflection now. With his sword still impaled through the general, he stepped back, releasing it. With one quick motion, he brought his other sword around with both hands and decapitated the general, sending his contorted, ugly head tumbling into the mud. Before the general's body dropped, Prince Mace had grabbed his other sword and stared viciously toward his father and the rest of the Highrock Clan.

"It's over! Let us stop this pointless fighting!" Prince Mace pleaded, looking at his people and then his father.

"You … Even being my son, I will not stand for this. Do not return home, Garon. You are exiled from the Highrock clan," Chief King Mace declared darkly, holding his still bleeding wounds.

"But father, there is another enemy out there," Prince Mace continued, taking a step toward his people.

"Silence! Never forget what you have done today. Because of you, the Highrock Clan has suffered and been deprived the vengeance it deserves. Goodbye, Garon," Chief King Mace replied, turning away from his son. "Retreat!"

Prince Mace watched as his people called him names, spat towards him, and began to retreat towards the tree line. He couldn't help but feel crushed, knowing in trying to save them he had lost them. Now, he truly was an outcast, an exile, and wouldn't be allowed home.

The cheering of the Narsho warriors behind him startled the prince, and he turned to see Anna still standing behind him. She had sheathed her swords and stared at him, not knowing what to say. Wanting to make sure he hadn't sacrificed everything in vain, he approached her, wanting to know more.

"I am Prince, er, well perhaps not that anymore. I am Garon Mace," Garon choked out, the impact of his loss starting to set in.

"I am Anna, a scout for the Narsho," Anna replied, extending her hand.

As they shook, Garon began looking at the nearby warriors. The Narsho seemed skeptical of him, which was understandable. From the way they stared, he once again felt like an outsider. However, he wagered the Narsho probably liked him more than his own people right about now.

"The Seer came to our home too and told of the threat. You've seen them?" Garon asked.

"Yes. In fact, we are going to discuss exactly what we saw now that we've won," Anna replied with trusting eyes.

"If you'll have me, I would like to be a part of this discussion. I know I've been exiled, but perhaps if I knew the full story, I could still convince my father," Garon suggested.

"It is not my decision, but given your peaceful intentions, I will vouch for you," Anna replied, turning and walking toward the Narsho village.

Garon followed close behind, not returning the stares the Narsho warriors were giving him. He couldn't avoid the sight of the nearby carnage, however. Hundreds of warriors from both sides had perished in what was arguably a useless battle. Their bodies, weapons, and armor littered the once open field in front of the Narsho village. Now that the battle was over, other warriors and clanspeople began searching and dealing with the dead. Others were already working on repairing the wall and putting out some of the fires started by Highrock archers' fire arrows.

"It's terrible," Garon muttered, looking down at his blood and mud-soaked feet.

"What was that?" Anna asked, slowing down to walk beside him.

"This fighting is terrible. I've been against it my whole life. But my father is blinded by hatred. I am sorry," Garon apologized, even though he knew he alone was helpless to change it.

"It is useless. We should be standing together against invaders, not fighting each other. But do not apologize, you do not lead the Highrock people," Anna answered, her words colored with mixed emotions.

Garon nodded, knowing she was right. Now he would never lead the Highrock people. In fact, he didn't know what would happen if his father were to pass, for there was no one else from the bloodline left. Unless his father had another child with someone else, the hereditary rule would come to an end. He shook his head as they entered the village, knowing it wasn't his concern any longer.

"Just answer me this, Garon. Why turn against your father, your people, like that? I cannot guarantee Chieftain Barod won't send you away from here. Why suddenly put yourself between the Highrock and Narsho people?" Anna asked as she stopped walking and turned to the former prince.

"Because I want what is best for my clan," Garon answered as they stopped. "When the Seer came, I believed him. Since you've witnessed that threat, I cannot stand by and let your people face it alone. Even if the Highrock Clan cannot see that now, I will still fight with whoever it takes to defeat this enemy. I am here because I believe it is the right thing to do."

"Then I'm sure you will be welcomed. Now come, there is much to do," Anna replied, patting him on the shoulder.

Garon followed closely behind, feeling sure he had made the right decision. Considering how she described the so-called Horrors, it seemed the Seer's warning was true. Knowing that even the Great Clan itself had once fallen, he wanted to ensure that fate didn't befall his people. Even if they didn't consider him to be a part of the Highrock Clan, he would still fight for them. For once in his life, Garon felt for certain he was finally on the right path.

Chapter 12

Valon found himself unable to even think as the ritual progressed; he could constantly sense the magic being used, distracting his every sense. Even sitting alone in his small home, nestled in his chair by his fireplace, he could find no solace. With each moment, he worried more about his master and all those mages who were assisting him.

He wanted to meditate during this time, not having anything else to do. Unfortunately, between his own mind and the magic disturbance from the nearby cave, he could only sit in slight torment. An old book lay open on the table next to him, its worn pages not calling to him. Wanting to give it another shot, he picked up the book and attempted to focus on reading.

The book he was trying to distract himself with was a copy of an ancient tome his master had in his tower that spoke of the goblins their ancestors of the Great Clan had faced. Valon was curious as to whether the book may have answers regarding the being that now invaded their lands, but so far, he couldn't even find evidence the goblins used to use magic; so far the book only said that they were quite simple, vicious, and lived in an even more primitive form of society than humans did. The one thing Valon found interesting was the Great Clan found that the goblins had disappeared after decades of fighting. The wording suggested the goblins either left or were defeated by someone else. It made it sound like the Great Clan didn't strike down the last goblin alive. Valon wondered if the devious Shadowalkers that had broken apart the Great Clan were what destroyed the goblins.

Valon shivered, recalling some of the details he had read about the Shadowalkers. While it was worth noting the authorless tome that his master had shown him potentially lacked credibility and accuracy, it did provide the most descriptive language of the terrible race his master had ever encountered.

They were described as 'foul, evil beasts with a bizarre appetite for flesh of all kinds.' They had sharp white teeth, which were sometimes the last thing a person would see, as they supposedly could blend in with the shadows and become almost invisible. Both their skin and eyes were as black as midnight, and the tome had even gone as far to describe them as otherworldly.

However, his master's initial farsight didn't give him that impression. Just after the great disturbance, they had immediately begun a farsight ritual. It was after this that his master saw what he could only describe as an 'infestation by a powerful entity.' Still, that infestation had worried the old Seer enough to go to the Highrock, Linta, Narsho, and Forud Clans, something he had never done in his entire life. It was then Valon knew how grave the threat was, and how powerful the magic his master had sensed.

As he sat back in his chair, he pondered the concept of farsight once more. Numerous times his master had described to him how it felt to utilize such a spell but the vague descriptions had only made him more perplexed. From the sounds of it, farsight was not more than allowing a mage to visually see another place or point in time; no, it wasn't that simple. That sort of sight was something Valon figured he could only truly understand when it was his turn.

Feeling restless, he stood from his chair and walked toward the front door. He suddenly felt stuffy, and the constant surges of magic from the cave were driving him mad. Opening the door to his small home, he thrust himself out into the cool yet humid evening air. He quickly glanced up towards the hill where the cave was, then turned away, knowing he had to follow his master's orders. He instead walked south down the village boardwalk, heading toward the exit. Valon wanted to clear his mind.

The swamp frogs were loud as he made his way toward the gate. Their clan's walls weren't large or strong around the village but made just tall enough to keep wildlife out. After all, nobody would want a swamp beast to come walking into their home.

Valon suddenly noticed a young man in brown robes standing at the gate, facing away toward the heart of the swamp outside the village. As Valon approached, he recognized the young man as Kynud. He chuckled to himself as he neared the young man without him even realizing it.

"Good evening," Valon greeted.

Kynud quickly spun around, instinctively holding his hand out as if to cast a spell at his elder. Seeing it was Valon, his cheeks grew red and embarrassment coated his face.

"Valon, sir! I'm so sorry," Kynud apologized.

"What for?" Valon asked, not wanting the kid to be hard on himself.

"For daydreaming! I was staring off into the swamp, imagining what sort of things lay hidden beneath it all," Kynud explained awkwardly.

"Don't be sorry for that. It's not as if threats to our village come from within often anyway. As long as you're looking out there, I'd say you're doing fine," Valon answered with a small smile.

Kynud looked relieved and stood awkwardly in front of Valon for a moment. He then realized the only reason Valon was here was to exit the gate, and quickly opened it.

"Thank you, sir," Kynud simply replied, not knowing what else to say.

"No, thank you for keeping guard. I'll be back shortly," Valon replied as he exited his clan's village.

He continued down the path, which turned to mud the moment he left the village. The Ancient Swamp had been the home to their clan since before the era of the Great Clan. The presence of magic was strong here, and even when the Great Clan thrived in a now destroyed city supposedly far west, their village had still been used as sanctuary for many wandering mages.

Valon continued into the swamp, large trees with hanging vines surrounding him on both sides. The swamp itself was a muddled brown-green color, some areas bubbling from mysterious gasses being released. While the smell was pungent and generally disliked, Valon was rather fond of it.

As he followed the winding path through the Ancient Swamp, the nearby frogs croaked to signal his presence. It was beginning to get dark, and Valon conjured a small ball of light from his hands. It slowly floated around him like a lazy cloud hanging in the sky, a bluish light that projected all around him, revealing whatever was ahead.

He was lost in a mix of thought and nostalgia as he slowly wandered down the old path of the Ancient Swamp. Valon had spent much time here as a child, exploring every inch of the swamp he could. He had always hoped to find some sort of buried treasure or secret society here. Given how enormous the swamp was, he still wondered even as an adult if such things may exist. However, there was one thing in the swamp that nobody knew the origin of.

A few minutes later Valon approached what most considered the heart of the swamp. From what they could tell, the center of the large mire was here. Standing directly in the center was an ancient and finely carved statue standing upon a block of fine white stone.

Valon looked at the statue, which seemed as mysterious and incredible as it had been the first time he laid eyes on it. It was carved to look like a thin, armored man and stood almost twenty feet tall. In one hand the statue held a curved sword, and in the other he held a book. He wore an elegant looking helmet, which appeared to have wings or ears of some sort made on the top. Considering some Chieftains had helmets with wings, it made him curious. Valon had always wondered if the things coming off the helmet were wings or ears, not that it made any difference. Still, the man seemed slender, and his body somehow more elegant looking than those of human clanspeople.

Both the statue and the stone it stood on had succumbed to the swamp around it. Valon walked forward, scraping off some of the swamp debris from the block of stone. While it appeared dim and was covered with moss and other growths on the outside, the stone underneath was surprisingly a fine white color. Despite being such a work of art, the elders of the Ancient Clan did not know where it had come from or who made it. The only thing they all agreed on was it had been there since before they were born, and their elders of the time didn't know the origin either. Valon had thought of many ideas over the years, but resigned to the fact that he may never know.

A few feet away from the statue was a large, ancient stump that had been there since Valon was a child. He walked to it now, sitting down on the old, many-ringed stump. He sat and enjoyed the silence, closing his eyes and pretending for a moment he was a child again. Back then, he didn't have any worries, responsibilities, or real reasons to feel conflicted or stressed. Now he felt as though the world may soon be thrust upon his shoulders.

Suddenly, he heard a strange bubbling.

"Good evening, Human," a deep yet peaceful voice said from somewhere nearby.

Valon's eyes shot open and he stood quickly from the stump. He looked all around, trying to see who had greeted him. However, all he saw was trees and typical swamp foliage all around him. Not even the frogs were croaking anymore.

"Hello?" Valon asked, curiously looking up towards the statue.

The voice began to laugh as he looked at the old statue. Valon now heard it was coming from the left of him. He directed his magical light to illuminate the area, but still saw nothing but trees, though upon closer inspection, he realized something about the trees looked off. Then, he watched as a knot on the tree opened, revealing a singular blue eye similarly colored to the Seers.

"Hello, Human," the tree repeated, its mouth illuminated with a the same magical blue as the Seer's eye.

"By the gods. Are you ... What are you?" Valon asked, not worrying if his lack of manners offended the tree.

"Older than you, Human, by centuries. I am Distichum of the Arboreals."

With that, the tree slowly stood from the swamp, water and mud draining from it. Valon watched in amazement as the roots of the tree acted as its legs, and the branches its arms. He had never heard or seen such a thing and wondered if he was hallucinating. After all, swamp gas could cause such things in prolonged periods. However, as he approached the tree-being, he knew what he saw was real.

"Hello, Distichum. I am Valon of the Ancient Clan. I have never met or even heard of an ... Arboreal, was it?" Valon slowly replied.

"I know, Valon. We prefer it that way. In fact, I am only here because of the dire situation our realm finds itself in," Distichum explained, scratching some moss from what looked like his chin.

"You mean the threat in the Cursed Lands? My master is currently using farsight to see how to stop it, or at least figure out what exactly it is," Valon replied.

"Ah, so that is the powerful magic I currently sense coming from your village. I am familiar with your Seer, Lorenz Mordou. He is powerful for a human. Farsight can be dangerous, however, and I'm surprised a human can withstand its effects," Distichum scowled.

"He can. And soon I will too," Valon replied, unsure of Distichum's feelings toward him.

"Well, be careful. Magic is a delicate, chaotic thing. But that aside, I'm here to warn you, Human. Your kind cannot defeat this strange foe," Distichum cautioned.

"You seem to say 'Human' quite a bit. I get the impression you do not like our race," Valon replied, getting the feeling he was being talked down to.

Distichum laughed to himself, shaking his entire body. He scratched his chin as he stared at Valon, his bark loudly rubbing together. Then he took another step and leaned forward, his entire body creaking.

"I do not have an opinion yet. Your race is young, but you remind me of those arrogant elves," Distichum explained, his voice lightening slightly as he realized he may have offended Valon.

"Elves?" Valon asked, having never heard the word before.

"Yes, the Holy Elven Empire. You were just staring at a statue of Imperator Ty'roel. I assumed you knew who they were," Distichum explained, his voice sounding both concerned and frustrated.

"Are they the Shadowalkers?" Valon asked, growing more confused.

"No, no, no. They are not those accursed Shadowalkers. They make the elves look like saints. Bah, I have made a mistake. I should not have revealed their existence to you," Distichum rambled, putting a leafy hand over his face. "The less you know, the better."

"What? Why?" Valon asked, growing frustrated with the tree.

"It is not my place. Our council made a decision to leave your people be and not interfere. I shouldn't even be here now, but I wanted to at least warn you, to tell you to bring your people together and leave this place. Even we are facing an absolute crisis, Valon. I beg of you, take your people and sail south. You cannot fight the evil stalking these lands, only escape," Distichum pleaded.

"But surely we can defeat this foe, right? What if our people worked together?" Valon asked.

"It wouldn't be enough. You may prolong it, hold it back, but from what we can tell once it takes root it cannot be stopped!" Distichum yelled out, his deep voice echoing through the swamp.

Valon didn't respond, chilled by the great tree's words. If such an ancient and seemingly intelligent race had no faith, then how could humans alone hope to stop them? He looked away, thinking of Distichum's words to sail south. The Ancient Clan didn't have any ships. Not only that, but he wasn't aware of any islands to the south.

"You say we should sail south?" Valon asked, turning back to the tree being.

"If you want to survive, I urge all you humans to flee. There is a great land across the sea, one where my people originated. It is a wild, enormous, savage land, but full of life," Distichum answered.

"I will mention it to my master, however we humans prefer to fight," Valon said.

"It is your choice. Now, I must leave you, Valon. If you wish for your people to survive, heed my warning. Goodbye, Human," Distichum said heavily, turning and walking away through the swamp.

"Thank you, great one," Valon replied softly, watching the great tree-being leave him.

As Distichum disappeared into the growing evening fog of the swamp, the frogs resumed their chorus. It seemed Valon was alone, and the words of Distichum echoed throughout his mind. Regardless, he'd have to tell his master about what he'd seen.

Valon quickly walked back toward the village, the fate of his people weighing heavily on his mind. He approached the warning with every part of logic he could; he wondered if the Arboreals had overestimated the threat, or perhaps were not a race of fighters. Just because Distichum said it was impossible didn't mean he was right. Or on the contrary, his evaluation had been entirely correct, and the only way to survive was to run. As he returned to his village, Valon was so concerned with the warning he hadn't even noticed the magic emanating from the cave had ceased.

Kynud opened the gate as he approached, greeting Valon as he walked through. Valon smiled and continued into the village, suddenly realizing there were many people out walking on the boardwalk. He knew the ritual must have concluded and picked up his pace as he headed towards the tower.

As he passed, he noticed many of his fellow clanspeople giving him strange looks. Their emotions seemed mixed, some looking sad, some unsure, some frustrated. Valon didn't have time to stop and speak to them, and pressed on, his leather boots thudding against the wood of the low boardwalk.

As he approached his master's tower, he noticed something incredibly strange. For the first time he could remember, the door had been left wide open. Valon slowly walked through the doorway, looking to see a white-haired man sitting in his master's chair facing away toward the fireplace. Considering he wore the typical brown Ancient Clan robes, Valon found himself wondering with concern who would let themselves in so brazenly.

"Excuse me," Valon said, staring intently at the man.

"Apprentice, I have been looking everywhere for you," the man replied.

"What? Master?" Valon asked, walking closer to the man.

Valon audibly gasped as his master turned towards him. His thick jet-black hair had become white as snow, and he looked as though he had aged another year since they had last seen each other mere hours before. The only thing that looked the same was his glowing blue magic-infused eye. Valon stared at his master in surprise.

"As you can see, the farsight took a bit of a toll on me," Seer Mordou chuckled with a small cough, his voice sounding strained.

"Master, by the gods! Are you alright?" Valon asked, sitting down across the table from his aged master.

"I am fine, simply tired. However, let us not talk about me. Let us talk about what comes next," Seer Mordou replied, not worried for his own health.

"What comes next? Was the ritual a success then?" Valon asked, still concerned for his master.

"It was," Seer Mordou replied, taking out his pipe and lighting it.

Valon sat in silence as his master smoked the pipe, wondering why he was being so silent. Valon waited for his master to speak, but the old man didn't seem to have anything to say. Finally, he couldn't sit by any longer.

"Well? What happened? What did you see? What should we do?" Valon questioned impatiently.

"We wait," Seer Mordou replied with a strange laugh.

"We wait?" Valon asked, stunned.

"For now, all we need to do is wait, my apprentice," Seer Mordou replied, appearing abnormally relaxed.

"Wait for what?" Valon continued, not satisfied.

Seer Mordou only chuckled, sitting back a little further and taking another large toke from his pipe. As Valon watched, he couldn't help but frown in confusion. His master seemed changed, and Valon couldn't tell whether it was complacency or confidence that oozed from the man in front of him.

"You will soon see. Now, what have you been up to this fine evening?" Seer Mordou asked with an interested look.

Valon didn't speak at first, still put off by his master's lack of caring. It was strange for Seer Mordou to act this way, and Valon only stared at his master for a few moments before remembering he had his own incredibly odd experience to share.

They spent the rest of that night going over Valon's story, recounting what had happened with his unexpected meeting with Distichum. Each time Valon tried to transition back to what his master had seen, Seer Mordou simply chuckled and playfully scolded his apprentice for changing the subject. It was an odd night, yet eventually Valon found it within himself to stop thinking about it and trust his master. For now, all he could do was follow along with the Seer's request to wait.

Chapter 13

Anna stared at Olaf, unable to speak. As their eyes locked, she noticed he looked upset. Normally she would try to ease him and make him feel better. After all, it wasn't his fault; however, she was stuck in a brief moment of shock.

"I'm sorry, Anna, I should have told you sooner. I would have told you yesterday, but you were so busy after the battle I figured you should sleep," Olaf apologized with a guilty frown.

"I just ... I ... Are you sure?" Anna stuttered, tearing up slightly.

"I am positive. Magic regarding that doesn't lie. I'd guess you are a couple months along, maybe a little more than that," Olaf replied solemnly.

"I see ... Does anyone else know?" Anna asked, wiping away a tear as she slowly rubbed her stomach.

"Only Chieftain Barod. He wanted to be here to tell you, but that poison has rendered him ... comatose ... as you know," Olaf answered with sorrowful eyes.

Anna closed her eyes as tears fell down her face. She was fraught with emotion, barely able to focus on her news. She knew she should be happy, knowing that somehow Fredrik's legacy and love would live on. However, he would never know. Not only that, but her child would never know his—or her—father.

"Do not apologize, Olaf, for you did the right thing. I would've still gone through with the mission anyway," Anna soothed, placing her hand on the old man's shoulder.

Olaf only nodded, not saying another word. Anna knew he was an empathetic person, perhaps even too empathetic, if it was possible. If there was truly a person who looked out for others more than himself, it was Olaf. That's what made him a great shaman.

"Now, I need to go. Thank you again, Olaf," Anna said, rising to leave his hut.

"Wait. Please, take this and have a spoonful every day," Olaf said, withdrawing a large vial from his worktable.

"I will," Anna affirmed, taking the foggy glass vial of blue liquid. "Thank you."

Olaf nodded and she walked from the hut. The bright sun hurt her eyes, and she quickly shielded them with her hand. It was surprisingly warm for this time of year, making her feel even more uncomfortable.

She looked to see Garon standing nearby against a post, nervously fiddling with something in his hands. Knowing she was somewhat responsible for his presence, she walked over to him. As she neared, they made eye contact, both slightly smiling.

"How are you doing?" Garon asked, knowing Anna was likely exhausted from her mission still.

"Pregnant," Anna replied quietly, still in disbelief.

Garon's eyes went wide and he failed to find words. He thought for a moment, unsure of what to say to the young woman he had barely known for a day.

"Oh, er, congratulations?" Garon spoke, as if asking a question.

"Wow, oh, I didn't mean to say that aloud," Anna said, shaking her head. "But thank you, it's just surprising…"

A few moments went by, and Garon didn't know how to reply. Anna was still staring off toward nothing, obviously deep in thought. He figured the least he could do was change the subject.

"You know, I'm actually surprised your people have a shaman," Garon remarked.

"Oh? Why does that surprise you?" Anna asked.

"I know your people dislike magic even more than we do," Garon replied, crossing his arms.

"Ha, dislike is a soft word. Many Narsho hate it," Anna snorted.

"Why is that? For example, my people think it's dishonorable. They also partially blame magic for causing the Great Clan to run from the shadows instead of fighting them," Garon explained.

"I see. The Narsho people hate magic because one of our chieftains from many decades ago was killed by a mage from the Ancient Clan. He considered the mage a friend and never saw it coming. They say the magic drove him to do it," Anna said with a shrug. "We call it the Great Betrayal."

"Interesting. I can see why there would be some hatred then," Garon replied, considering the story.

"Anyway, we should go to the Chieftain's Hall. We will be discussing what to do next," Anna said, beginning to walk.

"Ah, is Chieftain Barod awake?" Garon asked, feeling partially responsible for the chieftain's coma.

"Unfortunately, he is not. It seems your father's poison is a virulent one," Anna replied.

Garon nodded and followed her. Neither spoke as they walked through the bustling Narsho village. Many of the clanspeople stared at Garon as they passed, though he didn't get upset over it. Here, he was an obvious outsider, a red cloak still hung around his shoulders. Anna recognized he was at least here with good intentions, and trusted him for now.

Entering the hall, they found Guard Captain Jarult, Forud Chieftain Wooll, and an exhausted looking Titus surrounding a round table. They all turned as they saw Anna and Garon enter, displaying various emotions. Titus simply waved, sulking low in a chair at the far side of the table. It seemed to Anna that Titus's wounds from the previous battle were not only physical.

"Ah, Anna. We've been discussing what to do. Your and Titus's detailed accounts gave us a lot to think about," Guard Captain Jarult greeted, then noticing Garon behind her. "I see the former Highrock prince has joined us as well."

"Hello, Guard Captain. Yes, Garon hopes to somehow convince his father to join us in the fight. From what I've seen, we will need every warrior we can get," Anna replied as they approached the table.

"She's not wrong; with each warrior we lose, the Horrors seem to gain them in death," Titus grumbled from his chair.

"Most disturbing," Chieftain Wooll added, shaking his head.

There was a moment of silence as they all considered the implications of their comrades coming back to life and serving the enemy. Having seen it for herself, Anna would never forget the horrible sight. Seeing Fredrik like that had nearly broken her, but fortunately it seemed his soul had at least moved on from his body.

"Regardless, Chieftain Barod's final order was for me to do whatever possible to destroy this enemy. Since I am tasked with upholding his position until he awakes or…" Guard Captain Jarult trailed off, not wanting to admit the possibility. "Anyway, I am sending someone to both the Ancient and Linta Clans."

"A wise choice. And with them I will send my Champion, for both security and to ensure they understand how grave this threat is," Chieftain Wooll agreed.

"I will travel back to Highrock Village shortly. Perhaps I can help my father see our true enemy," Garon added quietly.

"While I doubt that will be possible, I commend you for wanting to try. Given you were exiled in front of all of us, I know how difficult that will be," Guard Captain Jarult said, his words honest but carrying a slight sting.

"I will try regardless," Garon answered.

"I would like to go to both the Ancient and Linta Clans," Anna abruptly said.

The room went silent as the men looked at each other, then back at Anna. Their looks seemed to show they thought they had either mistaken what she had said, or she had misspoken.

Titus, however, looked on with amazement at Anna. "How can you possibly have the energy?" he asked with incredulity.

"It's not a matter of energy, it's a matter of our future. If we don't act now, we won't have time," Anna urged.

"While I will not stop you from accompanying them to the villages, are you sure you're up for such a journey?" Guard Captain Jarult asked.

"At this point I've become used to the constant fatigue," Anna chuckled darkly to herself. "But besides Titus, and I guess young Falu, I'm the only person to have seen them in person."

"Well, if you think you can manage, I will not stop you. Does anyone else object to Anna being one of our representatives?" Guard Captain Jarult asked, looking at the others.

"Of course not. I've only recently met her and have already heard tales of her fierce determination," Chieftain Wooll smiled kindly.

"I certainly wouldn't get in her way," Titus chuckled, wincing from the prior day's wounds.

"Then it's settled. I planned on sending three warriors and an elder in addition to the Forud Champion. They are set to leave tomorrow at dawn. Will you be rested by then?" Guard Captain Jarult asked, keeping on task.

"I will be. I will leave with them," Anna nodded.

"Would you mind if I accompany them as well, Captain? At least, until I have to travel to Highrock Village, that is," Garon asked.

"Hm. I suppose that's fine," Guard Captain Jarult acquiesced, rubbing his well-trimmed moustache.

"Thank you," Garon replied, stepping back from the table.

"I would go, but unfortunately I need to reserve my strength for the fight to come," Titus said, shrugging his shoulders unhappily.

"Which is why our Champion shall accompany you should you run into any real trouble," Chieftain Wooll added. "His name is Goreth Destro, and he should be just outside if you wish to introduce yourselves. You won't be able to miss him."

"Now, get some rest. I'll want you all to travel as fast as possible, or at least as fast as the elder can go," Guard Captain Jarult said with a hint of command in his voice.

Anna nodded and headed for the exit, Garon close behind. As they departed, she saw who she imagined was the Forud Clan Champion standing close by. He wore plate armor similar to Titus's, except his was dyed blue—the signature Forud color—in certain spots. He had an imposing sword at his side and a large shield held on his back. Like the other Champions, he was exceptionally muscular, though far from handsome in any way, and his head was so bald it gleamed in the sun almost blindingly.

"Excuse me, are you Goreth Destro?" Anna asked as she and Garon approached the Champion.

"Yep," Goreth replied, a simple look on his face.

"My name is Anna Myhre, I'm a scout. I will be joining you tomorrow," Anna said.

"And I am Garon Mace. I will be joining you for a short time as well," Garon added.

As the two extended their hands toward the Forud Champion, Goreth nodded and slowly shook their hands. They stood there awkwardly, all waiting for the other to speak, but Goreth was quite content standing in silence.

"Well, I shall see you tomorrow then," Anna smiled.

"Take care," Garon added.

"See you tomorrow," Goreth nodded.

Anna quickly walked away, Garon next to her. She didn't say anything at first, not wanting to have the Champion hear her. However, she wasn't the first to start speaking about their last conversation.

"He's a simple one, isn't he?" Garon spoke, glancing back at Goreth.

"Sh! Don't let him hear you," Anna scolded, glancing back to confirm he hadn't.

"I'm not trying to be rude, I'm just being honest," Garon chuckled.

"Well, just because the man's simple doesn't mean we have to acknowledge it. I'm sure he is quite strong," Anna replied.

"I'm certain he is. It's often the simple ones who are most deadly in simple combat," Garon added. "Not to mention you have to be strong to wear that armor all day."

Anna didn't reply, not wanting to feed into the slightly arrogant outlook. Overall, she knew Garon was a kind man, and had enjoyed speaking with him since they met. However, his upbringing as a prince had likely imbued him with some attitude. Still, it wasn't a fraction as bad as how Titus could be.

They continued back towards Anna's home, walking through the busy dirt streets of the village. Since the battle, everyone in the clan had been keeping busy making repairs, tending to the wounded, and burying the dead. It was a lot of work, but there were plenty of clanspeople who were not warriors who contributed in this way.

"I've noticed you were using two swords to fight. Is that a style you often use?" Garon asked as they walked, breaking the silence.

"Not at all. I've played around with it in the past a bit. It was sort of a last-minute thing after I lost my buckler," Anna answered.

"Well, you had surprisingly good form for someone playing around. I was actually trained by a master in the style. I could practice with you, if you were interested in continuing on with that form," Garon mentioned, resting his hands on the pommels of his twin swords.

Anna looked back at him, piqued by his offer. She found that dual wielding was an efficient combat style;

139

she had seen Garon in battle and knew he was beyond proficient in such a form.

"Could we practice today?" Anna asked, determination in her eyes.

Garon blinked in surprise, not expecting her to agree so quickly. How she had any energy left was a mystery to him. However, he had seen her fight, and knew she was quite a fierce warrior who hadn't yet reached her full potential.

"Of course. Do you have any sparring swords?" Garon asked.

"We can use the real thing, if you can hold back from killing me," Anna teased as they approached her house.

"I'm fairly certain I can manage that," Garon replied with a chuckle.

Garon waited outside her small home as she walked inside to grab her swords. He had been surprised by the kindness she had offered him since they had met. She appeared to trust him, something that warmed his heart. While they had been enemies a day ago, now they would fight together alongside whatever came next. He smiled, thinking of how glorious the Great Clan must have been when all humans fought side by side instead of against each other.

While he had not ever actually trained someone himself, Garon thought back to his lesson with Trov; the old weapons-master had been a cold, concise teacher who often drew blood from Garon when they sparred. Trov had been a warrior for most of his life, until he suddenly left the clan as weapons master to explore Forthoton. When Trov returned, he wasn't the same. This was around the same time Garon was able to begin his own training. Trov managed to convince the king chief that he would teach Garon much better than their current weapons master, which turned out to be true.

As Anna came back out, Garon's first thought was how her swords were mismatched; one was longer and heavier than the other, and they probably differed in quality as well. While it wasn't ideal, he knew she may be limited from it.

"You're at a disadvantage by having two different swords, you know," Garon noted.

"Well this one is Titus's sword. He just keeps letting me use it," Anna said, shaking the smaller sword. "Why is it a disadvantage?"

"Only because you could not interchange them like I can with mine. If you were to train one way, then suddenly have both swords in opposite hands, you may find yourself being clumsy, unused to the change in weight and size. Real twin swords are like two halves of the same weapon, complimenting and completing each other," Garon explained.

"I see. Perhaps someday I will have my own twin swords," Anna replied.

"Perhaps. Now, where should we practice?" Garon asked, looking around.

"There's a small field close to the port. Follow me," Anna replied.

The two walked down the small hill of the village towards the port. Garon was surprised to see so many ships, not knowing the Narsho even had one. Since Highrock was a landlocked village, they had no use for sailing. The only other clan he knew of that had these sorts of ships was the Linta Clan.

As they reached a small open field, Anna readied herself. She knew Garon was a better fighter, but she wasn't going to go easy on him. So far, using two swords had been effective, and she wanted as much training as possible before the upcoming battle.

"Now, come at me with everything you have," Garon said, a sword in each hand.

"Gladly," Anna replied, before running at him.

The two trained for some time, Garon frequently surprised by Anna's natural talent. He shared pointers with her and other techniques he had learned from Trov.

Narsho onlookers were surprised by the sight, some taking time to cheer for Anna as they fought.

After their training, they returned to Anna's home for a meal and rest. Since Garon had no other place to stay, she made him a makeshift bed from straw and old blankets. She figured the former prince was less than enthused, but he did not complain. They went to sleep early, knowing they had a small journey ahead of them. Anna had trouble falling asleep, worrying about what the future held. Between the threat their clan faced and being pregnant, her head was a muddled mess. Training with Garon was the only time she had felt grounded and focused.

Still, there was nothing she could do at that moment, and it was that fact that gnawed at her, as time was of the essence. She worried about their journey to the Ancient Clan, not knowing what creatures lurked in the Ancient Swamp. She managed to find some solace in knowing whatever they would encounter wouldn't be as deadly as the Horrors that now ran rampant in the Cursed Lands.

After circling around these thoughts, her body finally ran out of energy and she nodded off, her last thoughts of Fredrik and her future child.

Chapter 14

As Anna and her companions walked through the wide-open field the following day, Anna was happy to feel the warm sun against her skin again. It was a cool day, and she had bundled up the best she could. Not only that, but the forests of their land were thick and blocked out much of the sunlight. Anna dreaded thinking about how cold winter could be, and knew it was only a couple months away. She only hoped this would all be over by then.

They now numbered seven people. Besides Anna, Garon, and the Forud Champion, they also were accompanied by four Narsho warriors and one of their village's elders. Anna had known Elder Roy Matkon for some years, as he was known to be one of the nicer of the bunch. Elders were not just old members of the Narsho Clan, they were also a chosen few who supervised education and community projects that the chieftain didn't have time or care much for. Not only that, but most were incredibly wise.

"There's so much land that's remained … untouched," Garon muttered from Anna's side.

"It's a beautiful sight," Anna added.

"Oh, it certainly is. Most of the trees around Highrock Village and the hill area have been cleared. From up there the trees are so distant. We don't have much to show for it, as many trees are burnt in our forges to produce more weaponry," Garon explained with a slightly sorrowful tone. "It seems war doesn't only waste human life."

Anna nodded, not saying anything. She was well aware of the cost of war. She had lost both family and friends fighting against the Highrock Clan. For all she knew, it could have been Garon who had killed them though she also knew it was pointless to dwell on it, as it would do nothing but further the cycle of violence.

"If only we could stop our ceaseless fighting," Elder Matkon sighed.

"Perhaps we will after we destroy the Horrors. I can't imagine my people would still seek Narsho blood after seeing such terrible beasts," Garon said, looking to the elder.

"Perhaps. However, our rivalry runs deep. I do wish to see it end in my lifetime, at least," Elder Matkon said hopefully.

"I will do everything I can. So far, your people have been nothing but kind to me, even if their kindness is simply leaving me be in peace," Garon replied genuinely.

"That's good to hear. I will pray to the gods for your success," Elder Matkon nodded with a small smile.

Anna wasn't sure if they could ever achieve peace. She had seen the hatred in Garon's father's eyes and in many of the Highrock warriors; they had been brought up to truly despise the Narsho people. That sort of indoctrination didn't vanish overnight.

Anna remembered the first time she had been told about the Highrock. She had been young, learning from a now deceased elder named George. He had taught them the Highrock Clan was misguided and hated them for reasons they likely no longer understood. She remembered wondering why people she didn't even know could hate her, and how odd it sounded, but not long afterward, her father was killed in battle. Since then, Anna had tried to retain George's teachings and stop herself from hating their ancestral enemies. It was not an easy thing to do. Meeting Garon, however, had made her realize that peace may yet be achieved.

As they crossed the field and headed back into the forest, Anna felt the cool lack of sun get to her again. She tried to focus on other things, such as the chirping of the birds around them, or what she would say when they arrived at the Ancient Clan. Still, her head would wander back to her pregnancy or how far the Horrors may have reached. Could they have their own scouts? Were they organized or more animalistic? For all she knew, they could be watching now.

Then she remembered the chilling voice she had heard. She didn't know whose voice it had been, or even how it reached her, but it had been terrifying. Something about it made her nauseous, and the way it spoke made it sound inhuman. But she had understood every word despite that. She wasn't sure if it was magic or something else, but she knew it was likely the voice of their leader.

Anna removed a small flask from her pocket, the blue liquid inside tossing around like an angry ocean. As she took a sip of it per the shaman's orders, she saw Elder Matkon looking at her. She watched as he hung back from the rest of the group to walk beside her.

"How far along are you?" Elder Matkon whispered so only Anna could hear.

"What?" Anna replied, not remembering having told him.

"Sorry, I recognize that potion quite easily. It's one of Olaf's finest creations," Elder Matkon explained, embarrassed he had surprised Anna.

"I don't know ... Not too long. A month, two perhaps," Anna replied, instinctively stroking her stomach.

"Ah, I see. Congratulations. I'm surprised you would join us on this journey, however," Elder Matkon added.

"Why? It doesn't slow me down," Anna countered, feeling slightly offended.

"Oh no, I know it doesn't. I simply mean, many in your situation wouldn't be here. If I may ask, why come with us?" Elder Matkon asked, voice still low.

Anna thought about the elder's words, knowing he wasn't trying to offend her and was merely interested in her motives. In fairness, her persistence had probably confused some people. She had already done her part, and she knew that—but, it wasn't over yet, not until everyone, including her unborn child, could be safe. For that, the Horrors had to be expelled from their land.

"Because I want to see this through. I was the first one to encounter the Horrors, and they took the love of my life from me…I won't stop until they're defeated and we have a safe future for all of us," Anna declared passionately.

Everyone had heard and turned to listen. After hearing her words, a fortified look of courage crested across their faces. Anna felt emboldened, ready to take on whatever lay ahead.

"We're with you, Scout Myhre," one of the Narsho warriors said from ahead with a hearty smile.

The other warriors grunted in agreement, including the Champion Goreth. Garon turned and gave Anna a smile, which she couldn't help reflecting. She was in good company, and she felt more confident than ever.

"A good answer, Anna Myhre," Elder Matkon answered with a grin.

They continued for some time before they reached the crossroads, a place where the rough footpaths from four villages connected. The paths themselves weren't too worn, as typically it made sense to travel a more direct route. Only walking to opposing villages would make someone take this route. The only reason they were here was to see Garon off.

"Well, it's time for us to part ways," Garon said as he stopped.

"Travel safely. Good luck with your father," Elder Matkon wished.

"Goodbye," Goreth said, patting Garon on the shoulder and walking past him.

Anna stopped in front of Garon, knowing he could make all the difference. She hadn't known him long, but she had already gotten to know him well. If anyone could stop the clans from fighting, it would be Garon. She wanted to see him succeed more than anything.

"Garon, it was nice meeting you, despite the situation. I hope you can talk sense into your father," Anna said, extending her hand.

"I hope I can talk sense into him too. I will do everything I can," Garon replied, shaking her hand.

"Then I hope to see you and your people soon," Anna smiled.

"I hope so too," Garon replied.

As they parted ways, Anna wondered if the exiled prince would be welcomed home. Killing the general had been one thing, but openly defying his father was likely the bigger crime. She wasn't sure if he would succeed, but her gut told her he likely wouldn't. Still, they needed every able-bodied warrior they had.

Their journey continued on quietly, nobody having much to say to each other. A couple of the Narsho warriors exchanged battle stories, each trying to one up the other. Surprisingly, Goreth told his own story regarding some bandits he once fought. It wasn't often anyone encountered bandits, as most people stayed within their clans their entire lives. Unsurprisingly, the story was told in the least elegant way possible and included more gore than Anna would have liked to have heard about. Even the calm and collected Elder Matkon seemed to wince at some of the Forud Champion's gruesome details, which he spoke of as if it were normal.

As they walked, they soon encountered a thin fog that lingered in the forest. With that, the slightest smell of a pungent swamp wafted through the air. Anna figured they must have finally reached the edge of the Ancient Swamp, as she didn't think there were any other swamps in Forthoton.

As they walked farther on, they reached the true beginning of the swamp; pools of festering water and sunken trees were all they could see in front of them. Anna had seen the swamp once in her life as a scout but had never traveled through it. As she stared over the soaked land, she had no idea how to proceed.

"Hm. There should be a sort of boardwalk around here somewhere," Elder Matkon pondered, walking close to the perimeter of the swampland.

"A what? Have you been here before?" Anna asked.

"The Ancient Clan built a wooden walkway so they may walk over the swamp rather than through it. Given we followed the crude footpath, I suspect there should be one close by. I visited once many, many years ago with one of their own leading us," Elder Matkon explained, staring off into the waters.

Anna and the rest continued to search, splitting up and walking around the swamp. As she stared into the water, she could see all sorts of movement. Bubbles, suspicious looking flora, and other things floated along the warm swamp water. She almost flinched when she spotted a large snake slither in front of her and into the water.

Looking over at the others, she saw Goreth staring intently at one patch of water. She approached him, knowing it may have just been a symptom of his relative simplicity. However, his face seemed anything but empty, and his brain was indeed working hard.

"Have you spotted something, Goreth?" Anna asked, standing next to him and following where his gaze.

"Something about this spot don't seem right," Goreth murmured.

Anna looked closer. The spot where he stared seemed normal enough; some reeds, water, and other typical plants native to such an environment stood quietly among the rest of the swamp. She knelt, looking closer. As she stared, she noticed something did seem off; she could just barely make out a vague outline of sorts, as if something may have been there.

"You see it?" Goreth mumbled.

"I think I do," Anna replied.

She looked around for a moment, grabbing a nearby stick. She then poked at the strange outline, and to her surprise the stick stopped in midair as if it hit something. She continued poking around to see how large the strange thing was. Whatever it was, it came right to the ground by her and extended forward beyond her reach.

Anna stood, dropping the stick and preparing herself. She carefully extended a leg over the water, took a deep breath, and then lowered her leg.

"Don't fall in," Goreth murmured, staring intently, preparing to grab Anna if the worst happened.

Anna's foot finally stopped, touching the invisible barrier. A moment later, a strange shimmering and light came from the invisible wood, revealing part of the boardwalk. Anna confidently stepped forward onto it, a little more of the boardwalk ahead becoming visible.

"What kind of sorcery is this?" Goreth asked lowly, seeming more disturbed than interested.

"We found something!" Anna yelled to the others, ignoring Goreth's discomfort.

She waited for the warriors and Elder Matkon to make their way over. As they noticed the shimmering, half-visible boardwalk, they were all equally stunned. Anna took a few more steps forward, more of the path revealing itself in front of her as she progressed.

"My, my; it seems they've concealed the path with magic. Very clever," Elder Matkon observed, following behind Anna.

"I don't trust it," Goreth added as he followed behind the Narsho warriors.

"I guess we follow the path into the swamp?" Anna asked, looking to her elder for approval.

"I suppose so. Lead on, Scout," Elder Matkon said with a small smile.

Anna nodded and followed the boardwalk through the murky swamp. It winded around the many trees and other obstacles of the swamp, slowly revealing itself more and more with each step. She looked behind them and noticed as they walked away, the boardwalk seemed to recede behind them, again concealing itself.

The group continued for another fifteen minutes, following the single path. They had no other choice but to follow it, and Anna wondered if it was even leading them in the right direction. The silence of the swamp had begun to worry her, and she caught herself looking nervously in every direction. She felt as though they were being watched. It didn't help that it was dark in the swamp, with only a few beams of sunlight making their way through both the clouds above and the trees.

Suddenly, they heard a scream, followed by Goreth shouting. Anna spun to see one of the Narsho warriors had been grabbed and was being dragged into the swamp. Goreth desperately tried to hold onto him, but the angle made it difficult to do so.

Anna looked to see a brown tentacle of sorts wrapped around the warrior's leg. She gasped, immediately thinking it was a Horror, but as she sprinted to help the man, she noticed that even the ugly tentacle emerging from the swamp wasn't a fraction as unnatural and hideous as the one she had been grabbed by.

"Is it one of … them?" Elder Matkon asked in panic.

Anna removed one of her swords and hacked at the tentacle as the other warriors struggled to save their friend. The tentacle quickly receded, red blood oozing from it. From what she could tell, this was not the product of a Horror. A moment later, her assumption was proven correct.

A slick, smooth creature emerged from the swamp. It had a long, strange mouth and its eyes were black. Its skin was brownish green, and it blended well with the swamp. It had at least eight other tentacles waving around it, in lieu of arms, and a nasty beak below two black eyes. While it seemed dangerous, Anna felt relieved to uncover the attacker's true identity was not a Horror.

"That's a swamp beast," Goreth said as he tossed the warrior back onto the boardwalk.

"A swamp beast?" Anna asked, sheathing her sword and taking out her bow.

"Aye. I think so," Goreth replied, his sword and shield at the ready.

The swamp beast let loose a deep, waterlogged cry and lunged at them. Its wavering tentacle arms came from all directions and began to smacked at the shieldless Narsho warriors. However, it failed to grab any of them, as its tentacles were subjected to the sharp deflections of their swords.

Anna let loose an arrow that struck the beast directly in its eye. It howled in pain, falling back into the swamp. It yelled one last time at them before retreating back into the swampy depths, red blood now floating on the surface of the water.

"Good work!" Elder Matkon yelled, taking in each member of the group.

"We should get moving," Goreth said monotonously, wiping blood from his sword.

"I agree. Who knows how many more there could be," Elder Matkon approved.

Anna nodded and continued ahead. It wasn't much longer until they came to a large chunk of land in the swamp, a strange yet elegant statue standing in the middle. Anna stopped to stare upon it, having never seen anything like it. She looked at the others, who seemed equally interested.

"Who do you suppose that is?" Anna asked aloud.

"Hm. Perhaps one of the gods? We may not worship them much anymore, but the Great Clan and clans before them did immensely. This does look quite old, after all," Elder Matkon theorized, approaching the statue.

"His helmet looks like that Highrock chief's," Goreth pointed out.

"You're right. I believe our own chieftain has a helmet similar, though he doesn't often wear it. I would imagine then this is one of the gods," Elder Matkon pondered, rubbing his hand through his hair.

Anna turned away from the statue, looking for the way forward. They now stood on what appeared to be a circle of land, and there were no boardwalks she could easily see. She figured they were hidden like the others. Before she went to investigate, she noticed footprints in the mud. Kneeling, she saw the footprints led to where she stood, then back towards the same direction. It was the opposite of where they had come, and she knew it couldn't have been one of theirs. She followed the prints to where the boardwalk should be and stepped forward. As expected, the boardwalk revealed itself. She turned to the others, wanting to leave the swamp.

"I found the path forward! Footprints lead this way!" Anna yelled.

The others stopped staring at the statue and followed her. They all walked over, looking through the slightly foggy swamp into the distance. Anna wasn't sure if it was the right way, but it was their best bet.

"I would expect no less from such a competent scout," Elder Matkon lauded.

Anna smiled and then proceeded down the hidden boardwalk. As they continued, they conversed of the gods and which one the statue depicted. Anna had never known much of the gods, although Fredrik had been interested. Fredrik had always been interested in all parts of the world around them. He used to tell stories he had heard about when the gods themselves used to walk among humans. She wondered if the ruined town they had found had something to do with the supposed gods. The only four she knew of were Ty'roel, Yrollshama, Svune, and Faraldo. She didn't know much beyond that, apart from the fact that Faraldo was supposedly a god of chaos and trickery.

She pondered the old stories until they noticed a tower ahead of them. It stood tall over the rest of the swamp and was beyond a wall and many other buildings. Behind it was a large hill. Anna figured this must have been the village of the Ancient Clan.

As they approached the gate, a young robed man stood, seemingly unsurprised with their presence. He wore a simple brown robe, and his hair had been cut short. He smiled at them as they approached.

"Hello there," Elder Matkon greeted, walking slightly ahead of Anna.

"Oh, hello! Wow, he was right ... Please, please enter" the young man nervously smiled, opening the large gate.

Elder Matkon nodded and entered. Anna was surprised with the lack of formality and followed close behind with the rest. As they entered, she was even more surprised by a large crowd of brown-robed people standing before them. They were all resting, surrounded by carts and their belongings. As they entered the village, Anna noticed two men standing at the front of the group; their robes had a silver trim around the arms and waist, with a symbol drawn on the front. They stepped forward, and Anna recognized the older man. His eye glowed blue, and his hair appeared to have had turned white. This was undoubtedly the Seer she had seen at their village that day, which felt so long ago now.

"Anna Myhre, Elder Matkon, Champion Goreth Destro, and other brave Narsho. We have been waiting for you," Seer Mordou smiled as he held his arms out. "We have much to discuss as we walk."

"As we walk?" Elder Matkon asked, confused.

"Why, yes. Our entire clan is ready to stand behind you and accompany you back to your village. After all, it is what needs to happen I'm afraid," Seer Mordou explained confidently. "If humanity, our people, are to survive, this is what we must do."

Chapter 15

Peering through the trees, Garon Mace stared at his home with mixed emotions. The flames of evening fires lit the village, and he could see a guard standing at the gate. He had been deciding whether to try to sneak in or simply announce his presence during his solo walk home. Now that he had arrived, he wasn't sure what to do.

He walked into the open, slowly approaching the gate. It took a moment before the guard saw him. By the time he recognized Garon, they were only feet apart. The young guard seemed confused and unsettled before the exiled prince even spoke.

"Good evening," Garon greeted.

"Prince Mace? You've been exiled. You aren't allowed here..." the guard said, lacking confidence.

"I know that. I'm sorry for the position I've put you in. I just want to speak to my father regarding a grave threat. I know you cannot let me in, but I beg of you, at least relay my message," Garon explained, knowing his people's fate may rest on this moment.

"A grave threat? Are the Narsho going to retaliate?" the guard asked worriedly.

Garon stared at him, unsure of what to say. At this moment, it would be so easy to lie and play upon their fear of the Narsho. After all, the rival clan was the only enemy they'd recognize. Garon didn't think the guard would respond to a threat as bizarre as the Horrors of which Anna had told him. Garon hated to lie to his people, but it would be the only chance he had to see his father and tell him the truth.

"They are. I stayed behind to hear them out, but I was wrong. I don't expect to be let back in; I just want to speak to my father, the chief king, and let him know what I heard," Garon lied, hating himself for it.

The guard nodded, unsure what to do. He paced for a moment before realizing this was not his call to make.

"Given the situation, I will ask. Please wait here and do not enter until I return," the guard instructed, again his voice revealing his uncertainty.

"Thank you. I will await your return," Garon nodded.

He watched as the guard went through the large wooden gate and latched it shut behind him. He wasn't sure if his father would believe his words, or even want to see him, but it was a risk he had to take, as the stakes were too high.

Garon took a seat on a nearby stump and stared at the sky. The stars above him looked as they always did, their lights glowing among the darkness of night. For a moment, Garon found himself lost in their brilliance. It looked like the largest city he could imagine, its lights reaching all the way down to him. He wondered if perhaps other people were up there in the heavens, watching over them. Or perhaps people like him looking back somehow. Were those stars other realms? The eyes of the gods? He certainly would never know. For now, they were his distraction.

Surprisingly, it didn't take long for the gate to open. As Garon stood, he was shocked to see his father and Lorag, the single remaining Highrock Champion. It seemed his father would stick to his decision to exile him, but at least he would listen.

"My son. I am surprised you have returned here. I thought you smart enough to understand what I meant by exiled," Chief King Mace said coldly, walking out from the gate.

Garon was shocked by his father's poor condition; he walked with a hunch, as if his wounds from fighting Chieftain Barod were worse than he thought. Not only that, the chief king's skin looked pale as it reflected off the torchlight.

"Father, Champion, I come bearing terrible news," Garon began, ignoring his father's comment.

"What news is that, traitor?" Lorag asked, crossing his large and crudely tattooed arms.

Chief King Mace held a weak hand in front of Lorag, stalling the Champion's words. Garon wasn't sure if his father simply didn't want to see his son disrespected, or if he was that intent on hearing the news. Either way, Garon knew his father may just walk away after finding out he had news about the Horrors instead of the Narsho.

"Answer him, Son. What news do you bring?" Chief King Mace asked with suspicion.

"I bring news of a grave threat to our, er, *your* clan," Garon began. "If it isn't defeated, all could be lost."

"Why do I get the feeling you aren't talking about the Narsho?" Chief King Mace asked, frowning in slight anger.

"Because I am not. I speak of a danger far greater than the Narsho or anything else. Father, the Seer was right; people have seen the creatures they call Horrors that lurk among the Cursed Lands. If we do not fight them, we will fall to them," Garon explained.

"Bah! You've lied to us. Such dishonor makes me ashamed to be your father. Goodbye, Garon," Chief King Mace snapped, turning away from his only son.

"No, Father!" Garon pleaded, stepping toward the man.

Lorag stepped between the two of them, putting his hand up. He had a cocky smile and thought that would be enough to stop Garon. However, it was not.

Garon grabbed Lorag and quickly employed a takedown move Trov had taught him long ago. It was the only hand-to-hand combat move he knew, but still, it was effective. Garon used his own leg to trip the Champion and grabbed his arm and swung the man full force over it. Not suspecting the exiled prince to fight back, Lorag went down quickly and loudly. Garon stepped around the temporarily crumpled man and lightly grabbed his father's shoulder, causing him to spin around in surprise.

"You dare put your hand on me? What are you thinking?" Chief King Mace roared with surprise and outrage.

"You need to listen to me! These creatures, these Horrors, they aren't like fighting a human. They infest the land around them, they take a hold of life and bend it to their will. Anna said they can even infest a brave warrior and turn them into something of their own! They didn't stand a chance when they fought them, and unless the clans all band together, we may all fall separately!" Garon pleaded, holding his father's shoulder tightly.

Garon watched as his father processed the words, appearing to be interested in what he had to say. He simply stared at his son for a moment, trying to understand exactly what he had just heard. For a moment, Garon thought he had gotten through to his father.

"You're saying the Narsho stood no chance against this foe?" Chief King Mace asked.

"They didn't! And neither will we unless—"

"Step away from our chief king!" Lorag yelled, lurching Garon harshly back. The Champion drew his greataxe from his back and stepped between father and son.

"Lorag, you are the sole Champion of the Highrock people. Do you not wish to protect them against those who would destroy them?" Garon asked, looking into the Champion's eyes.

"That is not for me to decide, exiled one. That is for my chief king to command," Lorag snarled, tightening the grip on his greataxe.

"Then Father, please listen! Those Horrors to the east in the Cursed Lands are coming unless we strike them down first! Anna thinks they serve some greater lord, but regardless they cannot be avoided!" Garon pleaded one final time.

"Enough! You have delivered your message. I will consider your words; however, I will never stand with the Narsho," Chief King Mace spoke proudly.

"Now, my son, you must leave, and do not return or you shall face much worse consequences than being exiled."

Garon's heart sank at the words. His father had heard him, but he would not join the other clans. He wasn't sure if his father would even do anything, but something about his words made him appear to take the threat seriously. Regardless, Garon hated having to leave his home permanently. He knew what being an exile meant.

"You heard him. Leave our village," Lorag growled.

Garon only nodded, turning away from the home he would likely never see again. He knew he had done his part, and everything he could possibly do. If his father truly cared for his people, he would send scouts to the Cursed Lands. He hoped his father had heard the emotion in his voice.

As Garon made his way through the dark forest, he knew he'd have to make camp soon. It would be too long of a walk back to the Narsho village, and the last thing he wanted was to run into trouble while he was alone and tired. He was just happy the moonlight was bright enough to illuminate the path ahead.

Thinking of the Narsho village, he knew he'd likely beat Anna back, considering she had to travel to two villages. He figured they'd still let him in regardless of her not being there, but she was the only person he had opened up to

He smiled as he thought of Anna, having enjoyed his brief time with her. It wasn't only her kindness he enjoyed, but her fierce determination that set her apart. She knew what was important and had the mental strength to set aside past grudges and unnecessary emotion. On top of all that, she was pregnant. She didn't let anything stop her.

Garon hadn't inquired about the father's identity, but figured he was no longer with her. Between what he had heard, he assumed it was the man Fredrik she had mentioned, which was likely the same Fredrik another

Narsho had referred to as dead. While Garon had only grown up with one parent, he knew Anna would be a far better parent than his father had been to him. He knew her child would be fine.

As the stars above guided Garon, he could only wonder at what would become of his people. Given the supposed strength of the Horrors, perhaps his father's concentration would shift toward them and away from the Narsho for once. Now, only time could tell, and Garon only hoped it wasn't too late—not just for his people, but for all the clans.

Chapter 16

As they walked, Valon couldn't shake the sense of dread that filled him after hearing Anna's descriptions. Despite all the texts, tomes, and other documents he had read over his life, Valon had never heard such a vivid, clear, and absolutely disturbing account. These strange creatures—Horrors as she called them—sounded world-ending. Not to mention the infestation they spread through the forest.

He looked back at the hundreds of people walking behind them. The entirety of the Ancient Clan—his people—had made the decision to flee their ancestral home to go to the Narsho village. It was their only choice considering everything that had happened, and had they stayed behind they would've perished on their own. At least, that's the conclusion they came to based on farsight and Distichum's warning.

Valon looked back to his master, who walked in front of him with Elder Matkon. While his master hadn't revealed his entire vision, or perhaps not understood it all, one thing was clear from it: what Seer Mordou saw and what the Arboreal had said had many similarities. Valon was surprised to hear that not even his master had met the secretive race of the Arboreals. However, the Seer believed his apprentice, and they concluded no clan was safe alone, and it made sense to move everyone to one village in case of the worst. If they had to flee, they could do so together. Now they just had to convince the Linta Clan to do the same.

Having acted strangely after the farsight, Valon still wondered what else his master had seen that he was withholding or couldn't put into words. All he had told Valon was the clans and their Champions had to unite to fight the threat, and that beyond the Cursed Lands on the east coast was a place that could help them. However, Seer Mordou was intent on having Valon keep the latter of that information to himself, as he only saw a select few going to these ruins. As for who these people were, so far Seer Mordou had only identified himself, Valon, Anna, and Goreth the Forud Champion. There were two more he claimed he could only truly see when they met. Whoever these mysterious two were, they weren't part of the Ancient Clan.

With a start, Valon realized Anna had spoken to him.

"I'm sorry, what was that?" Valon asked, looking at Anna walking beside him.

"I was asking about a creature we saw in the swamp," Anna replied.

"Oh. It wasn't a tree creature was it?" Valon asked, wondering if the mysterious Arboreals were on the move.

"A tree creature?" Anna asked, almost laughing at the absurdity.

"Oh, er, never mind then. What did it look like?" Valon asked, knowing many things lived in the swamp.

"It was aggressive, had tentacles, and tried dragging one of our warriors into the water," Anna replied.

"Ah, the swamp beasts? Did you not have a torch on you?" Valon asked, not even considering the cowardly animals a real threat.

"We didn't," Anna answered.

"That explains it. They're not very brave and are absolutely terrified of fire for some reason. The light we conjure from our magic is usually enough to do it. We always have conjured light anyway so we can see the boardwalks," Valon replied nonchalantly.

"So that's how you can see them! We were lucky Goreth somehow spotted enough of a shimmer to go on, otherwise we wouldn't have found you," Anna said frustratedly.

"Oh my, I didn't even think of that," Valon said, feeling almost embarrassed at his lack of foresight.

He wasn't used to being around those who didn't know how to use magic. Not having it was like missing a primary sense, for it allowed one to operate in a whole different sort of way. Valon couldn't imagine his life without it.

"Yes, it was strange," Anna replied, shaking her head.

"But you made it without our help, just as you should have," Seer Mordou said from in front of them, before turning back to his conversation with Elder Matkon.

"Does he really see the future?" Anna quietly asked Valon.

Valon nodded, not knowing how much detail to go into. Normally, he wouldn't bother wasting time telling a non-mage about magic. It would be like trying to explain sight to someone who couldn't see. Surely it would interest them, but since they didn't have the sense it would be impossible for them to grasp it. However, times had changed, and Valon wondered if Anna would be interested in learning the very basics of magic.

"He does, using a sort of spell or ability called farsight. Someday soon, I will be given that power and will become the next Seer of the Ancient Clan," Valon replied.

"That's ... Wow. It's hard to believe, but so far, he's been right. But I don't understand, if he can just see what happens, why not just tell everyone or do it?" Anna asked skeptically.

"Ah, because it doesn't work quite like that from what he tells me. You see, the future itself has many possibilities based on the actions we take. It takes time and focus to see your path, and even then, it is foggy, muddled in a myriad of branches and paths. But he is skilled enough to see our path, and prominent points, as it were. These points are things such as your arrival to our village, our uniting with your clan, and more. That, and he can see great distances away in our current time," Valon explained, finding it difficult to come up with the correct words.

"I think I understand … Somewhat. It sounds like a gift from the gods themselves," Anna replied.

"It really does," Valon agreed.

Valon wasn't sure if the gods existed anymore. He had always been skeptical, especially since he had never met someone who had ever had a godly encounter. However, after hearing that beings called elves had once existed here and that one was named Ty'roel, the same as a supposed god, Valon couldn't help but wonder about it all. Suddenly, they heard loud yelling from just ahead.

"What was that?" Anna asked, clenching the pommel of one of her swords.

"It sounded like someone ahead," Elder Matkon replied, looking at Anna.

"Come, we should see what is happening," Seer Mordou said, beginning to jog ahead.

They quickly followed him, leaving the rest of the group. The yelling continued, and they weaved through the forest to find a small field. In the middle of the grassy field's path was a large wagon being pulled by a now-deceased ox lying dead in a pool of its own blood. Three men and a middle-aged woman stood around the cart, surrounded by a few other creatures that Valon couldn't quite make out, as they were small and covered by tall grass.

"Hold on!" Elder Matkon yelled to the frightened people.

As they neared, Valon sensed something strange about the creatures in the grass. Unlike most of the animals of their realm, these ones contained a strange magic. In fact, it seemed like the magic from the farsight ritual that had transformed their fellow mage.

"Horrors. They're smaller, perhaps scouts," Anna said as she unsheathed her swords.

As the Horrors noticed them, two nearby stood on their hind legs. Valon quietly gasped at the site of their grotesque features. They had four legs like a wolf, but that was the end of the similarity. Their skin was purple, gnarled and coated with growths of all sorts. Their claws and teeth were sharp and vicious. Their heads barely had skinny elongated necks that came off their asymmetrical bodies. Their entire form looked like a sickly killing machine.

"Try to take one alive if you can!" Seer Mordou shouted to everyone.

Valon readied himself, looking to see a dozen more Horror scouts standing to assess the group. Their nasty form made it hard to even look at them, and their magic essence almost made Valon feel sick. It seemed even their souls were infected.

The Horrors dove back into the long grass, obscuring them from view. Valon watched as his master let loose a burst of magic energy towards some moving grass, hitting the Horror hard and sending it into the air a few feet. Next to him Anna had already managed to find one and had engaged it in combat.

Valon continued over to the people and quickly noticed they were adorned in yellow. Between that and the cart full of goods, he knew they were from the Linta Clan. The Linta weren't known for their fighting skill, and the three men looked noticeably afraid of the Horrors. However, it was the Linta woman that looked the fiercest. She stood ready with a bow, staring into the grass.

"Are you all alright?" Valon asked as he walked between the four of them, his eyes constantly searching for the still-prowling Horrors.

"We were ambushed!" one of the Linta Clan fighters replied.

"We're fine but are glad you're here to help with whatever these beasts are," the Linta woman answered, letting loose an arrow and striking a nearby Horror.

"Except our ox is dead! That and our cart is stuck in a patch of mud," another Linta fighter added.

Valon suddenly felt a presence behind him and turned to see a Horror jumping in midair at him. Valon barely dodged it in time, and the wily creature landed in the tall grass in front of him. Valon extended his arm and let loose a burst of magic energy, a streak of harsh blue light going forth and hitting the Horror in the head. The creature toppled over but managed to survive the magic blast and quickly squirmed its away from Valon.

"They're retreating!" Goreth yelled as his sword just barely missed a running Horror.

"Valon! Catch that one!" Seer Mordou yelled, pointing to a patch of moving grass nearby.

Valon looked to see a wounded Horror hobbling as fast as it could through the tall green grass, an arrow sticking into its harsh skin. It noticed Valon and tried to change course, but it was too close, and Valon began to focus his power.

A moment later, the Horror rose into the air, its legs frantically searching for ground. It realized what was happening and screeched loudly, flailing its body violently. Valon and the others slowly approached it, finally able to see one up close.

"Magic. You're the Ancient Clan then?" the Linta woman asked, looking at the others around them.

"Not all of us. My name is Anna, I am from the Narsho Clan," Anna greeted, extending to shake the woman's hand.

"I see. That's curious. My name is Becca. I am a Linta trader, and these three terrified men were my guards," Becca greeted, shaking Anna's hand.

"Our apologies, my lady. We aren't used to fighting ... those," one of the fighters said shakily.

Valon thought it was interesting they referred to her in such a way. He did recall hearing once of a Becca Yarmot, a relative of the Linta Chieftain Richard Yarmot. He wondered if this could be the same person, but it was not information he would reveal. He would leave it up to her, when the time was right.

"I am Seer Mordou of the Ancient Clan. We're fortunate we were close. In fact, we were heading to your village to speak to your chieftain," Seer Mordou said, smiling at Becca.

"Oh? The Ancient and Narsho Clans are working together? That's very curious … What are you speaking with our chieftain about?" Becca asked, looking almost suspicious

"About those," Seer Mordou said, pointing toward the still hovering Horror.

"What are they? Some sort of wild beast?" Becca asked, her brown eyes wide with a mix of fear and interest as she stared at the Horror.

"Much worse. This is by far the smallest I've seen. There are likely hundreds of them, if not more in the Cursed Lands. This is what Seer Mordou warned our clans about," Anna replied.

Becca looked at Anna, then back at Seer Mordou. It took a moment, but suddenly her memory came back. She shook her head, surprised she hadn't recognized him.

"I remember when you came to our village, Seer Mordou. We didn't believe a word you said, but now it's as plain as day with it here before us. If there are hundreds of them, what can we do?" Becca asked the group.

"We can stand together as one and fight," Anna replied.

"Well, then we should get back to our village. I don't know how we'll get the cart free," Becca said, looking at her stuck, heavy cart.

"We could try pushing it again," one of the Linta fighters offered.

"No, no. We can handle it. Valon, dispose of that beast," Seer Mordou ordered.

Valon nodded and imploded the magical force on the Horror. Its body crumpled and leaked black ooze as he dropped it to the ground. It seemed that sort of concentrated magic worked well on the creature. He wasn't sure if it was a certain part of it that needed to be killed, but normal attacks were not as effective.

"Good. Now, let's get that wagon out," Seer Mordou continued.

Valon nodded and the two of them lifted the cart using their magic enough to break it free from the mud pit and moved it close to them onto dry ground. Valon already knew what his master would suggest next, and it was an easy solution.

"We will have our clan use their power to push it. With so many of us, none will tire themselves from the magic, and we can get it back to your village," Seer Mordou offered. "If you'd allow us."

"That's very generous. Thank you, Seer Mordou. Thank all of you. Our chieftain will be told of your kindness," Becca thanked, shaking the Seer's hand.

Valon followed his master and brought their following clan over to the field. Given there were hundreds of them, all able to use basic magic, keeping the cart moving was easy. After all, basic levitation wasn't a difficult spell.

Two at a time would levitate the cart as they traveled to the Linta village. As soon as they felt any sign of fatigue, two more would step forward and move the cart. At one-point, Valon's parents took their turn, their magic strong as ever despite their aging bodies. Valon was proud of them and his entire clan; they had never harbored the negative emotions other clans held for them.

Valon chuckled to himself at the amazement of the non-mages. Anna, Goreth, Elder Matkon, Becca, and the other Linta and Narsho warriors were equally stunned and kept their eyes on the hovering cart almost the whole trip. Out of all of them, he could tell Anna was the most interested. He didn't want to approach her first, but he hoped she'd ask about using magic. Given how powerful and helpful magic was as a tool, he'd love the chance to teach other clans about it.

Fortunately for them, the trip to the Linta Clan village was quick and without conflict. Valon hadn't ever been to this village but had been told it was the largest of all the clans, given their focus on trading instead of war.

Surrounding the large village were large, rolling fields of wheat and other crops. It was far different from any of the other villages Valon had seen, and he noticed how peaceful it felt standing here. They followed the single path through the fields toward the village. As they neared, Valon was most surprised at the lack of walls surrounding the village, though he supposed it made sense, as they had no enemies, and there didn't seem to be any nasty wildlife in the area.

In fact, the surrounding valley was nothing but peaceful. It was far different from the dark, chaotic Ancient Swamp. Valon smiled as he gently ran his hand through the wheat of the field as he passed. His smile slowly vanished as he remembered Distichum's warning. If the Arboreal was correct, the Linta would have to leave their beautiful valley. Valon wasn't sure if it would come to that. For now, they'd have to at least talk the Linta into coming to the Narsho village, as it was the furthest from the Cursed Lands.

"Valon," Seer Mordou said, looking behind him.

"Yes, Master?" Valon answered.

"Speak with me a moment," Seer Mordou continued.

Valon quickly walked ahead of the others to his master, who was a few paces in front of everyone else. He wasn't sure what his master wanted to talk about, but obviously wanted privacy.

"Yes?" Valon asked, walking next to his master up the dirt path towards the village.

"That Linta woman, Becca, she is one of the people I saw at the ruins," Seer Mordou said quietly.

"Oh? That could make sense. I believe she is Becca Yarmot, a relative to Chieftain Yarmot," Valon replied, trying to put the puzzle together in his head.

He instinctively turned to see Becca speaking with Goreth. It was a surprising sight, as the Forud Champion was a quiet, simple man. It seemed she was able to open him up, and for the first time since Valon had briefly known Goreth, he saw the Forud man was smiling. It seemed they had a connection, which added to the mystery.

"I believe you are right, apprentice. She is most likely the very same. This is a good thing, as she can vouch for the situation now. Say nothing to her about my vision yet. I will wait until we arrive at the Narsho village before I have that conversation," Seer Mordou explained.

"Of course," Valon replied, knowing it would undoubtedly be a strange conversation.

Valon knew that despite everything, there was likely still skepticism about magic from the other clans. It would not be easy to convince the others they had to leave their people just before a great battle to pursue ancient ruins that may not even exist. Still, Valon had faith his master's plan would work out. For if it didn't, everything could be lost.

"Here, let me lead you in. My people will be surprised to see such a great mass coming and we don't want to alarm them," Becca said, stepping past Valon and Seer Mordou.

"Of course. I will instruct the rest to wait here, as only a few of us would like to speak with Chieftain Yarmot," Seer Mordou agreed.

Moments later, only a small group approached the village's outskirts. Valon followed his master alongside Elder Matkon, Anna, Becca, Goreth, and the Linta fighters. The remaining Narsho warriors waited behind with the rest of the Ancient Clan.

Without a gate, Valon wondered how they kept track of who went in and out of the village. It looked as if three roads led into the sprawling, messy looking village. The fourth side was on the ocean, and Valon could just barely make out what he assumed were tall masts from some of their ships.

As they walked by some of the homes, Valon was surprised to see how casual the Linta clanspeople were; they all smiled and waved, not worried about the random group of ragtag foreigners walking down the center of their village. Not only that, but they were all dressed vibrantly, and seemed to have a sort of personal wealth Valon hadn't noticed in other clans. Between the size and shape of the village, it was apparent that the Linta Clan were doing relatively better than all the others.

"This is much different from our home, isn't it, Anna?" Elder Matkon asked.

"It is. I'm surprised at the lack of guards, walls, and other defensive positions. This would be an easy village to capture," Anna replied, her eyes darting from building to building.

"True, but who would want to attack such a peaceful place that would openly trade with you"? Elder Matkon asked.

"The Horrors would," Anna replied darkly.

"Unfortunately, she is right. This is why it's imperative we are able to convince Chieftain Yarmot of the threat," Seer Mordou added.

Valon saw Becca looking noticeably worried. It was understandable, as her home was not set up in a way where they could defend against any sort of invader. She had just looked the enemy in the eyes, and it was as real to her as anyone else who had encountered them. And like Anna said, they were the smallest she had seen.

The group followed Becca through winding streets, the center of the village crowded with jovial Linta clanspeople. As they noticed them, a fair amount waved to Becca. Some even addressed her with the same sort of formality that the fighters did, confirming Valon's suspicions.

Finally, after walking for what seemed fifteen minutes through the massive village, they came to an impressively large two-story building. It was like nothing Valon had seen before architecturally. Besides the Seer's Tower, all the Ancient Clan buildings were one floor only. It wasn't easy to build such a building, let alone one so large.

"Please, wait out here a moment, I'll make sure our chieftain can speak to you," Becca said before walking through the large front double doors.

"Well, I certainly hope he can," Seer Mordou laughed, looking at the others.

"I hope so too. These people are at risk. Without walls or a proper guard, they will be easily overrun," Elder Matkon agreed, looking far more somber.

"Plus, they're the closest village to the Cursed Lands. Just look at how close those scouts were. But Elder, can we even take in so many people to our village?" Anna worriedly asked.

"Hm. That is not a question I like to think about. The Linta Clan is probably twice the size of our clan. We could possibly all fit behind the wall if necessary, though it would not be a viable living solution; but if, gods forbid, we must sail away from our homeland to escape, we will need every ship we can get," Elder Matkon replied, seeming troubled at his own conclusion.

Before anyone replied, Becca had opened the doors to the large hall. She waved them in, her hands moving quickly. Valon could see the worry in her eyes.

The group followed her into the huge hall. Large paintings, sculptures, and other unique pieces of art decorated the sides of the hall. Valon had never seen such art, let alone so much of it. The paintings that hung here were far better than any of those in his own village.

Sitting in an ornate throne at the end of the hall was a middle-aged man. He was overweight, not too tall, and had straight greasy hair down to his neck. He did have kind eyes, a jolly smile, and a scar running down the entire right side of his face.

"Hello, visitors!" Chieftain Yarmot greeted, slowly standing from his throne. "And welcome to our village!"

Seer Mordou and Elder Matkon looked at each other, not knowing who should speak first. They stared for a moment, whispered, and then looked back at the Linta Chieftain.

"Chieftain Yarmot, I am Seer Mordou of the Ancient Clan. It is a pleasure to meet you," Seer Mordou said with a small bow.

"And I am Elder Matkon of the Narsho Clan, representing Chieftain Barod. It is also an honor," Elder Matkon greeted, bowing like the Seer.

"So, my niece was right! Two clans coming together to see me. This is quite an unexpected meeting. She said it was dire, but I would've expected to see Chieftain Barod here himself to give the news," Chieftain Yarmot replied, sitting back on his throne.

Elder Matkon and Anna shared a glance, and Valon knew exactly what they were thinking. Given the circumstances, Valon hoped they would just tell the chieftain what happened to Barod. Now was a time of honesty, even if the news wasn't good.

"Unfortunately, Chieftain Barod is recovering from a nasty poison used by the Highrock Chief King when they attacked our village. He will likely live, but there was no possibility of him traveling. But do not confuse my being here with a lack of importance," Elder Matkon explained.

"I see … That is terrible news. Is this why you are here then? To ask for help to fight against the Highrock Clan?" Chieftain Yarmot asked, seemingly perturbed by the news.

"No, chieftain. We don't ask you to join our fight with the Highrock Clan. We ask for you to join the fight against an enemy far more dangerous, corrupting, and on your doorstep. What can only be described as Horrors are running amok in the Cursed Lands; in fact your niece here encountered some when we met," Elder Matkon explained.

"She briefly told me about them. Her description was terrifying. She said that they were much smaller than the ones you've come across, is that right?" Chieftain Yarmot asked, leaning his head on his pudgy hand.

"I personally haven't encountered them. But Scout Anna Myhre here has fought them multiple times and lived to tell the tale," Elder Matkon said, gesturing for Anna to step up next to him.

"Oh, I see. Hello, Scout Myhre," Chieftain Yarmot greeted.

"Hello, Chieftain; it is an honor," Anna replied.

"Please, tell me your story. I want to hear everything," Chieftain Yarmot insisted, waving for a nearby servant to fetch him some wine.

"Okay. I will spare no detail then," Anna said, preparing herself mentally.

Valon stood back and listened to Anna's tale once more. Her finding of seemingly ancient ruins, the tragedy of losing Fredrik to them, and then encountering the strange area from which they originated. The descriptions sent chills down Valon's spine, especially thinking about a dark forest where the trees merged together like some terrible mass. The story was just as he'd heard it previously from her. She did not exaggerate and was so well articulated that her descriptions made those listening rather uncomfortable. However, her mentioning of where the Horrors came from sounded a bit more detailed this time.

As Valon listened to her describing the strange, shimmering translucent look in the air, a memory of something he had read in an old tome long ago stirred in his mind. He closed his eyes, trying to focus on what he had read. Something spoke of a very similar thing in a similar context, but what could it have been?

"Are you alright, Apprentice?" Seer Mordou whispered quietly, as to not interrupt Anna.

"Her description of the shimmering air. It reminds me of something I've once read," Valon replied quietly, still trying to think hard.

"Not invisibility like with our boardwalks?" Seer Mordou asked.

"No. No, there was an old, old tome I read years ago. It was about explorers from the Great Clan who found something similar and recognized its magic," Valon replied, starting to remember.

"Hm, I think I recall that as well. Something about the gods, or land of the gods, wasn't it … hm…" Seer Mordou trailed off, his old mind losing track.

Between racking his brain and hearing his master speak of the land of the gods made him remember: the explorers from the Great Clan traveled far east to find a small camp by a strange, shimmering something in the air. It was there they supposedly met one of the gods, and even traveled through that shimmering air to where the gods supposedly came from. That was it! That magic was the magic of teleportation.

"I think it is a portal, master. A form of magical teleportation to another realm. The explorers from the Great Clan traveled through it to visit the land of the gods. It's even located east of the Great Clan technically. It might even be the same portal!" Valon said, not noticing his voice had raised volume a bit.

"What sort of godly land would send such horror to us…" Seer Mordou spoke quietly, trailing off.

Ecstatic to have figured out what it could be, Valon looked back at the group to see everyone staring at him. It seemed he had unknowingly interrupted their conversation. He didn't know how to respond.

"Are we missing something important?" Chieftain Yarmot asked with a chuckle.

"Apologies, chieftain. This is my apprentice, Valon, soon to be the next Seer of the Ancient Clan," Seer Mordou introduced.

"Greetings, Apprentice Valon. Do you have more information about this most … disturbing threat?" Chieftain Yarmot asked.

"I believe so," Valon began, stepping forward with everyone else. "I believe what Anna saw was a portal. A portal has been mentioned in an ancient tome in our possession, and is a magical method of transportation

NICHOLAS JOSLIN

called teleportation, which is not only instant, but can link great distances apart. Explorers from the Great Clan found what they called a portal to the far east during their time. Perhaps it is the same portal. It does make sense, as she describes Horrors coming out of thin air. Except they are not just appearing from nowhere, they are coming from a portal linked to what could be another realm."

Everyone became silent after Valon finished speaking. Not only were they not familiar with magic, but even Valon wasn't too familiar with what he just described. But the more he thought about it, the more sense it made. Yes, the horrors could be coming from another realm

"Another realm? Like the Dark Depths?" Chieftain Yarmot asked, unsure what to believe.

"I suppose that is a possibility. Perhaps that's where these wretches come from. Regardless, the threat is real. Given that these Horrors can take the bodies of the dead and dying and use them against us, we must consolidate our clans. Respectfully, chieftain, your city is not prepared for an attack. Although none of us are prepared for these beasts. We may have to flee our homes on ships, at least that's what Distichum told me," Valon replied, realizing he shouldn't have mentioned the living tree.

"Distichum? Who is that?" Chieftain Yarmot asked.

Despite knowing it sounded like a strange children's tale, Valon continued and told the story of Distichum and the supposed Arboreals to everyone in the room. Only his master had heard the tale, and everyone had equal confusion and disbelief on their faces as Valon spoke, though given how much else was going on, it seemed to fit right in.

"So … trees live, Horrors from another realm invade our world, and a chunk of land lies south of us across the ocean. In my forty-one years of living I have never felt more like a confused child in a land he doesn't know," Chieftain Yarmot chuckled, masking his unsettled feelings of confliction.

"Uncle, they are right. We cannot risk it. If they are wrong, or if we defeat them, we can always return here," Becca urged, believing everything.

"But to ask thousands of clanspeople to pick up and leave … that's not easy. We've never dealt with anything like this since the days of the Great Clan…" Chieftain Yarmot replied, suddenly looking to the servant that had stood quietly next to him the entire time. "Pil, what do you believe of these stories?"

The servant's eyes widened as he was put on the spot. He had obviously been listening the entire time, even forgetting to refill his chieftain's wine once. By the look on his face, Valon wondered if this was the first time he had ever been asked his opinion.

"Chieftain … I … well, I believe them. They have no reason to lie, not to mention your niece Lady Yarmot herself saw some of the creatures. Considering the Narsho and Ancient Clans stand here before us in unison, I would do what they ask. Oh, er, but that is just my humble opinion, of course…" Pil replied sheepishly.

"He is right, Chieftain. These are strange times. We must work together to save our people," Elder Matkon calmly added.

Valon watched the Linta chieftain rested his head in his hands for a moment, closing his eyes. He sat there in silence for close to a minute, causing those others in the room to glance nervously amongst themselves. However, Becca and Pil seemed to find his actions typical, and stood patiently. Finally, the chieftain looked back at them, and stood from his chair. He gritted his teeth and nodded as he looked at Elder Matkon and Seer Mordou.

"For the sake of my people, I know what I must do. It will not be easy, but it will be necessary by the sounds of it. In two days' time, I will take my clan and ships to your village, Elder Matkon. There we shall form a plan on how to secure our realm," Chieftain Yarmot said with certainty, downing his wine and setting his metal chalice firmly down on the throne.

"We are pleased to hear that. We will prepare our village for your arrival," Elder Matkon replied, trying to hide his enthusiasm.

"Then we will form a plan of attack," Seer Mordou added.

Valon felt relieved as he heard the words. They had succeeded in the first part of their mission. Now, they'd have to figure out how to fight back the strange threat that sought to destroy them. He stopped himself from worrying too much about the future, as there was nothing more he could do. For now, they were doing everything they could and were succeeding.

Chapter 17

It was the shuffling of items on a table that awoke Chieftain Barod. He coughed, rolling on his side and hanging over the bed. He looked up to see Olaf quickly walking towards him, vials in hand.

"Chieftain! I am so sorry to wake you. I was working on a better rejuvenation potion that may serve you well," Olaf apologized, shuffling over the crude wood floor towards him.

"Olaf, don't apologize. I can't sleep all the time. At some point I'll need to get out of this bed, or I'll be here for good," Chieftain Barod replied as he slowly sat up.

His entire body felt as though it were on fire, and every movement made him feel great pain. However, he still felt better with each passing day. In fact, he noticed he felt so much better he may be ready to stand.

He slowly moved his legs off the bed and onto the cool, wooden floor. He noticed his feet were grey and could see the discolored veins from the poison. He looked as terrible as he felt, but if he was still alive then he wouldn't be dying from the poison. He slowly began to put weight on his feet, and all his muscles burned in response.

"Chieftain, please take it slow! There is no rush," Olaf said, standing close to the chieftain.

As Chieftain Barod managed to stand, he noticed he felt weak. He had heard of bedridden people becoming weak over time, but he hadn't been here that long. Between the poison and lack of movement, he felt horrible. His entire body felt as though it had been torn apart and crudely put back together. He almost didn't feel like the same man he was even a mere week earlier.

"I'll be alright, I may just need to steady myself," Chieftain Barod replied, placing a hand on Olaf's shoulder.

"Please, it's the least I can do. The last thing we need is you falling and breaking a hip," Olaf half joked. "Is there much pain?"

"There is, unfortunately," Chieftain Barod replied, wincing.

Olaf looked at him with stern eyes, something Chieftain Barod wasn't used to getting from the old man. He did know that this look meant Olaf was serious, and sure of what he was going to say. He watched the wrinkles on the old shaman's head move as he spoke.

"Please, let me use some magic. I know you detest it, but I can at least relieve the pain. There is no harm in it," Olaf urged, grabbing his chieftain's arm.

Chieftain Barod stared at his old friend, considering his offer. Ever since he was a child, he had been told to hate magic. He had been told to not trust it, and to even be wary of their own shaman. He didn't want to be skeptical of one of his closest advisors, but it was so ingrained into his soul he could barely find the power within him to say yes. Finally, after much internal debate, Chieftain Barod nodded to Olaf, mumbling agreement.

Olaf placed his hand over Chieftain Barod's heart, closing his old, weary eyes. He slowly muttered something to himself, as if finding it difficult to remember exactly how to use such a spell. Moments later, the smallest specks of blue light squeezed out from Olaf's hand and into Chieftain Barod's chest. A quiet humming sound filled Chieftain Barod's private cabin, neither speaking a word besides Olaf's mumbling.

As the blue light embraced him, Chieftain Barod felt at peace. In fact, he had felt more at peace now than at any other point in his life. At least, besides the one other time he had to accept aid from Olaf. Even then, that was just a hard decision to trust in such a chaotic force like magic. However, that had been brief, a flash of magic. This was a much longer spell.

Some of Chieftain Barod's color returned to his faded, grey cheeks. He let go of Olaf, able to stand on his own. As the magic flowed through his body, he felt full of life. In fact, it was more than that; he felt full of a strange, yet peaceful sensation. The Narsho chieftain felt as though he was back in order.

Olaf stopped, stepping back from Chieftain Barod. The blue light of the magic quickly dissipated, leaving no trace of its existence beyond a rejuvenated chieftain. Olaf took a deep breath, slightly tired from the brief usage of magic. He smiled as soon as he noticed how his friend looked better.

"Olaf, my old friend, thank you. It wasn't easy for me to accept such magic, but I feel much better," Chieftain Barod replied. "At least, the pain is gone. I'm still exhausted."

"Of course, Jonis. Anything for you. That's quite a difficult form of magic to use. Despite its power, it will fade. While it can heal a wound and ease pain, that poison may be too complex for it. You may feel better, but take it easy," Olaf explained, sitting in a nearby chair. "Sorry, it just takes a bit out of me."

"Please, relax. You are welcome to stay here anytime," Chieftain Barod smiled.

Suddenly, a knocking came from the front door. The two men looked over, not expecting anybody, though Chieftain Barod could guess who it was. He walked over to the door and opened it, seeing Chieftain Wooll standing before him.

"By the gods! You look much better!" Chieftain Wooll beamed with a toothy smile.

"I feel much better. I have Olaf to thank for that," Chieftain Barod replied, gesturing to the shaman.

"Hah! Perhaps he could teach our shaman a few tricks," Chieftain Wooll chuckled.

Olaf slowly stood and approached the two men, motioning that he had to get through. He still seemed tired but dedicated.

"You can relax here if you want, Olaf," Chieftain Barod offered.

"Thank you, but I have other matters to attend to. That battle left many wounded, and my healers aren't as effective as I am. I will see you both later I'm sure. Remember to take it easy, Chieftain," Olaf said before shuffling away towards the village.

Chieftain Barod gestured for his fellow chieftain to take a seat in one of the chairs on his small patio. The two sat down, now facing the wide blue ocean. It was a peaceful sight, which is why Chieftain Barod had his home built here. He was the farthest away from the village, on a small point his people had dubbed "the chieftain's point." From here, he was only a few feet from the beach.

"It's so peaceful here, Barod. The ocean is truly something. Even when I'm home in our forest village I do not forget the ocean's beauty," Chieftain Wooll acknowledged.

"It is. Which is why I will fight to defend it with everything I have. I only wish I wasn't so weak for the battle to come," Chieftain Barod replied.

"Ah, well leading isn't just about brute strength. It's about wisdom, too," Chieftain Wooll said, taking an ornate pipe from his pocket.

Chieftain Barod nodded in agreement, watching his old friend stuff the pipe full of tobacco. The Forud people had large tobacco farms, a plant that Chieftain Barod had never much appreciated. He didn't enjoy smoking like his fellow chieftain, who didn't bother to offer, already knowing this about his friend.

"I do wish to apologize to you, old friend," Chieftain Wooll said, taking a puff from his pipe.

"Apologize? What for?" Chieftain Barod asked.

"I feel partially responsible for you almost dying. Had we stood together with you earlier, the Highrock may have never attacked your home and you may have not gotten poisoned. Allies should stand and fight alongside each other, even if their reasons aren't as strong," Chieftain Wooll explained, some sadness in his old grey eyes.

Chieftain Barod had always been conflicted with their alliance. He understood why Wooll wouldn't want to get involved, but with their help they may have been in a better position. But there was no sense dwelling on the past, not now.

"Thank you, but do not feel responsible. I understand why you've never fought the Highrock Clan. After all, I wish we didn't have to fight them. We were once all part of the same clan after all, those many generations ago. That hatred they harbor comes from a grudge older than any of us. So please, my friend, do not be sorry," Chieftain Barod replied with a small smile.

"I wish you didn't have to fight them as well. I sometimes used to dream of us all reuniting and again becoming the Great Clan … Have you ever been to the ruins of the Great City far to the North?" Chieftain Wooll asked.

"No, I have never made it there. I have always wanted to, but it's a long journey, is it not?" Chieftain Wool answered.

"It is. Over a week's walk from our village, even longer from yours. I went there a few years ago with some scouts. There must have been tens of thousands of clanspeople, all living together in a massive, well, city. Most all of it has been destroyed or withered away to nothing. But there's enough to paint a picture of our past," Chieftain Wooll explained, peacefully puffing from his pipe. "Perhaps someday we can venture there together and see our people's past."

"I'd like that," Chieftain Barod smiled, hoping it would be a possibility.

Chieftain Barod had the same dream. Humans were stronger together, and their small clans were only a half-exposed shadow of what the Great Clan had been. If they had all still been united, maybe this new threat could have already been defeated.

"Well, I will convince my people to fight against both the Horrors and the Highrock Clan if they continue on with their war. It's late, I know, but I doubt your fight with them is over," Chieftain Wooll offered. "In fact, I have sent a couple of my guards to bring all my people here, as requested."

"Thank you, Herold. I'm sure that fight isn't over. I would be surprised if they fought alongside us against the Horrors," Chieftain Barod thanked.

"No, I doubt they will … I wonder if we will even see that Garon boy again. Prince or not, exile means exile," Chieftain Wooll added.

Chieftain Barod wondered the same thing. He hadn't met Garon yet, but based on what everyone had said, he was trustworthy. Apparently, Anna liked the man, and if anyone was a good judge of character it was her. He hoped the boy would be able to convince his father, but Chieftain Barod had seen the hatred in the chief king's eyes.

"I hope we do. We will need everyone we can get. I wonder how our people are faring with the Ancient and Linta Clans?" Chieftain Barod pondered.

"Hard to say, but I have faith. Elder Matkon seems like a good man, and Anna is strong willed and determined. Between the two of them, I'm sure they'll be able to make their case," Chieftain Wooll said, taking a long puff of his pipe. "However, if they are successful, this village is going to be a bit crowded."

Chieftain Barod hadn't thought about how many people his village could handle. The Narsho Clan was larger than the Highrock Clan, and not by much. The other clans were all larger, and it would be difficult to house them here. He wasn't sure how many lived with the Ancient Clan due to their secrecy, but it made the most sense to bring them all together. If anything, they could settle outside the wall and they could fortify another perimeter.

"It will be, but if the Horrors really can possess the bodies of the dead, then we'll need to keep our people together. Otherwise, they'll hunt us down one by one, taking us whenever we are weak," Chieftain Barod replied, staring out at the ocean.

"You are not wrong," Chieftain Wooll said, also gazing out to sea.

The two talked about more casual topics for a while, trying their best to take a moment to relax. They knew the path ahead would be troublesome, and they would need to conserve their strength and not overthink things.

Eventually, Chieftain Barod felt the pain return; the fires of old poison began to burn again, but not as hot as before. The magic had at least relieved some pain. Chieftain Barod had no idea how magic worked, but he couldn't deny its effectiveness.

As the two chieftains retold stories from their youth, they didn't even hear the young man walk up next to them. Only when he cleared his throat did the two look over. To Chieftain Barod, the black-haired man with a well-trimmed goatee was a stranger. His clothes were nice, and his swords seemed to be made of the highest-grade metal. A red cloak was draped from his shoulders.

"Exiled Prince Garon Mace, you return," Chieftain Wooll said, not standing but still extending his hand toward the prince.

"Chieftain Wooll," Garon greeted, shaking the man's hand.

Recalling the battle, Chieftain Barod remembered seeing the young man fighting alongside his people. Part of him wanted to hate the young man, an enemy to the Narsho, his father a poison-wielding coward, but he was level-headed enough to cut through such petty thoughts.

"I am Chieftain Barod of the Narsho Clan. It is nice to finally meet you, Prince Mace," Chieftain Barod greeted, extending his arm toward his former enemy.

"I am a prince no more. Please, call me Garon. It is an honor to meet you, Chieftain Barod. Your people speak of you with absolute respect," Garon greeted, shaking the chieftain's hand.

Shaking Garon's hand, Chieftain Barod noted how the younger man had come to terms with his new role in the world—from prince to outcast; it seemed Garon had lost everything. Still, he stood before the chieftain with a sense of pride. It was obvious the exiled prince had not given up, though it was also apparent he had been unable to convince his people to fight alongside them.

"A pleasure, Garon," Chieftain Barod corrected.

"Did you have any luck with your father?" Chieftain Wooll asked.

"Unfortunately, I did not. He is too far gone in his hatred. He would not listen," Garon answered, his voice slightly wavering.

"That is unfortunate, though I did not think you would be successful. No offense to you, Garon," Chieftain Wooll replied, sitting back and stroking his white beard.

"We will have to make do with who we do have then," Chieftain Barod added.

"I will stay and fight alongside you, for my people's sake," Garon said, saluting the chieftains. "Is there anything I can do to help now?"

Chieftain Barod thought for a moment, figuring out the best thing Garon could do. While Garon was still an outsider; he would be tolerated by anyone if their chieftain vouched for him. He had seen the man's excellent swordsmanship but knew he had fought Narsho warriors not even a week before. It would be worth the risk if his people could learn anything new from him.

"There is, actually. Go to the barracks and find Guard Captain Jarult. Tell him I've sent you to be a trainer for anyone willing to improve their skills with a sword. Most will not trust you, but some may be willing to put their feud aside if they desire self-improvement enough," Chieftain Barod told.

"Then I will go at once. Thank you, Chieftains," Garon said with a small bow.

The two didn't talk until Garon had walked away. Chieftain Barod could tell that the young man truly had the best intentions. It was a shame he didn't lead his people. It appeared Chief King Mace had failed to indoctrinate his son like he must have been as a child.

"He seems like a good lad," Chieftain Wooll said, looking over at his friend.

"Seems like it. A fierce warrior at heart too," Chieftain Barod agreed.

The two old friends trailed off into stories of the past once more. As they stared out at the ocean, they remembered better times from years past. They had both faced their fair share of challenges in their long lives, but nothing with the magnitude of what was to come. The Highrock Clan, bandits, beasts, food shortages, and illness were nothing compared to the potential danger Anna had described. But for now, they simply relaxed, talking with each other like they were young men again as they gazed over the beautiful orange sunset.

Chapter 18

Sitting peacefully on the grassy knoll, Anna looked over the thousands of people camped out around her home. It was a sight to behold, as these thousands were from different clans with different backgrounds. Now the Ancient, Linta, and Forud Clans had joined together here at the Narsho Village. She wondered if the Great Clan had started out like this.

She took a sip of the tincture Olaf had refilled for her, which supposedly was the best thing for her pregnancy. Despite it being early on, she could feel it. She placed her hand gently on her barely changed stomach, hoping they would win the battle to come.

It had been days since she had returned, and the Linta Clan had only just arrived. Before they did, she had taken the time to rest and keep to herself. She hadn't seen anyone besides Chieftain Barod, Olaf, and a few other scouts since she had been back. Due to the chaos of their overpopulated village, she had been staying outside the walls during the day. She always felt better out in nature, surrounded by peace.

She looked across the village towards the sea, counting the masts standing tall over their now bustling harbor. Two dozen ships of varying sizes were crammed in the port and surrounding waters, the most of which being Linta ships. Considering the warnings to leave, they hadn't stopped the construction of the ships. Now, Linta and Narsho shipbuilders worked together to create more ships capable of transporting their large population. Anna wasn't sure if they'd be able to take more than a third of the people with the current ships; if anything, only the young, old, and fragile of the clan would escape while the warriors stayed behind. She shuddered at the thought and thought of more pleasant things.

A few minutes went by before she saw someone making their way towards her. It took her a moment to recognize the burly man as Titus. She wasn't used to seeing the Champion in plain clothes and unarmed. As she stared, their eyes connected, and he picked up the pace.

She hadn't seen Titus since she had left, but he looked far more motivated and full life than he had when last she saw him. It seemed he had gotten his much-needed rest and was ready for the battle to come. She said nothing, waiting for him to approach.

"If only I could've found you in the dining hall," Titus said half-jokingly as he finished climbing up the small knoll.

"You wouldn't catch me there right now. I fear we have more hungry mouths than we have food," Anna replied, standing to shake Titus's hand.

As they shook hands, she noticed the Champion was out of breath. Perhaps he hadn't quite gotten the relaxation he had needed. There was no time for it now, however, as the battle neared.

"You may be right…" Titus said, taking a moment to catch his breath.

"I know you didn't come all the way over here just to talk to me. What's going on?" Anna asked with a small chuckle.

"They are preparing a meeting with everyone. All the chieftains, the Seer, the elders, everyone who's anyone is there," Titus answered, standing straight and regaining his proud composure.

"I see. Am I part of that everyone?" Anna asked.

"Of course you are. Chieftain Barod sent me to find you. I just wish you weren't camped up all the way over here," Titus replied, again only partially joking.

"The village is far too busy for my taste. Scouts prefer it out here. At least I do," Anna replied, looking at the massive crowds in the distance.

She could see where they were trying to build a secondary wall, or at least a sort of defensive perimeter around everyone. Even with many of the other clanspeople inside the village, there was still a camp almost as large as the village itself right outside the gate.

Now they were taking whatever spare wood and other material they found to secure themselves.

Anna wasn't sure if it would be effective, but it would at least slow down the Horrors if they somehow made it here. She looked back at her belongings on the ground and gathered them, knowing her people once again needed her. She knew this may be the very last time she spent on the knoll overlooking the village, the place where she and Fredrik first kissed.

"I agree. The warriors from the other clans are weak too. You can tell they haven't fought as frequently as us, let alone as intensely," Titus said.

He looked at Anna and waited until she had gathered her things. They began walking back down toward the bustling village. As they walked, Titus continued speaking about his issue with the other warriors. It seemed he had little faith in their new allies, though he did at least recognize they were far better than nothing.

Approaching the hastily constructed and incomplete new wall, they were greeted by a few Ancient Clan mages using their magic to construct the barrier. The clanspeople from other clans would bring them the supplies and the mages would place it down. Anna felt hope seeing the clans work together so well.

However, seeing the conditions of some of the clanspeople pressed that hope boot-first back into the ground. As they walked through the tent city, she saw many of the clanspeople were confused, sick, or otherwise unhappy. It was understandable, after all; to be told they had to suddenly leave their homes with whatever they could carry was a hard thing to deal with. Then to be camped out with people they didn't know or perhaps even trust was difficult. Not only did it strain families, but it strained the clan as a whole. After all, they probably didn't realize or possibly even believe in the threat that existed so close nearby.

As they rounded the last corner before reaching the Narsho wall, Anna spotted a large group of warriors training together just outside the gate. As she and Titus approached, she made eye contact with one of the people training them. As she saw the red cape behind him float through the air as he turned to see her, she couldn't help but smile.

"Anna!" Garon called out, saying something to the warriors in front of him and coming her way.

"Is that the Highrock prince?" Titus asked, squinting at the young man.

"Not anymore," Anna replied, still smiling.

She quickly walked toward him, and as they neared, she felt the urge to hug him. He must have had the same urge, and the two quickly hugged, both then realizing it might have looked strange. As they backed away, Anna had to fight the smile from her face with great mental strength.

"I'm surprised I haven't seen you yet! Are you doing well?" Garon asked, his eyes darting toward the much larger Titus a few times.

"As well as I can. I'm just ready to finally put an end to all of this," Anna said, fierce with determination.

"I can see that. I believe we are ready too. The warriors seem ready for a fight," Garon agreed.

"They've got you training them, huh? Could be worse, I suppose," Titus added with some attitude.

Anna made a small face at Titus before looking back to Garon. She wanted to ask how his trip home had gone, but she already knew the answer. She had known the answer before he had even left.

"We're about to attend a meeting to determine our plan. I think you should join us," Anna said to Garon.

"I see. I would be happy to join," Garon replied. "Let me send my warriors to another trainer."

Anna nodded and watched Garon go back and speak to the group of mixed warriors he had been training. Warriors from all clans stood in front of him, some young and some old. Seeing them all together was a sight to behold.

"You trust him?" Titus asked quietly.

"I do. Completely," Anna replied, not inviting any more of that conversation.

"Alright, I'm ready," Garon said as he approached the two.

"Then let's get a move on before they start without us," Titus grumbled, walking past Anna and Garon.

They followed Titus through the gates and into the very busy Narsho Village. Clanspeople from every clan crowded the paths, most having something to do to keep occupied. Those who didn't stood by, looking almost sour from the situation.

As they reached the Chieftain's Hall, the three arrived the same time as Seer Mordou and Valon. Nearing each other, Anna noticed the Seer was staring at Garon, as if lost in a trance. His smoldering magically blue eye was locked on the Highrock exile.

"That man with the blue eye, that's the Seer isn't it?" Garon asked Anna.

"It is. You haven't met him yet? He seems to recognize you," Anna replied.

"I haven't … Perhaps he's seen me in one of his visions," Garon added.

"Anna, Titus, hello!" Seer Mordou greeted, still staring at Garon.

"It's nice to see you," Valon added with a kind nod.

"It's good to see you both," Anna greeted in return.

She watched as Titus simply nodded toward them before turning and walking into the Chieftain's Hall. She wondered what his problem was; the Narsho Champion almost seemed disappointed that Garon was alive and well. She figured it was just his instinct to distrust Highrock clanspeople.

"Seer Mordou, I am Garon Mace, formerly of the Highrock Clan. I remember you coming to our village. I am sorry we didn't listen then," Garon apologized.

"Please, do not be sorry. You are here now, and that is all that matters. Garon, this is Valon, my apprentice and soon-to-be Seer of the Ancient Clan," Seer Mordou introduced.

As the men shook hands, Anna noticed Valon seemed nervous after his master mentioned him becoming Seer. She had gotten to know him a little during their traveling, and she had come to respect the man's intellect. If anything, he lacked confidence. Although to be fair, Anna had no idea what becoming a Seer entailed. From their brief conversations, it seemed like a great responsibility.

"Anna, Garon, I must speak with you both after this meeting," Seer Mordou began, keeping his voice down. "During my farsight, I saw something you need to hear about."

"Oh? What was it?" Garon asked.

"We shouldn't talk about this yet. There are others who must join us. After the meeting, follow us outside so we may speak," Seer Mordou suggested.

"Okay. We will," Anna agreed, looking to Garon.

"Certainly," Garon affirmed.

"Good. Now, shall we?" Seer Mordou said, holding the door open to the hall.

Anna entered the hall alongside the others, seeing that it was already full of people. She spotted Chieftains Barod, Wooll, and Yarmot speaking between themselves at the head of the table already. Becca Yarmot and Goreth Destro were sitting across the table from each other, staring into each other's eyes as they spoke. Anna was surprised to see the simple, quiet Forud Champion acting so bubbly, but figured he must have found Becca attractive. It surprised her even more that the feeling appeared to be mutual, and was happy for the two.

Seated around the table and standing behind each other were the Narsho Elders and other clanspeople from the Forud and Linta Clans. Guard Captain Jarult and Olaf spoke quietly to each other behind Chieftain Barod in the back of the hall, both as loyal to their chieftain as always. Suddenly, someone nearby called her name. She looked to see Elder Matkon approaching her.

"Elder Matkon, hello," Anna greeted, feeling uncomfortable as more eyes were drawn to her.

"We're happy you've made it! Your experience with the Horrors is unmatched, after all," Elder Matkon said with a nervous smile.

"Psh, barely," Titus said from nearby.

Anna ignored the comment and followed Elder Matkon. He brought her close to the head of the table, near the chieftains. There was one seat open, which he urged her to sit in. As she did so, Garon stood behind her, not saying a word. She looked over to see Titus at the far end of the room, looking upset. It was then Anna realized she was sitting in what was normally his chair. She looked away, not wanting to appear as though she was gloating. After all, she did respect Titus. She didn't want to take his place at all and wouldn't have asked for this seat. She only knew why she was chosen now, and that was solely for her stories and experience in the Cursed Lands.

"Well, it looks as though everyone is here," Chieftain Barod said, standing from the table.

"Gather their attention," Chieftain Wooll said with a chuckle.

Anna watched as Chieftain Barod slammed his fist down on the wooden table the same way he always did to begin a meeting. The Narsho didn't move, expecting such a loud sound. Those from other clans nearly jumped out of their seat, all of them closing their mouths and looking to Chieftain Barod.

"My, my, that's one way to begin," Chieftain Yarmot said, his large hands enveloping the arms of his chair.

"Welcome, everyone," his voice boomed across the table. "I am glad we are sitting here as allies. In fact, seeing everyone together makes me wonder if this is how the Great Clan felt," Chieftain Barod began, getting some sounds of approval at his words.

"I'm sure it was," Chieftain Wooll muttered mainly to himself with a small smile.

"Now, like the Great Clan, we face a threat that could put an end to all of us. While most of us haven't seen these Horrors in person yet, some of us have. Of those, only a handful have survived to tell the tale. You've already been told of their strength, their cruelty, and their sickly infestation of our land. Now we as a temporarily unified clan must decide a plan of attack, for if we don't, we may fall like our ancestors did!" Chieftain Barod spoke loudly, his voice echoing with authority through the hall.

"And unfortunately, we do not have a choice in the matter. Even if we do not want to fight, we must," Chieftain Yarmot added, looking primarily toward his advisors.

"Exactly. We are all in this together now. You might have also heard we may have to leave Forthoton, our home, and sail south. This is why you have seen ships under construction. Our people are our priority, and we must ensure their survival at all cost," Chieftain Barod continued.

"But how do we know there is land to the south? What proof do we have?" a Narsho Elder asked.

Anna knew there would be hesitation about leaving. For that, they only had the visions of the Ancient Clan and the supposed run-in with a creature called an Arboreal. It was hardly the evidence they'd want, but Anna knew better than to distrust the Seer's visions at this point.

"The Seer of the Ancient Clan has seen it, and his apprentice has spoken with a mystical being claiming there is land south." Chieftain Barod replied with confidence.

"And there are maps! I remember seeing a map in my young years showing land to south," Chieftain Wooll added, trying to help his friend convince those around them even though deep down he was lying.

Anna could tell Chieftain Wooll was lying, but it was for good reason. She had seen how the Horrors afflicted the forests; their corruption seemed to live, to control whatever it could and turn it into something they could use. She didn't see why it wouldn't spread throughout all of Forthoton. If that was the case, they had no choice but to flee. She watched as the Narsho Elder leaned back in his chair, somewhat satisfied with the answer he received.

"But that is not our first choice. First we must lead every warrior we can muster to the Cursed Lands and attempt to destroy this enemy!" Chieftain Barod urged.

"Who will lead them?" a Linta advisor asked, her question genuine.

"Who will lead them?" Chieftain Wooll asked almost mockingly as he stood. "We will lead them!"

Anna watched Chieftain Wooll place his hand on Chieftain Barod's shoulder, both looking full of vigor. In fact, she was surprised Chieftain Barod was looking so well. She figured Olaf must have convinced him to allow the use of magic.

"Well then, who will lead the clanspeople back here?" A Forud advisor asked with concern.

It was a good question, and Anna worried the warrior's unrest may spread throughout the village. They barely had enough food as it was, and they couldn't remain here too long before they'd have to either return home or travel somewhere else. She raised an eyebrow as the Linta Chieftain quickly stood up on his thick legs.

"I am obviously not a fighter. But, if there is one thing I can do, it's manage a large village. I will stay behind and address the concerns of those clanspeople remaining here," Chieftain Yarmot soothed calmly.

"And I'd trust Chieftain Yarmot to do a fine job leading in my stead. Who here takes issue with this plan?" Chieftain Barod asked, his old eyes smoldering with intimidation.

Nobody spoke a word, and Anna realized they must have now figured out how out of options they were. It seemed like a fine plan, and despite Chieftain Yarmot being friendly and competent, she didn't know how he'd fare leading so many different people. The Linta Clan's people seemed far different from the rough and gruff Narsho.

"I will also lead my mages into battle. You will need us to close the portal from which these Horrors came," Seer Mordou said over the sounds of muffled whispering.

"Good! The more power we have the better. Now, we must discuss when we leave and how we will approach. Let's get into the details," Chieftain Barod said, sitting back down.

Anna watched Chieftain Wooll nod and sit. She knew the two chieftains were fierce warriors but worried what would happen if they were lost in battle. Should any clan lose their leader, they may begin to feel underrepresented and want to leave their temporary alliance. However, she knew these issues were not for her to worry about.

She stayed silent for the meeting, never being asked about her experiences. By now, most everyone had been told about what lay in waiting for them in the Cursed Lands anyway. There was some bickering between everyone, but they realized they had no choice and quickly agreed on a plan.

The entirety of their combined warriors would leave in two days' time for the Cursed Lands. Then, they would establish an outpost and send scouts to see if the enemy had any weaknesses. All warriors would be sent with only a few dozen left behind to keep order and watch over the village. Anna wasn't sure about the all-or-nothing strategy, and hoped the Horrors weren't smart enough to attack their village.

After the meeting, everyone had their brief words with each other and then departed the uncomfortably warm hall. Anna and Garon silently followed Seer Mordou and Valon outside back into the cooler evening air, wondering what he wanted to talk to them about. As they walked, she noticed both Becca and Goreth were following them. In fact, the two looked as surprised by their presence as they did to the others.

Seer Mordou stopped as they reached a quiet patch of grass located between two nearby homes. With everyone out on the street talking loudly, they were perfectly able to speak without any other ears hearing. They all circled up, waiting for the Seer to speak.

"Thank you for following me here. I know this appears to be a random group of people to you, but I have seen you all in my last farsight," Seer Mordou began, looking at each member of the group.

"Seen us? What do you mean?" Anna asked, her finger wrapped around her red hair.

"I have seen all of us standing together in a place far east of here, even farther than the Cursed Lands on the east coast of our realm. There, we will discover something that will grant us great power, which we need to fight back these Horrors," Seer Mordou explained.

"A place? Like those ruins I found?" Anna asked, trying to visualize what he had seen. "White stone buildings of great design, right?"

"Yes, yes exactly! But a large ruined city farther east than that. It is there we may find what we need to defeat these invaders," Seer Mordou continued, looking at each of his Champions.

"Do you mean weaponry?" Goreth asked, scratching his chin suspiciously.

"I think he means something else," Garon added.

"Precisely. It wasn't quite traditional weaponry; some sort of strong magic calls out to me. We must leave now, as we must travel farther than our armies do. This way we can reach them before they engage the Horrors in battle," Seer Mordou explained.

"And I only just arrived," Becca joked, shaking her head. "I will follow you, Seer. For my people's sake."

"I too will follow. I can't turn down a chance for better weaponry," Goreth said, looking into Becca's eyes.

"I will do whatever is necessary to end this, once and for all," Anna agreed.

"Perhaps I will find a way to save my people in the process. I too will join you," Garon affirmed.

"I follow you wherever you lead, Master," Valon said obediently.

Seer Mordou smiled, his blue eye appearing to glow even brighter. He took some parchment from beneath his robe and handed a sheet to each of the group except Valon.

As Anna grabbed it, she began reading the old words. It appeared to be some sort of explanation of magic. She looked at Garon, who stared at her with excitement.

"Then take these and study them. These sheets explain the very basics of tapping into and using the magic that flows around us. I know it is typically forbidden in your clans, but I believe we will need this if we are to be successful. We shall leave tomorrow morning at dawn. Say goodbye to whomever you need and meet at the center gate tomorrow morning," Seer Mordou ordered his new Champions.

Everyone nodded, and the group separated. Anna and Garon walked back to her home, both reading the papers given to them by the Seer. Anna found the words interesting, but incredibly strange. She wasn't sure how she felt about using magic, but they would at least have to try.

"These notes are so odd. Supposedly magic flows all around us, unseen and untouchable … and we can interact only using our minds? How odd," Garon rambled as they walked.

"It is odd. But if it is what we need to win, I will do everything I can," Anna replied.

The two entered her home, their eyes still glued to the interesting yet complicated words on the parchment. They barely spoke as they continued reading, and almost an hour of this studious silence went by before either attempted using magic. The words went into great detail about the state of mind needed, the focus needed, and the basic understanding of how magic flowed. The ideas and training described therein were not something someone could find themselves, at least not quickly. Anna had never read such interesting, yet thick writing.

Garon, comprehension dawning, set his paper down gently on the table beside him. He stood from Anna's chair, closing his eyes. As she watched, she thought she could see some small blue flecks in the air around him.

"I ... I think I understand," Garon slowly said.

Anna didn't respond, not wanting to break her friend's focus. The parchment spoke of a few basic spells, the most recommended being the wisplight spell. This allowed the user to create a magic wisp of light that also revealed objects hidden by basic invisibility. This was the spell the Ancient Clan used in the swamp.

Suddenly, the small flecks of blue formed a small, gentle floating ball in the air next to his head. As the magic coalesced, Anna's small home was filled with an unnatural blue light. Garon had done it, he had successfully used magic. Anna figured if anyone could, it would be him. The exiled prince was incredibly smart and had a strong will.

"Open your eyes," Anna said softly.

Garon opened his eyes to see his wisplight slowly dancing through the air around him. He brought his hand close to it, intrigued by his creation. His handsome smile forced Anna to grin in unison as they both admired what was possibly the first spell ever cast within the Narsho village by anyone other than Olaf.

"It's incredible ... I can feel it, the magic. I can also feel the draw from my energy—my body—that this takes

… It seems magic really does flow through all of us," Garon smiled.

He stared at the wisplight and waved his hand through the air dramatically. Then, as quickly as it had appeared, it vanished, scattering tiny specs of blue aside that quickly disappeared from their vision. He chuckled, sitting back in the chair and looking at the parchment.

"That was great," Anna complimented.

"Not too bad for the easiest spell they recommend. You should give it a try. Come on," Garon urged playfully.

"Maybe," Anna replied, looking back at her parchment.

The next spell the author recommended was basic levitation of a small object. In a good mood, Anna thought it would be entertaining to try to one-up Garon. She eyed a chunk of bread sitting on the table next to them and closed her eyes.

Like the instructions said, she pictured the flow of magic around them, how its essence touched every object, both living and inanimate. She pictured bridging the magic of her being to the bread and focused her mind to use that bridge as if it were another appendage to simply raise the bread.

She slowly opened her eyes and noticed the bread had begun to lightly shake on the table. Garon didn't bother to look next to him, expecting a similar wisplight to appear. He watched Anna intently, not seeing the bread slowly rise into the air next to his head.

"Ah, well it was a good try I suppose. I thought I saw some sort of magical blue flecks in the air," Garon consoled, still unaware a piece of bread was hovering inches from his head.

"Look to your left," Anna quietly said, still focusing her newfound ability.

Garon looked and lurched back as his nose almost touched the levitating bread. He burst out laughing, shaking his head at his brief fear. His laughter being contagious, Anna laughed as well, breaking her focus and dropping the bread back on the table.

"I see, trying to show off, eh?" Garon laughed. "Not bad, Anna, not bad."

"Maybe a little," Anna laughed.

At that moment, Anna forgot the many woes of their world. She laughed with Garon, enjoying his company greatly. She didn't have many people she trusted, or even talked to that much now. For the first time since Fredrik's death, she didn't feel entirely alone.

They continued practicing basic magic for the rest of the evening, constantly trying to outdo the other. At one point, Anna even launched a small bolt of pure magic at one of her pots in the kitchen, which exploded into a puff of flour and shards of former pottery. This only elicited more laughter from the two.

Eventually, the novices felt too exhausted to continue. Between a long day and the beginning of magic usage, they had little energy to spare. Anna almost offered Garon to sleep in her bed instead of wherever he was staying so that he would have a good night's rest, but she didn't get the chance to ask before he got up to leave.

As they bid farewell, Anna felt the sense of dread that frequently plagued her return. She found it difficult to fall asleep that night, thinking about the great path ahead and the battles they would soon face. A single tear fell from her eye as she thought about Fredrik, who she knew was never coming back. She gently clutched her stomach, whispering to her future child as she faded off into a tumultuous sleep.

***

Becca waited for the voices inside the newly constructed shack to slow before she finally knocked. As she did, the mutterings inside ceased, and she could hear footsteps quickly approaching her from inside. She stood up straight, trying to project confidence to whoever would be answering.

Cora, an advisor to Chieftain Yarmot, answered. The serious look across her face quickly lightened as she recognized Becca, and immediately opened the door wide.

"Who is it?" Chieftain Yarmot asked with frustration.

"Ah, hello, Becca!" Cora greeted kindly, closing the door behind Becca.

Becca didn't speak as she walked in the dimly lit shack, sensing the obvious tension in the room. While she wouldn't ask, she could assume it was from the outcome of the meeting. The Linta Clan had given up everything based on the whims of other clans.

"Becca, good evening! I'm glad you've come to visit me in my new palace," Chieftain Yarmot laughed, trying to lighten the mood for his beloved niece.

"I was going to say, this is quite an impressive place," Becca chuckled, looking around and noticing the poorly constructed floorboards were coated in dirt, and the roof had small gaps that let in the moonlight.

"I should be going, Chieftain," Cora quickly suggested, wanting to leave the family alone. "Goodnight, Becca."

"Yes, get some rest, Cora. We shall discuss more tomorrow," Chieftain Yarmot replied, waving weakly at his advisor.

"Goodnight, Cora," Becca added.

Becca didn't speak again until Cora left, not wanting to accidentally spark a new argument with her news. She knew it would be difficult to convince her uncle that she had to follow the Seer, and Cora would likely be even less enthused with the idea.

Given the fact her father had disappeared at sea when she was young, and her mother had passed from sickness only a couple years later, Becca had been raised primarily by her uncle, who had already become the chieftain by that time. Cora had also already been an advisor, and often helped take care of Becca when he was too busy with his duties.

"So, what brings my favorite niece to me tonight?" Chieftain Yarmot asked, his mind still partially occupied with his previous conversation.

"Seer Mordou wants me and some of the others to follow him east tomorrow morning. He thinks we can find … a weapon or some magic to aid us in battle," Becca explained, finding it hard to summarize something she didn't even fully understand yet.

Chieftain Yarmot's eyes went wide upon hearing the news, instantly torn away from his other thoughts. He tried to speak a couple times, raising his finger as if to object. However, each time he stopped himself, remembering that Becca was old enough and smart enough to make her own decisions. Finally, he found the words he sought.

"Becca … there is much I do not understand right now, though I am continually convinced by overwhelming evidence to trust those fellow clans that we stand with. However, the risks of traveling that way with a small group are obvious. What does the Seer hope to find? Why does he need you?" Chieftain Yarmot slowly questioned.

"Well, from what I understand, it's more the fact he has foreseen it that makes it important. When he sees this path using his magic, it means we must follow it if we hope to win. He saw me, Anna Myhre, the former Highrock Prince, Garon, the Forud Champion Goreth, his apprentice, and himself all standing at a strange place to the far east, just beyond the Cursed Lands. It is there we will find some sort of magic that can help us," Becca explained slowly.

"I see … So, if the Seer is to lead us to victory, we must follow the path he sees. I don't quite understand it fully, but there is much about all of this I do not understand. Let me ask you this final question, then. Is your gut telling you to go?" Chieftain Yarmot asked.

"It is. Something in me tells me that I need to go," Becca replied.

Chieftain Yarmot simply nodded, the smallest of smiles appearing on his face as he looked at the ground. He appeared almost sad, which confused Becca. It took a moment, but he finally looked back up at her, a small tear in his eye.

"When the voice within you calls out, you must listen. Your father ignored that voice the day he disappeared out to sea. I remember him being torn, his gut telling him to stay behind and his sense of duty telling him to go out on the fishing boat with his men. I didn't weigh in at the time, wanting the decision to be his own. So, I will tell you now what I should have told him then … trust in yourself, Becca. Trust your inner-voice and go with Seer Mordou. I believe in you," Chieftain Yarmot explained, trying hard to keep his emotions in check.

Becca teared up at her uncle's words, barely able to remember her father. She quickly wiped away the tears and ran forward to hug her only living family. She couldn't ask for a better uncle, or a better chieftain.

"Thank you," Becca quietly said as they let go.

"No, thank you. You've always done more than your share for this Clan, Becca. I know we're different than the others, not having the same warriors, the same fighting culture …We haven't had a Linta Clan Champion for well over a hundred years, perhaps longer. I cannot even remember the name of the last champion. Perhaps it's time we change that," Chieftain Yarmot began, pride in his eyes.

"What do you mean?" Becca slowly asked, wiping away a final tear.

Chieftain Yarmot turned toward his chair, searching for something. As he looked around, he muttered to himself, unable to find what he was looking for. Finally, he took the empty chalice from where he had been sitting and turned back toward his niece.

"You'll have to excuse my lack of formality here, but I seemed to have misplaced my sword. Anyway, this will do," Chieftain Yarmot chuckled, holding the wine encrusted chalice high before him. "Becca Yarmot, I,

Chieftain of the Linta Clan, hereby dub thee the Champion of the Linta Clan."

Becca couldn't help but smile as he slowly tapped each of her shoulders with the chalice, chuckling at his actions as an uncle, but also feeling extremely honored by his declaration as a chieftain. She couldn't have expected such a response, but felt more confident than ever before.

"Thank you, Chieftain. You honor me greatly," Becca replied formally.

"And you honor not only this clan, but our family. Your parents would be so proud ... I have kept you long enough. Now go, Champion Becca Yarmot, and succeed in your quest, and get some rest before tomorrow."

"I will not fail you, or the Linta Clan. Thank you, Uncle, for everything," Becca replied, filled with emotion.

She could feel more tears coming from various emotion and didn't want to embarrass herself in front of her uncle. She turned, walking toward the door and leaving her uncle behind. As she opened the door and began to walk through, she turned to see him sitting back in his chair, raising the chalice toward her with a large grin on his face. She smiled back and closed the door behind her, seeing her uncle for what may be the final time.

Chapter 19

Chief King Mace stood in absolute darkness, only red eyes visible in the distance. Had he not been full of such vengeance and hatred, he would surely be fearful of where he was. However, his clan needed him to be strong, and he had found someone who could make them all strong.

Having heard whispering, he had called out loudly to speak with their leader. Now he waited, glancing back over his shoulder at the sunlight far in the distance. He took another step forward on the fleshy surface, calling out once more.

"I am Chief King Mace of the Highrock Clan! I know you're out there! I can see your eyes! I can hear your whispers! I want to discuss an alliance!" Chief King Mace yelled, still filled with enough righteousness to override his sense of fear.

He watched as a set of red eyes neared him in the darkness. As they came closer, he rested his hand on the axe he now kept in lieu of his mace. He watched as the humanoid figure approached him, now wishing he had brought a torch.

"Reveal yourself!" Chief King Mace yelled, wielding his axe.

Suddenly the pitch-black forest erupted in a deep red and green color. The flesh-coated trees glowed through the artificial darkness that had been created around them. Chief King Mace froze, stunned by the unnatural and disturbing sight, though he quickly realized the man standing before him wore Narsho armor and colors.

"Narsho! What are you doing here?" Chief King Mace yelled, wanting to strike down the strange looking man with his axe.

The man chuckled, slowly moving his hand down his smooth purplish, veiny cheeks and then through his golden blond hair. He took a step closer, smiling with sharp teeth and staring into the eyes of the chief king.

Chief King Mace froze, stunned with the man's appearance. Through the red eyes he thought he could see the smallest hints of blue. It was apparent this was no real Narsho man, at least not anymore.

"Chief King Mace," the man spoke.

As the Horror-infused man spoke, a deeper, darker voice echoed throughout all the forest around them like a sinister echo. Chief King Mace felt his blood run cold but stood strong and eyed down the strange man.

"Yes. Are you the leader?" Chief King Mace asked, easing his grip on the axe slightly.

As the man laughed, so did the entire forest. The dark, disturbing cackles cut through the chief king like the sharpest of blades. He felt terrified, but still sought an audience with the enemy the Narsho feared so much.

"I am. I am everything you see here. Every human, every beast, every tree; they are all mine," the voice boomed.

Chief King Mace looked to see dozens of beasts emerging from behind the trees, with a few more sickly humans following.

"Who ... What are you?" Chief King Mace asked, his voice lowering slightly.

"I have had many names from many tongues, but I prefer my birth name, Xerannu. It is a pleasure to meet you, Chief King Mace," the voices boomed as the man standing before the chief king extended his arm.

The chieftain begrudgingly shook the man's incredibly warm, unnerving hand. He quickly wiped his hand on his clothing afterward, a warm slime stuck to it. He wasn't sure what was going on, but he could tell whoever this being was, it had power, power that he wanted.

"Xerannu ... I seek an alliance. The Narsho clan, they are our ancestral enemies. Together my clan of warriors and your … creatures, can defeat them," Chief King Mace offered.

"You think I need an alliance?" Xerannu's many voices boomed as the man in front of him laughed.

The red and green glow from the trees vibrated as the entire forest erupted in sickly, chaotic laughter. The mocking tone made the chief king angry, but he knew he needed the being's assistance.

"No, I need an alliance. Perhaps if you help us achieve victory, I can help you," Chief King Mace spoke over the laughter.

The laughter stopped, and the man in front of him curiously scratched his chin. A sharp, toothy smile warped over the man's visage as he began working out details in his head.

"Chief King, I hear your plea. If you accept my gift, I can make both you and your people stronger than you could ever be on your own. In return, all I ask is for you to aid me in the great battle I shall someday face," Xerannu spoke, completely stable and without any tone.

"Your gift? What do you mean?" Chief King Mace asked suspiciously.

"Do you want to defeat the Narsho or not, chief king? My gift will make the Highrock Clan the strongest clan of humans this world has ever seen. All you have to do is accept it," Xerannu explained with a strangely delighted tone.

"I do want to defeat them. I accept your gift, Xerannu, and so do my people," Chief King Mace proudly said, standing straight and staring into the red eyes of the man before him.

"Just as I predicted," Xerannu said shortly. "Now kneel."

Chief King Mace slowly knelt on the fleshy surface, hating to kneel before anyone. He felt the urge to vomit at the nasty sensation, his bony knee pressing deep within the purplish black floor of the forest. He stared up toward the man controlled by Xerannu and waited for the supposed gift.

"It may be more effective when the host is still living, but not quite as enjoyable," Xerannu said quietly as the entire forest silenced.

Suddenly, the man lurched forward and tackled Chief King Mace into the fleshy ground. Before the old man could act, a hideous fleshy tube shot out from the man's mouth into his own. Chief King Mace could feel it latching onto the back of his throat, and he tried to cry out in terror, but he couldn't speak as his mouth was pumped full of foul ichor.

"Calm yourself, Chief King. This will give you the power you seek," Xerannu's voices chuckled from the forest.

The glowing red trees began to dim, and Chief King Mace felt his own strength fading fast. In that brief moment, all he could feel was a combination of regret and terror. As the man pressed his body onto the chief king, Xerannu laughed.

"Now you can give all your people my gift, and you will do so as soon as you return!" Xerannu commanded. "Just as I planned!"

Chief King Mace's eyes teared up as he thought of his ancestors. They would be disgusted by him, even disturbed. Where was his honor, his pride? He was going to die here and fail his ancestors. He closed his eyes, feeling the world fading around him.

In his very last moments of sickening reflection, he thought of Garon; he had failed his son, had failed him ever since he was a child. He pictured Garon's face, trying to cry out as he slowly suffocated. The last words the chief king tried to speak were, "I am so sorry, my son."

Chapter 20

Garon winced as a gush of hot, tarry blood splattered his face. He quickly wiped it off with the back of his hand as he stepped back from his foe. He stared at the gurgling Horror, its malformed head barely hanging by threads of putrid flesh. As it fell, Garon took the smallest moment to savor his brief victory before looking to the next target.

Even with the magic of Seer Mordou and Valon, the fight against the Horrors was taking everything they had. Garon looked over at the two mages, who were now looking fatigued as they assaulted their foes with deadly magic. Sharp streaks of blue and an accompanying crackling sound blasted through Horror after Horror, but their numbers were too high, though they appeared to be holding their own, Garon realized.

"They never end!" Goreth yelled over as he bashed a Horror with his heavy shield.

"Keep fighting! We have no other choice now!" Anna replied, her skill with dual wielding looking sharp.

Garon looked back to a shambling Horror closing on him, practically foaming at the mouth. This particular one had three arms, two being on the same side, all of which had bladelike claws emerging from the end. It hissed at Garon as it swung at him.

Garon prepared to attack, not afraid of his enemy. The Horrors may have been designed to fight, but they all had a flaw of some sort that could be exploited. Some of them were slow, others were clumsy, and a few were just weak. Plus, fortunately none of them seemed too smart. So far, none had used any weapons beyond their body either. He figured their strength lay in their great numbers.

"Garon! Behind you!" Becca yelled as she released an arrow toward her target.

Garon turned to see a smaller Horror running on all fours at him. He had to fully dive on the ground just to avoid it, tumbling over a corpse of a recently slain monster. He quickly stood just in time to parry the sharp claw of his foe.

The Horror hissed again, flailing all three of its arms at the former prince. Garon parried a few of the blows before finding an opening and cutting all three of the being's arms off in quick succession. More tarry, black blood burst out, and the beast roared in pain. Knowing that wouldn't finish it off, Garon quickly decapitated this foe as well, sending it toppling over into the rocky ground.

Just as that one fell, the smaller one jumped at him again. This time, Garon was not quick enough, and was knocked on his back on the rocky ground. He couldn't help but let out a brief cry of pain, and gasped as the air was knocked out of him.

The Horror jumped on his chest and brought its head close, howling at him. Garon tried to grab for his swords, but they had both landed just out of reach. As the beast tried to pin Garon's arms, it lunged its head towards the former prince's neck.

Garon managed to break his arms free and stop the beast from tearing into his neck. He barely held back the ravenous beast, rancid saliva spraying on his face. Gritting his teeth, Garon tried to push his foe off, but was failing. The beast's head was closing towards his exposed neck.

Suddenly, a crackling bolt of blue energy struck the beast's head and sent it flying off Garon's sore body. Hitting so close to his face, the magic had assaulted Garon's own senses, causing his vision to go white before readjusting, and he could smell a something vile from the impact.

He stumbled to his feet, seeing it had been Valon who had saved him. The two made eye contact and nodded, knowing their fight was not over yet. There were still more Horrors, but Garon noticed their numbers were thinning.

"They're almost defeated! Keep fighting!" Garon yelled.

As he looked to each of his companions, Garon noticed Anna's skill with two swords was improving greatly. He smiled slightly, finding her form alluring, but his thoughts were quickly interrupted by a more primal looking Horror that ran at him, growling madly.

The group fought with all their might and finally found themselves victorious. The last of the attackers fell to the bow of Becca Yarmot, who gracefully struck the gnarled head of a Horror dead center. As the final foe fell to the ground, they all stood in silence, waiting to see if any more would run out from the nearby treeline. Fortunately, none did.

"We've strayed too close to the corrupted forest," Anna said over tired breath.

"I believe you are correct. Come, we should traverse farther away before we rest," Seer Mordou agreed, looking so fatigued that even his glowing blue eye seemed less intense.

They continued their journey, keeping just out of sight of the newly infected forest at all times. Tired from the unforeseen fight, no one spoke and simply continued to walk where the Seer led them.

Garon trusted the Seer but wondered if the man knew where he was leading them. They were deep in the Cursed Lands now, far deeper than he figured anyone had been in a long time. In fact, the landscape itself showed no signs of human interaction. Besides the ever-growing corrupted forest, the rest of the trees, boulders, and other resources were untouched. The grass was long, the peaceful wildlife abundant, and they constantly had to create their own path through the overgrowing flora.

They had been traveling for days now, and that had been the second fight with Horrors they had encountered. The first had only been against a few of the creatures, but this time they had slain easily two dozen, if not more.

Garon had also noticed the Horror-afflicted forest grew in an equal circle. Having kept track of their path against the stars at night, it seemed the forest was growing quickly. No doubt, the epicenter of the horrible place was what Anna had seen. The worst part was Anna claimed the corrupted forest had grown immensely in diameter since the last time she had been to the Cursed Lands not long ago. It was obvious this wasn't a problem they could ignore, as with each creeping moment the corruption of the Horrors engulfed more and more of their world.

"Those things are disturbing. I've never seen or fought anything like them," Becca said in a worried voice.

"Fortunately, they're not too tough," Goreth replied, feigning nonchalance to impress Becca.

"They may not be dangerous alone, but it is their numbers that ought to concern you. I have a feeling far more are hiding in those woods than we know," Seer Mordou replied.

"Then why wouldn't more attack?" Goreth asked in confusion.

"They may not want to reveal themselves," Valon pointed out. "Anna mentioned a voice; there is a chance someone or something is controlling them all."

"That's what I find disturbing," Garon replied.

"You have no idea," Anna agreed quietly, thinking about Fredrik's walking corpse.

They continued up a large hill for almost an hour until they eventually reached a revealing outlook. As the sight before them unfolded, everyone either gasped or mumbled a voice of concern at the terrible sight.

"Look at that..." Anna whispered with wide eyes

Garon felt his heart sink as he saw the scale of what they were dealing with.

From high on the hill, they could see the true magnitude of the corrupted forest. The circular black mass expanded as far as they could see forward, and most of what they could see left or right of them.

"By the gods … Perhaps Distichum was right," Seer Mordou said, looking at his apprentice. "Perhaps our land is lost."

Garon didn't know what to say, his eyes locked on the terrible sight before them. From here, he could barely make out some individual trees on the very edge of the corrupted land. It was engulfing everything, and even the open areas had been coated in a patch of growth that extended from tree to tree. It looked as though a world-ending plague was enveloping their entire world, and they were powerless to stop it.

"We can't just give up, we owe it to all our clanspeople," Anna said, looking at the others for agreement.

"She's right. This is our home; we can't give up without a fight," Becca agreed.

"Master, if we close the portal, will the forest return to its normal state?" Valon asked.

"That, I do not know. All I know is we are nearing the place I saw my vision. Not too much farther east now," Seer Mordou said, seeming nervous.

"Are you sure? How do you know where we are going?" Garon asked, knowing time was of the essence.

"I can sense magic lingering from that direction. It is what called out to me in my last farsight. We are going in the correct direction, do not worry," Seer Mordou replied, seeming unhappy to be questioned.

Before Garon could respond, something caught his eye. He turned to see the corrupted forest had begun to glow slightly red. As he stared, he noticed the trees on the far edge of the corrupted part of the forest near them had turned red. As it happened, Garon could feel the slightest sensation from somewhere around him, but was unable to process it. However, the two mages were able to do so.

"By the gods!" Seer Mordou yelled, placing his head in his hands.

"Master! What is that ungodly energy?" Valon asked in desperation, looking all around them.

"The forest!" Garon yelled, wondering what the sensation was they had felt.

"I can feel it too, barely. Like a bile in the back of my throat," Anna said, looking toward the glowing forest.

"Aye, I can as well. Is it magic?" Goreth asked.

"It must be," Becca replied.

Garon had no idea what to do and looked between his traveling companions. He wanted to help the mages but didn't know what to say or do. Suddenly, he could hear a voice somewhere in the distance. No, there were two voices.

"Do you hear the voices?" Garon asked, looking at everyone else.

"Voices? What voices do you hear?" Valon asked, still overwhelmed by the magic.

"Seer Mordou! Your eye!" Anna yelled.

Garon noticed it as soon as she spoke. The Seer's glowing blue eye was beginning to turn almost purple, the same red from the forest affecting it. Garon had no idea why the man's eye glowed like that, but he had figured it was something to do with farsight.

"Master!" Valon gasped.

"I can hear them too, Garon. But, how can you? You are not powerful enough. How can you possibly witness such magic?" Seer Mordou asked aloud.

"But what do you hear?" Becca asked impatiently.

"Muddled voices," Garon softly replied, trying hard to hear wherever the voices came from.

"Dark, conspiring voices," Seer Mordou added.

"I can barely make them out now too," Valon added. "It took me a moment, but I found them."

"Found voices? How?" Goreth asked puzzledly.

"The magic that's flowing around us, it's being altered, being used, like voices traveling in the wind," Valon explained, focusing more on the magic than on Goreth.

Garon found something familiar about one of the voices. That voice was old, cold, yet full of resolve. The other voice was dark, wretched, and full of pain. He could barely comprehend even hearing them, as it was nothing like hearing with his ears. No, this was a sense, something beyond a normal person.

"It's becoming clearer now," Valon added, looking to his master and appearing visibly in less pain.

"Yes, I can almost hear them now," Seer Mordou slowly spoke.

"Who is it?" Becca asked.

"Is it the Horrors?" Anna added.

A few more moments of silence passed before anyone answered. Then, suddenly, all their answers came at once in a gush of magic. Even the evening air blew hard and tossed leaves and other debris around in that moment of clarity.

"Xerannu," Seer Mordou repeated.

"Father?" Garon asked at the same time, looking around instinctively for his father.

Then as quickly as it had begun, it stopped. The red and green glow faded from the forest and the Seer's eye, and the flow of dark magic stopped, like they had been thrust back into their own time, cut off from the answers they sought.

Garon fell to his knees, tears running down his cheeks. He had seen, or rather sensed what had just happened. It made absolute sense; his father, fueled by nothing except hatred and vengeance, would seek any enemy of the Narsho. He understood his father's ambitions, but this was a step too far.

"Garon!" Anna yelled, running over and placing a hand on his shoulder.

"What's going on?" Seer Mordou asked, regaining his focus.

Garon couldn't reply, thinking only of his father. He should have expected this, should have seen it coming. He had told his father about the one thing the Narsho actually feared. It was his fault his father had done this and had forsaken his people. Until he heard one last tiny wisp of magic whisper into his ear.

"I am so sorry, my son."

Garon began to cry, feeling the fear and confusion in his father's words. No, it hadn't been some sort of justice-fueled rage that had caused his father to seek such allies. It was desperation. His father had thought he had only achieved failure his whole life, and now, in one final act of desperation, he had sought out whoever he could to win. Garon could tell his father had done this to prove to his son he was not the failure he assumed Garon thought he was. Yes, in some twisted way, Chief King Mace had done all of this for his son, for his family, for all that ever carried the surname Mace. His sacrifice, while having damned himself and his people, was done in the name of his ancestors and son.

Chapter 21

"By the gods, Barod, look at that," Chieftain Wooll
fretted, taking a large puff of his pipe.

"It's even worse than I remember," Titus gawked.

Chieftain Barod did not reply, but stared at the terrible
sight before them. The corrupted forest Anna had spoken
of was fleshy, twisted, and oozing with unnatural life. A
terrible darkness emanated from the corrupted forest. He
tried to think of something, anything to say to his
comrades and thousands of fighters marching behind him.
But for the first time in his life, Chieftain Barod was truly
speechless.

"Bah, I wish Goreth was here. I can't believe we let
the Seer take them off on some strange hunt," Chieftain
Wooll added, crossing his arms.

"Shall we set up camp here, Chieftain?" Guard
Captain Jarult asked, noticing how quiet Barod had been.

"Oh, yes, we must make camp here. We cannot go into
that forest until we are ready for a great fight," Chieftain
Barod said, trying to snap himself out of it. "Make sure
this position is as fortified as possible."

Guard Captain Jarult nodded, quickly turning and
barking orders to the many troops behind him. Chieftain
Wooll turned to his second-in-command and gave the
same orders. It seemed they both agreed this was as good
as any spot. The corrupted forest was about one hundred
yards away, though constantly expanding in size.

For almost an hour they had peace. In that brief time,
the warriors had set up their small canvas tents and began
to work on creating a rudimentary wall around their
enormous encampment. It wasn't easy to create an
outpost quickly, but they knew this peace was only
temporary. Plus, the mages of the Ancient Clan were able
to speed up construction immensely. Unfortunately, all
that work attracted attention.

A small horde of Horrors burst forth from their
gnarled forest and charged at the front of the incomplete

encampment. As Chieftain Barod finally laid eyes on the enemy he had heard so much about, he found himself again stunned silent. They were uglier and more otherworldly than he had pictured.

A group of Ancient Clan mages had been working when the Horrors attacked, and together unleashed enough magic to slay their foes before they even made it to the crude, incomplete wall. There had only been twenty or so Horrors, and now they all lay slain just feet from the wall.

Chieftain Barod was equally impressed and disturbed at the power of the mages, for they cut down their foes with relative ease, not even having to engage them physically. However, Chieftain Barod had a feeling he knew what the Horrors were doing; that small attack was simply to test their defenses and nothing more. This was not a victory to praise, but a reason to be concerned. Their next attack would likely be far more dangerous.

"They're reckless creatures, aren't they?" Chieftain Wooll asked, staring off into the dark forest ahead.

"Perhaps. Or whoever commands them does not care if they return," Chieftain Barod replied thoughtfully.

Given the sheer number of warriors and assistance of the mages, the encampment's progress was quickly furthered. In addition to the resources they bought, healthy trees from behind them were cut and used to begin a palisade wall, and for a temporary hall for the chieftains and their advisors.

Nobody had bothered to count how many humans now stood together in this sprawling encampment, but Chieftain Barod guessed it was in the thousands. The Forud Clan had the most warriors to spare, with the Narsho just behind them. The Linta Clan had a fair number of fighters they could supply, but they weren't as well trained. Finally, a few hundred Ancient Clan ages of appropriate fighting age and ability had joined them. Chieftain Barod felt odd fighting alongside the mages, as well as slightly guilty that almost half their population had agreed to fight. However, it was a necessity, as only together did they stand a chance.

The next attack arrived just before the sun set over the encampment. This time, the Horrors arrived in both greater numbers and ability. Unfortunately, the allied clans suffered a few losses from this attack.

Chieftain Barod ran to the gate as his warriors yelled they were under attack. By now, platforms had been constructed just touching the inside of the palisade wall up which his archers and mages could climb to keep watch. While it gave them a good line of sight, it also made them targets. This made them the first to fall.

As Chieftain Barod approached the section of wall closest to the forest, a few mages and archers lay dead in the dirt with sharp, organic spikes impaled in their heads. They had died quickly, not even having a chance. Chieftain Barod knelt next to one of the bodies, quickly examining the projectile. It was like nothing he had ever seen. It was not an arrow or anything else he had ever used and looked as though it came directly off the body of one of the Horrors. As he examined it, warriors began yelling from outside the wall.

He worked his way through the gate behind a line of troops to see a dark mass of mangled Horrors running through the field. As they ran, some tall, lankier Horrors in the back of the formation began to raise their misshapen arms and shoot something forth. A few warriors in the front of the formation fell, being impaled in their necks and heads. That's when Chieftain Barod realized his assumption was correct and knew the Horrors' attacks were also ranged.

"Shields at the front of the formation! Keep them up!" Chieftain Barod yelled to his men.

"What sort of terrible attack is that? How can they do that?" Chieftain Wooll asked, placing his winged helmet on his head, a piece of armor handed down from the time of the Great Clan.

"I don't know. But you have the right idea," Chieftain Barod said, placing his own finely crafted and ancestral helmet on his head.

Before he could give any orders, his warriors clashed with the Horrors. Terrible sounds of claws hitting metal and flesh filled the air, quickly followed by the screams of warriors who hadn't expected such a fierce enemy. Chieftain Barod drew his battleaxe, ready for whatever followed. He watched as more of his warriors poured from the crude gates to engage the enemy. He couldn't help but flinch each time a Horror howled or hissed, their sounds unnatural and vicious.

His archers had limited effect but managed to take down the remaining spike-shooters that lingered on the edge of the corrupted forest. Their line was also holding fast, preventing the Horrors from pushing them back within their walls. Chieftain Barod knew they would not want to hide behind the walls, as it was not only a sign of weakness, but left them sitting ducks. Chieftain Barod also knew this attack was not their final either; the Horrors had attacked from a single side, again likely a test to gauge the strength of the clans. He hated waiting, but they couldn't press into the forest yet.

Eventually, the few remaining Horrors fled back into the woods, leaving their deceased and dying pack behind without second thought. It was their actions that disturbed Chieftain Barod, as they seemed as intelligent as a human but without any sense of comradery or worry for their own being. They attacked with absolute focus, as if puppets on a string.

"Get the wounded back in camp!" Chieftain Wooll yelled to the men.

"Wait!" Chieftain Barod responded.

"What?" Chieftain Wooll asked with shock.

"We cannot bring them in yet. Anna said that Bernol changed on their way back after a wound from one of them. If we bring them into the camp, they could transform and attack from within. That could be their plan," Chieftain Barod explained, realizing he had never told his friend this frightening truth.

"He what? By the gods! Even if that is true, we cannot leave them out here. They need help!" Chieftain Wooll urged.

"I know, I know. We must keep them supervised then, or at least together in one place in case the worst happens. We must also tell those guarding them of the possibility," Chieftain Barod agreed.

"Then I will do so myself. Some of those men and women out there screaming for help are mine! I will ensure they get the help they need and do not threaten our encampment," Chieftain Wooll replied eagerly, brushing past his friend and into the fray. "Get the wounded out of there!"

Chieftain Barod watched as just over a dozen wounded soldiers were hauled off the blood-soaked battlefield. Chieftain Wooll stepped in, grabbing a man and holding him over his shoulder.

Titus ran up behind him and nearly knocked him over. "Chieftain!" the Champion said, wearing his now refurbished plate armor.

"What is it?" Chieftain Barod asked, slowly turning around.

"The dead archers and mages! They've already begun to turn! Just like when I was with Anna!" Titus yelled, pointing back toward the fray inside the camp.

Chieftain Barod's blood went cold as he remembered Anna's tale. He turned back to his friend and noticed the defeated clan warriors on the ground were seizing and returning to life. He had known of this possibility, but not that it could happen so fast.

Their skin split in some parts as their bodies festered and grew. Bones burst from their flesh as whatever corruption that the afflicted the Horrors overtook their recently deceased bodies. A small blood-red and infectious-green glow emanated around them in the dusk of the new evening.

"Wooll!" Chieftain Barod yelled, running towards his oldest friend. "Behind you!"

Chieftain Wooll heard the yelling, and then noticed the glowing bodies of the nine warriors that were turning close to him. Still holding a fallen Forud troop, he almost lost his balance trying to hold on.

Chieftain Barod flew over the ground between them, but it wasn't fast enough. The dead transformed too quickly, and he watched as one close to Wooll lurched forward, gnarled sharp hands ready to kill.

He felt helpless as he watched Chieftain Wooll try to deflect the blows of the afflicted warrior, unable to act quickly enough due to the extra weight of the warrior he carried. Despite his skill and strength, the creature finally got a hit in moments before Barod could try to save his friend. The afflicted warrior slashed Chieftain Wooll's arm, knocking his axe from his hand. Despite this, the chieftain held stubbornly to his fallen comrade, managing to leap away without dropping him. It was then Chieftain Barod reached his friend and decapitated the twisted warrior with a single blow.

Titus and a few other warriors were just behind him and made quick work of the other risen clanspeople. They all had to fight back urges of sickness at the terrible sight, muttering at the brutality of it all.

Chieftain Barod did not stop escorting Wooll until they were safely within the walls. Even then his adrenaline was running, and he couldn't stop searching for new enemies. Given how the corruption of the Horrors spread, enemies could be anywhere.

"By the gods, it got me," Chieftain Wooll grumbled as he handed off the wounded Forud to a nearby warrior.

"Herold, your arm; that needs healing now!" Chieftain Barod exclaimed, noticing the river of blood now soaking his arm.

"Chieftains!" a nearby Ancient Clan mage yelled as he quickly walked over.

Chieftain Barod said nothing, waiting for the old man to approach. As he did, the chieftain first noticed a pale scar under his left eye. The man seemed frail yet walked with determination. His brown robes were already covered in blood.

"I can heal his arm. I have been healing my entire life," the old man said with a small smile.

"I won't argue against that. Please, do what you can, old man" Chieftain Wooll laughed, kneeling next to the man and catching his breath.

"Thank you," Chieftain Barod added quietly, too preoccupied with his friend possibly turning.

The old man simply nodded as he gently placed his hand over Chieftain Wooll's wound. A blue light emerged from his hand, small wisps of magic fragmenting away and disappearing. A small hum accompanied it as the blue light enveloped his arm. As he continued, however, a strange red light glowed from his wound.

"What? There's magic already inside of you?" the old man asked.

"So that's how they turn then, is it?" Chieftain Wooll asked aloud, shaking his head.

"Turn?" the old man asked, looking at Chieftain Barod.

"Yes. We must keep an eye on all the wounded. It seems some, or perhaps all, will transform into a Horror if they are wounded by one. The dead always seem to transform … Can you help him?" Chieftain Barod explained, desperation in his voice.

"I can try," the man replied nervously.

The blue light intensified and began to push the red light back, but a few moments later, it stopped and the healer's hand was forced away. He shook his hand as though in pain and looked with great concern at Chieftain Wooll's arm. While it had been mostly healed, there was still a dim red light emanating from a small scratch in the center. The veins around the area looked slightly blackened as well.

"I cannot dispel whatever magic this may be. I believe I have slowed it down, but nobody here will be able to completely remove whatever that is. I am sorry…" the old man said, a small tear forming in his eye.

"No, no, don't be sorry. I'll be fine for now," Chieftain Wooll said, standing back up. "Could you tell the other healers about this? Our wounded will likely have the same… affliction."

"Of course. I will go now, Chieftain," the old man nodded, still upset.

Chieftain Barod didn't know what to say to his friend and could only think of all the ways this could have been avoided; if he hadn't stopped Wooll from going to the wounded, if perhaps he had joined his friend, so many things could have changed the course of events and led to a different outcome.

"Herold … I am so sorry…" Chieftain Barod said with a heavy heart, placing his hand gently on his oldest friend's shoulder.

"Jonis…" Chieftain Wooll said, using the name he hadn't used since they were young. "Do not apologize, this isn't your doing."

"I should have realized it sooner! I should have been at your side!" Chieftain Barod yelled, drawing stares from nearby warriors.

"No, it isn't your fault, friend. You cannot always be by my side, just as I have not always been by yours. Now I can imagine the suffering your people have gone through since we did not stand by you in your time of need. For that, I am the one who is sorry," Chieftain Wooll explained, taking his pipe from his pocket.

Chieftain Barod barely fought off tears as he saw the look of acceptance in his friend's eyes. As Chieftain Wooll lit and took a puff from his pipe, he closed his eyes as if it would be his last. The sight almost made Chieftain Barod hopeless, but he remembered it wasn't over yet.

The most powerful users of magic were not with them and would be returning soon.

"No, Herold. Don't apologize. We shouldn't dwell on the past," Chieftain Barod urged, putting out his hand toward his friend and signaling he wanted the pipe. "Seer Mordou can help us."

Lifting an eyebrow, Chieftain Wooll handed his friend the pipe. He said nothing as Chieftain Barod took a large puff of it but couldn't help a chuckle as his friend coughed from his inexperience in smoking. As he took back the pipe, Chieftain Wooll's look of defeat was replaced with rising hope.

"You are right. We can only look forward now. I hope they return shortly, for all of our sakes," Chieftain Wooll agreed with an exhale of light smoke.

"They will return and aid us, I am sure of it," Chieftain Barod insisted, trying with all his might to remain hopeful.

Suddenly, Titus came crashing toward them, barely stopping in time before knocking the two over. He was out of breath and his eyes were wide with terror. Chieftain Barod had never seen his Champion like this.

"Titus! What is it?" Chieftain Barod asked.

"Chieftains, please, you need to see this," Titus replied, then ran back toward the gate while gesturing for them to follow. The chieftains did so.

As they reached the gate, the nearby guards opened it, looking equally horrified. Chieftain Barod stopped next to Titus, who pointed out toward the tree line of the corrupted forest. Being dusk, it was hard to see exactly what he was pointing at, but then he saw it, feeling goosebumps assault his body.

"By the gods…" Chieftain Wooll muttered from beside them.

Standing just outside the tree line was a large line of Highrock warriors, except these were not the Highrock that they had fought recently—no, these warriors had been corrupted to the bone. Their skin was sickly purple, their eyes glowed red, their bodies seemed taller and more muscular than they had been. However, something was different about them compared to normal horrors; these warriors still had some shred of humanity about them.

Despite their transformation, the corrupted Highrock warriors stood tall and proud as they had before, wielding the same weapons and wearing the same now barely fitting armor they always had. They all wore a look of arrogance and bloodlust, staring at the encampment with a rage unlike any they ever had before.

"They've transformed … But they look relatively humanlike still," Titus uttered, sickened by the sight.

As they made eye contact with Chieftain Barod, the semi-Horrors quickly turned in one simultaneous motion. It was an impressive display, and a brief sound of gnarled flesh and metal rang out as they did. Then they marched back into the dark forest, only their red eyes illuminating their path.

"For our sake, I hope Seer Mordou returns soon," Chieftain Wooll muttered.

Chieftain Barod stared into the forest, wondering if his life-long enemy had finally given into his madness. Chief King Mace had been consumed by his hatred long ago, but he had always kept his clan safe and did care about them. Now it seemed the chief king had finally fallen to his hatred and resorted to the most dishonorable and desperate measures possible. Sickened, Chieftain Barod walked back inside the encampment, hoping Anna and the rest of her party would return soon.

Chapter 22

As she stared upon it, Anna could only dream of what sort of people lived in such a large, well-constructed city. Passing through great now-crumbling walls made of the same elegant, white stone, nobody spoke a word. While the city looked to have been ransacked at some point due to most all the buildings having been damaged beyond age, it was large and intact enough to give them a picture of how it used to look. Large circular decaying towers stood along the walls, some in better condition than others. The city's hundreds of homes varied in their structural integrity, some crumpled into nothing but dust and others remaining almost entirely intact. Regardless, they were all covered in vines and other creeping flora that were determined to reclaim the city for the earth.

Like the town Anna had found, the main road down the center of the city was made with fine cobblestone, though this city was enormous compared to the town, and various smaller cobblestone paths led away. Still, the similarities in architecture were undeniable.

As she looked to her right, Anna could see the city's port and the ocean in the distance. She wondered if there were any ships here, or anyone still hiding within the homes around them. She was stunned that such a city existed in their realm.

"Is this the home of the Great Clan?" Goreth asked, eyes wide as he turned to look at the city around him.

"No, the Great City is far, far west of here. I traveled there once," Garon answered. "It was large, but nothing compared to this. Our greatest structures were made of rough, grey stone. But most were wood. This white stone, whatever it is, looks to be something entirely different."

"Precisely. I've been thinking a lot about this since we've been traveling," Valon began, a tome open in his hands. "I believe this was the home of what Distichum called the Holy Elven Empire."

"Elves? The ones you told us may be the gods our ancestors spoke of?" Anna asked, walking over and touching a white stone wall of a nearby home.

"Exactly. I have been theorizing that it was the elves who settled this land long ago. These ruins could be their cities. Their advanced civilization could be why our ancestors referred to them as gods," Valon explained, speaking faster with excitement.

"If that's true, where did they go?" Anna asked, a lock of hair curled around her finger.

"That I do not know. Perhaps the Shadowalkers of old destroyed them like they did our Great Clan, or perhaps they just left. I only wonder if their people are from here, or came here, perhaps from the land to the south," Valon pondered.

"Or they came through a portal," Seer Mordou pointed out with a cheeky smile as he led them down the cobblestone path.

"Perhaps they did, from the supposed land of the gods," Valon added quietly.

"Now, we are getting close to the source of the magic. Can you sense it too, Valon?" Seer Mordou asked.

"Perhaps, but it is not great. I think you made a connection in farsight, Master," Valon replied.

"I believe that is a possibility," Seer Mordou replied, hastening his pace.

As Anna followed, her mind was cluttered with the fantastical, seemingly unreal information. In a matter of weeks her entire view of the world had been shattered, replaced with knowledge that proved to be almost too much, but her motivation to see an end to the Horrors prevented her from thinking on it excessively. For now, her mind was focused on her goal.

As they neared a larger two-story building, they noticed there were fragments of a wooden door that once stood in the doorway lying just outside on the ground. Only small pieces remained, but it looked as though it had been ripped off the hinge.

"Look, weapons," Goreth said, pointing to a few heavily rusted swords partially engulfed by the grass.

Seer Mordou held out his hand and brought the sword from the ground using magic. It split under the pressure, and he released it and let it fall back to the ground. Based on its decomposition, they had been here a long time.

"I'm surprised any swords remain at all. It seems there was a battle here quite long ago," Seer Mordou said, kneeling down and looking at some armor fragments.

"I wish we had time to search the entire city," Valon said, shaking his head.

"Unfortunately, we do not. We must press onwards, for we are close," Seer Mordou added, starting to walk again.

"My uncle would be intrigued by all of this," Becca said quietly.

"As would Chieftain Wooll," Goreth agreed, walking next to Becca.

Anna turned to see Garon staring off into the distance. Ever since they had witnessed the surge of magic coming from the corrupted forest, he had been quiet. She knew the reason but wasn't sure if she should pry. However, he only seemed to be getting worse.

As they walked together, Garon didn't speak. He only followed behind Goreth, eyes ahead and barely blinking. Finally, Anna realized she had to say something; she cared about Garon and knew he wouldn't fight as effectively now.

"Garon, are you alright?" Anna asked, placing her hand gently on his arm.

Garon stopped, turning to Anna and trying hard not to frown. The smallest of tears emerged from his eye before he quickly wiped it away. He took a deep breath, obviously torn from what he had witnessed the day before.

"No, I'm not. I could've saved my father; I could've stopped him. I should've stayed behind and done something. Is his blood not on my hands?" Garon said, staring at his hands out in front of him.

"No, Garon. It isn't," Anna replied, taking his cold hands in hers. "I saw the hatred in your father's eyes; you did everything you could."

"Did I? I told him about the Horrors. If I hadn't done that, he wouldn't have … sought them as allies…" Garon choked, picturing the worst.

"But that was his terrible choice, not yours. You warned him and tried to broker peace between the clans. Garon, you did everything you possibly could, and your father wouldn't listen. Don't blame yourself. Now the only thing you can do to help your clan is press forward and defeat the Horrors," Anna reasoned, holding Garon's hands tightly.

He stared into her eyes, knowing deep down she was right. He found it hard to admit, not wanting to come to the realization that his father would forsake his own people just for vengeance. However, Anna's words and genuine care helped him realize it wasn't his fault, it was only his father's.

"Thank you, Anna. Your words do help," Garon said, wiping a final tear from his eye.

"I'm glad. Now, we must go; if we want to help our people, we need to uncover whatever the Seer is looking for," Anna urged, gently patting her friend's back.

Garon nodded and the two quickly walked to catch up with the group. Anna didn't mention Garon's father again, knowing he was likely in a better place. There was nothing they could do now, and she thought Garon might have finally realized that truth as well. Not only that, but she hoped Garon knew who his father truly had been. Chief King Mace had lived in hatred his entire life and would do anything to destroy his enemies, even consorting with darkness itself.

They caught up to the others and continued onward down the cobblestone path. The ruins of the sprawling city surrounded them, smashed white stone scattered amongst the street from the destroyed buildings. Anna figured this had to have been from fighting, knowing the mere passage of time wouldn't have caused such damage.

To Anna, it felt like being in a completely foreign world, all the buildings so different from the clan's shacks and halls, and the signs being in a language they could not read. Multiple times they stopped to read signposts but failed to translate any of the strange language. The letters looked odd to Anna, who had enough basic literacy of her own language to realize she didn't' understand this one. The letters of the elves were sharp, bold, and often symmetrical.

Finally, Seer Mordou stopped as they reached a large grassy area. Surrounding it was a short metal fence. As they approached, Anna quickly noticed innumerable gravestones almost touching each other. The graveyard sprawled for many streets in all directions, and she spotted a large rectangular building far in the center. She guessed that building was where the Seer was leading them.

"We are close. I believe the power lies just through this graveyard," Seer Mordou said, eyeing the building in the distance.

"Mildly disturbing," Becca chuckled.

"But what could be here, Master? I sense it too now, but I do not see anything," Valon asked, looking all around them.

"We will soon find out," Seer Mordou replied, opening the rusty graveyard gate.

They continued into the long-abandoned graveyard, many of the tombstones coated in a layer of creeping flora. It appeared undisturbed, even during whatever battle had occurred here. Anna felt slightly spooked as they walked, wondering if Horrors could raise the long dead to fight beside them as well.

As they reached the rectangular building, Anna noticed there were no doors. It was a solid, windowless building that stood directly in the center of the overgrown graveyard. Despite this, she could sense something off about it.

"Is this it?" Garon asked, placing his hand against the cool white, vine-covered stone.

"I believe so ... But something isn't right," Seer Mordou replied.

"Where's the door?" Goreth asked, crossing his arms and eyeballing the building.

"Good question," Becca replied, walking around the side of the building.

Anna stared at the building that wasn't much larger than her home. If this was where they were supposed to go, then why wasn't there anything here? She racked her brain, studying the bare building. Then, she remembered her basic magic training.

"Could there be an illusion?" Anna asked Valon.

"Good question! Let us check," Valon said with a surprised smile.

Anna watched as Valon quickly conjured a wisplight. It floated in front of him, glowing blue and reflecting off the building. She followed Valon as he slowly walked around the perimeter, and they both stopped as a strange shimmering appeared roughly the size of a large door on one of the sides.

"We've found something!" Valon shouted to the others.

As they all walked over, Anna tried touching the stone and half expected to reach through. Her hand stopped as she rubbed against the cold stone, but she could slightly sense the magic of the illusion.

"Interesting," Seer Mordou marveled as he approached. "It is a partial illusion, but I believe the stone itself must be moved."

Valon nodded at his master and the two held out their hands. They began to shake the stone, and now they could all clearly see the outline of the hidden door. They continued for some more time before Anna realized the two couldn't do it alone.

She held out her hands and remembered the notes on levitation. She figured a similar mindset was needed to push things and focused her mind on pushing the stone back. As she began, Garon smiled and stood next to her. Quickly after, Becca and Goreth followed, standing and using the same basic magic.

With the combined power of the six members, blue wisps of energy struck against the door and revealed a layer of shimmering gold. As they continued their flow of magic, the blue eventually overwhelmed the gold and pierced its way through. As it did, the door slowly scraped open, revealing a room inside.

"Excellent work!" Seer Mordou praised, almost clapping as they all stopped.

"That was strange, Master. It looked to be protected by magic, but it was gold in color..." Valon noted suspiciously. "But now I can sense that magic even easier. It's right below us."

"Yes, we must press on!" Seer Mordou declared with excitement.

Anna watched as Seer Mordou and Valon entered the dark room. She quickly followed, the others just behind her. Before anyone could conjure a wisplight, the torches on the walls began glowing with golden flame. Anna could sense the magic around them, and found it felt different from what she had briefly trained with.

The walls of the room inside had more indiscernible writing on them, and an old stone stairway led down into darkness. As it was the only way to go, Seer Mordou began to walk down the stairway, causing more torches to automatically light. They followed him down, descending into the unknown.

"This is so interesting. How have we never found this city?" Garon whispered.

"Everyone was too afraid of the Cursed Lands. Fredrik and I were the first to travel there in our lives, supposedly" Anna replied, finally able to say his name without choking up.

"None of our people ever traveled there either," Becca added.

"Why would anyone want to anyway?" Goreth asked.

"There wasn't much reason until now," Valon answered from ahead of them.

Minutes went by as they descended the stairs. Part way through, the stairs turned and continued down in a different direction. Various urns stood abandoned in this small flat section, but nobody dared look inside. They continued downward, closing in on the source of the mysterious magic.

Finally, the stairs ended, and a flat hallway led to an enormous, dark chamber. As the six humans entered, torches on the walls and hanging braziers from the incredibly high ceiling flashed to life in a simultaneous explosion of gold magic. Their flames all burned gold, silently but with an imposing presence.

As the light revealed the chamber, they noticed the room was filled with interesting objects. In the center of the large cylindrical room was a large rectangular stone object that Anna thought looked like a casket. Surrounding the casket on the edge of the rooms were seven tall stone statues of strange looking people. The bodies of the statues were taller and thinner than humans, but still muscular. However, the first thing Anna noticed were their ears, which were tall and pointed.

Next to the statues were large metal footlockers. They had no locks, latches, or any other way to open them. Anna squinted and saw there were more strange letters written on the storage containers. They were large, and she wondered what was inside.

"By the gods … This is magnificent," Seer Mordou said with awe.

"Those statues, they're just like the one of Imperator Ty'roel in the Great Swamp, but of different elves," Valon murmured, captivated with the statues.

"So, these are the elves then?" Garon asked, approaching one of a fierce looking elven men with two swords.

"According to Distichum, yes. This is likely a mausoleum of the Holy Elven Empire," Valon replied, walking toward the strange casket in the center. "The Great Clan had much smaller mausoleums from what I've read."

Anna followed Valon, looking at the floor. The stones of the room had been cut in large circles within each other, like looking at the wood of a stump. She wondered if that was of any significance.

"Wow, look at the ceiling," Becca whispered from next to Goreth.

Anna looked up to see the circular vaulted ceiling had been painted in its entirety. The outer parts depicted heavily armored warriors fighting each other. As she stared at the art, she noticed half of the warriors wore elegant, white armor with gold trim and the warriors they fought wore sharp black armor. While the warriors fought, unarmored beings argued in the middle, some with fair skin and golden eyes the others with dark, grey skin and red eyes. The artwork intrigued Anna, but she had no idea what or who it was meant to portray.

"How very interesting. Could those darker elves be the Shadowalkers our ancestors fought?" Valon asked, looking at his master.

"Perhaps … But unfortunately we don't have time for that. Valon, the magic is right here, in this, well, casket," Seer Mordou said, his hands hovering over the stone casket.

"What is it?" Goreth asked, looking worried.

"I have a feeling we're about to find out," Garon added, walking over and standing next to Anna.

They all watched as Seer Mordou began to use his own magic over the casket. Tendrils of blue magic gracefully left his fingers and began to disperse on the casket. As they did, the casket began to glow gold like all the other magic they had witnessed here. Anna kept one hand on the pommel of her main sword, ready for whatever might come next. The blue and gold magic seemed to bounce off each other, doing nothing. Valon went to step in but Seer Mordou protested, holding one hand up briefly. He was focused, and soon blue magic coated the entire coffin.

Then, with a sudden burst of energy, all the magic erupted outward, the gold and blue exploding forth and shattering into dozens of shards that disappeared in the air. The power of it physically moved everyone, causing most to take a step back. Anna grasped the grip of her sword, expecting to be ambushed. Luckily, nothing of that sort happened. First, the arm of the middle statue at the farthest point of the room from the stairs raised upwards. Anna noticed it had an hourglass that was activated as it was raised. The sand inside the orange glass began to run slowly.

Before anyone could comment on the oddity, the stone under the casket brought it upwards into the air at an angle so that one could easily step in, or out of it. It shook momentarily, and there was a brief pop as the casket opened, the cover falling loudly to the floor in front of them. It revealed a thick golden layer of visible magic shimmering in the opening of the casket.

They all took a step forward, and Anna stared at the strange aura. Just behind the aura was a face. Not just a face, but an entire body that had been preserved in the casket. Then, with a snap and sizzle, the golden barrier that separated humans from elf disappeared. The eyes of the old elven woman opened, and she gasped for air. Anna couldn't help but gasp at the sight of another being that wasn't human, and gripped her sword firmly, ready for anything.

Chapter 23

Licking the wine from his lips, Chieftain Yarmot savored the peaceful moment, for he knew it would not last. He stared out at the many ships in the small Narsho port and docked out at sea. They were just about to finish what would be their twenty-ninth ship, making this the largest fleet any of the clans had ever seen. Still, it wasn't nearly enough for their entire population to flee with, and Chieftain Yarmot knew this well.

He stood upon a watchtower overlooking the port, watching as ship twenty-nine had its finishing touches done. It wouldn't be long before the overworked shipbuilders would roll the ship off the logs that held it and into the water below. Still, it was the most minor of victories, and wasn't enough for the Linta Chieftain.

"Chieftain, the ship builders are fading. We've perhaps been working them too hard," Cora suggested.

"I know, I know," Chieftain Yarmot replied, taking another large gulp of wine and emptying the chalice. "But we haven't a choice."

"But surely we don't need this many?" Cora asked.

Chieftain Yarmot quickly poured more wine from the nearby bottle before his servant, Pil, could do so. His chubby hands shook slightly, spilling a few tiny droplets on the rough wooden table of the tower.

"I'm sorry, my lord," Pil apologized.

"Quiet, Pil, you've done nothing wrong," Chieftain Yarmot snapped, realizing he was far more stressed than he had thought.

"Chieftain, are you alright?" Cora asked.

"No, Cora, I am not. You see all those ships? Those almost twenty-nine ships? That's not even half of what we would need to safely evacuate everyone from our allied clans," Chieftain Yarmot replied, trying hard to regain his composure.

"But surely we are not actually going to sail away from our homes?" Cora asked, almost laughing at the idea.

"We will do whatever we must to survive, even if it means sailing south to some unknown land," Chieftain Yarmot replied unhappily. "If we get word to sail away, that's what we must do."

"Excuse me, Chieftain, but that's insanity. It's strange enough we've all come here to pack ourselves within the city for some threat barely anyone has seen. But to pick up and leave? Our people won't do that," Cora said, hands on her hips.

"They will if they truly respect their chieftain," Chieftain Yarmot grumbled, turning and looking back at the port. "Plus, look at our history; if our Great Clan had not run from their home, we might not even be sitting here right now."

His blood almost boiled with stress over the idea of his clan refusing to follow him. Not once during his entire rule as chieftain had he experienced any dissent among his people. Although to be fair, the greatest challenge he had previously faced as chieftain was an issue regarding a large group of encroaching raptors. The stress of that event didn't even compare to the current issues at hand.

"Push with all you've got!" a foreman yelled from below the tower.

Chieftain Yarmot peered over the wooden railing of the tower to watch the many shipbuilders pushing the newly built ship off the logs and into the water. With their combined strength, they pushed the newly constructed wooden ship into the light blue shallow water. One worker climbed aboard to ensure it didn't crash.

The workers cheered, clapping and yelling as the boat slowly drifted out. However, as they all watched, they realized something was wrong; as the boat drifted, it lowered into the water. The worker on the boat yelled, realizing it was sinking.

"No, not now," Chieftain Yarmot uttered, his eyes locked on the sinking ship as he took another swig of wine.

"Oh, no," Cora whispered from behind him.

They watched as the man on the boat panicked, running below deck to see what the issue was. Chieftain Yarmot knew it was possible for the boat to be fixed, assuming the worker had the proper supplies aboard. He waited with bated breath, watching the ship slowly sink.

The workers back on the shore had already prepared a rowboat and started out, filled with wooden buckets and patching supplies. They quickly rowed toward the nearby ship, all yelling to their comrade who was still below deck. Suddenly, the worker aboard the boat reappeared above deck, his arms in the air as he yelled a victory cry. Chieftain Yarmot let out a sigh as he noticed the ship had stopped sinking. Still, he kept his eyes on the workers until they had all boarded the ship and gone below deck with their buckets.

As they started to bail the water, Chieftain Yarmot turned away. He felt ill thinking of the close call, knowing if the ship had sunk it would mean less of their people could escape if the time finally came. Chieftain Yarmot sat on the nearby wooden stool, placing his hands on the table and letting his body relax for a moment. While he knew logically he couldn't do much more than wait for news from the other chieftains, he wanted to do more. However, everything here was out of his skill set. Given the longstanding peace of the Linta Clan, Chieftain Yarmot hadn't done anything relating to war in his entire life. He only hoped the village wouldn't face any attacks before the others returned, if they returned.

He shuddered at the thought of defeat, bringing his cup to his mouth and realizing there was no wine left. As he went to pour more, he found there was none left in the bottle. He simply stared at it, lost in deep thought.

"Do you need another bottle, Chieftain?" Pil asked attentively.

Chieftain Yarmot didn't respond immediately, simply staring at the empty bottle. He felt lost, worried about what the future held. He slowly stood and walked toward the nearby ladder leading down from the tower.

"No, thank you. I'm going to go back to the Chieftain's Hall. Alone," Chieftain Yarmot answered, still lost in thought.

Walking quickly, he tried to avoid contact with anyone in the village. However, by keeping his head down, he nearly ran into Olaf. As he stopped, he made eye contact with the old man.

"Ah, Chieftain Yarmot, how are you?" Olaf kindly greeted.

"Oh, Olaf, right? I am, er, fine. Just heading back to the Chieftain's Hall to take care of some things," Chieftain Yarmot almost stuttered.

"Hm. Excuse me for saying so, but you seem stressed, Chieftain," Olaf slowly said, trying his hardest not to offend the man.

"I suppose I might be. These are trying times," Chieftain Yarmot replied, inching away from Olaf.

"Well, I can brew you a relaxant, if you desire. I have a potion that could greatly help you," Olaf offered generously. "Warriors of ours sometimes take it after battle to calm down."

Hearing about battle only made Chieftain Yarmot more nervous. He practically felt sick, and couldn't think of drinking anything right now, especially a mystery potion from another clan's shaman. He let out a small, sickly burp, and shook his head.

"Er, no thank you, Olaf. I will be all set. I should be off. Much to do, I'm afraid," Chieftain Yarmot said with a fake smile.

"Alright then. Come find me if you change your mind," Olaf replied with a slightly worried look.

"Of course," Chieftain Yarmot added as he quickly walked away.

As he slowly made his way back, Chieftain Yarmot's mind was clouded with self-doubt and worry. All he could think about was seeing this far overpopulated, undefended city become subject to an attack. He himself had never fought in battle and was not some war hero like Chieftain Barod. No, if that day did come, he would only be able to sit idly by and watch as his people were torn apart by a horrible foe. As he sat alone in the Chieftain's Hall, Chieftain Yarmot dozed off, soon plagued by vivid wine-induced nightmares of a possible future.

Chapter 24

"What the!" Goreth yelled, jumping back and grabbing his shield from the floor.

"It's an elf!" Valon blurted.

The elf quickly lurched forward from the casket, the humans jumping back to give her space. Her skin was withered, old, literally hanging from her bones. Her hair was ancient white, thinly clinging to life upon her head. As she looked at the small group, Anna made eye contact with her. The elf still had eyes like a human, except the colored part was bright gold. Anna got the feeling that long ago, this elf was probably the epitome of what humans considered beauty.

"She... she is the source of magic," Seer Mordou slowly spoke, holding his hands in front of him to show he was unarmed.

"*Ty'lo joir feun?*" the elf quickly spoke confusedly.

"Er, what did she say?" asked Becca, also confused.

"Perhaps that's the language we've seen on the signs and walls," Garon replied, trying to look non-threatening.

"Hello, do you speak Clansi?" Seer Mordou asked slowly, his glowing blue eye tinged with flickers of gold.

The old elf-woman seemed to understand and began looking all around her. As her eyes found the hourglass, she stared at it. As she watched the sand fall, it seemed everything was coming back to her. She turned and looked back at the humans standing before her, her golden eyes filled with concern.

"Clansi? Do you mean Lowborn?" the elf asked hesitantly, still unsure if she had responded in the correct language.

"Er, perhaps. Regardless we understand your words," Seer Mordou answered quickly.

"But you are all humans ... Why are you here?" the elf asked.

"We are here because of a vision I had during my last farsight. I saw us in this room and connected with a strange magic. You appear to be the magic that reached out to me," Seer Mordou answered.

The elf woman stared at him, rubbing her wrinkled chin. She turned to stare at the other humans one by one, perplexed by the situation. It seemed she truly had no idea what was going on. As Valon and the elf's eyes met, he could tell there was sadness within the old elf's eyes. She seemed almost disappointed that a mere group of humans stood before her. He watched as the elf woman then looked around the room once more before looking at Seer Mordou.

"You say you, a human, used farsight? Very curious ... But you still haven't truly answered my question. Why are you here?" the elf asked, her sad eyes turning suspicious.

"I suppose we are here for help. Our clans, our people, face a dangerous threat. We sought your magic to aid us against our foes. I am Seer Mordou of the Ancient Clan," Seer Mordou greeted kindly, looking to the others to introduce themselves.

"I am Valon of the Ancient Clan, apprentice to Seer Mordou," Valon added.

"Hello, I'm Becca Yarmot of the Linta Clan," Becca briefly greeted with a smile.

"I'm Goreth Destro of the Forud Clan," Goreth murmured, still in shock.

"I am Garon Mace ... formerly of the Highrock Clan," Garon nearly stuttered.

"And I am Anna Myhre of the Narsho Clan," Anna greeted kindly.

Valon watched as the elf appeared intrigued, knowing something about the information she had just heard. She stared into the distance, not speaking for a few moments. Finally, she looked back at the Seer, ready to speak.

"I am High Priestess Hy'ria of the Holy Elven Empire … I would say it is a pleasure, but I expected to see the faces of my own people standing before me," Hy'ria greeted calmly.

"Why would you expect to see your own people?" Valon asked with great curiosity.

Hy'ria took a deep breath and glanced back at the hourglass. Barely a tenth of it had fallen below so far. It was apparent the timer meant something to her.

"They were supposed to come get me after the city fell … Tell me, what year is it to your people? Have you any idea?" Hy'ria asked.

The six humans looked at each other, not knowing what to say. None of the clans had kept time in any true way. They hadn't had a real point to, and Valon had no response for the elf besides an excuse.

"We haven't quite kept time in the way you would. It has been probably close to two hundred years since our Great Clan fell. As for your people, we only just found out you even existed within the past week. Your city above has begun to be reclaimed by the land itself…" Valon answered, knowing she wouldn't want to hear it.

"Great Clan? Your people … unified?" Hy'ria asked with surprise.

"They did for over a hundred years, until the Shadowalkers fragmented them apart," Seer Mordou answered with equal surprise.

"Shadowalkers? Do you perhaps mean them?" Hy'ria asked, pointing towards the black armored warriors painted on the ceiling.

"That we do not know. They disappeared around the same time the Great Clan fell apart. We only have record that they could disappear into the shadows and were a cruel foe," Valon cut in.

"Then it seems we fought the same enemy. I only wonder why they let you live, or what drew their attention away…" Hy'ria replied.

Valon watched as Hy'ria glanced back at the ever-moving hourglass. Her long ears flinched as she watched the sand pour down. It bothered her greatly.

"What is that hourglass, er, ma'am?" Goreth fumbled.

"That is the timer until my death," Hy'ria replied with a grim, partially defeated smile.

"Your death? But how?" Valon asked startled by the news.

"You see, it started with the elves you call Shadowalkers. I do not have time to explain our past, but they attacked this city with the intent to slay us all. I was the High Priestess of this city, which we called Ruol. An assassin plunged his blade into me, but my dutiful priests managed to find a way to save me. They sealed me in here, the Mausoleum of Saints, with magic keeping my body alive until our people returned with someone strong enough to save me," Hy'ria explained, revealing a magically sealed wound in her chest.

"No ... You mean, by opening your casket we have doomed you?" Seer Mordou asked, looking sick.

"Theoretically, yes. You do not have the magic to save me. However, based on how much time has passed I do not believe anyone was ever going to come for me. If anything, you have done me a favor, and now my spirit may pass onto the next life instead of remaining here in limbo for as long as magic flows," Hy'ria explained, coming to the realization.

There was an awkward silence, and nobody spoke. Valon felt his heart drop as he realized the old elf would soon perish. He could tell that Hy'ria hadn't fully come to terms with her fate and was disappointed her people had never come. Now it wouldn't be long until she faded away.

"Regardless, I am sorry Hy'ria ... We all are. We had no idea. We are only here for magic to help us," Seer Mordou apologized.

"In your fight against the Shadowalkers?" Hy'ria asked.

"No. In our fight against the Horrors, against Xerannu," Seer Mordou answered.

"Xerannu? I have never heard that name before. What sort of being is he?" Hy'ria asked, again glancing at the hourglass.

"We have not yet seen him, only his spawned Horrors. They infest our land, taking over all life and binding it to his will. We believe he controls them all, and comes from a portal from another realm," Seer Mordou explained.

As he mentioned the portal, Valon noticed the elf's eyes go wide. In fact, she looked horrified at the description. She quickly recovered and tried to compose herself.

"That worries me greatly. Is the portal west? What sort of magic does this Xerannu use?" Hy'ria questioned.

"Yes, it is. But what do you mean sort of magic?" Seer Mordou asked, not understanding the question.

"Sort of magic?" Valon asked aloud.

"Yes! What ... essence of magic? Primordial? Holy? Unholy? Biotic? Which of the four is predominantly his style?" Hy'ria asked impatiently, knowing her time was nearing.

"What? Essence? I am not sure what you mean," Seer Mordou replied, flabbergasted.

"You use farsight to look forward in time but do not know of the basic essences of the flows of magic? You humans always fascinated me. Such primal, yet complex beings," Hy'ria chuckled grimly as she shook her head. "Seer, the flows of magic around us consist of those four kinds of essence."

"I-I ... I've never heard such a thing," Seer Mordou choked, looking defeated.

"None of us have," Valon added, putting a hand on his master's shoulder.

"My, my ... Fresh slates. I wish I had the time to teach you, but alas I do not. You people have been using primordial magic, the most basic yet still very useful magic of the flows. We mainly use holy magic, the most powerful and useful magic that exists. The Shadowalkers disagree and use a wretched form of magic we only call unholy. Then, there exists biotic magic, that is the magic of life, nature, and druids that spend far too much time in the forests," Hy'ria explained as if speaking to children. "The colors are usually a dead giveaway."

"Colors? Like how magic is blue?" Valon asked, trying hard to follow.

"Correct. Holy appears gold, unholy red, and biotic green. Of course, that can vary, and they can overlap, but typically that is what you see when magic interacts with the world around it," Hy'ria explained.

Valon was beginning to understand, but it was unlike anything had ever learned. None of his texts had mentioned anything beyond colors of magic, but he had assumed that existed for detailing purposes only. He stared at her. Hy'ria noticed the group's confusion and rubbed her temple as if she had a headache.

"Okay, well, er, Xerannu and the Horror magic appears red, although there is some green too. Mainly red, however," Seer Mordou rambled, trying to make sense of it all.

"Unholy and biotic? How disturbing. You may have primordial magic, but you will need holy magic if you are to save your people," Hy'ria replied, staring off into the distance again.

"So how do we get holy magic, High Priestess? How do we use it?" Valon asked.

"Through years and years of dedicated training under a priestess," Hy'ria chuckled darkly, shaking her head.

"But we don't have time," Garon said from behind Valon.

"No, there must be some other way," Seer Mordou agreed, looking at Hy'ria for answers.

Anna watched as the elf stared at the hourglass, now half of it gone. She seemed visibly more fatigued than when she had emerged, as if her body was fading. As Hy'ria turned back, she had a look of satisfaction, fear, and accomplishment on her face.

"There is. I can imbue my power into all of you and give you the holy strength needed to cleanse your land of this pestilence," Hy'ria murmured, knowing what it meant.

"Then I must ask this of you, Hy'ria, otherwise our people will all die!" Seer Mordou urged, taking a step toward the elf.

"I will not survive the ritual, but perhaps it is the best use of my power in my final moments. Please, give me a moment, and ready yourselves for a great change," Hy'ria said quietly, turning and walking toward the statue holding the hourglass.

Hy'ria's words made Valon feel almost guilty, noting the acceptance of death in the old elf's words. Whether she gave them all her power or not, she was still going to die. Regardless, he knew it wasn't an easy thing to accept. Her death was imminent.

"Valon," Seer Mordou began, placing his hands on his apprentice's shoulders and staring into his eyes.

"Master?" Valon asked, ever at the ready.

"It is time," Seer Mordou uttered with confidence.

"So it finally is…" Valon began, his eyes shifting from intrigue to focus. "What must I do, Master?"

"Simply prepare yourself. I do not know what her holy magic will do to us, so I must give you farsight now. It is a simple and quick process but will likely leave you stunned momentarily. After this, you will lead the Ancient Clan, and I will no longer be your master," Seer Mordou answered with a satisfied smile. "After this, you will likely be the most powerful human mage alive."

Valon nodded, wondering what the process would entail. He knew there was no way to really prepare, to imagine what he would experience. However, his nature was to try to ready himself for whatever came. As he looked at his master, Valon knew he would have to trust him.

"Then I am ready, Master," Valon answered confidently.

The others each took a few steps back from the mages, having no idea what was going to happen. Anna and Garon spoke quietly amongst themselves, neither taking their eyes off the master and apprentice. Becca and Goreth did the same, but their hands had bumped into each other and they now loosely held each other's fingers.

"Then let us not delay. Keep your eyes open for a moment," Seer Mordou grinned, ignoring the rest of the group.

Valon watched as his master's glowing left eye stared into him, as if reaching into his soul. Then, suddenly, he watched the magic within his master burst forth and strike his eyes. It wasn't a painful thing, but it did contain a magic power that was rivaled by nothing Valon had ever encountered.

Time warped as a powerful, ancient magic flowed through Valon's entire being. His normal vision disappeared, and he found visions of his life flowing before him, all around him. He did not panic as his entire reality cracked and reformed around him, seeing familiar things flashing before him—spraining his ankle as a young boy, being selected to train under Seer Mordou, accidentally blowing a hole in his home practicing magic, his first kiss with Lora Fenn, his final birthday as he reached adulthood, so many memories flashed before his eyes. He smiled at the memories, both good and bad, gaining an innate understanding of how time and magic reacted with each other. He was magically and spiritually no longer in the mausoleum.

As his memories continued, he noticed they increased in speed, almost becoming a blur. He tried to maintain his mental acuity, to not panic, but as the blur increased, he did find the overwhelming visions much to handle. He began to breath quicker, having to kneel on the unseen ground to stabilize himself.

He briefly saw the portal, then the Narsho village, his father, a strange land made of sand and odd-looking mountains, short men, green creatures, destruction, reconstruction, and a sprawling city of stone and metal. Then the future before him increased to an incomprehensible speed, and he was unable to distinguish anything.

Valon held his head, feeling as though reality itself was trying to expel him from existence, as if he were an unwelcome guest. Just before he reached a point of panic, he heard his master's voice from somewhere far away; he remembered his training, his master's confidence in him, and the future that still needed him. Valon gritted his teeth and slowly stood back up, filled with determination and purpose. As the magic flowed through his entire being, Valon stood fast. He did not waver as cosmic forces beyond his true understanding imbued themselves within him.

Then, without warning, the visions stopped, and nothing but darkness followed. He looked all around, seeing nothing but an absolute void. He then realized it was cold, far colder than anything he had ever felt. He shivered, freezing, but did not give up. As the darkness engulfed him, Valon stayed strong, ready for whatever came next. For the briefest of moments, he thought he felt a presence with them. Then, as fast as it had begun, it faded away.

The world around him slowly reappeared in a haze of color and light. The first thing he noticed was Seer Mordou standing before him, having not moved the entire time. As his former master removed his hands from Valon's shoulders, the flaming blue light in his eye dwindled, leaving nothing but a thin layer of blue.

Valon immediately noticed he felt stronger in all aspects, feeling an even more powerful connection with magic. He felt the presence of magic with him, and he could sense nearby sources with absolute ease. He had never felt so sharp in his entire life.

As he looked around at his companions, he saw they were staring at him with great curiosity. In fact, he noticed Goreth's mouth was almost wide open in surprise. It took a moment before he found the words to speak.

"Master? Is it finished?" Seer Valon slowly asked.

"It is, but I am no longer your master. You are now the Seer of the Ancient Clan. I may still be a Seer, however you are The Seer. But, Valon, something has gone rather … differently from when I was given the ability," Seer Mordou began, more intrigued than worried.

"His eye…" Anna mumbled from behind Seer Mordou.

"My eye? Does it glow blue now?" Valon asked, holding out his hand in front of him but not seeing anything.

"Er, it glows, but it glows gold like this supposed holy magic, not blue," Seer Mordou answered, scratching his chin as he stared at his former apprentice.

Hy'ria laughed from behind Valon as she walked back to the humans. He turned to see her with a tall, silver staff. She shook her head, seeming to laugh directly at them.

"What has happened, High Priestess?" Seer Mordou asked firmly yet respectfully.

"Oh, you humans never cease to surprise me. Seers, the holy magic that emanates here is immense. Not only is my power radiating to you, but this entire city was constructed on a flowline. Holy magic is strong here, the strongest of this continent. Farsight, as you have just given it, draws from whatever magic is nearby. Yes, it is primordial in nature, but can and has been imbued with holy as well. That is why your eye now glows gold, for holy magic has been mixed into the power Seer Mordou has given you, which if anything is beneficial," Hy'ria explained almost mockingly.

"I-I see," Valon said, staring down at his empty hands, unsure of what this new information meant.

"I will acknowledge the quality of training you must have been given in order to achieve farsight at such a young age and not instantly fall to the flows of magic," Hy'ria admitted with a small smile. "You humans do surprise me."

"Young age? He is over thirty years old!" Seer Mordou scoffed.

"Yes, and had I pursued farsight in my long life, I would have not done so before my one hundred and twentieth birthday. Succumbing to that sort of insanity is one of the worst ways to go. Now speaking of time, I am running short of it. If you humans are ready, I will give you all the last of my power. I cannot quite control how much goes to whom given the time, but you will all have the holy strength you will need to fight your new enemy. Now, shall we begin?" Hy'ria asked, hitting her silver staff on the ground.

The humans looked at each other, some more nervous than others. Anna hesitantly rubbed her stomach, looking concerned for obvious reasons. However, none of them stepped back or turned away, all ready to fulfill their roles.

"I believe we are," Seer Mordou responded, briefly looking at everyone else.

"Good. I want you, Seer Valon, to have my staff after I pass on," Hy'ria explained.

"Your staff? I would be honored," Valon nodded respectfully.

"It will enhance your magic greatly. Not only that, but it has enough power to fracture the flows of magic and create a portal one last time. Use it wisely," Hy'ria insisted, practically pushing the silver staff into Valon's hands.

"Incredible ... We shall be in your debt, High Priestess," Valon thanked.

"As long as you embrace all that the holy flow of magic has to offer, you need not be indebted. Now come, all of you hold hands and form a circle," Hy'ria urged, holding out her withered hands.

Valon set the staff gently on the ground and took her hand. Seer Mordou took the other of the old elf's hands, and the other humans stepped in and completed the circle. Before anyone could speak, holy magic began to radiate from the high priestess.

The powerful, ancient magic surged through the arms and bodies of the new Champions, each of them reacting to the efflux of power differently. As it continued, a gold pool of magic formed between them, the source being the fading elf.

Valon could feel his great power continue to grow, and the knowledge of new spells flowed into his mind. He looked over to see his master keeping a monotonous face, his blue eye pulsating gold. The other humans looked stunned, feeling a sensation they had never remotely felt before. Valon only hoped their lack of training wouldn't cause them to suffer, though he doubted it, as the embrace of the holy magic felt warm, understanding, and almost a sentient force on its own.

Valon felt Hy'ria's grip loosening, and he looked over to see her eyes had closed. As if fate itself suddenly converged, the hourglass had emptied the moment she completed her ritual, and Hy'ria left their realm. As her body went limp, Valon kneeled to catch her.

She felt light in his arms, and her look of disappointment and confusion had been replaced by one of peace. He stood, carrying her lifeless, light body in his hands and looked to the coffin nearby. He didn't want to leave someone as powerful as her lying on the floor.

As he walked over, small strands of holy magic began to travel out of Hy'ria's body. He stopped, feeling her body becoming lighter. More golden pillars of holy light left her, and moments later Valon felt no more of her weight.

He slowly let go as her body drifted upwards, slowly unraveling into a golden, glistening thread. He smiled at the breathtaking sight, Hy'ria's entire body finally disappearing into floating magic. Then, without warning, the magic merged into one large pillar, traveled upwards a few feet and imploded in on itself, disappearing from the mausoleum completely.

"By the gods..." Seer Mordou mumbled, walking next to his former apprentice.

"That was ... I've never seen anything like it," Valon said, turning around to face his companions.

The rest of them looked even more surprised than him, trapped in a confusing feeling of newfound power and witnessing such a sight. It was undoubtedly the most notable moment any of them had ever witnessed.

"I can feel the power," Garon said, small beams of holy light dancing from his fingertips as he raised his hands before his face.

"I do too," Anna added. "I feel warm."

"The spells that we've just learned are so fascinating. This holy magic is far from what we are used to using," Seer Mordou said, looking mainly at Valon.

"I agree," Valon replied, slowly picking up Hy'ria's staff from the ground.

"So, we can really create a portal with that?" Becca asked.

"Supposedly. But I do not believe now is the time we should use it," Valon answered, staring at the elegant yet simple staff.

"Why not?" Goreth asked bluntly.

"I do not feel it is the time," Valon answered.

"Then we must go back to our people. They have certainly reached the corrupted forest by now!" Anna urged, remembering the rest of their clans.

"I agree. We must not delay," Garon added.

"Then let us make haste! With our newfound power, we may be able to defeat this Xerannu and drive the Horrors from our realm!" Seer Mordou ordered, his eye returning to its blue color.

They quickly made their way from the mausoleum, the glowing torches turning dark as they walked away from them. They wasted no time climbing the large staircase, and as they reached the top, the stairs back down returned to their state of absolute darkness.

Before they left the building, they all briefly discussed the spells and other things they had been gifted. Valon was surprised that such knowledge and power could be given so freely, especially since the others had only used magic for a few days. Had they been given farsight, they would have likely perished or lost their mind. Something about holy magic was different from their primordial magic, and it seemed exceptionally strong.

From blessings, to healing, to purifying, to using concentrated holy power, they had all been gifted over a dozen powerful spells. Valon felt more powerful than he could ever comprehend, and the visions of his newly gifted farsight lingered in his mind.

As they walked back through the ruined elven city, Valon turned to his master. He was surprised his master had been so quiet, especially considering the circumstances. He hadn't once even asked how the ritual had gone. Finally, Valon couldn't take the silence any longer.

"Mas—, Seer Mordou, I wanted to ask you something regarding your transfer of farsight," Valon began, seeing his former master lost in thought.

"Yes?" Seer Mordou asked.

"When it was given to you, did you see your life too? I saw my past, what could be my future, and who knows what else flashing before my eyes. Then there was darkness, such cold darkness," Valon explained, shivering as he remembered the void.

"Ah, it was so long ago now, Valon. I do believe I had glimpses of the future, yes. But darkness, I do not remember that. My old master did not tell me about his experience, as his master did not speak of his either. You see, it is a strange thing to come to terms with. I may have small visions, glimpses of the future, but the true power of farsight now lies within you. Part of my connection is severed now, and the power that flowed through me no longer exists in its old form. Forgive my lack of interaction with you, but it's stranger than I would have thought," Seer Mordou said.

"Do not apologize, I should apologize for asking. I didn't consider that, your point of view and what you've given up, I mean. If anything, I should thank you for allowing me to lead our people and become the next Seer. I will not fail you, Master," Valon replied.

"I know you will not, for that is why I chose and trained you. My only hope is that your power surpasses my own and you can lead our people to peace and unity. Now, prepare yourself, as all your power will be needed to close this portal," Seer Mordou smiled.

Valon only nodded in return, knowing so much of his life still lay before him. Now he would be tasked with leading the Ancient Clan. Now, he would have to utilize farsight and search their realm for threats, disasters, and whatever else would befall them. Now that the time had arrived, Valon no longer felt nervous and unsure of himself. No, Valon felt more confident than ever. As a mix of primordial and holy power flowed through his body, Valon felt more powerful than he could have ever imagined. He was ready for whatever came next, even if it tested every part of his being.

Chapter 25

"Incoming! Heads down!" Guard Captain Jarult boomed, hoisting a large shield over his head.

Chieftain Barod braced for impact of the arrows, holding his own shield over his own head and the torchbearer next to him. He glanced over his shoulder to see a weak Chieftain Wooll barely able to hold his own shield. Looking at the other men near him, it was obvious their morale was broken, and the attack had failed. He hated to give the order but knew that he had to.

"Retreat! Back to the encampment! Do not break formation!" Chieftain Barod ordered loudly over the fray.

The warriors repeated the message to their comrades, and their shield formation retreated out of the dark forest. As they did, arrows rained upon them from the afflicted Highrock warriors deeper in the forest.

Chieftain Barod watched as unprotected torchbearers were struck by arrows, their torches falling onto the living ground and singeing the flesh. As it happened, a tentacle would rise from within the ground and wrap itself around the torch, creating a horrible smell of burning flesh and returning that area to darkness.

After a long night of barely any sleep, Chieftain Barod and Wooll had decided to assault the Horrors within the forest. They had made it quite a distance before they were attacked; they had successfully repelled these Horrors only to come under attack by arrows from the corrupted warriors of the Highrock Clan.

Chieftain Barod knew it was the right call to retreat, but was angered to see his warriors begin to break formation and run for their lives. As another wave of arrows came, many warriors were struck and fell onto the fleshy ground. Unprotected by their comrades' shields, the torchbearers tried to unsuccessfully hold their weapons and torches in front of their faces and were slain quickly.

"Hold formation, you cowards!" Guard Captain Jarult yelled.

Despite the command, the warriors began to flee even faster back towards the morning light coming from far in the distance. As they sprinted, Horrors flanked from behind the side trees to engage them, picking off fleeing soldiers one by one.

Chieftain Barod ran as fast as he could, knowing he had left a line of mages in case this exact event happened. If they could reach that line, they would be able to retreat without excess casualties.

Chaos brewed around him as warriors were dragged away by the quick Horrors or fell as arrows continued to rain on them. Chieftain Barod saw Wooll trying to drag a fallen torchbearer who had been struck by an arrow. As always, his old friend would leave no warrior behind.

"Let me help you," Chieftain Barod said, grabbing the other man's arm while he held his shield over himself.

"This is a slaughter, Barod," Chieftain Wooll coughed, trace amounts of blood running down his lower lip.

"I know! We need to make it back to the mages. They should be just ahead!" Chieftain Barod barked, the stress finally getting to him.

They continued dragging the groaning man across the fleshy ground, his voice far surpassed by the screams of warriors fighting and dying. Two times Chieftain Barod had to hack away gnarled tentacles that had grabbed the man's legs, his axe covered in black, tarry blood.

Then the forest lit up with blue light. They had reached the defensive line of mages who had sent their almost one hundred wisplights into the air around the area. Now that it was illuminated and the mages had appeared, the warriors regained some morale and began to regroup.

As they neared, two mages ran out and took the place of Chieftains Barod and Wooll, quickly healing the man and dragging him back behind their line. Another mage approached them, and this time Chieftain Barod recognized him as the assigned leader of the group.

"What are your orders, Chieftain?" the mage asked, surprisingly calm.

"We must retreat to the encampment. We were assaulted by arrows. Do what you can to keep them at bay and we will all fall back together," Chieftain Barod replied.

The mage nodded, and the three ran back to the other mages. A torrent of warriors followed behind, some pushing their way through the mages and sprinting towards daylight. Their retreat had fallen into absolute chaos, and it was turning into every man for themselves.

The majority of the mages combined their magic to create a sort of wall of magic above the retreating warriors. As they did, the arrows slowed significantly as they passed through, harmlessly falling to the ground.

Chieftain Barod's head turned back toward the enemy as he heard a sharp scream. He quickly noticed a dead Narsho warrior woman lying dead on the ground, and close to her was a group of warriors encircled by Horrors. In the middle he noticed Guard Captain Jarult barking orders to his group of failing warriors.

"We need to help them!" Chieftain Barod pointed to the nearby warriors and mages.

"We cannot maintain such a field of magic and attack at the same time," the mage said with a frown.

"Fine. Then keep those arrows off us," Chieftain Barod ordered as he and a few warriors began to push through the retreating warriors.

"Don't leave me behind," Chieftain Wooll chuckled with a small cough.

"I wouldn't dream of it," Chieftain Barod grumbled, still disappointed at his retreating warriors.

As they made it through the last of the warriors, almost two dozen Horrors stood between them and Guard

Captain Jarult's group. They were slightly outnumbered, but at least the arrows had stopped striking.

They charged into the Horrors, their axes and swords cutting into the gnarled flesh of the monsters. The human warriors screamed with both courage and terror, looking into the red eyes of a truly terrible foe.

Chieftain Barod roared as he struck his battle axe into a Horror, quickly bringing around his shield and bashing the creature on the ground. Before it had a chance to recover, he leapt toward it, hacking his axe into the neck of the creature. It hissed and squirmed, managing to crawl a few feet before succumbing to its injuries as tarry blood seeped out.

Chieftain Barod made eye contact with Guard Captain Jarult, and the two began to work their groups toward each other. Most of the warriors held their own against the Horrors, able to take at least one or two down before they were bested. However, unlike the Horrors, more warriors weren't coming to replace those lost.

Despite their disadvantage, they managed to regroup with the guard captain's warriors, and they began to retreat through the enemy. As he looked around, Chieftain Barod noticed most of the warriors were wounded. He could only wonder if they would turn like the others did. He noticed Chieftain Wooll had a severely wounded Linta Clan fighter's arm around his shoulders as he helped walk the man to safety. He smiled, knowing his friend always put others in need before himself.

A few of the mages not holding the barrier cast spells at the Horrors around them, sending them flying with forceful magic. As they neared the defensive perimeter, Chieftain Barod felt hopeful again. While the battle had been lost, they could at least fall back to the encampment and hope the others had returned with something useful, and they could attack once more. However, an instant later, his hope was permanently crushed.

A group of lanky looking Horrors shot up from the ground, their bodies bending in disturbing ways. They raised their arms and unleashed a barrage of spikes toward the group, making sure to avoid the visible magic barrier.

Chieftain Barod raised his shield, stopping any of the spikes from reaching him. He watched as the mages ran forward and sent their own attack flying over the group and hitting the lanky Horrors, but as the chieftain looked back toward the others, he saw something that tore his old heart in two. Kneeling on a fleshy, bloody ground, his oldest friend, held his neck, two knotted spikes from the monsters piercing clean through. His hands clenched around the fatal wound, and his eyes stared into Chieftain Barod's.

"No! Wooll!" Chieftain Barod cried, running to his friend.

"Chieftain! We need to keep moving or we'll be surrounded!" Guard Captain Jarult yelled as he fought off the encroaching monsters.

As he knelt before his dying friend, silent tears fell from his face. Chieftain Wooll looked in obvious pain yet had a strange calm about him. He slowly let go of his neck, blood pouring between where gnarled Horror spikes met flesh. Chieftain Wooll looked to his friend, using up all his strength to speak two final words.

"End me."

Chieftain Barod stared at his friend, feeling time almost freeze around them. The shouts and orders around him twisted into a muddled incomprehensible nothing, and for a moment he forgot where he even was. His grip failed and his battleaxe started to slide from his hand, but as Chieftain Wooll's eyes began to close, he knew what would befall his friend if he did not grant him his dying wish.

"You are my brother, Herold. I am so sorry," Chieftain Barod choked out, trying to numb himself for what he had to do next.

As Chieftain Wooll's eyelids closed, Barod clenched his teeth and fought against his every pull to stop. With a heavy, mournful swing, Chieftain Barod delivered to his oldest friend, his unrelated brother, his final wish. He cried out as he lost the only real family he had left, quickly turning away from the sight that would break him if he saw it. At least Chieftain Wooll would rest in peace.

Guard Captain Jarult's saddened face was close to Barod's, already dragging his shoulder back. As warriors fell around them and sizzling bolts of magical energy shot past them, Chieftain Barod felt almost lifeless. He followed close behind his guard captain, who still led him by the shoulder. Finally, they made it to the defensive line, which was beginning to falter as more Horrors flanked the sides. The mages had begun to form a horseshoe shape, being pressed together on all fronts except behind them. If they were to be encircled, it would be the end of them all.

As Guard Captain Jarult yelled to him, Chieftain Barod couldn't make out the words. Part of him was still too disassociated to comprehend it. All he could think about was Herold Wooll, the great man they had all lost. His mind replayed memories in his head of their time together, decades on decades quickly spiraling through his mind. Then, one memory forced itself into the mental stage of his mind.

Chieftain Barod recalled when they were barely teenagers, many years after meeting at a festival and many before either would be chosen as chieftains of their respective clans for their various accolades. He remembered the day Wooll had lost his father. It was especially tragic because only a week later, Herold Wooll would go on to win the Forud Tests of Strength, the tournament that first caused the Forud Council to look at him with interest.

Lying sick in bed, Herold's father had begged his son to continue and not let his death slow him down. Chieftain Barod had not lost a parent at this time but could see the immense hurt in his friend's eyes. Herold's father could see this too, which is why he almost angrily insisted his son take no longer than a minute to mourn his death before returning to his routine. He urged that if Herold truly wanted to make his father proud, he would force himself forward. And that was exactly what Chieftain Wooll had done.

As the mayhem around him continued and more looked to him for orders, Chieftain Barod knew what he had to do; he had seen the last look on Chieftain Wooll's face, and knew it was the same as the man's father before him. Chieftain Barod realized his minute was up, and the world around him cleared once more.

"Retreat! Everyone fall back in formation!" Chieftain Barod boomed, wiping a final tear from his cheek.

"You heard the chieftain! Tighten up that line!" Guard Captain Jarult yelled, turning and running toward the other end of the mages' line.

Slowly and steadily, the remaining warriors and mages fell back and retreated out of the forest. As daylight finally struck them, they realized the encampment was only just behind them. The Horrors surprisingly did not follow them, and the arrows had stopped from the Highrock warriors. They all turned and ran to the encampment, the mages exhausted from using so much sustained magic.

As Chieftain Barod made it to the gates, he didn't enter until every possible warrior and mage was safely inside. Guard Captain Jarult protested when it came to the two of them, and Chieftain Barod pushed him through and followed him. As the gates closed behind them, it was as if there was a collective sigh of relief.

"Chieftain … I am sorry about Wooll," Guard Captain Jarult frowned, shaking his head. "I should've done something."

"No, there was nothing you could do. That was a slaughter," Chieftain Barod replied out of breath.

"What? Where is Chieftain Wooll?" a nearby Forud warrior asked.

Guard Captain Jarult looked nervously at his chieftain, not wanting to be the one to break the news. Without their chieftain, Chieftain Barod wondered if they would continue to fight. He wouldn't force them to stay, as he couldn't without wasting his own men. He only hoped seeing the threat would force them to stay.

"He is dead. He fell trying to save others," Chieftain Barod answered slowly.

"Dead? Oh, no," the Forud warrior uttered, quickly turning to his comrades and sharing the news.

The news of his death spread quickly through camp. Whispers turned to yelling as the camp erupted in a mix of confusion and sorrow. The Forud Clan warriors looked stunned, lost, not knowing who to report to if their chieftain was gone. Chieftain Barod realized he had to step in now.

"Chieftain Wooll might be gone, but his sacrifice to help others should not go in vain!" he boomed, walking over and climbing on top of a nearby table.

"But how can we win?" a voice shouted from somewhere in the forming crowd.

"We can win through our determination and skill in combat! They might have numbers, but they do not have skill! Unless we want that terrible infestation to overtake our entire realm, we must fight! Chieftain Wooll did not stop until the very end, and neither should any one of us! If we stand together as one unified clan, we can push through those Horrors and end this once and for all!" Chieftain Barod yelled to the crowd around him.

He watched as the crowd murmured to themselves, some obviously hesitant to listen to what he had to say. He felt he had their attention but needed to inspire them somehow as he wasn't sure if they had it in them. But given the circumstances, he had to try something.

"Think of your family, your friends, anyone you care about. Think about what these monsters will do to them if we do not stop them!" Chieftain Barod urged.

"Soon, a group of powerful Champions will return with weapons we need to finish this fight!"

"Weapons? What weapons?" a Forud woman asked from near the front of the crowd.

Chieftain Barod didn't reply immediately, not knowing exactly what Seer Mordou would bring. He had barely been told anything beyond the fact some sort of power or weapon lay on the east coast that would turn them into great Champions of magic. He did not know when they would be back, or even if they would.

"Something, something that can defeat our foes!" Chieftain Barod stammered.

As the crowd erupted into furious arguing, Chieftain Barod felt he was failing them. But before he could say another word, he noticed the gate opening. He climbed off the table, seeing six figures walking through. His prayers had been answered; the Champions had returned.

"Look!" Guard Captain Jarult yelled, trying to get the crowd's attention.

Chieftain Barod stared at them, slowly walking forward. As he did, he saw Seer Mordou smiling from the front of the group. He watched as the mage raised his arms, causing the others to do so as well. Chieftain Barod stopped, his distrust of magic once again seeping into his mind.

He watched as the six conjured a large pool of gold colored magic. It grew and shimmered in the air, coalescing and fermenting into a vibrant looking ocean. Part of him hated seeing the magic, but as he made eye contact with Anna, he knew it would be alright.

Suddenly, the magic burst apart into a tidal wave of golden energy. It first hit Chieftain Barod, then flowed over the crowd of people and then into the rest of the encampment. As it did, it made a strange soothing sound.

Chieftain Barod immediately felt warm, rejuvenated, and emotionally stable once more. Not only did his morale return, but the crowd of warriors also erupted in cries of joy and eagerness to fight on. He did not move as the six approached him, all smiling with confidence.

"Anna," Chieftain Barod smiled, looking to his scout.

"Chieftain, let's finish this," Anna grinned with a tough smile.

Chapter 26

Garon was filled with righteous fire as they cut their way through the corrupted forest. After hearing that his people had been turned to fight alongside the Horrors and Xerannu, he had found himself unable to do anything but fight. Even now, in the heart of what could be their final battle, he did not do anything but surrender to the bloodlust.

Still, he had yet to actually see his people. Only the arrows of their distant, ever-retreating archers allowed him to confirm what he had heard was true, although nobody had seen the bulk of the warriors in some time, and he wondered where they lurked.

He let loose a blazing burst of holy magic, not only cleansing the ground of the flesh but burning whatever organic material stood before him. The afflicted did not appear as though they could be saved, and now they would engulf all who stood before them in holy flame. However, as they cleared a swath of forest as they traveled inwards to wherever Xerannu lurked, he could feel his energy draining from so much usage.

After returning to the camp amidst Chieftain Barod's speech, every warrior and mage now fought behind the six Champions, their morale at an all-time high. Between seeing such power on their side, plus no longer having to fight in darkness, the allied clanspeople fought at their best.

"How close are we to the center?" Valon asked, looking over at Anna.

"I do not know. This is not the way we came," Anna replied as she bathed two nearby trees in holy fire.

"I believe we are getting close," Garon grumbled, somehow able to feel his father's presence ahead.

As a group of burly Horrors ran towards him from behind some nearby trees, Garon unleashed a fiery torrent of holy energy. He watched with indifference as the holy magic burned the Horrors alive, practically melting them to the bone.

"By the gods, this magic is so powerful," Seer Mordou uttered, impressed with Garon's ability.

"At least it is against these shambling monsters," Valon added, unleashing his own rain of holy fire on another group.

"But I can feel myself becoming fatigued from using it," Becca said as she cleaned some ground.

"Me too," Goreth yawned.

"Then we must be efficient. I do not know if this magic will remain with us, or return as strongly if it does," Seer Mordou cautioned.

Garon watched as Guard Captain Jarult made his way through the formation and approached their group. He wasn't sure who to address, so looked between all of them as he spoke.

"We need help back there! We're being flanked!" Guard Captain Jarult expressed loudly.

"I will go. The Forud Clan must not lose more of its own," Goreth grumbled, thinking of Chieftain Wooll.

"I will come too," Becca added, walking behind him.

Garon turned back to face more Horrors and let loose another barrage of magic. With each spell cast, he felt as though some sort of being, or consciousness reached out to him. Each time he used holy magic he wanted to use more, to cleanse more of the realm. He ignored it, wondering if it had something to do with Hy'ria.

As they continued to burn their way through the sickened forest, they came to a line of humanoids standing behind one with a crown. Garon instantly recognized his people, despite their entire bodies being warped by whatever disease the Horrors spread. He stopped, suddenly making eye contact with his father's terrible red eyes.

The others stopped next to him, and as they did, the Horrors stopped attacking the warriors and mages behind them. There was a strange silence in the air, not even the sounds of nature lingering here.

Garon watched as his father led his few people to the edge of their forest, all of them standing ready to fight. Then, his father took a few more steps out into the sunlight, revealing his warped form.

"My son! You serve the wrong magic and wrong leaders!" Chief King Mace boomed with a sickly tone.

Garon stepped a few feet beyond his friends, not far from his father now. A voice deep within his head told him to engulf his father in holy flame, but he couldn't bring himself to do so, not yet anyway.

"And who do you serve, Father? Xerannu?" Garon asked loudly, resting his hands on his twin blades.

He watched his father frown at the mention of the name. It seemed his father hadn't expected him to know of his true master.

"Xerannu is my ally, not my master!" Chief King Mace yelled, waving his bloodied axe through the air.

"Is that so?" a dark, deep voice boomed throughout the forest loudly.

Garon could feel a cold, haunting entity somewhere nearby. He looked all around but couldn't see anything, but he did notice the eyes of every Horror, Highrock archer, and his father glowed bright red.

Chief King Mace forcibly knelt to the ground, trying and failing to stay standing. His bones slightly cracked as he was forced to look down, as if kneeling before some invisible leader. He looked as though he was trying and failing to speak.

"Xerannu! Show yourself!" Seer Mordou yelled loudly, coming to stand next to Garon.

"I am all around you, weak human. In every tree, in each of my thralls, in all the Highrock Clan. I am everything, and soon I will be your world!" Xerannu boomed, striking fear into all who stood opposing him.

"But why are you here? Why are you doing this?" Valon yelled from behind.

"To save us all, fool! Do you not know what other terrible threats exist in this celestial realm of ours? What I do, I do to save all life! For only under me can life continue to thrive," Xerannu explained, his voice gurgling from all around them.

"What are you talking about? What other threats?" Seer Mordou asked, his golden eye flickering with red and green as Xerannu's presence cut through them all.

"I do not have time to explain, nor should I have to such weaklings. I will give you one chance, all of you. Surrender yourselves to me, and together we can create an army like no other and find peace," Xerannu offered, his voice oozing with temptation.

"Never!" Anna yelled, walking forth and standing next to Garon. "We will never surrender to you, monster!"

Garon and Anna shared a look, each reminding the other why they fought. Garon looked back, raising his hand towards his father. He knew it was too late, but he had to stop his father's suffering. He let loose a flaming bolt of holy magic at his father, trying to ignore the sadness creeping into him.

Then, suddenly, the magic bolt dissipated. As it shattered into small disappearing flecks, a greenish red field revealed itself around Garon's father. As it happened, Xerannu let loose a deep cackle.

"If you want to kill your father, you will have to do so with your own two hands," Xerannu chuckled.

"Then so be it," Garon said darkly, unsheathing his twin blades.

As he walked towards his father, he watched the controlled man stand once more, axe at the ready. He stood still, waiting for Garon to come to him. However, as Garon walked, he felt someone run from behind and grab his arm.

"Wait," Anna said quietly, holding Garon back.

"What is it?" Garon asked impatiently, turning and looking to his friend.

"It's a trap. He wants you to fight him up close. If anything, Xerannu wants to dominate you like all the others. You can't let that blood on your father's axe cut into you," Anna answered, letting go of Garon.

"Don't worry, it won't," Garon answered, turning around and continuing toward his father.

"You've failed your people, Garon. They are mine. This entire land is mine," Chief King Mace and Xerannu spoke in unison.

Garon ignored the obvious taunt and ran at his father. As he swung his blades, he felt holy power coursing through his body. As his blades met his father's axe, the opposing magics crackled as they touched. Each of the two men were now filled with power that was not their own.

Magic aside, Garon had always been a far better fighter than his father. This was quickly realized as his twin blades danced with ease around his father's replacement weapon. Only the magical power emanating around his father, and the fact he didn't want to say goodbye, were stopping him from ending the chief king.

"You were always a disappointment to me," the influenced Chief King Mace growled.

Garon ignored it, knowing he had to finish this fight before Xerannu could warp his own mind. He nimbly dodged a flurry of desperate hacks from his father's axe and readied himself, preparing to end the sick being that posed as his father.

Filled with a righteous fury, Garon used everything he had to overwhelm the corrupted chief king. He managed to break through his father's parrying ability and sever his weapon-wielding arm. This only caused the inhuman imposter to hiss like an animal and flail his other arm at Garon.

"The Highrock Clan will soon have its revenge!" Chief King Mace rambled violently.

"If you're still in there somewhere, rest in peace, Father," Garon uttered softly, ignoring the crazed man.

Infused with holy light, Garon brought his swords across his chest, and when his father approached him, he slashed outward, decapitating him in one quick move. He could feel his father's energy disappear, and as he did, red and green strands leapt from his father's body and dissipated into the woods.

Garon felt no pain or sorrow, knowing his father had truly died that night days ago. If anything, his father's soul would be free. Not even a single tear fell from his eye as he turned away from his father's corpse.

"You would kill your own father for glory. Have you no shame?" Xerannu asked, trying to warp Garon's mind.

Garon looked up to see the Highrock archers staring at him, looks of contempt across their faces. It was the same look he had seen his entire life. However, there weren't many archers, and the warriors were not present. He couldn't help but wonder where the rest of his people were.

"Xerannu, where are the rest of my people? I demand to know!" Garon shouted, looking toward the almost three dozen archers standing not far from him.

Xerannu laughed, his sickly voice causing the trees to glow slightly before subsiding. Garon ignored it and continued staring ahead. As he did, he wondered if his corrupted father's final words had any meaning.

"You just heard your father say it, dear Garon. They are going to have their revenge on the Narsho Clan. They, along with a legion of my thralls, should be arriving there shortly. Then your people will get the revenge they've always wanted, and your homes will burn to the ground," Xerannu laughed.

Garon gasped and turned back to his fellow Champions. Upon hearing this, panic spread throughout the army of unified clans. He quickly ran back to the others, who were already discussing what to do. The

273

chieftain, guard captain, and other Champions had joined them. As he approached, Anna very lightly held his hand, knowing what he had just done was more difficult than he would admit.

"You will not return to your village in time, so you must make a choice. Press forward and fail or return to your people and try to save what you can," Xerannu boomed. "Just know that with whatever you choose, I will still win. Even if you close my portal, the manifestation will only get worse without my presence to guide my forces! My gift will spread throughout this land!"

"He doesn't mean … Is it too late?" Seer Mordou asked aloud.

"Search the future, Seer!" Xerannu boomed mockingly. "Your land is lost, whether I am defeated or not! Regardless, it is over for you!"

Garon watched as the Horrors that had surrounded their army retreated back to the forest where the Highrock archers stood. As Xerannu's thralls fell back, a reddish haze fell over the forest. Based on the energy, Garon felt it would dampen the effect of their holy magic.

"We must save our people!" Chieftain Barod urged, looking primarily at Seer Mordou.

"I fear the only way to save them is to leave this land. Regardless if the portal is closed, our home is lost," Valon added solemnly.

"What? Are you trying to tell me we are fighting for nothing?" Titus asked angrily, pushing his way into the group.

"No, not at all. We must close the portal and we must sail south. That is the only way our people will survive," Valon began. "I'm afraid I need to return to the Narsho village to warn the others. Fortunately, Hy'ria's staff has one portal left in it to get us there before our enemy."

Garon shook his head, realizing their task had now turned into a suicide mission. Not only he knew it, but the others did as well. Whoever continued onwards to fight would be left behind in a dying land.

"Then that is what we shall do," Chieftain Barod slowly declared.

"But Chieftain!" Guard Captain Jarult protested.

"Jarult! He is right, the Seers have not been wrong yet. Now we must trust and listen to them if we want our people to survive. I want you to travel back through the portal with Valon and three-quarters of our forces. I must stay and fight, and see this to its bitter end," Chieftain Barod ordered.

"I will not leave your side, Chieftain; I too want to fight," Titus declared.

"Then you will stay and fight until our end, Titus," Chieftain Barod replied, turning from Titus back to Jarult. "Now find those who wish to go and those who will stay."

Guard Captain Jarult nodded and quickly ran back to his comrades, who were eagerly awaiting orders. He spread the new information, crushing the his men's previous morale.

Garon didn't like the thought of losing Valon, easily the most powerful of all of them. However, he was the Seer, and he knew it had to be done. Thinking of his people attacking the Narsho, Garon sighed, knowing his father might finally get his way.

There was a solemn silence between them as they watched the warriors and mages split into who would go and who would stay. Given the fact that every warrior, either wounded or healthy, had left the encampment meant that every able-bodied human now stood before them. The majority would go defend the village and escape off their doomed land, and just over two hundred and fifty remaining warriors and mages would stay behind to help finish the assault and close the portal. They all knew what their choices meant, and a heavy weight hung around them.

Garon watched as Seer Mordou and Valon embraced each other, both knowing this would likely be the last time they would ever see each other. Of everything that had happened, today, he found this sight to be the most heart-wrenching of all. He hadn't known either man for very long, but he could feel the respect and friendship the former master and apprentice shared.

"Seer Valon, I expect you to lead our people to their new home safely and proudly, for you are no longer only the Seer of the Ancient Clan, you are the Seer of the Allied Clans. Lead them well," Seer Mordou ordered as he let go of Valon.

"I will remember all you have taught me. Our people's lives lay in all of your hands now," Valon said, now looking to the other Champions.

Valon first shook the hand of Chieftain Barod, exchanging a mutual nod. He then shook Titus's hand, and moved onto Becca and Goreth. He shared some words of magic wisdom to the two, shaking their hands.

"Anna, are you sure you don't want to return with us? I know you are pregnant after all," Valon asked respectfully.

"No, Valon. My place is here with my chieftain. I must finish this. We will be fine," Anna said as she shook the Seer's hand, her other hand lightly brushing against her stomach.

Finally, Valon approached Garon, the Seer's gold eye burning brightly with holy magic. He didn't know what to say but grasped the man's hand.

"I applaud your choice to join us in the true fight, Garon. I am sorry for what has befallen your father and your people. If I can spare them somehow, I will. Otherwise, I will do what is necessary to save our people," Valon consoled as they let go.

"Thank you. Good luck, Valon," Garon replied.

Valon nodded and turned to Guard Captain Jarult. They spoke for a moment, all eyes of the warriors and mages on them. It seemed their time to part ways had come.

Garon watched as Valon hit the staff on the ground, wisps of holy magic letting loose from it. They formed a shimmering vertical pool in front of him, a thin layer of gold finally revealing the Narsho village. As it appeared, even Garon could feel the immense power it was drawing. It was about ten feet tall, and twenty feet wide.

"Quickly, men! Into the portal!" Guard Captain Jarult yelled, smiling at his chieftain with pride one last time. "Charge!"

Garon watched as Guard Captain Jarult ran into the shimmering pool of magic and disappeared into it. Valon waved to them one final time and stepped in afterwards, he and the staff disappearing for good. The other warriors and mages followed behind, yelling as they ran into the shimmering light and vanished.

As the majority of their forces vanished into the portal, Garon knew it was up to them now. If they failed to do their part, Xerannu's forces would continue to spread unchecked. He wasn't sure if the being was bluffing about making things worse, but Garon figured it couldn't get much worse.

Moments after the last warrior ran through the portal, it began to sizzle loudly and collapse in on itself. It erupted with golden light, sending a small wave of power out from it. Now they were truly cut off and on their own.

"Warriors! Mages! We must press forward and finish this!" Chieftain Barod yelled.

Those behind them roared in agreement, ready for anything. Their swords, axes, and magic were at the ready, knowing this would likely be where they died, but it didn't matter, as they had seen what could take the lives of their loved ones if left unchecked.

"Now, let us go. We must destroy this Xerannu and save our people!" Chieftain Barod ordered, looking to his Champions.

"I will follow you to the end," Titus said, saluting his chieftain.

Garon prepared himself, knowing his own end may be around the corner. Despite that, it didn't dissuade him from walking forward toward the corrupted forest. Everything he had ever lived for was now gone except his new friends. Everyone he had left to fight for was now standing beside him, ready to fight the same foe.

Garon's resolve was bolstered as he marched alongside his friends toward the forest where their enemy waited. Perhaps if they defeated Xerannu, his people could yet be saved, although deep down he knew that was not likely the case. Still, he had enough to fight for, and Garon Mace would give everything he had to help save the Allied Clans.

Chapter 27

As Valon stumbled from the portal, it took him a moment to collect himself. His entire body felt hot, and the cool drops of harvest season rain felt soothing on his warm skin. As the warriors began pouring through the portal, he moved away, stepping next to a dazed Guard Captain Jarult.

"By ... the gods ... that was ... ohh," Guard Captain Jarult moaned, hunched over his knees, hair already damp with rain.

Valon nodded in agreement, still feeling odd from the portal. He could tell they had traveled using nothing more than holy magic, and he wondered if it would leave any lasting effects on those who had traveled through. However, that was far from important right now.

"We need to prepare for the attack. There's no telling how close they are," Valon urged, shaking his head. "We also need to prepare the ships to sail."

"Of course. I will ready our defenses and send warriors to begin the evacuation," Guard Captain Jarult agreed, stopping and staring off toward the portal. "It just doesn't feel real."

"No. No, it doesn't," Valon concurred, watching as warriors and mages alike poured from the portal.

Valon noticed two familiar faces among the mages emerging from the portal. He almost gasped as he recognized his parents stepping out. He had assumed they would remain in the Narsho village instead of fighting. He spared no time running over to them.

"Mother! Father! You were at the encampment?" Valon asked loudly, retroactively worrying for his parents' wellbeing, despite them standing before them.

"Indeed, Son! We couldn't stand idle and let our son fight alone," Valon's father smiled, then noticed his son's gold eye.

"By the gods, your eye!" Valon's mother gasped. "Why is it gold?"

Valon chuckled, hugging both of his parents. As they walked back together with the horde of clanspeople, he explained everything that had happened. He told them of the elves, the various flows of magic, and every strange thing he had seen. Out of everything they had been told, they were most interested in the fact their son had finally become the Seer. By the time they reached the Chieftain's Hall, he had told them everything.

"To think our own son has finally become the Seer of the Ancient Clan. We are so proud," Valon's mother smiled.

"Indeed, we are. Now, what are your orders, Seer?" Valon's father chuckled.

"I want you two to head to the ships to help our people evacuate. Heal whoever you can, for we still have wounded. Do whatever you can; we will need to leave this place soon," Valon ordered, taking his role seriously.

"Are you certain, dear? We can still fight," Valon's mother asked.

"I am certain. I will do my best to hold them off with the others, but if we are overwhelmed, you must set sail, even if we are overcome. Otherwise, I will see you at the port," Valon explained, at least wanting his parents to escape their dying land.

"Then we shall do as you say," Valon's father nodded.

"Long live the Seer," Valon's mother smiled, hugging her son.

Valon hugged his mother then his father, knowing this was not a true goodbye. He had already seen glimpses of his mother sailing south with him and knew their plan would succeed. At least, it would succeed if they all did what was necessary.

As his parents headed through the bustling village and toward the docks, he saw Chieftain Yarmot exiting the Chieftain's Hall. The rotund man staggered slightly, as if he had been drinking. As he noticed Valon, he briefly stopped, shocked by the Seer's glowing eye, then continued walking again.

"My, my—Valon, right? I have heard from Guard Captain Jarult that you are the new ... Seer is it?" Chieftain Yarmot questioned with a hiccup.

"I am. It is good to see you, Chieftain Yarmot," Valon greeted, shaking the chieftain's sweaty hand. "Has Guard Captain Jarult explained the threat we face?"

As Valon asked the question, Chieftain Yarmot groaned as if he were in pain. He held a facade of confidence on his face, but Valon knew how the man truly felt. He could see the fear in the Linta chieftain's eyes, the lack of confidence the man had in not only himself, but everyone else.

"He did. The evacuation is underway, and I have ordered our remaining forces to hold the line at this gate," Chieftain Yarmot replied with a high, stressed voice.

Valon looked toward the hastily constructed wall in the distance. He knew it would be foolish to try to hold such a larger, less fortified position. However, now they only had the Narsho village between them and the docks, meaning if they didn't hold, some of the clanspeople may not be evacuated.

"We do have another problem," Chieftain Yarmot admitted.

"What other problem?" Valon asked slowly.

"It is impossible to fit everyone on the ship. We can barely fit the people we have here, but even that would be pushing it. Once the others return, there's no way we will be able to save everyone," Chieftain Yarmot panicked.

Valon realized the chieftain hadn't been fully informed of the situation, that Becca and many others were staying behind to finish the fight. While he would normally approach the situation tactfully, Valon knew they were short on time.

"Chieftain, the others are not coming back. This is it. We have been told to set sail without them. They are going to find a way to close the portal," Valon finally admitted, seeing the chieftain's eyes open in shock.

"They're ... they're not coming back? I assumed the attack had failed and you were split up. Did they not follow you here?" Chieftain Yarmot questioned.

"No, they did not. We took a portal back and traveled here instantaneously so we could defend against the coming attack. They continue to fight against Xerannu, the leader of those Horrors. They will not return ... I am sorry, Chieftain Yarmot," Valon explained empathetically.

"But Becca, my beautiful niece. Oh, gods. My wonderful Becca. And what of my fighters that did not return? Their loved ones will ... Oh, gods!" Chieftain Yarmot agonized, turning away from Valon.

Before Valon could console him, Guard Captain Jarult ran to them. He looked nervous, and the look on his face already told Valon what was happening. He quickly spoke, looking primarily at Valon instead of the slightly sobbing chieftain.

"The enemy has already arrived."

Valon only nodded, following the guard captain back towards the front gate. The positioned warriors and mages let them through, quickly moving aside for their superiors. They all whispered between each other, clearly disturbed by the sight outside the gate.

Finally, they reached the first line of shield-bearing warriors and mages behind them, who glared nervously at their enemy across the scarred battlefield. They made way for Valon and Jarult, whispering about how powerful Valon supposedly was.

Valon couldn't help but feel sickened as he stared at their foe across the muddy battlefield. The entirety of the Highrock Clan stood opposite them, all wielding weapons and donning whatever armor still fit their warped bodies.

Standing in front of them was a single line of nearly two dozen of bulky, giant Horrors which stood close to twenty feet tall. They were thick, tough, and Valon figured were being used as meat shields. He remembered once seeing a drawing of clay golems that looked similarly, and he shuddered at the thought of living flesh. As he sized up their enemies, Valon then noticed a single man emerge from between the flesh golems.

The Highrock man stood tall, adorned in well-crafted plate armor and wielded a large greataxe. From here, Valon could barely discern that the blade was coated in tarry black blood. It seemed it had been placed there on purpose, likely to infect anyone who was wounded. He could only surmise the other Highrock warriors had the same trick. Even with the light rain, the blood was thick enough to stay on the blade, at least for now.

"Lorag … the Highrock Champion," Valon muttered, staring at the dangerous foe.

"I've heard of his brutality, but if Glora fell, he surely will too," Jarult replied confidently.

"Look, their blades are coated in the blood of the afflicted. Any wounds will lead to infection unless I can cleanse them, and I will be too busy holding them off to do that," Valon whispered quietly to Jarult.

"Damn the Highrock. They know no honor. Is there no way you can teach that, er, spell to the other mages of yours?" Jarult asked quietly.

"Unfortunately, I cannot right now. I am not sure if I ever could, but if I can it would take far, far longer than we have," Valon replied.

"Damn. They probably have even more Horrors behind them too. They outnumber us. We need to evacuate the village," Jarult grumbled, wielding his battleaxe and placing his helmet over his head.

"I believe I may have a way to prevent them from breaching our line. There is one spell I have been given that can create a barrier of holy magic. It is immensely powerful and could hold them back indefinitely. The problem is it will take time to conjure. You wouldn't have my aid in battle, as I would have to focus my power solely on creating the barrier," Valon added, looking at Jarult for his thoughts.

"I see … If you really think you can create a barrier, then we can buy you the time you need. Either way, we will lose many brave men and women here, but if you can create a barrier, our warriors will be able to escape without sacrifice. Are you sure this is possible, Seer?" Guard Captain Jarult asked.

"Yes, it can be done," Valon replied, knowing what he had to do.

"Then we will hold them off, I swear it," Jarult promised.

Valon simply nodded and held Hy'ria's staff in his hands. He closed his eyes, searching his memory for the spell among the many holy-infused spells Hy'ria had given them. The spell would conjure a blazing wall of pure holy magic that could surround the entire village. It wasn't only large in size, but in power as well. Valon knew he would have the power required, but it would take time. However, he agreed with Jarult, and knew the shield would allow any remaining warriors to escape without worrying about being chased by the enemy.

Focusing his power, he began to draw from the flows of holy magic. He could feel the fiery warmth of the magic flow through him as though he were a mere conduit, and began to form in the field not far in front of him. Brief flashes of unrequested farsight hit him as he began, and he saw he was on the right path. Now, if his warriors could just hold the enemy off long enough, they could finally escape their doomed home.

***

Guard Captain Jarult took a deep breath, looking away from the now meditating Seer next to him. He could feel the burning red eyes of his enemy on his back as he faced his own troops. As the Allied Clan's mix of fighters from all tribes stood before him, he knew he needed to boost their morale like his chieftain would.

"Warriors! Mages! Get ready for the fight of your life! All our people rely on us! Your friends, your family, your brothers and sisters in arms, they need you now more than ever to fight with all you have! Do not let our chieftain's and other allies' sacrifices be in vain! You no longer fight for your own clan, you fight for humanity, for the Allied Clans!" Jarult boomed, his voice echoing through the formation. "Now, let us charge the enemy!"

Jarult turned as the warriors yelled in response. He held his battleaxe high over his head; he knew this would be the last thing the Highrock would expect. He pounded the battleaxe against his shield, then pointed toward their foe. On cue, his warriors charged past him and Valon, and he joined the front line. Jarult's blood pumped as he rushed the startled enemy. However, they quickly responded with their own charge, all the Horrors and afflicted Highrock warriors following behind the lumbering flesh golems. Horrible, blood-curdling roars came from their enemy as they bellowed out in an animalistic rage. The sound of the flesh golems was the worst, their entire being a creation against nature itself.

Jarult's teeth clashed together as he eyed his closing enemy, more horrifying than any he had ever faced. Everything was on the line now, and he would not fail his people. He would not fail his chieftain. He clenched his weapons, knowing even one strike against him could be fatal in a matter of moments. This was the day he had trained for his entire life.

Dozens of sparking magic missiles flew over their heads as they ran, striking the flesh golems that slowly shambled toward them. Given the immense size and strength of the golems, they had to be targeted one at a time. As the first golem fell, it shook the nearby ground, startling all around it

As a second golem fell, an opening was created just before the forces merged. Both forces advanced toward each other, both knowing this was the end. Then, chaos erupted as they clashed in an explosion of metal, bone, and flesh.

Jarult was filled with a passion for his people as he charged his first target, bashing an afflicted Highrock warrior with his shield. As the warrior stumbled back, it made a terrible roar, tendrils emerging from its mouth. It charged at him, red eyes full of systematic hate.

Undisturbed by the corrupted warrior, Jarult roared his own battle cry, inspiring those around him to do the same. He leapt toward the afflicted warrior, bringing his axe down and chopping through the hand of his foe. Black blood sprayed from the wound, vicious and defiled in color. Jarult continued his attack, deftly striking multiple blows against the terrible being. The warrior couldn't keep up and was struck more times in its knotted flesh that bulged from its armor. It wailed, attracting the attention of a nearby flesh golem. As it looked over, Jarult made eye contact with the horrible beast. Busy with other foes, the untargeted flesh golem lurched over at him, swinging its thick arms like a clumsy child swatting bugs. It knocked warriors of both sides to the ground into the muddy, blood-encrusted battlefield. However, Jarult dodged to the side, avoiding the wrath of the simple monster.

Missing its target, the flesh golem wailed in annoyance. It swung again, but this time Jarult was prepared with a bold idea. He slung his shield around his back and grasped a dagger in his other hand, ready for the arm swinging his way. He leapt forward and jumped onto it, stabbing his dagger and battleaxe into the gnarled purple flesh of the being.

The golem cried out in confusion, swinging its arms and trying to shake him off. Jarult clung on for dear life, hoping his weapons would hold. As the golem stopped, he climbed up the arm, using his battleaxe and dagger as climbing tools. With each forceful stab, tarry blood seeped from the wound of the monster, causing it to wail and shake its arms slower and slower. Jarult grinned maniacally, surprised his plan was working as he neared the barely definable head of the golem. With his target in sight, Jarult pushed himself, using all the strength he had to stay on the flailing golem. As he reached the top of the arm, he could see the bloodshot red eyes of the terrible beast staring at him.

"You loathsome monster!" Jarult growled as he climbed atop the shoulder.

He ran at the golem's head, barely dodging the foe's other arm swinging and missing him. Filled with adrenaline, he dove off the shoulder and into the air, screaming at the monster. His aim was true as his weapons plunged into the beast's eyes. Screaming with rage at those who would seek to destroy his people, Jarult hacked violently at the golem's face. Before the golem could swipe him off, Jarult struck a fatal blow.

The golem wailed in desperation, then began to stumble on its stubby legs. It wavered like a tree in a heavy storm, finally losing its power to live. It took a few more steps, knocking over nearby warriors of both sides before it finally slipped in a muddy patch and collapsed backwards.

Jarult braced himself against the golem as it slammed to the ground, catching a few unlucky Horrors under its large body. He laughed in triumph, and a few nearby warriors cheered as they saw his victory. However, it was short lived, as more Highrock warriors were running towards him. As his troops clashed with the enemy, death began to consume the area. Both the living and the afflicted fell, causing the ground to be littered with both bodies and equipment. Jarult ignored the carnage, knowing he could do nothing beyond fight. As he glanced back towards Valon, he was glad to see gold light shimmering in the sky; the spell was working but needed more time.

"Keep fighting! Narsho, Forud, Ancient! Fight in the name of the Allied Clans! For everyone you love!" Jarult called out, looking to any of his troops that could hear him.

This time, less of the fighters yelled out in response, their morale slowly weakening against an endless force. They might have had magic and skill on their side, but the numbers and savage fighting of their enemy were wearing them down. Not only that, but as each of the living fell, they returned as an enemy.

The battle raged, and Jarult cut down Horror, Highrock, and turned allies, each kill reducing his will to fight by a miniscule amount. He didn't consciously realize it, but fighting such a horrible, vicious enemy and seeing his allies turned against him was damaging to his mind.

Time flowed sickeningly slow as Jarult fought, practically losing himself to the battle. There were immense casualties on both sides, and many of his allies had been lost by the time the last flesh golem fell. While more of them hadn't appeared, smaller Horrors of all shapes and sizes ran from the woods, their numbers limitless, though they didn't form as much of a threat as the afflicted Highrock, who were dangerous with their blood-coated weaponry.

Jarult couldn't stop his sanity from being tested as he watched the fallen bodies of his comrades warp and twist into such gruesome enemies; as he gazed across the great battle in front of him, he recognized one of the fallen as their loyal gate guard. It was the same guard that first met with Seer Mordou. On that night, they had laughed as they sent the Seer off, thinking the man was nothing more than a lunatic from a clan of fools. As Jarult felt his heart sink at the sight of the afflicted young man, he was filled with doubt, wondering if it was partially his fault for ignoring the Seer like the others.

His mind was soon interrupted by a throwing axe just barely missing his head. A surge of adrenaline shocking him, he looked to see Lorag barreling towards him, cutting down two warriors and a mage in the process. The Champion had already been muscular, but the strange affliction given to them warped his body to be almost double the size he had been. Now, the afflicted Champion had become a being of pure, gnarled hatred. Jarult withdrew his shield from his back, ready for true combat.

"Narsho dog!" Lorag yelled sweeping his greataxe low and taking down a nearby Forud warrior as he ran.

Jarult bashed his battleaxe against his shield, staring into the menacing red eyes of Lorag. He waited, letting his foe come to him. He watched as Lorag brought his greataxe over his head, putting his unnatural strength behind the upcoming swing.

Jarult held up his shield to deflect the blow, not expecting such a hard hit. As the greataxe connected harshly with his shield, it struck hard enough to split it in two. The force of the blow sent a violent vibration up his arm, and Jarult dropped the broken shield. He quickly took a step back, realizing his enemy was too strong to parry safely.

As Lorag swung his large greataxe with ease, Jarult found it difficult to keep dodging. He was becoming fatigued and knew the afflicted Champion could likely continue on without issue. This wasn't a fight he could prolong, as only he tired like a normal human.

"You're weak, Narsho!" Lorag bellowed arrogantly, swinging his axe cruelly at Jarult.

"You inhuman fiend!" Jarult snapped back, barely jumping out of the way of the attacks.

"What I am now is better than a mere human," Lorag yelled, his eyes red with unholy magic.

Jarult went on the offensive, using all he had to keep Lorag on his toes. He repeatedly swung his battleaxe, Lorag parrying it with his large greataxe or simply letting it hit into his armor and unnaturally thick, purplish skin. Then, with one harsh swing, Jarult lodged his axe into the Champion's gut; instead of keeling over in pain, Lorag looked even more motivated.

"That almost tickles," Lorag grinned viciously.

Jarult cursed to himself, his confidence wavering. As the two locked eyes, they both paced from side to side, each hoping the other would make a move. Jarult knew the only way to stop Lorag would be to deliver a death blow. That was easier said than done.

Lorag faked toward Jarult and laughed cruelly as Jarult flinched. He was toying with Jarult, like an arrogant predator fooling around with its prey before he consumed it. To Jarult, however, this was his enemy's weakness—his arrogance would be his downfall.

"You have no honor! Your ancestors would be ashamed that you call yourself Highrock!" Jarult taunted, beating his chest once with his free hand.

"You dare tell me I have no honor, Narsho?" Lorag snapped, grasping his greataxe and rushing toward Jarult.

Watching his foe charge him, Jarult readied himself. Tarry blood still coated Lorag's axe, almost hardened at this point. He briefly looked at the battle around him, his troops falling to their foes. Jarult realized he had to end this now.

Lorag swung deadly, sweeping strikes toward Jarult, each filled with more malice than the last. Jarult dodged the first few, waiting for an opening. Then, as Lorag overextended one slash, Jarult made his move. He leapt towards the man, intent on beating the greataxe back. Unfortunately, Lorag's unnatural strength truly showed itself as he swung back the other direction at an inhuman speed.

Lorag stumbled to stop himself from running into the axe, but it was too late. The topmost part of the greataxe's blade cut through his metal breastplate and slightly into his flesh, though it did not stop the brave guard captain, who then lurched forward and continued his assault.

This time, Lorag couldn't bring his hands in front of him in time to stop his foe. He yelled in anger as he realized his blunder. Jarult grabbed his battle axe with both hands, screaming loudly as he stared into the eyes of his foe, then, using every ounce of strength he had, he brought his axe down into the center of Lorag's warped face in one clean, mighty motion.

Lorag cried out in an unnatural, wretched manner as he dropped his greataxe and stumbled back a few steps. His grotesque arms slowly reached up toward the weapon lodged in his face, but it was far too late for the afflicted Highrock Champion now, as his tarry blood slowly oozed from the wound. Lorag's hands fell back to his side, and he sunk to his knees. He tried to say something unintelligible before collapsing onto his back, his wretched soul finally free from his corrupted body.

Jarult said nothing as he ripped his weapon from his opponent's face, blood spraying forth from the grievous wound. Ignoring the chaos, he looked down at his own wound, noticing the black blood of the greataxe had been smeared on the punctured breastplate. He knew unless Valon could save him, he was a dead man walking; however, despite this grim realization, Jarult found himself filled with the will to fight. Now, he could fight recklessly and with everything he had, knowing his fate was likely sealed.

Jarult roared at the heavens, letting the chaos of battle overtake him. In his rage, he cut down Horrors and Highrock with ease, moving across the battlefield like a dangerous predator. For some reason, the enemies didn't detect him as easily. He aided his own troops, helping them double team foes and slow down the enemy. Still, more Horrors came, and his warriors and mages alike fell to the enemy, and it was only when his mages fell that the battle took a sharp decline in their favor. As the first Ancient Clan mage was reborn in unholy, festering darkness, an aura so vile permeated through the air that even non-mages could sense it. Jarult watched in shock as the risen mage lifted his arm and shot forth a blast of red, sizzling energy.

Jarult didn't even have time to warn the target and watched in horror as the man was struck harshly by the bolt of magic. He toppled over, a clear hole burnt through his armor and cloth down to his skin, which now bubbled horribly. He cried out in pain, unable to move.

"By the gods…" Jarult murmured, looking to a nearby mage.

"Mages! Target our risen comrades!" the mage near him shouted, realizing the same threat.

While Jarult continued to fight, it appeared the enemy had also realized the risen mages' potential. As a result, the Horrors and afflicted Highrock targeted the mages even more ferociously, desperately charging through the Narsho, Forud, and Linta warriors to get to them.

As the Allied Clan was slowly pushed back toward the village, it appeared their defense was shattering, but as Jarult looked toward the golden energy that was now just behind him, it seemed the spell was almost complete. They just needed to hold them off a little longer.

"Keep fighting! We are almost there!" Jarult yelled loudly.

As he yelled, Jarult felt a moment of weakness overtake him. He stumbled behind the fighting line and almost fell to the ground, catching himself on a knee. His chest burned terribly, and his head felt increasingly cloudy. He forced himself to stand, but noticed he felt a strange presence around him.

"Join us, Jarult," a deep voice whispered from far away.

Jarult turned in fear, not knowing what he was experiencing. The voice carried a power to it and sounded like it came from all directions simultaneously. He took his helmet off and wiped a pool of sweat from his forehead, suddenly feeling ill. Then the voice spoke again, his chest burning awfully at the same time.

"We need you, Guard Captain," the voice said slightly louder.

Jarult wiped his eyes, desperately looking around. He hoped to see someone standing by him, something that meant he wouldn't become whatever was befalling him. However, the only thing he saw were partially transparent greenish red strands connecting all the enemies.

He stared in a confused stupor, seeing that they all connected into one larger strand that led off to the east. He had never seen anything like it, and simply watched it with intrigue as the battle around him started to vanish. Just as he went to take a step toward it all, he was pulled back, an arm under both of his own.

Jarult tried to struggle, to break free of his captors. He looked to either side, seeing pale white, dark-eyed people taking him. He tried to wriggle free, but it was no good. Then, he looked back to see a flaming wall of terrible golden energy. The sight instilled fear in him, and he tried desperately to flail free, but it was no good, and his abductors dragged him through the magical barrier.

The flame seared his mind for a moment, but then quickly stopped. He blinked his eyes and realized he was back within the barrier, surrounded by his warriors and mages. He looked to see his captors were a Narsho man and Forud woman, who let go of him as he found strength to stand; as he did, he found his chest still hurt, and his own blood oozed from the wound.

Just before Jarult was Valon, holding a silver staff at the center of the great barrier. Valon turned and made eye contact with him, realizing the man was dying. Jarult stumbled forward but found his strength rapidly declining. He fell to the ground, beginning to succumb to his wounds.

***

Valon instinctively leaned toward Jarult but knew he couldn't let go of the staff. As he felt the great holy magic flow through him, he realized he was merely a conduit of a greater power, and that if he left now, the barrier would collapse and the Horrors and afflicted Highrock that now stood outside it would break through.

"Get to the ships! Now!" Valon yelled to the surviving warriors and mages. "Prepare to purge any wounded that may become afflicted if I cannot heal them in time!"

They seemed hesitant, especially at the idea of killing their wounded comrades. However, the brave fighters had just seen what would become of the wounded, and knew it was their only choice. As they all ran toward the docks, Valon looked back to Jarult.

"We ... did it," Jarult coughed, slowly looking up from the ground at Valon.

"Just hold on, Jarult! Once they leave, I can drop this barrier and help you," Valon said, realizing the impossibility of his words.

Then, just as the humanity inside of him panicked, a brief burst of farsight struck into his mind. He knew he would not die here but did not see how he would escape. Moments like these frustrated him greatly, as he could see the end of the road, just not how to get there. Then, as he tried to think of a plan, he noticed a handful of Ancient Clan mages walking through the gate toward him. Among them were his parents.

"My son! We must go!" Valon's father yelled, running to him.

"I cannot go, Father! I must channel this spell to keep the barrier up!" Valon replied.

"But how will you escape?" Valon's mother asked with great worry in her eyes.

"I will manage. Please, take Jarult and go," Valon urged, knowing even his parents could do nothing for the dying man.

"But we do not have your holy power, my son. We cannot save him or any of the other wounded," Valon's father said.

Valon's grip on the staff slightly loosened, knowing his father was right. He tried to come up with a plan, anything he could do to escape. Surely, there had to be something he could do. Alas, he knew in his heart that someone had to be here to channel the spell—he had to be here.

"I cannot leave. If I let go of this staff, the barrier will collapse. This staff is a sort of amplifier of magic, not a source of it. Please, you all must go," Valon urged his parents and other mages before him.

There was a moment of silence as Valon's parents looked at each other, as if making a decision. Valon watched in confusion, not knowing what they were doing. Then his father stepped forward, a look of peace in his eyes.

"I will take your place, Valon," Valon's father declared.

"What? No, Father! I cannot let you!" Valon replied, his heart sinking at the thought.

"Yes, my son. You may be the Seer of our clan, but I am still your father. I will take your place so you may lead your people and save the wounded!" Valon's father insisted, stepping forward and grabbing hold of Hy'ria's staff.

As his father took it, Valon felt the burden of flowing magic lessen. He watched as part of it flowed through his father, the old man having to brace himself against its power. Watching this, Valon realized this was how it was supposed to happen, which caused sorrow to quickly envelop him. This was how they would succeed.

"Yes, Father ... I will do as you ask," Valon choked, tearing up as he let go of the silver staff.

Valon felt the holy magic sever its connection from him and instead use his father. His father winced in pain as the power burst through him. Still, he smiled, looking at his son with nothing but love and pride.

Valon's mother quickly ran to her husband, embracing and kissing him. She held her head against his, keeping her goodbye brief. She turned away, knowing her husband was making the ultimate sacrifice.

Valon, too, hugged his father, embracing him for the final time. His mind spun with things he wanted to say but knew they didn't have the time. His father would not last forever, and when he did fall the afflicted enemies would run rampant through the village, desperately searching for their enemies. Valon couldn't stop tears running down his face as he hugged his father, but finally had to let go; he had much to do and would keep his goodbye short, knowing it would only hurt more to prolong it.

"I love you so much … I couldn't be any prouder to call you my father," Valon spoke mournfully, backing away from his father.

"Indeed, my son. and I am proud of the man you've become. I will love you and your mother forever … Now go, lead our people to their new home," Valon's father replied, keeping his tone of courage.

Valon simply nodded, knowing he had to leave. He couldn't help but notice the horde of Horrors and afflicted Highrock staring at him from the other side of the barrier. If they dared to cross now, they would likely be incinerated alive in a second. They had no choice but to wait. He knew their rage would build, and his father would be the only target left. He shook his head, trying to fight the guilt that had already found him. He had no other choice now.

Turning his attention to Jarult, he knelt and touched the man's breastplate. He could feel the corruption growing inside him, and quickly projected a flash of holy magic into the man. This would at least hold him over until they were aboard the ship. Then he could take his time to cure the man and whoever else was stable enough.

Valon slowly picked up the loyal guard captain, who was now unconscious. He looked to his mother and the other mages, who gazed somberly toward his father. As they noticed their Seer, they quickly began to walk toward the port, knowing the time had come.

"We must go," Valon said to his mother.

"I know…" Valon's mother began to cry, looking as sad as she was proud.

Valon followed his mother toward the port where only one ship remained, the others out at sea at a safe distance.

With Jarult in his arms, Valon felt the literal weight of his people on him, though it was not as damning a burden as he thought; now he was filled with newfound power as well as the wisdom of his former master. Now, Valon felt he could accomplish anything.

As he quickly strode towards the port, Valon could not help but wonder what the fate of his comrades who still fought Xerannu would be, or his father's. While he wouldn't allow his personal feelings to stop him, he couldn't prevent his human emotions from constantly piercing his mind. Still, each person had their own role to play in this realm, something not only Seer Mordou had taught him but also something he had come to realize from farsight already. As he walked confidently towards the ship that would lead them to their future, Valon was ready to do whatever it took for his people.

Chapter 28

Sweat poured down Anna's brow as she continued her barrage of holy magic unto her enemies. With each passing second, she could feel the fatigue of its usage draining her. Still, they were this close, and she would push herself to the very end. She knew if her child was to have a safe life, then their enemies would have to be destroyed, and she wanted to be there to witness it. She wanted revenge for Fredrik.

Unable to purge the forest of the corruption, the remaining warriors and mages had no choice but to continue into it as it was. Their holy magic illuminated the darkness, still effective on the Horrors that continued to assault them. Now only the Horrors remained, as they had slain the few Highrock archers. Still, Anna could only wonder how those back at the village fared.

It was slow moving as they cut their way through the Horrors. Now, only five holy-imbued mages remained, Valon having traveled back. Their formation roughly resembled a square, and each took a side alongside many warriors and mages while one rested in the middle, using far less power to mend wounds and bless their warriors. They continued this cycle as they slowly made their way to the heart of their enemy, yet their numbers continued to thin, for the constant assaults by the Horrors slowly chipped away from them. Not to mention any warrior that was entangled by a tentacle or incapacitated in any way had to be left behind if not quickly saved. It was a race against time now, and they had to reach the portal before they were out of troops completely. While their magic was powerful, they could not fight Xerannu's thralls alone.

"Keep moving! Hold those beasts back!" Chieftain Barod yelled from behind Anna, primarily looking to the handful of soldiers and mages left in their formation.

"We are so close, I can sense it," Seer Mordou said, taking Anna's place.

"I can sense it too," Anna replied, allowing Seer Mordou to step in.

She returned to the middle of the bustling, crazed formation, pushing through at least ten warriors until she reached the center. They were tired, some scared, others still having fight in them. She knew there was a chance they could all die here, even before they closed the portal. However, if they did nothing they would certainly perish. She was sure every one of her comrades in arms knew that too now.

As one Linta Clan fighter came to her with an injury, Anna noticed the woman around her age looked utterly defeated. Anna didn't say anything at first, examining the wound on the woman's arm. It was a nasty gash, filled with whatever poison Xerannu spread through the veins of his thralls. Anna began the purifying spell, knowing it would take up to a minute to cleanse the woman.

They had to continue walking slowly to stay centered in the formation, making it more difficult for Anna to concentrate. Despite the many obstacles, she cured the woman of the affliction and healed the wound enough so that it wouldn't continue to bleed. However, as she went to send the woman back, she knew she had to say something.

"Thank you for your bravery," Anna softly spoke, placing her hand gently on the woman's arm.

"This is a nightmare…" the woman replied, barely holding it together.

"It is, but we are surviving. How many have you killed?" Anna asked bluntly.

"What?" the woman asked, wiping a couple tears from her eye.

"How many Horrors have you slain?" Anna repeated.

"I don't know ... I don't keep track. Perhaps a couple dozen or more? Why?" the woman asked, her curiosity replacing her fear.

"Then that's a couple dozen that will no longer attack us. That's a couple dozen that will not hunt down our friends, our family. Had you even said you only killed a single enemy I would commend you," Anna explained, trying her best to motivate the woman. "If we each do that, we will push back these foes and put an end to them for good!"

The woman nodded, sniffling one last time. As she processed Anna's reasoning in her, some of her morale returned. It wasn't much, but it was enough for her to grit her teeth and replace her lack of hope with a reason to keep fighting.

"I see. Thank you," the woman said, readying her battleaxe to keep fighting.

"No, thank you. Fight strong, Linta," Anna nodded with respect.

The woman returned the nod and moved back into the formation. Anna watched as the cycle of warriors continued as well, trying to keep any one person from becoming too exhausted. It wasn't perfect, but it was the best they could do while remaining flanked.

As more time went on, it was soon Anna's time to relieve the head of the formation. She again pushed her way through the warriors, having to walk quickly to keep up. Luckily, she did feel a bit restored and ready to fight more. Finally, she found Goreth leading the way, flanked by Forud warriors that cheered on their Champion.

Goreth destroyed any Horror that came within his field of vision, projecting his holy magic like a single blade of holy fire that continued to sweep in front of him. He did not speak or even acknowledge his fellow clansmen that flanked him, completely absorbed in the mission at hand.

"Goreth," Anna said loudly over the cheering, tapping him on the shoulder.

Goreth nodded and uttered a small grunt. He slowly withdrew his magic, watching as the Horrors ran forward to seize the moment of opportunity. He and Anna quickly changed places, and Anna let loose concentrated bolts of holy power. The magic was far too quick for the Horrors to avoid, and she pierced the attackers with relative ease. As it happened, the Forud warriors next to her cheered.

"Look at that light ahead; we must be close," Goreth said before he left, pointing over Anna's shoulder in the distance.

As Anna saw it, she froze. In that moment she remembered the last time she had been there, seeing Fredrik and watching her clansmen die. Her mind being torn away from the moment, Anna's magic began to fade, and as she lost focus, she almost tripped over a flesh-covered root on the ground.

Seeing the opportunity, more Horrors charged from behind nearby trees, their shapes and sizes varying. However, this time some of them were recognizable. Some of the attackers looked to be raptors that had been corrupted by Xerannu. The afflicted raptors quickly ran to the front of their group, their cries wicked and warped.

"By the gods … miss? Mage? Are you alright?" A nervous Forud asked, tightening his grip on his spear and shield.

The words reached Anna, and she quickly snapped herself out of it. Upon seeing the great raptors afflicted, she felt sickened. They were fierce, primal beasts, but they did not deserve such a fate. She targeted them and let loose a torrent of holy power. As her power struck them, however, they did not instantly die like the Horrors. No, something was slightly different about them, and they managed to press onward toward the group and were closing in fast.

"What? How did it survive that?" the panicking Forud warrior asked.

"I don't know. Brace yourselves!" Anna yelled.

Their pace almost stopped as they raised their shields and spears. Anna continued her barrage, taking down two of the six vicious, afflicted raptors. The other four made it and leapt onto the warriors, Anna being pushed behind them as she had no shield or armor like them. Despite spears piercing their bodies, the afflicted raptors attacked their foes with a frenzy of mangled claws and chipped teeth. They were somehow even more violent than normal raptors, ripping and tearing at the humans before them.

The other lines of the formation ran forward to engage the raptors but found it difficult to get close. The four swung their heavy, leathery tails at them and knocked the warriors back. Other mages used primordial magic and sent bolts at the beasts. As it struck them, it wasn't too effective, but did manage to force them to stumble off their prey. Luckily, one of the raptors far from her was taken down through an exhaustive effort of mages and warriors.

Anna attacked again, dissuaded by her poor effectiveness. As she glanced into the eyes of the closest raptor, she swore she could see torment in the beasts, as if they were still aware enough to know they were being controlled. That sight caused Anna to try the boldest move of the battle. She slowly walked forward to the raptor, using her holy light to calm it, much to the surprise of all near her; despite their protests, she pressed onwards. Only one voice made her reconsider her actions, but she didn't let it stop her.

Having heard the commotion, the side flank had sent Garon to check in on the front.

"Anna!" Garon yelled, ready to strike down the raptor in front of her.

"Wait!" Anna yelled in response, only feet from the beast.

As her eyes and the raptor's locked, she could tell the beast was truly a slave to Xerannu. She was not face to face with it and stared up a few inches at the taller beast. She gently placed her hand on its head, rubbing between the top section just above its nose. Then, she began the same cleansing spell she had used on the wounded fighters.

The flows of magic around her hissed as opposing magics met, forced together by two separate wills. She could feel Xerannu's presence and knew the entity wouldn't let one of his thrall go. However, she knew this was one of many beings he controlled and he couldn't focus on saving a single raptor.

She poured her energy into her magic, sparks of magic flinging violently from her hand and the temporarily debilitated raptor. She ignored the chaos around her as the other two raptors still fought warriors and more Horrors followed. By now the formation was close behind her, waiting for the result.

"You're cleansing it, aren't you?" Garon asked between attacks, giving her cover.

"Yes. I can sense its pain. I can free it," Anna answered.

Finally, her magic found its way through and ripped the influence of Xerannu's unholy magic from the beast. Then, she purged the remaining biotic magic, green flecks of magic falling from the raptor. As it happened, its form began to change. Anna watched as the beast slowly returned to its normal form, losing its gnarled purple skin and being replaced with its normal grey, feather-covered skin. Its red eyes slowly lost their torment and revealed the simple, primal eyes the raptor normally had. It made a low sound with its voice, coming to its natural senses. It had been restored to its natural state, at least for that brief moment.

As Anna saw the raptor return to how it had been before Xerannu's influence, a thought popped into her head. She suddenly thought of a spell that had been gifted to her that allowed her to imbue beings with holy light, empowering them and making them a force for good. She remembered the spell and figured this would be a good time to test it. As she began, holy magic poured from her being.

"Anna? What are you doing?" Garon asked skeptically.

"Trying something," Anna replied shortly, focusing on imbuing the raptor with holy magic.

She let the flow of holy magic run through her and into the raptor, which squealed in discomfort. She persisted, something telling her what she was doing was right. Finally, enough magic had been siphoned into the raptor, and it was enveloped in golden light. It roared once, sounding in great pain. Anna stepped back, something warm within her telling her she was making the right decision.

Then, the veil lifted, and the light around the raptor shattered. The creature roared again, this time a battle cry. Its skin had gone completely white, devoid of any color, and its feathers and eyes had turned gold. Anna could feel the magic she had given the raptor and smiled in delight at the sight of the powerful beast of good.

This attracted the other two raptors, who now noticed their changed comrade. They roared, and ran at the holy raptor, their red eyes as tormented as their kin's. The holy raptor leapt forward, ready to fight.

"By the gods..." Chieftain Barod mumbled in awe as he approached behind Anna.

The imbued raptor dove at the first of the two assailants, diving on it and knocking it to the ground. It showed no mercy as it ripped and tore through what was once its kin, roaring in triumph as it quickly dispatched its first foe.

The second afflicted raptor swung at its holy-imbued relative, ripping into its pale skin. Light, golden blood dripped out, and the raptor cried out in fury. It dove onto the warped raptor, biting the neck of the dark beast. The dark raptor tried to fight back, gouging its claws into its holy-imbued kin, but it was not strong enough and was tossed aside as Anna's experiment proved successful.

"It's so powerful. Can you control it?" Garon asked, staring at the raptor.

Anna didn't reply but reached out with her mind to the raptor. She used her magic to give it orders to continue attacking every Horror it saw. Then, a moment later, it followed her command. The raptor roared, ignoring its wounds and running towards nearby Horrors and tearing them apart.

"It's making us an easier path; let's keep moving!" Anna shouted to the others, the concentration of holy magic slowly fading from her.

The formation tightened and they continued through the forest towards daylight, still fending off attacks from the other sides. However, with the front path being cleared by the vicious raptor Anna had saved, they could move faster.

As they approached the light ahead, Anna fought her mind to stay focused. She knew the body of Fredrik was still out there. Not only that, but there was a chance she could bring him back. If she could save a raptor, she could perhaps save him. She didn't want to let hope overcome her, but it was difficult. With this newfound power, anything seemed possible.

Finally, the front of the formation plunged into daylight, following the bloody path of the raptor. Having fought easily a hundred Horrors, the great beast was beginning to slow. Its golden blood dripped from it as it fought, leaving a path of black and gold blood through the forest. Anna could do no more for it, knowing it would soon meet its end. Swarmed by ruthless Horrors, it soon fell to the ground. As it did, the Horrors continued to attack it, filled with hatred. Then, as its eyelids fell over its golden eyes, its body caught ablaze in a white-hot fire. The holy magic that imbued it collapsed in on itself, burning every nearby Horror in a blaze. Anna, however, was more focused on the shimmering portal from which Horrors continuously emerged.

"Champions! Regroup!" Seer Mordou yelled, appearing behind Anna.

"Warriors! Cover them!" Chieftain Barod ordered in addition.

Goreth and Becca moved through the formation to stand alongside Anna, Garon, Seer Mordou, Chieftain Barod, and Titus. They all looked onto the portal with intrigue and disgust. This was the vile source of their realm's illness. It was here, and only here, they could fix it.

"As terrible as I remember it," Titus growled.

"So that's it, isn't it?" Garon asked. "The source of corruption that took my people…"

"Seer, how do we destroy it?" Chieftain Barod asked, placing his hand on the man's shoulder.

"Now that I am a bit unsure of. As far as I am aware, there is no 'close portal' spell. I do have some ideas, however," Seer Mordou replied, nervously rubbing his chin as he gazed upon the shimmering anomaly.

"Well, please do whatever you can, and fast. Our people cannot hold out forever!" Chieftain Barod implored, looking back at their dwindling formation.

"Of course. Now, I believe if we all bombard it with holy magic and simultaneously use primordial magic to physically close it, we may have the desired outcome," Seer Mordou theorized, looking at each of his Champions.

As the Seer continued to speak, Anna felt a presence coming from the portal. She tried to ignore it, knowing it was likely a trick. However, the fighting at the front line stopped, and a yell from a Narsho warrior stole her attention.

"By the gods … Fredrik?" a man said from the front line.

Anna immediately turned and pushed her way through the formation. As she walked between two warriors, she saw what had caused the commotion: standing in the middle of the trampled field between them and the portal was Fredrik; however, this time, there was no facade of humanity, and he looked as twisted as any other afflicted being.

Anna gasped at the sight of her former lover, and she slowly stumbled towards him. With her new power she was sure she could cleanse him, save him from this terrible affliction. She ignored the yelling of her comrades, as the Horrors had all disappeared from the front line and were no longer coming from the portal. She was ready for a fight but needed to try to save him.

"H-help," Fredrik gurgled terribly, his red eyes wavering.

"Fredrik!" Anna yelled, running toward him with newfound hope.

Then, in an instant, her hope was shattered into terrible pieces. In a gory, magic-infused explosion, Fredrik's body erupted. Parts went flying as unholy power decimated his body, red wisps of magic flying forth. It was gruesome, brutal, and left a permanent scar on Anna's soul.

"No!" Anna wailed, dropping to her knees.

"You thought I would allow you to save him?" Xerannu's voice cackled.

She stared ahead at the portal, which now glowed in a sickening greenish red aura. She couldn't speak, too scarred from what she had just witnessed. However, her sight did not fail her, and a large Horror emerged from the portal, a sword still lodged in its body. As Anna laid eyes upon the Horror, she immediately recognized it, as well as her sword.

"You monster," Anna muttered angrily, still unable to stand.

"Monster? You do not understand, Anna. I am far from that. I exist to stop monsters, to bind them to my will. I bring order to savage lands and fortify them for what is to come. If you fools cut me off from this world, then every beast here will lose itself in animalistic hedonism. Only under my control can my thralls function in an orderly fashion," Xerannu's voice boomed, bursts of warm odd-smelling wind coming from the portal.

"Liar! You are the one giving into your primal urges!" Garon yelled, running to Anna.

As he helped her stand, Anna felt hope return. Gazing into Garon's eyes, she knew she had other reasons to continue the fight now. She touched her hand to her stomach, knowing Fredrik would live on only if she survived. It took a moment, but she finally regained her composure, realizing Fredrik had been lost the moment they assaulted the portal.

Xerannu did not respond, and the large sword-stabbed Horror ran full speed at Anna. She took Garon's hand and looked into his eyes once more. Becca, Goreth, and Seer Mordou ran to her, all linking hands. Together, they could easily defeat any foe.

As the rabid Horror sprinted towards them, others began to pour from the portal. Xerannu chuckled deeply as he watched the mortals hold hands. He did not realize they were readying to use their power in perfect unison.

As Anna let loose her wrath of holy magic, so did her allies. Together, they emitted a godly beam of holy magic that pierced through every Horror in front of them, instantly obliterating them into ash. Even Anna's old sword stuck inside the Horror vanished, caught in the incredible beam. The light continued until it struck the portal, and as it did, they lifted their arms to bring it to the center of the shimmering mass. At first, nothing happened beyond the slight wavering of the portal, but the Horrors did stop emerging, and a golden light wisped around the portal.

"Why is nothing happening?" Becca asked.

"I-I don't know. This should work. We should have the power. Unless…" Seer Mordou began, almost looking pale form his own thought.

"Unless what?" Garon asked.

"Unless we need mages on both sides of the portal," Seer Mordou answered grimly.

As he voiced his thought, their torrent of magic ceased. They all immediately knew the implication of such a thing. They knew whoever went through would be going on a one-way trip. Despite this, Anna was the first to volunteer.

"I will go through," Anna declared, her decision already made.

"Then I will go with you," Garon quickly added.

"What? No, Anna, I will go," Becca insisted.

"No, I will!" Goreth urged.

As they began to bicker, Chieftain Barod and Titus joined the argument. Anna knew they were wasting time and grabbed Garon's hand. She led him towards the portal, ready to put an end to Xerannu if this was what it took. As they walked, Garon stopped her and looked into her eyes.

"I will follow you anywhere," Garon softly said, his eyes almost glimmering with holy magic.

"Good," Anna said with a small smile.

She held Garon's hands tightly, looking into his eyes. Then, without delay, she continued towards the portal that led to an unknown world. They didn't stop as the others yelled, and just as she reached the portal, Seer Mordou ran to them.

"I am joining you. The power of us three will be enough to fend for ourselves. We shall leave the rest of our troops to Becca and Goreth," Seer Mordou explained as he walked past them.

"Wait!" a voice boomed.

Anna turned to see Chieftain Barod standing nearby, his muscular old form looking tired. Titus joined him as well, crossing his muscular armored arms. She quickly ran back to him, wanting to say goodbye to her clan.

"Anna, your sacrifices will not be forgotten. You are a true Narsho," Chieftain Barod declared as he shook her hand. "Titus, what do you think?"

"I would be honored to share the title," Titus said with a hearty smile.

"What do you mean?" Anna asked as she shook Titus's hand.

"Anna Myhre, I grant you the honor of Champion of the Narsho Clan. May you fight boldly for our people, and may you know victory!" Chieftain Barod smiled with satisfaction. "You deserve it."

"If we somehow make it out of these forests, I will tell tales of Champion Anna, the Holy Warrior," Titus chuckled darkly, knowing deep inside it was unlikely.

"And I will tell my child tales of Champion Titus the Brave and the honorable Chieftain Barod," Anna replied, beaming at the honor.

"Then go, Champion, and let us end this," Chieftain Barod ordered kindly.

Anna nodded and ran back to the others. Garon took her hand, and they walked towards the portal. Seer Mordou did not hesitate as he stepped through, vanishing from sight. Small golden flecks jumped from the shimmering air where he had entered.

"Are you ready?" Garon asked.

"Yes."

The two quickly ran through the portal, and Anna felt a brief flash of power surge through her body. There was a strange light, and a moment later she emerged, her vision blurry. She and Garon still held on to each other, inseparable to the magic.

It took her a moment to regain her senses, but instantly realized they were no longer in their own realm of Forthoton. Afflicted trees stood close in the distance, but they were strange in shape, thick at the base and thinned towards the top, their branches looped and strange. While they were still covered by the affliction of Xerannu, they were definitely not the trees of their home.

"Where could we possibly be?" Garon wondered, grabbing Anna's hand a little tighter.

"Come! We must close the portal!" Seer Mordou yelled, readying himself as he faced the portal.

Anna and Garon quickly ran to him, Anna taking the man's hand. She waited for instruction, knowing this was the Seer's area of expertise. As she looked around, she found it odd there were no Horrors nearby.

"Focus every drop of power you have! We will bring this portal down from both sides!" Seer Mordou yelled.

Together, they streamed unrivaled power at the portal, their three beams of magic conjoining into one. Sparks of blue and gold fell from it as it struck the dark portal, making a cacophony of bizarre sounds. This time, their efforts were not in vain.

The portal began to waver, its entire shimmering form waving like a flag in the wind. Slowly, it began to shrink down from the sky, pops of red and green coming from the portal like pustules of an infection being purged. As it happened, Anna began to feel triumphant. The portal trembled and collapsed on itself, the shimmering of its existence rapidly falling from the sky. Then, a moment later, it erupted in energy. The three quickly enveloped themselves in holy magic, which shielded them from the eruption. The burst of energy lasted a few seconds, toppling afflicted trees and ripping the fleshy covering from the ground around them. Finally, when it was over, they felt a presence around them. Anna realized it was Xerannu.

"You fools! You will pay dearly for this!" Xerannu boomed. "You may have removed me from your world, but you will never remove my gift! Now, you are stuck here with me."

"The portal is closed!" Seer Mordou yelled in victory.

"We've done it!" Garon beamed.

"But he's still out there. Wherever we are," Anna said grimly.

She turned and let go of Garon's hand as she prepared herself for battle. She was exhausted, but they were not done yet. Strange looking Horrors began to gather at the tree line. They almost looked like humans, but with odd faces. They had sharp, oddly shaped blades and wore strange armor. However, their red eyes gave away their allegiance to Xerannu.

"Our fight is not over yet," Seer Mordou said, readying himself.

"No, but we can take solace in knowing our people are safe," Garon added.

"That is all I ever wanted," Anna said with a small smile.

"Then come, let us continue the fight against Xerannu for as long as we can," Seer Mordou said, looking proudly at the two mages next to him.

As the afflicted beings from the forest charged them, Anna readied herself, ready to do whatever it took to bring her friends and her unborn child to safety, filled with triumphant hope, knowing Xerannu could be beaten, and that her people were safe. Now, she had an even greater reason to fight, which only strengthened her resolve in the face of her enemy.

Anna and Garon took each other's hands as Seer Mordou prepared himself, standing together against Xerannu's thralls.

***

Chieftain Barod fought with every last bit of energy he had, taking down one Horror after another as the ritual continued. He was exhausted, and his old body couldn't take the exertion. As he looked at his army, he saw only twenty or so warriors remaining, all of them Narsho. The sight tore at his heart, but seeing Titus continue to strike down their enemies filled him with some hope.

"Back! Closer to our mages!" Chieftain Barod yelled.

The tired warriors followed his orders, and they moved back to be only feet in front of the mages. Chieftain Barod was proud of his people, of everyone who had fought such a vicious foe. However, their losses were immense, and he knew they would likely not escape.

"Look!" Goreth yelled from behind him, channeling fierce magic.

"Yes! It's collapsing!" Becca cheered.

Chieftain Barod turned to watch the portal collapse. It was violent, even showing malice as it fell. As it did, the Horrors that had been assaulting them shrieked and fell to the ground, clenching their heads.

"They're stopping. They look to be in pain," Titus said in bewilderment.

"That is either a very good, or very bad thing," Chieftain Barod grumbled.

The portal erupted in an explosive fashion, and the energy burst out in all directions. Becca and Goreth tried their best to shield their comrades against it, barely being able to do so. Still, they managed to hold on. The terrible energies tore apart the Horrors that had surrounded the portal, leaving them not much more than a gooey mess on the newly revealed dirt. Trees along the edge of the forest exploded, splintering harshly as energy tore them to pieces. The wave finally stopped, revealing great carnage around them.

"It's over," Titus whispered.

Chieftain Barod watched as the dead whose bodies remained intact began to rise, warping into nasty Horrors. However, this time their eyes glowed green, not red. He watched a nearby Narsho rise into such a Horror, and he felt sickened.

"No, I don't believe it is," Chieftain Barod added.

The creatures began to cry out like the most primal of beings and attacked each other. More emerged from the forest, drawn in by the explosion. Now, all the afflicted eyes glowed green, and looked more primal than they did tormented. As some noticed the group, they charged toward them. The ones that didn't fight each other attacked the humans like wild animals.

"The fight isn't over!" Chieftain Barod boomed.

He looked back to see Becca and Goreth exhausted, sharing a long kiss. Finally, they strode forth together, ready to use their holy power until the end. They held each other's hands, both of their eyes filled with golden determination.

"I will fight by your side until the end, Chieftain," Titus pledged, saluting his chieftain.

"I wouldn't have anyone else," Chieftain Barod replied, knowing the end was near.

Swarmed by primal beasts, they would fight until the very end. While the Horrors now fought each other, their numbers were still too great. Not only that, but they fought with a newfound independence, almost random rage that made them harder to incapacitate. Still, they defeated numerous foes as they tried to escape the afflicted forest.

Chieftain Barod watched as Titus protected him to the bitter end, swinging his greatsword with everything he had. Finally, he was out of energy, and his armor and large weapon slowed him too much. He dropped to his knees, fighting off the primal beasts with his hands. One last time, Titus, the Narsho Champion saluted his chieftain.

Unsure of where Goreth and Becca had gone, Chieftain Barod knew his time was next. Despite this, he fought bravely, not giving in. He knew that with each kill, their old land would be that much safer.

Chieftain Barod's final thoughts were of Herold Wooll, knowing his friend's sacrifice had helped them save their realm. At least now Xerannu had been cut off, and their people sailing south would make it. As he fell, the great Narsho Chieftain was not afraid, for he was filled with too much pride for his people. Not just the Narsho, but for the Forud, Linta, and Ancient Clans.

United as one, they had defeated the worst foe they had ever seen. Together, they had been victorious.

***

After the incredible explosion in the far distance, the Horrors began to turn on each other, eyes glowing green with newfound madness. Valon's father lost his focus and the barrier began to collapse. It slowly fell, golden light imploding on itself and searing the ground beneath it. He smiled, knowing he had given them enough time to escape. Not only that, but he could feel the flows of magic change, meaning the portal had been closed. They had won.

Valon's father fell onto his old knees, dropping the silver staff by his side. He was beyond exhausted, and his old skin had begun to turn white. He knew his time had come and watched as a primal Horror turned to him with nasty interest. But then something happened, stopping the Horror from getting its meal. A golden light enveloped Valon's father's entire body. He felt warm, safe, and happy. As his vision faded, he swore he could see golden winged people descend from above.

"I love both of you," Valon's father whispered with one final smile as his body was taken from their realm.

And so, his body ascended to the heavens, his sacrifices having not gone unnoticed. Nothing remained of him where he had kneeled previously, except for Hyria's staff. Still infused with holy magic, the staff would remain untouched for much time; Valon's father would not be the last to wield the powerful artifact.

Epilogue

Coated in a layer of otherworldly fog, Valon could make out a trio of heroes. They stood in unison, proof of success lying behind their back. Surrounded by new foes, they prepared for the worst. He squinted as shadows appeared on the ground in front of them, and then noticed something soared above them, diving to the ground. As the leathery birdlike shadows descended towards the trio, he watched in interest, but then the sound of creaking wood startled him, and he watched as the image before him clouded in impenetrable fog.

Valon shot up from his slumber, breathing heavily. He looked around his quarters, searching for a trio that wasn't there. He slowly stood, seeing that light shone through the windows of his small cabin. Above he could hear footsteps, remembering where he was. He felt exhausted, having expended every droplet of energy he had to save as many as he could from Xerannu's influence. Fortunately, very few succumbed to their wounds, although Valon still hated not being able to save them all. He stretched, then approached the door.

He walked from the stale room into salty air, taking a deep breath. He rubbed his eyes, trying to make sense of his vision. It was difficult to discern anything from it, but he thought one of the trio was Seer Mordou. If anything, it was a sign he was still alive.

"Good morning," a familial voice calmly called out to him.

Valon looked across the deck to see Guard Captain Jarult leaning over the ship's railing, and next to him were Olaf and his own mother. He walked over, his mind slowly awakening.

"Hello, Seer," Olaf smiled.

"Hello, everyone," Valon replied, wondering how long they had been awake.

"Valon, now that we have a moment, thank you for saving me," Jarult thanked, extending his hand toward his Seer.

"Don't thank me; I should thank you for putting your life on the line to buy me—to buy everyone—time," Valon replied, shaking the man's hand.

"Of course. Anything for our people," Jarult answered proudly.

Valon knew they had been successful. As they had sailed away from their land days ago, they all had seen the explosion in the far, far distance. Not only that, but he could sense how the flows of magic had changed; the portal had closed, and their world was safe. However, he could still sense the lingering, dangerous biotic magic of Xerannu from their land and knew it would never be the same. They could not return, as it was too dangerous. He did not dare to try to use his power to look back at their land, not yet.

"I wonder if any of them live," Olaf said somberly.

"I believe at least three do, my former master included. Perhaps once I have the energy and once we reach dry land, I will perform a ritual of farsight," Valon replied.

"How far is land?" Jarult asked.

"I will not lie, I do not know. Weeks, months, regardless we have the supplies if we ration well. We will endure; I can see it," Valon answered, looking at the many ships around them.

"Very good. Come, Olaf, let us check in with our ship's captain," Jarult suggested, patting the old shaman on the back.

Olaf nodded and the two walked away, leaving Valon alone with his mother. He could tell she was melancholy, reminding him he hadn't had a chance to mourn for his father. Now that he had time and energy, his father's death hit him harder than before.

"I will miss your father greatly," Valon's mother smiled, tears trickling down her face.

"I know. I will too," Valon added, hugging his mother.

"He is so proud of you; we both are. Our son, Seer of the Ancient Clan. No, Seer of the Allied Clans. You have a great task before you, Son, but I have no doubt you can deliver our people to their new home," Valon's mother said, looking out into the ocean.

As Valon glanced over the great oceans none of his people had ever seen before today, he knew she was right. He had been tasked with the survival of all humans, of all clans except the Highrock. Before he had become the Seer and been given holy magic, he would have dreaded such a moment of importance, but now as he gazed out toward where their new home lay, he felt absolute confidence, the strength of holy magic coursing through him. His gold eye glowed brightly.

"Thank you, Mother. I will not fail you. Any of you."

Author's Note

Thank you so much for taking the time to read my book. I am very proud of *Rise of the Champions*, and am already in the early stages of planning a sequel. While I will be busy at law school for the next few years, I will certainly not be giving up my writing, and will be spending my spare time doing so. This is one of my true passions, and I hope to continue on with sequels to existing content and new content over the years.

If you've made it this far, I hope you've enjoyed this book. If you have, I would be very grateful if you could leave a review on Amazon (or on other sites such as goodreads) if you ever had the time. In today's world, reviews are exceptionally important, especially for new authors.

Regardless, I welcome all feedback whether it be positive or negative. I'm still new to all of this and encourage you to reach out to me on the book if you desire. Only through growth can we slowly work towards perfection.

A big thank you to Kayla Henley for your wonderful editing and feedback; you've helped not only this book's quality greatly, but my writing as well.

Thank you Alexandre Douanier AKA "Mr. Panka" for your gorgeous cover illustration, I couldn't ask for something more eye-catching.

About the Author

Nicholas Joslin is an avid writer who has enjoyed writing his whole life. After graduating from Keene State College in 2017, he began working as a property manager and set his sights on finishing his first novel, *The Forgotten Sorcerer*, which was self-published in 2018. With sequels and other smaller projects in the works, he will continue to focus on his writing in his spare time. More information and updates can be found at www.nicholasjoslin.com.

Want to contact the author?

Email: nickjoslinwriting@gmail.com
On the web: www.nicholasjoslin.com
On Twitter: @Xerannu

www.ingramcontent.com/pod-product-compliance
Lightning Source LLC
Chambersburg PA
CBHW051959240626
47153CB00005B/1816